Enjoy t

ESCAPE TO KILLALOMA

DEBRA CURRIE

ESCAPE TO KILLALOMA

Printed in Canada

ISBN: 978-1-4866-1670-1

Word Alive Press
119 De Baets Street Winnipeg, MB R2J 3R9
www.wordalivepress.ca

WORD ALIVE PRESS

MIX
Paper from responsible sources
FSC www.fsc.org FSC® C016245

Cataloguing in Publication information may be obtained from Library and Archives Canada.

To my loving husband Steve, who is my safe place.
To my children, Sarah, Michael, Matthew and Erin
who always challenge me to be a better mom,
I thank you all.

ACKNOWLEDGEMENTS

I would like to thank Word Alive Press for publishing my book. Thanks goes out to Jen Jendavs-Hedlin, my publishing consultant for her many emails that encouraged me to publish *Escape To Killaloma* with their company. Thanks also to Marina Reis, my project manager who walked me through each step of the publishing process and made me feel at ease. Sheila Beauprie, my friend, it goes without saying that I never would have been able to write this book without your insight and help. For working tirelessly on my behalf, I thank you.

CONTENTS

ESCAPE TO KILLALOMA

PROLOGUE

The sounds came to him as if through a long tunnel. They reverberated off the walls and assailed his senses. He ran for his life, knowing that if he were to stop, it could mean his death. Amid the cacophony, he could distinguish a more sinister sound. It was the flutter of leathery wings beating louder and louder as they approached from behind. The smell of sulphur was overpowering and mindless laughter mocked his every step. The hair on his neck bristled as he stumbled once, and then found his footing. Tears squeezed out of the corners of his eyes as he blindly reached for the light that beckoned him. It was bright, so bright it made his head spin and pain shot behind his eyes like a thousand starbursts.

In the midst of the light, there she stood. Soft edges, muted colours...face surrounded by light. "She must be an angel," he thought in the back of his mind. She was saying something to him. "What was that? Please, say it again! I can't hear you.". He tried to speak these words but nothing came out of his mouth but a garbled jumble of sounds. His tongue felt like it had been glued in place and his lips felt like rubber. "I must be dead, and this must be heaven," he thought as he fought to come out of the fog that held him in its grip.

The smell of sulphur had diminished but had been replaced by something even more disturbing. Was it urine? There was also a hint of disinfectant. This couldn't be heaven. Then where was he, he wondered absently? He realized now that the sounds he was hearing were coming from his own throat. He was screaming. Why? He began to struggle. Maybe this bright place wasn't any better than the dark one he had just left behind. His arms and legs were paralyzed. No matter how hard he tried, he couldn't move his limbs. Thankfully, unconsciousness overtook him and mercifully, his mind went blank. His struggling ceased and the sounds of screaming abated. The furrows on his brow relaxed and all the tension drained away from his body…

CHAPTER ONE
LIFE IN BURKESHIRE

Kate Harmon had worked in the Klindale Detox Centre for almost two years. She had seen a lot of broken lives before, but something about the man before her touched the deepest recesses of her heart. She could almost feel his pain as a physical hurt inside her own soul. Her spirit was in turmoil as she sent her prayers heavenward for the well-being of this man. Kate didn't know what God had planned, but she did know this man needed prayer desperately. She could feel the evil surrounding him, but could also feel the deep peace of God which enveloped her, like a warm blanket.

Kate had been a nurse for five years now. The first three years had been spent on the surgical floor at Mercy General Hospital in her small hometown of Burkeshire. It wasn't large as hospitals go, but her job had always been satisfying. She was well-loved by all who knew her, both in the hospital and in the unobtrusive white building one block from her home which housed the congregation of "Morningstar Christian Fellowship." Kate had practically been raised there. She had attended regularly with her parents, Bob and Betty; her brother Edward and sister Eva.

Becoming a Sunday school teacher was a natural step after she had gone as far as she could go in the teen class. She remembered sitting one Sunday in the pew when she was twelve. The message preached by Pastor David Wilkes that week was about salvation, and as she listened, Kate could feel her heart go to mush inside of her. She knew God was calling her to go up to the front of the church. As she walked down the aisle she could feel the warm glow of the smiles surrounding her and the longing and love she had for Jesus. As she knelt at the altar with tears pouring down her cheeks, she was filled to overflowing with God's Holy Spirit and in that brief moment, she gave her heart away to her Lord. As the old song, "Just As I Am" was finishing, Kate knew that her life would never be the same again.

Although Betty and Bob were both Christians, their oldest children for some unknown reason had pulled away from the church. Edward and Eva were both university students at the time and the flash and glitter that the world had to offer them was too enticing to pass up. Their faith wasn't strong enough at that point in their lives to withstand adversity and to be set apart and separate from the world. They may never have known it, but Betty had always covered all three of her children in prayer. She was confident that eventually they would come back to the church and their Christian faith, which had blossomed in their lives at an earlier age. She also knew that a faith untried was no faith at all.

Betty prayed fervently for young Kate who was at an impressionable age and could easily be swayed by her older siblings' antics. She really had no fears because Kate had always been different. She had such a quiet and gentle spirit and was always offering to help anyone, anytime. It was just this kind of character that probably gave her the strength and endurance to get through the harrowing sickness and subsequent death of her most cherished friend and confidante, her father.

As she stood looking down at the man before her, she remembered another man lying in the hospital when she was nineteen years old. All of the details were etched forever in her mind and had not diminished in the years since then. She could picture the day four months before he died, when the family had gone on an outing to a friend's cottage. As they sat down after lunch, her mother brought everyone some lemonade. That afternoon had been of the 3H variety…hot, hazy and humid! They were all grateful to be sitting in the shade of a small forest of birch and maple trees. The birds were singing such festive songs. Crickets chirped by the stream, cicadas kept up their symphony of buzzing and the sun was shimmering on the surface of the river below. A mother duck was slowly gliding through the waters, making barely a ripple behind her. Struggling to keep up, was a string of five ducklings. Everything was so peaceful…the day, the view, the surroundings and the company.

Why then did she feel such a sense of foreboding? Something wasn't right. Her mom and dad were casting furtive glances at each other and her heart caught a skip inside her breast. Her mind went numb as her father began to speak. He seemed to be talking from far away. Everything seemed so surreal. And then it struck her like a knife being twisted in her gut. Those words he said so quietly.

"We've brought you to this place today to share some disturbing news with you," her father began. "As you all know, I've been to see the doctor quite a bit lately. I had an x-ray, a CT scan and an MRI. I also saw a specialist in Andover. It's been confirmed that I have terminal lung cancer, and it's in the advanced stage. Your mother and I have dreaded telling you, and decided we would give you the news in this peaceful spot. It's always been a special place to come since you were little. We wanted you to feel God's presence here, so you could understand that he is in this situation as well."

With those dreadful words, the peace of that place was forever shattered. Kate's mind screamed out a resounding—NO! This just couldn't be happening! Not to her dad. She got up so quickly that the chair snapped closed behind her and she ran down to the water's edge. Here was the stillness and serenity she yearned for. In her anguish she cried out to her Lord.

"Why, Father? Why? He's never hurt anyone in his life and he loves you so much. You can't let this happen. I claim a healing for him in Jesus' name!" Her voice came back to her from across the waters, and the sound of its simpering noise nauseated her. As she begged for forgiveness, she once again heard that still, small voice which she treasured so much. It came unbidden to the back of her mind.

"Be still my child, and know that I am God. I love him too!"

The sound soothed her furiously beating heart. As Kate once again came back to reality, she could feel a peace that surpassed all understanding wash over her. She turned on her heel and headed back to face whatever pain lay ahead. She knew now that she could meet anything head on as long as God was there to bring her strength and comfort.

She once again joined the small circle that was her family, went over to her dad, wrapped her arms gently about his neck and kissed his forehead.

"I love you Dad, and with God's help we'll all get through this together," she said softly.

He smiled at her then, with relief on his features. She then went over and hugged her mother, bringing with her words of comfort. Next came Eva and Edward. That day, their tears brought cleansing and as their prayers lifted up towards heaven, they were fortified. The doctors had said he might have six months or maybe even one year. That wasn't long, but they vowed to make the most of the time they still had together.

CHAPTER TWO
SOUL SEARCHING

A scream brought her back to the present. She looked with compassion upon the man before her. He'd been brought into the Detox Centre four days earlier, and had yet to focus in on reality. He was still in that world in between, where he fought his own personal demons. Earlier she had thought he was actually looking right at her but then he had slipped once more into oblivion. His arms and legs were being restrained so he wouldn't hurt himself. He had apparently been found by a neighbour, who had gone to check up on him. He'd been sitting in a lawn chair by the pool with his head hanging off to one side. A forty-ounce bottle of gin lay tilted haphazardly beside him, and a razor-sharp hunting knife had fallen to the ground under his right hand. His left wrist had been slashed deeply but when he had lost consciousness his arm had fallen and been pinned to his side, thus staunching a major flow of blood. The wallet in his pocket said he was Peter Carson M.D. She wondered what his story was and why a doctor who apparently had the world by the tail, would want to take his own life. She had driven past his house to try to glean some clue as to the depths of this man. What had led him to pick up that hunting knife?

Peter lived in one of the finest neighbourhoods in the city. It was very affluent, and only families of high standing were allowed into it. The houses along this quiet strip of beauty were large, and opulent. Well-manicured lawns were all surrounded with meticulously maintained landscaping. You could just catch a glimpse of tennis courts and pool fences in the backyards of many, and the double and triple car garages housed a vast assortment of Porsches, Jaguars, and family Suburbans.

Obviously this man had a family, by the tire swing hanging sullenly from the tree in the side yard, but Kate couldn't fathom why no one had come to see him. The picture in his wallet had shown a beautiful woman laying beneath an umbrella, with a small blond-haired child toddling around her. The girl was precious. You could tell she was well looked after, wearing a designer sun-suit, sandals and a long pig tail cascading down her back. In better times, she could almost imagine the resemblance of her in this man before her. He was cleaned up now, but had been a real sight when they brought him in. His face had about six days worth of growth on it, and his neatly trimmed blond hair was dirty and matted. He obviously hadn't bathed in days and the odour emanating from him had been nauseating.

Kate opened the drapes to let the last vestiges of sunlight bring some warmth to the room. The rooms were tastefully decorated with simple flowered borders and dusty rose-coloured paint. Years of research had shown the specialists, that these soft warm colours had a calming influence on the residents in the Centre. The people who came here were called residents not patients, so they would maintain some semblance of dignity and self-esteem. It reduced recovery time and helped speed their return to society. Many selfless people spent hours of their personal time volunteering at the Klindale Detox Centre. There were doctors and nurses to fix the body; a Christian psychiatrist to help bring healing to the mind; people to help find the residents a place to stay upon their release if needed, and jobs if they didn't have one. Continuing out-patient care for one year was standard operating procedure at the facility. This greatly increased their rate of success. This was Mike Collins job. He pastored the church across the street and due to his remarkable love and patience, had led many residents to the Lord. He still found time to spend at least an hour a day on his knees to intercede for the hundreds of men, women and teens who had gone through the doors of the Centre. He was well liked and no one felt threatened by his vocation because he was so casual and down to earth. A friendly smile usually graced his face and he always had a word of encouragement for everyone he met.

On this day, Mike had come to see one person in particular. As he walked into the room he wasn't surprised to see Kate sitting beside Peter's bed, praying. He had seen her here faithfully, day after day. Mike was here today for the same reason. The man needed God's protection. Of all the residents here, Peter Carson had yet to regain full consciousness. It had been at least four days, and still he was barely functioning on his own. He was fighting something horrible in his life. Mike and Kate were both aware of Peter's need for prayer cover, so he stood beside her and together they prayed for deliverance from the evil one and for the spiritual cleansing of Peter.

Most of the residents were unaware that they were covered in prayer on a regular basis. Fifteen minutes later, the two left the Centre for the day.

"Why don't you join Marg and me for dinner, Kate? I know it's been a long day for you, and she's cooking your favourite... meatballs with pineapple."

The temptation was too much, so Kate followed Mike across the road to the church manse. Marg and Mike had four children. Elizabeth was seven, the twins Kevin and Kyle were six and little Joanne was almost five. If nothing else, mealtime at the Collins' household was certainly memorable. Every mouthful seemed to be punctuated by non-stop chatter. The home rang with laughter. This was always a welcome change for Kate. She was used to living alone in a one-bedroom apartment, six blocks away.

After the supper dishes were cleared away and the children were off playing in another part of the house, the three adults sat around the table for some more serious talk.

"How's your mother making out Kate? Has she decided whether or not she's going to move here?" asked Marg.

"She still claims that she'd rather live alone than move to the city. Edward and Eva and their families don't live far from mom and she seems to be quite content with her life. She got her prayers answered when my brother and sister finally came back to the church last year. Edward hasn't made a personal commitment to Jesus yet, but at least mom got him through the doors," laughed Kate.

After forty-five minutes and another cup of tea, Kate was on her way home. She crossed the street and got into her car, which was in the lot beside the Detox Centre. She looked fondly around the interior. It was a 1982 Spirit put out by American Motors, and it was still her first car. It wasn't as if she were a world traveller or anything like that.

The Centre was about four miles from the downtown core, therefore it wasn't as busy. It was also a lifetime away from the disgusting skin shops, crude movie houses and the street prostitutes and vagrants that graced its sidewalks and back alleys. This small piece of the city where she worked seemed to be sheltered from the realities of downtown. As she pulled out onto the street, she glanced up at the second floor of the Detox Centre. His light, third from the end, was still on. She wondered if he had come to his senses yet.

"Lord, I pray you would watch over Peter Carson and surround him with your holy angels tonight. Keep his mind safe from the evil that is threatening him. In Jesus' name I pray. Amen!"

She sent her prayer upward, and drove away silently. She was exhausted and looked forward to a nice hot bath and a comfortable bed. She thought of the pleasant evening she had tonight. The Collins family had sort of adopted Kate since she came to Klindale over two years ago, and they brought the music of laughter back into her heart. Marg had invited Kate to their church about nine months earlier. It was simply called "Cornerstone Fellowship," and was a non-denominational church, which had great appeal to Kate. She had been very discouraged in her search for a new church home, although she had been to several in Klindale.

The first church had appeared friendly enough in the beginning. The people welcomed her with open arms until they found out she didn't "speak in tongues." Kate knew it was a spiritual gift and not everyone had the same gifts. She remembered what Paul had written in First Corinthians. She had looked it up just to give herself some peace of mind.

It said: "I thank God that I speak in tongues more than all of you. But in the church I would rather speak five intelligible words to instruct others than ten thousand words in a tongue." That church, however, had insisted she would speak in tongues. So they prayed with her; anointed her head with oil and laid hands on her. Still, nothing happened, so they said she obviously wasn't praying hard enough or perhaps she had some sin in her life that she hadn't asked forgiveness for. She quickly left that church with the feeling of having an inferior Christian walk compared to the others, and questioning her own faith.

The next church had a "just name it and claim it" policy. It preached health and prosperity. All you had to do was pray in "Jesus' name". They used it like a mantra. Again Kate became disillusioned because she felt the name of Jesus shouldn't be thrown around so loosely. He deserved to be treated better than that. He was not just a genie in a bottle that you could conjure up on a whim. He didn't live in a box where you could pull him out whenever you wanted something. They also went so far as to say that if you didn't get what you were praying for, then you must have sin in your life, which was hindering the prayer process. She fairly ran out of their building.

Her next try found her in a church filled with noise. That was an understatement. Throughout the sermon and especially the prayer time, the din was unbelievable and people were constantly yelling out: "Praise the Lord! Hallelujah! Thank you Jesus! And "Amen, brother John!"

Kate found herself in the back of the church praying: "I'm sorry Lord, but I just can't concentrate on you right now! I can't even hear myself think! I won't hear you speaking to me even if you holler in my ear."

That was the last time for that church as well. Several churches she found had "feel good" doctrines. Many people thought you constantly needed to have those "warm fuzzy feelings" from God's Holy Spirit. Kate knew there had to be more to Christianity than what had thus far been offered her. She had also tried one church that looked like it had potential but mentioned nothing about Jesus, or salvation, or the fact that these two things went hand in hand.

Finally Marg had come by and invited her to their church. She tried to keep an open mind when she entered the front doors and the first thing she noticed was the warm welcome given her. Next came a time of singing praise songs where Kate felt her spirit soar. Mike was an excellent teacher and preacher, so the message he gave had all the necessary elements for salvation, personal growth, and how to take your Christianity with you into your everyday life. The scripture readings were perfect in relation to the message, and the music ministered to the deepest parts of her soul. Here Kate found a place where she could have a healthy balance in her Christian walk. It had equal parts of praise and worship, prayer, fellowship and sound biblical teaching.

Kate had been reunited with her best friend here as well. She missed Katya so much. She had gone to Sweden three weeks earlier to look after her mother, who was ill. She was due back in two days, and Kate couldn't wait for her return. Katya and Kate were closer than sisters. They could talk about absolutely everything and had similar interests. They both liked reading, swimming, skating, and most of all they both loved Jesus. They were always there for each other with words of encouragement, incentives to excel at whatever they were doing, or just tears and hugs as they struggled together in their Christian walk.

As she climbed into bed that evening, she thought about all the talks the two of them had shared over the years since they had been together. They had met in nursing school and were reunited when Kate moved to Klindale. Although they didn't have any hands-on experience, the new Detox Centre had been willing to hire the both of them on a trial run because they had gotten such high marks while in training. It had proven to be a wise move for the Centre, because the two young women had brought something special with them. Their personalities were so different.

Kate was loving, quiet, compassionate and gentle while Katya was more outgoing, boisterous, and full of mischief and life. For some reason, they complimented each other perfectly. They were both hard workers, and always brought smiles to people's faces. The residents loved the two girls, and most wondered what they had that made them so very different. They didn't understand why there was a bounce to their step and such a sparkle and light in their eyes. All they had to do was ask though, and either girl would have given a ready answer as to where their joy came from. It came from having a heart full of God's Spirit, and they wanted others to have what they had.

Kate felt something rough and warm grate on her cheek and her face broke out in a sleep-filled smile. Tiger, her kitten, was licking her and she laughed as she rubbed his belly and scratched him behind the ears. She got up and made them both some breakfast. Today was Kate's day off, so she decided that first she would go outside with the kitten for a while and then maybe do some light house cleaning. And then, maybe she would go for a bike ride up by Bayside Park. The more she tried to bury herself in the busyness of her day though, the more Peter came to her mind. She was unable to help herself and was so very confused by the thoughts going through her head. That's why she wanted to talk to Katya. She needed to tell someone what she was feeling.

Kate found herself a little bit attracted to Peter for some unfathomable reason. She hadn't even spoken to him as of yet but every time she looked at him, something stirred deep inside her heart. What disturbed her most was the fact that he was obviously married and really was in a pathetic state. He had big problems, which Kate was not prepared to deal with.

Kate grabbed her bicycle from under the stairs and took it out into glorious sunshine. What a beautiful day it was. There was just a slight breeze as she peddled away from the house, where she lived in the back. Her destination was two miles away and the ride was exhilarating. As she rode into Bayside Park, she headed onto the right hand bike trail. It wound through the middle of the park, which was decidedly darker, due to a full umbrella of foliage overhead from the numerous large trees. Sunlight filtered through the leaves and the place had an aura of peacefulness.

She came out at the south end where the trail meandered along the bank of the Granger River, so named for Thomas Granger who owned a huge chunk of property on the river. He came from old money, and was a retired judge. Kate guessed that with enough money, anybody could have a river named after them. She got off her bike and sat down beside the water. It was now after the lunch hour so the park wasn't very busy. The moms with small children didn't usually come near the water so she enjoyed the relative quietness.

As she gazed out at the sun glistening off the water, it brought back to her mind the day at the cottage years ago when her father had talked about his illness. No one knew that day just how little time he had left. Over the next three months they had travelled, gone for long drives, and as a family, had drawn closer together. By this time her dad had lost 37 pounds, his skin was pasty looking and his steps had slowed measurably. One thing that remained visibly ingrained in her mind was his attitude. Bob still had a smile for everyone despite his pain, and many words of encouragement for those who had come by to encourage him. It seemed ironic that a man as sick as he was would be the one to bring comfort, peace and love to others, but Kate knew that her father spent a couple of hours a day in prayer. It was God who sustained Bob and never left his side. He had such a peace in his heart because he knew where he was going.

When he was finally admitted to the hospital for the remainder of the illness, she remembered how he had led his night nurse to the Lord. Kate smiled with pride as she remembered how animated her dad had been when he told his family what had happened. The evening duties had slowed and the nurse had gone from room to room to make sure the patients were comfortable enough for the night. She had worked on the "Sunlight Wing" for the past fifteen years. Because she had watched so many patients dying and had seen so much death, you'd have thought she would have become hardened to it all, to protect her own mind. But Janice Foley had a soft heart. She worked with dedication and compassion towards every single person on that floor. She'd seen the whole spectrum of emotions such as anger, disbelief, bewilderment, pain, anguish, fear and hate. Seldom, if ever, did she recall anyone going through pain with joy! This was unheard of. She had determined to find out what this man had, that most others didn't.

She went into Bob's room on the pretence of filling his water jug. He had been praying beside the bed and she didn't want to disturb him. As she quietly turned to leave, he gently called her back. "Something is bothering you tonight Janice. What is it?" he asked her. She was nervous and her cheeks held the faint flush of embarrassment. She stammered, and finally just blurted out what was on her mind.

"I hope you aren't offended by what I'm going to say, but I need your help in understanding something. I've seen the pain you've been going through and yet you never seem to be overwhelmed by it. I've seen others around you cry in their desperation and fear of death, yet you still radiate joy. Forgive me if I'm being forward, but where are you able to find joy in such an adverse situation. Please help me to understand," she pleaded with him as her eyes misted over. With a voice filled with the love of God, he calmly told her what she needed to hear.

"Janice," he began. "I have Jesus in my heart and I know where I'm going when this old body is finished with me."

He could clearly see that she didn't understand so over the next few days he took her slowly through the salvation process. He told her how she had to first admit that she was a sinner. Then she had to be willing to repent or turn away from her sins. Next, she had to believe that Jesus Christ died for her on the cross, and rose from the grave three days later. Then through prayer, she had to invite Jesus Christ to come into her life as her personal Lord and Saviour. Janice finally said she understood, so one evening, both patient and nurse bowed their heads right in the middle of that hospital room and prayed God's Holy Spirit into her heart.

That had given Kate's dad such a lift. She swore to herself the next day, that she had never seen his eyes sparkle more, or his grin get any wider. In the following three weeks, the transforming change in Janice had been amazing too. Kate wasn't surprised. She had seen many times, how a life could be changed with Jesus in it.

CHAPTER THREE
PETER RECALLS

The squawking of a gull overhead brought Kate back to the present. She skipped a smooth flat stone on the water's surface and got her bike from under the tree. She backtracked and headed home for another quiet dinner with Tiger and the television. On her way, she stopped by the small family-owned grocery store on the corner of her street. She had been a regular customer since moving to Klindale and was known by name. Andrew Card and his wife Sylvia had two adorable children; Colin, who was twelve and Carrie who was eight years old. Andrew looked up when the little bell on the door tinkled.

"Good afternoon Kate. Have you been enjoying your day off?" he asked her with a smile.

"Actually, it was very peaceful," she replied. "I went for a really great ride through the park this afternoon and just about nodded off on the side of the river. It wasn't very busy for a change, so I had the place all to myself for about an hour."

"Katya should be home soon, shouldn't she?" Andrew inquired.

"Yes, she'll be back some time tomorrow afternoon. Her plane is supposed to arrive at 4:00 p.m. She said she would call me the minute she gets in. I had best get myself some groceries before you close up shop around me," she laughed.

When Kate got home she let Tiger out for a run and got supper going. She decided on something light and just had a bowl of soup and a grilled cheese sandwich. Kate still found it difficult to make meals for only one person. It seemed like such a waste to make a casserole or anything like that because she didn't have a very big freezer and didn't like the same dish over and over again.

After supper she called her mom like she did every Wednesday night and found out all the latest news from her old hometown. She hung up feeling good, and sat down to watch television. The news was on and she really wasn't paying much attention until she heard some words that got her focused in a hurry.

"When asked what she thought about her ex-husband regaining consciousness today, Annette Carson replied brutally that she didn't care whether he lived or died."

"He was nothing but a lousy drunk and a murderer," she replied. The female commentator went on to say how it was too bad that the governor's daughter had to be subjected to such tawdry media coverage due to Peter's foolishness.

"Let's face it," said Annette. "He's just another of the city's hopeless rehab cases that the taxpayers are babysitting. It's a disgrace, but someone told me that Peter has a private suite, and is enjoying his paid vacation immensely," she concluded.

The commentator was caught by surprise by her vehemence. "And that's it for Channel 10 News at 7 p.m." she stammered. "You can catch more of this story by staying tuned to this station for news at 11. We'll keep you updated!"

Kate just sat there with her mouth agape. Her heart was thumping straight through her chest like a caged bird ready to take flight. Two things registered in her mind at once. The first was "murderer," and the second was "ex-husband." So he wasn't married now, but he had killed someone. That made matters even worse for Peter. He really did need prayer. That must have been the reason why Kate's spirit had been so agitated. She knew something wasn't right in the man's life besides the fact that he was in a detoxification clinic. She got right to her knees and prayed in earnest for the next half-hour, for this man who had so recently made such an impact in her life. A couple of pieces to the puzzle of this virtual stranger were now in place. Kate remembered also that the news commentator had mentioned that Peter was now awake. She didn't know if this could be true or not, because obviously they had gotten the information about his room all wrong. They had made it sound like Peter was staying at the Hilton Hotel, so maybe they didn't know where he really was. That was a possibility. There was no point in knocking herself out about it. She had to be at work by 8:30 a.m. because she was on the 9-5 shift.

Tomorrow was also the day of Katya's return, so Kate knew she would probably be up late tomorrow night, hearing about all the details of her trip. She let Tiger in, washed her dish and pots and then hurried off to bed. She never realized how tired she really was. One minute she was pulling the soft cotton quilt up to her chin and the next minute, she was out like a light.

The next day Kate arose and was greeted at the window by rain, thunder and lightning. "Great day," she mumbled to Tiger around a half-eaten piece of raisin toast. By the time she had run through the front doors of the Centre, she was thoroughly soaked. She thought taking the car would be a smart idea, but nevertheless, she was drenched. Kate changed into a fresh uniform from her bag and quickly dried her hair under the hand dryer in the ladies washroom.

Drs. David Waters, Derek Campbell, and Martin Graydon were on with her today, along with a staff of eight other nurses. There was one doctor and three nurses for each of the three floors, which consisted of nine rooms each. There was only one bed per room so residents in various stages of affliction and recovery wouldn't be able to disturb the others. Each person had the mental, spiritual and physical parts of their bodies ministered to. When they left this place, they had to have a new outlook on life or else they would be seen again and again. Kate went about her duties of getting the residents washed and ready for their morning seminar on "Improved Self Esteem."

As she cleaned up the soiled bedding and gown in Peter's room, she glanced up and saw that he was watching her. That darned flush went to her cheeks again and she spoke quickly to hide her embarrassment.

"Welcome back, Dr. Carson," she stammered. "We've all been very concerned about you. May I get you anything?"

"I could use some water please," he croaked from a throat that hadn't been used for several days. "I really am dry."

Peter obviously wasn't sure why he was in this place, and he was staring at her quite frankly. Kate left to get some ice for his water jug as he contemplated his surroundings. He had recognized her right away. She was the angel from his dream. So it was no dream at all. It was still very fuzzy in his mind, but he did remember the fear and the darkness, and something trying to catch up to him. Then he recalled the instant of bright light and this young nurse. He didn't know what was different about her, but he was instantly attracted to her in a way he had never experienced before. He couldn't figure it out.

She was not someone you would call beautiful, but she somehow had beauty. She didn't have the body of a runway model, but she was graceful and poised. For a man who could have had any woman, anytime, he wondered about this plain woman's magnetism. She wore no make-up and neither did she need any. Her name could be called "plain Jane" yet there was something about her. It was her eyes, he decided. There was some kind of sparkle about them. They actually looked alive. He was curious, and wondered what was different about her. He had lived with a whole spectrum of eyes all of his life. He'd seen eyes filled with passion, eyes of hate, eyes of greed, eyes of ice and finally just "dead" eyes. Those were the eyes which had lost all hope of life and living. Those eyes had stared back at him as he saw himself in the mirror the night he tried to take his own life.

He wanted to ask her why there was such a glint in her eyes. Peter looked down at the bandage wrapped around his wrist. There was a dull throb there, so he knew his wrist really had been slashed. How had he been found before death overtook him and more importantly, who had found him? He felt like his life was already ended so why was he still here? It made him more than a little angry that his suicide had been thwarted. He couldn't do anything right!

He thought about the final scene that had been played out with Annette, four months ago. She had spewed forth such hate and ugliness from deep within her black soul, that he could still feel the chill of her accusations towards him. He wondered how they could have been married for eight years and really not known each other. He had loved Annette when they first got married. He was fresh out of medical school when they met at a party given by a mutual acquaintance of the two. The attraction had been purely physical for both of them, but they figured it must be love. They were joined five months later in a lavish wedding display, typical of those who had money, or wanted other people to think they did.

She was used to having whatever she wanted and now that Peter was an established doctor working full time at one of the largest hospitals in the city, she wanted it all. The more he bought her, the more she wanted. She wanted her "daddy" and her debutante friends to see that she had it made in the shade all on her own. Although he was exhausted quite often from the long hours he put in, Annette wouldn't pass up any opportunity to do the party scene. There were always cocktail parties and the like, so it seemed a natural progression to start having drinks in the evenings they spent together…and then drinking even when they were by themselves. She drank during luncheons with her so-called friends and then tried to cover up her drunkenness with breath mints and lies. She was fooling nobody!

She began to use more and more make-up to cover up the ravages of drink. Due to weight gain from the alcohol, she began to purge herself after meals. The noise of her retching turned his stomach as well. A tummy tuck here, lyposuction there, and she always managed to look pretty good. Although Peter wasn't a fall down drunk back then, he had become an alcoholic and his work was starting to show the effects of late nights. He couldn't quite hide the slight tremor in his hands anymore. The two of them eventually tried to cut down a bit. Their lives were empty and meaningless to him. To try and mend their eroding relationship and restore the love in their marriage, they decided to start a family.

One year later, they had a beautiful fair-haired daughter who they named Bethany. Annette had actually refrained from drinking throughout most of her pregnancy. When she failed miserably at breast-feeding; listened to endless colic cries in the night and changed scores of filthy diapers, she was ready to make a concerted effort at drowning her sorrows in a bottle of gin. Peter did have to give her credit though. Bethany always wore the latest designer clothes and was clean and healthy looking. Peter still liked to have a few "social drinks" when they were out. Others might have jokingly called him a party animal, but in truth, he was an alcoholic. The only thing that really mattered to him in life was his little girl though. He worshipped and adored her. She held his heart in her tiny hand.

He remembered teaching her to ride a tricycle and then the day he took the training wheels off and she had laughingly left the safety of his hand to go it alone up the long driveway. He could still hear her call out to him with such pride in her voice.

"Look Daddy," she cried out with delight. "I'm big now. I can do it all by myself!" His heart had swelled with love for this unbelievable treasure of theirs.

Well, it wasn't doing him any good dwelling on such things. His little girl and his wife were both gone now. It was thinking too much, which had landed him here in the first place. He was brought out of his reverie by soft footsteps beside his bedside.

"Sorry I took so long Dr. Carson. There was an emergency at the end of the hall," Kate said quickly.

"Seeing that you seem to know all about me, tell me what your name is so I don't have to keep calling you "nurse."

"My name is Kate. I've been your nurse for part of the last six days since you were brought in," she shyly replied.

He was terrified by the fact that he had been out to lunch for so many days; days which were lost to him forever. They would never be recaptured and inwardly he was glad of that. He vaguely thought of the frightening black dreams and shook his head at the violent images that threatened to overrun his every waking moment. Kate was looking at him with a face that registered compassion. He wondered why she should care what happened to him. She knew nothing about who Peter Carson was and if she knew she would probably run out of the room in revulsion and disgust. He didn't want to think anymore. What he really wanted was a good stiff drink, not a glass of water. He didn't want to remember. There was pain in remembering. Pain and extreme hurt.

"I think I want to go to sleep now, Kate. All of a sudden I feel really tired. Perhaps we can talk again, later on. Good night or good morning, or whatever it is."

He knew he was tripping over his tongue and felt totally foolish and awkward. Thankfully Kate was retreating out of the room, so he could be alone to reflect on this predicament he had gotten himself into. "Why couldn't you just let me die?" he silently screamed out to God. This just isn't fair he thought wildly. He felt like a trapped animal in a cage with no doors. There was no escape from the prison his mind had created, as he looked about with feelings of panic and dread. Was it ever going to get any better, he wondered?

He remembered when Annette had left him. She had slapped his face and cut his heart to the quick when she had screamed out that sickening word, "MURDERER!" That was the last he'd seen of her. He had withdrawn completely from life, and had become a recluse. He drowned himself in drink and as the weeks went by, he began to miss more and more time at work. When Peter did show up, he was useless because of his bleary sleepless eyes and shaking hands. The hospital had resigned itself to his deterioration, and he was finally put on medical leave without apology or fanfare, to get himself cleaned up. For the past two months he had tried without success to drink himself to death. When that had failed, he tried the hunting knife in final desperation. There'd been so much loss. Total fatigue was weighting his body to the bed. He slowly drifted into grateful oblivion. Then the nightmare began replaying in his head...the party, the free-flowing booze, the baby-sitter's house, the accident, the blood, the screams...his own now...the wail of sirens. Thankfully he sunk deeper within himself and found...absolutely nothing!

CHAPTER FOUR
LIFE IN DETOX

Much later that evening, Kate and Katya finished their second pot of tea. Her friend looked relaxed and wonderful. Katya had been very upset about her mother before she left, but the time spent ministering to her had finally made the worry lines on her forehead disappear. Katya was three years older than Kate's twenty-nine years. Both were still unmarried, because they hadn't found anyone that they wanted to spend the rest of their lives with. It was so hard to find good Christian men. There weren't a lot out there and the good ones were usually taken.

Katya had been filling Kate's head with pictures of all aspects of Swedish life for the past hour and a half with a face full of animation. Her eyes twinkled with mirth as she recalled humorous stories of things that had happened to her. The Nilsson family appeared to be fairly eccentric, which had given Katya such endearing qualities in her own character. Kate laughed along with her and knew now what had been missing in her life for the past few weeks. It was Katya's laughter. It was infectious and brought smiles to anyone who was within earshot of her. Finally, tired and winded, Katya decided to get some sleep at her own place.

"I'm suffering from jet lag," she said around a huge yawn. "Luckily I don't have to be back to work until Monday. When do you have to work, Kate?" she asked.

"I work tomorrow, get Saturday and Sunday off, and go back on Monday. Then we can be back together as the fearsome twosome," Kate joked. "When I'm through work tomorrow, maybe we can go out for supper. There's still a lot of stuff I want to talk to you about, but I know you're tired right now. We'll wait until tomorrow night, okay?" she added.

"I'd like that, Kate. I have tons of laundry, banking, bills to pay and all that stuff that piles up after three weeks of neglect. I'll definitely be ready for a meal by then. See you tomorrow at six then. I'll pick you up. Bye love! I sure missed you," Katya said as she gave Kate a bear hug and took her leave.

Kate crawled wearily into bed that night and sleep quickly overtook her. She had a blissfully dreamless night until the early light of dawn began seeping around the blinds. Then a story unfolded in the recesses of her mind, conjuring up all sorts of imagery and emotion within her. The place was somehow familiar and vague at the same time. She was riding her bike and had stopped on a large hill. When Kate first moved to the city, she had biked all over the place while she was applying for jobs.

She had seen this place somewhere on one of those excursions, but she couldn't quite remember where or when. There were two large lions perched upon wide stone pillars, which flanked the thick iron rungs of a massive gate. There was a curved sign overhead. She had to back up to read it and in her sleep-enhanced state she wondered why she could possibly be here of all places. It read "Birch Cemetery." This was strange, and not just a little bit scary. She felt an unreasonable urge to take a walk in this ethereal place. Kate had discarded her bike beside a high stone wall and timidly walked through the gates. It was as if the outside world never existed in here.

The trees and the pine needle blanket covering the ground, muffled all exterior noise. There were no car horns, no squealing tires, no life whatsoever, save that of the birds above and the lone gnarled grounds keeper. The earth was spongy underfoot and as she was drawn deeper into the centre of the property, she began to feel unnerved.

"Don't be alarmed, my child. I have something you need to see, to fully understand the man you've been thinking about."

Kate wheeled around like a cornered animal and standing before her was the most blinding light she'd ever seen. Kate shielded her eyes and prostrated herself on the ground.

"What do you want from me?" she stammered.

"I'm simply a messenger, Kate. You can stand up. I've been sent to show you something in this place. It will enable you to help the man get his life back. Follow me, please."

Meekly Kate arose and followed the huge man before her. Light emanated off amazingly white hair and skin of bronze. He had eyes like flames that burned right into her soul. He had to be an angel she thought with amazement. Her rational mind mocked that idea, but the spirit within her nevertheless confirmed him as real. All of a sudden he stopped and moved off to one side. There before her was a small white tombstone. Obviously it hadn't been there for very long. There was an enormous bouquet of roses, which had dried into brittle brown petals adorning the base of the stone and obscuring the words etched there. Two words did stand out in blazing starkness against the darkened background. It simply read "Sleep, Bethany."

Tiger licked her face and Kate unwillingly awakened. She sat up in bed, stroking her pet and wondering what her dream had meant. God was obviously trying to tell her something and the answer would be found in the cemetery. At once the idea both frightened and pleased Kate. God wanted to use her in Peter's healing process and she was grateful for answered prayers. She had been looking for a way to help him. Kate never wondered how she knew without a doubt that the angel meant Peter. Silently, she wondered who Bethany was, but she knew God had taken her to the cemetery in the first place, so she would trust her Lord. Everything would be done according to His Will and purpose. Of that, she was quite certain.

Kate got up and prepared herself for the workday ahead. On her way to the Centre, she determined to find the cemetery if it took her all weekend. She was sure that Katya would want to help. One of the residents under her care was going home today. They would have a small prayer time for him in the tiny chapel on the third floor.

Going home was a hard thing for most residents. They definitely didn't leave as the same person. Some left as new creatures in Christ who had turned their lives over to their Saviour. Some left in great fear and had doubts like: "Will I be able to get my job back? Will I be tempted once again to substance abuse? Will my family ever forgive me and forget the awful past, as I'm now a different person than I was before?"

These things racked the minds of the departing residents and made some even physically ill, due to anxiety. That's why Kate loved her job so much. The need was great, and she felt humbled to work here. The words of Jesus came softly to her.

"Truly I say to you, whatever you did for one of the least of these, you did for me."

Those words brought her comfort in the more difficult times. She would picture Jesus in her mind and would imagine him ministering and healing, in this place. What a role model Christians had in Him. The standards were high, but the rewards more than made up for it.

She greeted Thomas Dillon who was at the desk on the main floor. Thomas was a retired accountant who volunteered his time twice a week. He was a gentle giant who topped six feet, four inches. Thomas' wife had passed away two years earlier and although he had a smile for everyone, there was still a haunting sadness in his eyes. Kate made sure she brought him homemade muffins once a week, and it was a standing game between them that he had to guess what kind she had made.

"Good morning to you Thomas. The city actually smells fresh after the rain yesterday. That's a novel idea, isn't it?" she quipped. "I almost drove down Main Street earlier just to remind myself that I wasn't in a small town anymore."

He laughed and rolled his eyes at her. She took the stairs two at a time to the second floor. It wasn't much in the way of workout but it was better than nothing. She found herself remembering the dream she had earlier this morning, but decided to push it to the back burner until work was over. She needed to be focused, to be effective.

Kate began her morning by discussing last night's happenings with her colleagues at the nursing station.

"So Dave Whiton leaves us today, eh Kate?" asked Susan Haywood. "I'll try to get my work finished on time so I can join you in the chapel for prayer at 11:00 a.m." she said.

"That would be great," Kate replied. "Where two or more gather in Jesus' name, there he will be in their midst."

"Dave is going to need Him," said Sharon Marshall.

"Well, if there's nothing more needed of me, I'm going to get started. I've got a busy day ahead of me," said Kate. She went to room 208 first, where Amos Parkins was staying. He was a dear old man, who had lived on the streets for about thirty years. As the cold nights of winter approached each year, Amos took up permanent residence for the duration of the season. He did have a drinking problem so Amos had a legitimate reason for being here. Everyone knew that if he wasn't here where he would be safe, he would probably be found dead on the streets somewhere. All he really needed was a kind person to listen to him and some love and compassion. He reminded Kate of an old sea captain with his tanned and weather-beaten face.

"Good morning, Amos. I hear you put in a really good night last night. We've got Dave going home this morning, so I won't have much time to spend with you before lunch," said Kate.

"That's all right Miss Kate. I'm going to be reading from that book you brought me last week. I'm just about finished too," he replied with unmistakable pride in his voice.

"Well, that's really great, Amos. I have lots more where that one came from. When you're single, you seem to get a lot of reading done," she laughed.

Kate listened while he told a couple of his infamous stories. Amos could spin a yarn with the best of them. He had seen and heard a lot in his seventy odd years, and had a whole truck load of stories in which to draw from. If Kate didn't have to work, she knew she could listen to him for hours.

"I'll have to leave for a bit, and then I'll be back", she replied apologetically.

She hesitated outside of room 209 just long enough to say a quick prayer. Smiling as she went through the door she said, "Good morning Peter. I see you got your tubes and wires pulled out this morning. Would you like to get up and go for a short walk?"

Peter seemed to be far away this morning and very withdrawn. She knew from the look on his face that he hadn't heard a word she had said. She reached out and touched his hand. He seemed to snap out of his reverie, and registered surprise at seeing her. There was a hint of tears still glistening on his cheek and Kate's breath caught in her throat as her heart went out to him.

What thoughts could possibly be going through his mind, she wondered. She thought about the tiny white tombstone, but knew she couldn't say anything about "Bethany". For some reason, she knew it wasn't time yet. He wasn't ready. She repeated her earlier words to him and he agreed to go for a walk. They slowly went down the hall to the bright, airy sitting room. Everyone in the Centre was on a first name basis because it helped people recover faster. They felt better about themselves knowing someone cared enough to call them by their first name.

"Do you feel like talking, Peter?" she asked. You seem a little distracted this morning."

"I know you won't be able to understand this Kate but I'm angry because I'm here. I mean because I'm still alive. I've seen you praying several times and it makes me mad because right now I'm very angry at God. I should have died that night but He wouldn't let me. Life for me is finished and hopeless and I don't want to keep enduring it. Now do you know what I'm struggling with?" he retorted.

"I won't claim to know what you're going through Peter, because I'd be lying to you. I can see you are in pain. I do know there are many people praying for you and things are going to get better. Please believe that. God must not be finished with you, or you would have died that night in the chair. You must have a powerful angel watching over you Peter. There's an old saying which states that God doesn't make junk. We are all special and unique. We are all made in God's image and are loved by Him, as are you, Peter. You've been given a second chance at life," she said, hoping that he would understand what it was that she was getting at.

"You don't really believe all that do you?" he asked.

"With all my heart and soul," she replied without a moment's hesitation. He had been watching her face for several minutes now and couldn't fathom what was happening there. Her eyes were dancing and appeared to be on fire with the passion of her convictions. There was something alive in there. He tried to grasp his thoughts. Peter's heart was stirring inside his chest and for the second time in one week he wondered about this woman. He wanted to get back to the room, and do some thinking about what she had said. As they stood to leave, Peter blurted out what was bothering him.

"Your eyes," he began. "There's something about your eyes. I can't really describe it. What is it that you have, that makes your eyes like that?" he asked with a frown on his face.

Her soft laughter sounded like wind chimes on a summer's eve. It was gentle, yet musical. "God's Holy Spirit lives inside me Peter. I asked Jesus to be the Lord of my life over 15 years ago and he's still changing me, after all this time. You see Christianity isn't just about going to church once in a while, or being a "good person" or helping others. Although these things are all good, it isn't what being a follower of Christ is about. We don't get to heaven by anything we do, only by what He has already done for us on the cross. Most people don't realize this, though. They figure that if you can chalk up enough brownie points in this life, God will be beholden to them and will feel obligated to cough up salvation on a platter. The terrible thing is that they'll die for these ideas, because a personal commitment to Christ is the only way for salvation," she said with great inflection in her voice.

Peter didn't know if he believed all of what she said or not, but he decided she had given him some food for thought. He entered his room and hesitated in the doorway long enough to ask Kate to stop by and talk some more about her God.

"I'd like that Peter," she said with conviction. "I'm sorry if I get a little carried away when I talk about Jesus. It's just that He's my life and I want everyone to have what I have. I'll definitely talk to you again." She smiled goodbye, hurried down the hall to the elevators and pushed the button for the third floor. Her cheeks were warm to the touch. She ducked into the elevator and took a deep breath. Kate couldn't believe she had just blurted all that out so fast. But now that her faith was out in the open, she hoped that Peter would respond to God in a positive way. She left the elevator and made her way to the tiny chapel.

Mike Collins and two nurses from other floors, had already arrived and were seated in a circle at the front of the room. It was simply decorated with a dark rich wood adorning the walls and pot lights in the ceiling, to cut the glare. The overall feeling was one of warmth, quiet and reverence. Kate made her way to the front.

"Good morning, guys. Sharon will be up in a sec. There was just some last minute paperwork to finish off and she said she wanted to look after it," said Mike. "How are you Kate? I hear Katya got back yesterday. You must be so glad." Kate nodded her agreement as Sharon and Dave walked in behind her.

"Here's the guest of honour now!" said Mike. "Please take a seat, friends and we'll begin. Dave, you've been here for the past five weeks. You have been through a living hell and have survived. There are many temptations out on the streets and you are going to need a lot of prayer cover. You will probably feel like you can take on the whole world at first, but you must realize that in all innocence, your family and friends may try to get you to compromise what you have learned here over the last while.

They won't understand they're hurting you, so that's why you must always be on guard. There's a passage in the bible that says, "Satan is prowling about looking for someone to devour." Be aware of your surroundings and stick to your daily routine as much as possible. If you have a routine in place, it will be harder to stray, and your life will be more manageable. Now let's join hands and bow our heads in prayer."

As they lifted their voices up, God's peace washed over all present and Dave knew that he wouldn't be leaving this place alone. After a short time of fellowship, they broke up and went their separate ways. Mike walked Dave to the first floor, while Kate grabbed his small bag that housed a few paltry items. She followed after them and wished Dave good luck and best wishes. He walked out those front doors to the waiting taxi with his one small bag and never looked back. He just focused straight ahead to his new future. That was as it should be, thought Kate with a faint smile.

CHAPTER FIVE
KATYA GOES HOME

Kate finished off her day, and looked forward to the weekend. Kate had almost forgotten her dinner engagement with Katya. She drove home and got ready. While she waited for her friend, Kate thought about what she would be doing tomorrow. She checked the phone book to see if there was a Birch Cemetery listed. It was a long shot, but definitely worth a try. She found what she was looking for right away, as her finger dragged down the list. The words practically jumped off the page. She wrote down the address and determined that she would go there early in the morning. The door opened with a bang and in walked Katya. They had dropped the amenities of knocking on the door, a long time ago.

"Hi Kate," she said as she fairly bounded into the room.

Kate wondered where she got her energy from. Katya would be thirty-three in February, and she had the endurance of a twenty year old. That's life she thought to herself. If she mentioned it to Katya, her friend would probably laugh in her face.

"Well don't we just look like a pair of old librarians," smirked Kate.

They both laughed then, until the tears ran down their faces. Both were wearing very conservative looking suits with a white blouse, and pumps. While Kate preferred skirts, Katya loved to wear slacks. Tiger thought they were both nuts and ran under the bed. When they could both contain themselves, they left for "La Maison Rouge." It had excellent French onion soup and chicken done in a mushroom and wine sauce that was to die for. The two women usually ate there every couple of months and they were always welcomed as old regulars. When you lived in a large city it was really nice to feel like you were known. After their meal was finished, the waiter just refilled their coffee cups for the next forty-five minutes. He stood back and smiled as he watched the two women. Whatever they were talking about, sure had them animated. Their hands were going as fast as their lips.

Paul always liked to imagine what each of his customers was talking about. He figured they were probably working women who'd been separated for a while, hence, the animation. He went smugly back to work praising himself for his clever deductions. Perhaps one day he would write a play about life in the city or some such thing. He chuckled and started clearing a table. The women got up and left. Paul watched out the large front window as the taller of the two unlocked the door of the car across the street. An older model car drove slowly by the restaurant, blocking his view of the women. When he would be asked later, he wouldn't be able to tell what the colour and make of the car was, or the description of its occupants.

What caught his attention and made him go to the front window in the first place was the glint of street light bouncing off something metallic. And then he heard it. It sounded like firecrackers, but the screams told him differently. People in the restaurant were looking around at each other and getting up to look out the window. When the vehicle passed, Paul could still see the car across the street. The woman that had been unlocking the door was slowly sinking to her knees. Her hands seemed to claw the air as she reached for an imaginary hand to hold.

The other woman ran around the car to support her friend. Her mouth was open to scream, but the only sounds escaping her throat were a soft whimpering, like that of a small, frightened animal. Paul ran then, as he was finally shocked into action. Cars were stopping on the street and the sound of sirens was getting louder. Paul knelt beside the woman on the ground and gently put her head in his lap. She fairly went limp in his arms and although she wasn't speaking it was her eyes that made Paul examine her more closely. They registered pain, shock and bewilderment. She was lying in an ever-widening pool of blood. His heart went out to the other girl who was shaking like a leaf. She was mumbling something under her breath, which he couldn't quite catch. He placed his fingers on the woman's neck and could feel a fluttery pulse.

The ambulance and police car pulled up to the curb simultaneously. Paul watched as the woman was loaded into the back of the ambulance and then just stared at its retreating taillights. He felt numb with shock. People on the sidewalk were all talking at once, as they tried to tell the two officers what they had seen. Paul waited in line. Tonight he really had a story to tell. Who knew? Maybe someday he would write a book. The other woman was ushered into the back of the cruiser. She was sobbing hysterically.

Kate sat staring straight ahead, as she thought back on the evening. It had begun so wonderfully, but had ended in a nightmare. She shook her head as tears fell softly from her eyes. Kate felt her heart fluttering in her chest as she fumbled in her purse for a Kleenex. She couldn't believe what she had witnessed. Katya had been home for only a matter of hours and now…nothing. She prayed in earnest that God would surround her with his mighty angels. If she were to lose Katya, it would be like losing a part of herself. Kate felt violated, like her life had just been chewed up and spit out. There was one thing that would be forever etched in her mind no matter what happened before this night drew to a close. That face! His eyes had a fevered look and his lips had been brought back in a… she searched for a word. A snarl was what he had. Kate felt the gooseflesh rising at the nape of her neck just thinking about it. It had obviously been a random drive by shooting. Kate would never be able to fathom why though. In less than a minute, Kate's world had been ripped apart and Katya's blood had been forced out of a gaping hole in her chest to blanket the sidewalk with her warmth.

They had talked about everything over dinner. It had all been so perfect. If they'd only stayed for one more cup of coffee, she thought to herself. Maybe none of this would have happened. The siren from the ambulance grew louder as the police cruiser turned the corner and quickly approached from behind. The lights from the emergency entrance to the hospital were just up ahead. With a jolt, they came to an abrupt stop. Automatic doors swished silently open as Kate approached on the run. The sounds of orders being barked out were the first things she heard.

Katya was being wheeled quickly down the hall towards a row of dark brown elevators. As Kate ran down the hall after them, she watched as the elevator doors closed around the stretcher. She looked around in sheer panic when a strong arm gently grasped her wrist.

"Slow down now, Miss. They've taken her up to surgery. It looks like they may be a while. There's a waiting room at the end of this hall. You can stay in there and they'll come out and let you know how she's doing whenever they can," said the kindly looking police officer.

He seemed genuinely concerned about her friend, so Kate just gave him a wan smile and headed down the hall towards the waiting room. She slumped into the nearest chair, dejected and alone. She guessed correctly that it would just be a waiting game now. Kate knew she had to get a grip on things, or she was going to lose it. Phone calls needed to be made, so she reached into her bag to grab her cell phone. That's when she got a good look at herself and felt her stomach drop. In the harsh light the blood almost looked black and it was all over her white blouse. Her hands started to shake uncontrollably and she began to cry again.

When she pulled herself together, she called Mike Collins' house. "Please come to the hospital right away Mike. I'm at Western General. Katya was shot outside of the restaurant and she's in surgery right now. She's in bad shape, Mike. I could use some support. I'll explain everything when you get here. Maybe I will have heard something positive by then."

She could hear Mike talking to Marg in the background. He was back on the line in a second. "I'll be right there," he said without preamble.

Mike drove as quickly as possible and was in the parking lot of the hospital within ten minutes. He found Kate in the waiting room. As soon as she saw him come in she started to sob again. Mike could see the blood all over the front of her and he just reached over to her and took her in his arms and held her while she cried. Finally, when the sobbing had subsided, he extricated himself gently.

"What happened tonight Kate? Where's Katya? Is she going to be all right?"

Kate blew her nose and wiped her puffy eyes with a tissue. She had a splitting headache and was exhausted from the questioning by the police. They had tried to pick her brain clean of details concerning what kind of car it was and what the occupants of the car had looked like. She hadn't wanted to remember the details but also knew they would never leave her. The boy's face was ingrained in her mind. Kate still couldn't understand where such hate could come from in such a young man.

She remembered her teenage years with joy and looked back with only fond memories. What was wrong with society nowadays, she wondered? The one detective had casually replied that it was normal for the hundreds of kids who were a part of the many street gangs in the city. They were angry at life itself and everyone, from parents to the school system, to the myriad of law enforcement officers. All were feeling the brunt of that anger first hand. Kate realized that although she had been brought up and raised in a Christian home, she had lacked one thing in her life, and that was exposure. She had been sheltered from a lot of the terrible things that went on in her world and was thus unprepared for the violence and hate. It caught her by surprise and forced her to face reality head on. Kate didn't like what she saw.

Now as the two of them sat in the waiting room, Kate found the words pouring out in a torrent. She needed to talk and Mike was a really good listener. When she had drained herself of all emotion, she looked up from hands that she just now realized were red and sore from rubbing and twisting them continuously. They decided that it was not a good idea to upset Katya's mother, as she wasn't in the best of health and any premature worrying might be harmful for her. They would wait and see what the outcome of the surgery was, before they called.

"I'll take you home now if you want, Kate. I can call you as soon as I hear anything. You look exhausted. It's going to be some time yet by the sounds of it," Mike said with compassion in his voice.

But there was no way Kate was going to leave until she had news one way or the other. Four hours later, a tired looking surgeon padded quietly towards them wearing a sweat covered gown and hospital green slippers over his outdoor shoes. His face was covered in perspiration and his brow was furrowed. Kate and Mike looked quietly at each other as the doctor began to speak.

"Your friend was in pretty bad shape when she came in and she had lost a lot of blood. She's presently in I.C.U. in critical condition. The bullet entered just to the left of her right shoulder blade and went through her one lung and damaged part of the ribcage. I have to tell you that it doesn't look very good for her. We have done our best, but only a miracle can save her now. I'm truly sorry."

As he turned his back on them, they could hear him mumble about it being such a waste. Well, if it was a miracle that was needed, then they would pray for Katya until that miracle happened. Again Kate struggled with the concept of prayer.

She would pray then. But she was torn. Should she pray for healing if God wanted to take her home, or should she pray that God would take her home quickly, so she didn't suffer? She decided to just pray for her best friend from the depths of her heart and as she laid Katya before the foot of God's throne in her mind, she felt a sense of peace wash over her. Whatever the outcome, Katya was in the best possible hands. When Kate felt like she was strong enough, she tugged Mike to his feet and started leading him towards the elevators.

"It's time Mike. I need to see her if I can. I feel like time is running out for her."

Mike agreed and followed closely behind her. They stopped for directions on the fourth floor. A pleasant faced woman at the nurses' station looked with compassion at Kate and pointed down a long corridor to their right. Slowly, but with purpose, they made their way down the hall to the intensive care unit. They were only allowed to see her from the safety of the doorway. Although Kate had imagined what her friend would look like, she was nevertheless unprepared for the shock that awaited her. Katya's skin was pale and shiny. There were bags and monitors everywhere and beeps were going on and off in a rhythmic pattern. A large bandage covered her chest and her shallow breathing barely moved the thin blanket. Kate wanted to hold her hand but realized that she was still contaminated with Katya's blood. Looking at her friend, she couldn't even see an eyelid flutter or a finger twitch. She prayed for her where she stood. Mike rested against the wall with his head bent in prayer.

All of a sudden a faint smile appeared on Katya's mouth and collectively they heard an audible gasp. Then there was nothing as the monitors started whining and they registered a flat line. Kate finally broke as she knew that Katya was gone. Doctors and nurses began hurrying into the intensive care unit and tried in vain to revive her but it was over in no time and Kate heard a doctor call out the time of her death. She turned and fell into Mike's arms. Mike gave her support as she called Katya's mom and explained as calmly as she could what had happened. Then Mike drove her home.

Katya's car had been impounded by the police to aid in their investigation so they didn't have to worry about moving that right now. Kate said goodnight to Mike and thanked him for being there for her. Right now, all she wanted was some peace and quiet to think things through. She opened her apartment door and turned on the light. Tiger rubbed up against her leg, vying for her attention. Kate slowly slid down the wall and sat on the thick rug in the hallway. She pulled the kitten onto her lap and slowly rocked him back and forth while the tears flowed freely.

Kate contemplated going back home. She knew her mother would be happy with that decision but Kate was torn. She had made a life for herself in the city and wasn't sure if she was ready to run home with her tail between her legs at the first sign of trouble. She also had the uneasy feeling that she had to stick around for something. Her spirit was telling her to stay put. The time wasn't right to leave. Kate decided she would heed that still, small voice. It never led her astray.

The phone jarred her awake at nine o'clock the next morning. She ached all over and realized she was still on the floor.

"Hi Honey, it's Mom. I was thinking during the night and wondered if you'd like to come home for a while. I would love to have you, you know!" she said enthusiastically.

"Gee Mom," she began. "I would really like that, but I think it's going to have to be some other time. I just feel like being alone for a bit. I hope you're not offended Mom. You know how much I love you," she said timidly.

They talked for a bit longer and then Kate hung up. She decided to go for a bike ride. That ought to get her head clear and focused, she thought.

The last day of September had arrived bright and sunny. The temperature hovered around the sixty-eight degree mark. Winter was on its way, but she certainly loved this time of year the best. She inhaled deeply of the rich perfume of fresh air and was grateful as it filled her lungs with the hint of new beginnings. She decided to just ride and see where she ended up. She headed up the drive and turned right. Kate drove aimlessly up and down several streets, finally ending up in a part of the city she wasn't overly familiar with. She began climbing a steep hill. Kate crested the peak winded and sweating profusely, and then froze. There on a curved sign were the words "Birch Cemetery." It was flanked by two wide pillars, with a large lion perched on each.

The detail was amazing to Kate. It was exactly like it had been in her dream. She knew exactly where to go from here. The bike discarded and forgotten, Kate made her way anxiously to the centre of the property. She let out a squeal when someone stepped out from behind a large headstone.

"Excuse me, Miss. I didn't mean to startle you," the gnarled old grounds-keeper said, as he headed away from her. The hair stood up on her neck as she stared at his retreating back. She looked at the stones around her. There it was right ahead, just like Kate remembered.

A tiny white headstone with dead flowers around its base lay almost at her feet. There in bold letters was the simple inscription, "Sleep, Bethany." She wondered who Bethany was. She got down on all fours and gently brushed the brittle flowers away. Her breath caught in her throat and tears welled in her eyes. It read, "Beloved daughter of Peter and Annette Carson. "God watch over you, precious one." The date read 1987-1993. She was only six.

When Annette called Peter a murderer on the television the other night, she was obviously referring to the death of their daughter. She didn't believe Peter would have killed his little girl intentionally, so it must have been an accident. No wonder he was in bad shape. The death was recent, according to the dates, so he was still going through the grieving process. Well, she thought bitterly. They had something in common after all. This piece of the puzzle made it easier to understand how to treat Peter. Now she knew why he was so withdrawn, and her heart went out to him. Somehow, he had accidentally killed his only child. How tragic, she thought. Now that her Lord had led her here, she wondered what He wanted her to do with this information. Kate trusted that God would show her in His time.

Kate left the way she had come, grabbed her bike and headed back towards the park entrance. She wanted to sit on the riverbank and do some thinking. As Kate found her favorite spot, she wrapped her arms around her legs and closed her eyes. She was angry and needed to deal with her emotions. Why did God allow her best friend to die? He could have brought healing to her, but didn't. The real basis of her anger was directed at the boy who had killed her. There was no purpose or reason to what he had done. It was simply a malicious act.

"Lord," she prayed. "I'm really hurting and I need to be able to forgive this boy for the terrible thing he has done. Create in me a new heart and give me peace, in place of this turmoil. In Jesus' name I pray. Amen!"

She stayed still for quite some time to await God's reply, if there was to be one. At first she thought it was just her own mind, but then she quickly recognized the voice instructing and bringing comfort. "All things work together for good, for those who love me and are called according to my purpose. Be patient child. Some good will come of this senseless violence," replied her Lord.

His Spirit enveloped her then and she felt thankful to Him for giving her such a good friend, if only for a short time. She was thankful to Jesus for being her best of friends, and knew that He would never leave her nor forsake her. He would always love her unconditionally and she felt blessed. Forgiving the young man however, would take a bit of time. With renewed strength, she felt it was time to leave. It surprised her a little, that over an hour had passed by so quickly. Kate knew she could face anything now, with her Lord by her side, sustaining her.

CHAPTER SIX
THE CALL

Meanwhile, Paul, the waiter from the restaurant, also had the day off. He had been too traumatized by last night's events to jump right back into work. He wished he knew how the young woman was doing. He'd heard her tell the detective that her name was Kate. Paul wanted to apologize to her. He felt so useless last night because he couldn't do anything for her friend. He'd never felt so helpless before, like he'd been stripped naked before an audience. No fancy words now; no fancy clothes; no fancy ideas. He had been forced to face himself for what he really was…just an insignificant and lonely young man who had been finally slapped in the face with a big dose of reality.

He was grateful that no one had been there to witness him crying himself to sleep like a baby. Paul remembered watching Kate last night. He figured she'd been praying, while her friend lay slowly bleeding to death. What he couldn't figure out, was what he had seen in both of their faces. The one woman had smiled at her friend, even though she was obviously suffering greatly. The other one had a deep sadness etched in her face while still displaying tenderness and compassion in her eyes which he felt was beyond her years.

These two women were very different from those he was used to being around and he wished there was someone he could talk to about it. What did they have that he didn't have? After witnessing such a horrible waste of human life last night, he decided today he needed to see something vibrant, and alive. He reasoned that Payton Street would show him life at its best; full of excitement and fast-paced action. So that's where he headed. Paul walked because it wasn't overly far from where he lived. It was in a rundown section of the city. Paul's whole life had been an act. He tried to make people think he had wealth, wisdom, class, and talent, but in truth, he had none of those things. He lived a lie.

Paul headed east on Payton, and slowed his pace. Now here was life, he thought to himself. The long sidewalks that ran parallel to each other were done in red brick-work, much to the chagrin of the taxpayers. Trees had been planted to give the flavour of a small town, but it couldn't mask the deeper problem. The farther one walked away from the centre core, the more cheap-looking the shops became. The sidewalks changed back into pitted concrete, with its cracks and flaws. Less care was taken to detail here.

The expensive salons, restaurants and boutiques, dwindled into cafés, smoke shops, cheap movie houses, and bars with signs that screamed out to passersby that inside were "Girls, Girls, Girls!" It kind of reminded Paul of a woman he had once seen in her seventies. She had lipstick smeared around her mouth and rouge with powder caked on her cheeks. Where eyebrows had long since disappeared or turned gray, she had painted some on with black pencil. Her hair had been dyed so many times that it had a blue and yellow tinge to it. She had tried in vain to cover up the lines that had deepened with time. Instead of showing the world the true beauty that God had created in her, she had desecrated it with garish paint. She had tried to recapture a bygone era and had failed miserably.

He remembered reading once about a whitewashed tomb somewhere. That woman had been like that. All the paint did was gloss over the cracks and decay. The street he now walked had the same kind of story attached to it. The shopkeepers had tried to use the brightly lit signs, wind chimes, and streamers to cover up the evil that ate away at the insides. It sickened Paul, as he looked around and saw his city for what it really was. He saw the prostitutes on the corners; the gang members skulking around in groups; the homeless vagrants pushing carts filled with treasures found in the dumpsters; and the drug dealers huddling in the back alleys. He turned right at the corner of Westwood and Payton. Paul felt like he had to get away from the filth caused by human beings who had lost all hope of a better life.

Many blocks away, he slowed his step, with the sounds of the city fading in the distance. Paul looked around for the first time, at this part of the city. He'd never had any reason to venture this far before. He looked up at a fairly new brick building before him. The sign read, "Klindale Detox Centre." Paul wondered why he had never heard of the place before this. After seeing the downtown today, in all its tainted glory, he imagined this place must really get some business. Across the street was a rather small, unassuming church called "Cornerstone." It was led by a Pastor Mike Collins, or so the sign out front said. Paul felt drawn to the front doors and it frightened him a bit. He had never stepped inside a church before and it seemed intimidating.

He was torn between a "should I?" or "shouldn't I?" mentality. Just then, Mike crossed the street. He was on his way back from the Centre. He could sense the man's hesitation and decided to approach him.

"I'm Mike Collins. Some people just call me Pastor Mike. Do you want to go inside for a bit? I could get you a cup of coffee and we could talk. I'd certainly welcome some company this afternoon."

Paul looked at the man in front of him. He wasn't like any minister he'd ever seen. This guy looked "normal," just like any other person on the street. He needed something and rightly assumed this man might be able to help him, so he quietly followed Mike up the steps, through the sanctuary, and into the tiny kitchen located at the back of the church. It wasn't what you would call fancy by any stretch of the imagination, but it was clean and decidedly friendly. Paul didn't speak while Mike prepared the coffee for them. He just didn't know what to say. Mike was obviously speaking to Paul, so he quit his daydreaming and focused on what he was saying.

"I'm afraid I'm not the best of company today," he began. "I lost a very good friend last night to a horrible drive by shooting. She was a really special person and everyone in my congregation loved her dearly. Her name was Katya, and she was gunned down by some punk who just happened to be driving by. He didn't even know her," Mike said as he tried to keep the bitterness out of his voice. "I need to pray for the street gangs. They seem to be literally getting away with murder and what they really need is the transformation which can only come from having Jesus in your heart."

Paul stared at Mike with his mouth hanging open. What were the odds? Could they be thinking about the same woman from the restaurant?

"Did this lady have a friend named Kate?" Paul ventured. Now it was Mike's turn to stare in surprise at Paul.

"How on earth did you know that?" he asked.

"I am a waiter at the restaurant the two ate at last night. I watched the whole thing happen, and then ran right outside to see if I could help. But there was nothing I could do," he added sadly. "I've just been walking around aimlessly today, trying to deal with what I witnessed. I hope you won't mind me saying this, but"...he hesitated for just a moment. "She had a smile on her face even though you could tell she was dying. That's what I've been really struggling with, Pastor Mike. It was her smile that has me so baffled," said Paul.

Then Mike's face lit right up. He looked at the young man before him. He said a quick prayer heavenward. "Lord, please give me the words this man needs to hear." For the next three quarters of an hour, Mike told Paul about how Katya's smile came from having a personal relationship with Jesus and how she knew with assurance where she was going if it was the Lord's will to take her home. He told him about where Katya's blessed hope came from and finally, how he too, could have the same thing.

It was right at that point when Paul realized that his life was absolutely empty. All he did was get up, work, eat, sleep, get up, work, eat, sleep and on occasion, party and sleep. It was all a monotonous repetition. It made him wonder what the point of it all was. Why was he here, in this world? What was the purpose? What was the point? Eventually you just died anyway. He voiced his thoughts to Mike, who left the room for a couple of minutes.

He returned with a bible and opened it to the book of Ecclesiastes. He told Paul about how King Solomon, the man who had much wisdom in human terms, had struggled with exactly the same stuff. He went further by telling him how Adam had brought sin into the world and subsequently, death. He talked about how Jesus had come into the world to take our sins upon his own body when He was nailed to the cross. He ended by telling Paul how Jesus conquered death, as seen by his resurrection and how that had finally opened the way to God. The barriers had come down and people were reconciled with God once and for all.

Paul then asked Mike if somehow he could have a relationship with Jesus. Would Jesus even accept someone like himself? Mike asked Paul to kneel beside him by the kitchen table, and right then and there, Paul gave Jesus the heart that he had been holding back from him all these years. He openly wept at the immediate cleansing relief he felt.

Something wonderful had just happened as a result of Katya's untimely death thought Mike. All things really do work together for good, he smiled inwardly. Wait until Kate hears about this, he thought. It was certain to bring a smile to her face and some peace to her troubled soul. Mike invited Paul to join them for worship the following morning and he watched as the man left with a new purpose in life. He shook his head and thought of all that had transpired in the last twenty-four hours.

"Thank you for Katya, Lord, and the gift that you just allowed me to share with someone else," he muttered under his breath as he went to his office to prepare for the Sunday service.

The next day came quickly and with it came a church that was filled to capacity. Katya's mom was unable to travel, so they would be having a service in her hometown. Kate looked around at the sea of faces present. By this point in time, everyone knew about Katya's death. For someone who had lived in the city for only a couple of years, Katya sure had made an impact. There were people from work and the church whom she recognized, but many others she didn't. When people came up to Kate and introduced themselves, she found out that one was a baker down Katya's street; one was the owner of the laundromat; and a couple were sales clerks from the grocery store that she shopped at. Kate noticed with amazement, that people from all walks of life had been impacted by her friend. Once again, she thanked God for Katya, as she sat down to hear the message Mike had for them.

There wasn't a dry eye in the place as the choir sang "Amazing Grace," but what was most noticeable to the people who had come into the church for maybe the first time in their lives, was the smiles on the faces of many of the church folk. They would later ask themselves how people could smile when it was obviously a memorial service. What could they possibly be happy about? Didn't they realize that Katya was gone for good? If Kate could read their minds, she would have told them that now Katya was sitting at the feet of her Lord. She was with Jesus. That's how her friends could find joy in their hearts, in the midst of this tragedy. Kate would have told them this had she known, but thankfully, Mike said all that needed to be said in his message.

The words spoken, and the songs that were sung made hearts soar that day and everyone present had felt that someone or something very powerful had been in their midst. As the people began filing out the front doors, Kate saw a man she recognized, but just couldn't place. He introduced himself as Paul, the waiter from the restaurant. Now it all came flooding back into Kate's memory. She thanked him for holding Katya up that night, and he thanked her for opening his eyes to the love and compassion of Jesus.

He could see that she clearly didn't understand what he was talking about, so he told her about how he had ended up here the day before, and how Mike had led him to the Lord. Kate couldn't believe what she was hearing. "Katya, are you listening to this," she said within her heart. She was so full of love for her friend that she couldn't voice her thoughts right now. She just squeezed Paul's hand, as the tears silently filled her eyes. Kate smiled apologetically and walked quickly away to her car. She needed time to think.

CHAPTER SEVEN
SHARING HER FAITH

She decided to take a couple more days off before she went back to work. Kate spent a lot of that time in the park. As the days progressed, the temperature steadily dropped. She wouldn't be surprised if there was snow within the next few weeks. As she sat staring at the river, Kate thought about her dad who had passed away so many years ago. She could recall the details as if it were yesterday and supposed that Katya's passing had brought these old memories to the forefront.

She could picture the clinical hospital ward, where her dad had spent his last weeks on this earth. She had watched a vital healthy man practically disappear before her very eyes. His skin was like thin dry parchment and hung in folds around his bones like it was exhausted from the fight. His eyes had been like darkened orbs, as he lost all of his body fat. Her heart had rebelled against such a cruel, debilitating disease that would literally ruin her father like that. Right up until the end though, it would be Bob that got everyone else through the ordeal.

The whole family had been with him until it was all over. They had cried, prayed and loved together. She remembered how his breathing had become very shallow and sporadic and they had all moved to the head of his bed to lovingly touch him one last time. He seemed to look past them at something near the ceiling behind their heads and he nodded once, softly sighed, and was gone. That had been it. One second he was there and the next he was gone. It was all so final and had left her with the terrible ache that comes from losing one so close. His service had been a lot like Katya's, though. There was still tears and grief, but added to that was the blessed hope of a man who knew where he was going. Kate couldn't begin to imagine what it would be like to go through the death of a loved one without having the peaceful assurance that came from having a relationship with Christ. That would be horrible, she thought.

People with no hope found that death had a big period at the end of the word, not a comma. It was the end, not the beginning of something infinitely more beautiful. She felt compassion towards unbelievers. They had hard hearts that needed to be broken before the Spirit of God could enter in and the travesty of it all, was that they were ignorant of what was happening in their lives. Satan made sure of that. He didn't want them knowing about Jesus and his way to salvation. It was tragic, but made Kate even more determined to share her faith with whoever would listen.

Her thoughts then traveled to the present and Peter Carson. Kate felt her spirit urging her to go to him. She knew that it would soon be time to confront him about Bethany. She figured that God had wanted her to deal with Katya's death before she could go forward. Life must go on, she thought with a new purpose. She finished off her last day at home, and decided that she would go back to work with renewed vigor and a greater respect than ever for life. Who but God, knew how much time each person had been given. The important thing was what one did with that time.

When Kate returned to work, she put all of her energy into the tasks at hand. After a week and a half at the Centre, Peter was coming along nicely. The shaking had subsided measurably and the greyish pall had left his face to be replaced by a healthy pink. Although he was still in fairly low spirits, he didn't appear to be as withdrawn as he had been. Peter had overheard two nurses talking in the hallway a few days earlier and therefore knew of the terrible thing that had happened to Kate's friend. He genuinely liked Kate and it saddened him further that she was unhappy. He wished he could say something to give her comfort but felt he could do her nothing but harm. All he ever did was hurt people, he reasoned.

Maybe one day he would become a whole man again and be of some use to society. Perhaps he would be able to find work again, although he didn't know where. Peter knew that the hospital where he worked before would never rehire him. He had lost too much credibility. But there were hundreds of other options available, he knew. There were clinics and family practice, sports complexes and yes, even centres such as this one. The sky was the limit if he was willing to work at it. He had been a good doctor before the booze and knew he could be again, in time.

Peter heard a soft shoe fall as Kate walked in the door. He wanted to say something to her, but was a little unsure of himself. Oh well, he thought. I may just as well jump right into it. "Hi Kate," he began lamely. "Could we talk for just a few minutes?"

"Sure Peter," she said as she began to straighten up his room. They both had something to say to each other.

"I was really sorry to hear about your friend. I overheard some nurses talking about it yesterday. Although I didn't know her, it must have been truly horrible for you," he said.

"It was, Peter. She was my dearest friend, and when she was taken, I felt like a part of me had been taken as well. The only thing that comforts me, is knowing where she is," Kate replied with a sad smile.

"I'm sorry if you think me foolish, but how can you be comforted knowing your friend is dead?" Peter asked quizzically.

"You misunderstand me," she said. "I know Katya is with her Lord and that's where my comfort comes from." Kate hesitated for the briefest of moments and then rushed on. "Peter, I don't mean to change the subject or to pry, but I've seen something that I need to get off my chest. It's been eating me up. The other day I was in the Birch Cemetery and was wandering around just looking at the headstones. I saw a small white headstone." She swallowed and hurried on. "I think it was your daughter's stone, Peter…" she trailed off.

Tears sprung to his eyes as pictures of Bethany flashed unbidden in his mind. "So, you know!" he said quietly. "I haven't talked about her with anyone since she's been gone. It's just been too painful. I'm afraid that's why I started drinking heavier than usual. I thought that in drunken oblivion, I wouldn't have to remember anything. But I was wrong, because things only got worse. I was drinking the night Bethany died, you know," he confided.

He paused to collect his thoughts and keep his emotions in check. Inside he was beginning to notice the lightening of his heart while feeling the pleasant release of tension, which came from getting rid of heavy burdening guilt and shame.

"My wife Annette and I had been drinking too much at a party over four months ago. I shouldn't have been driving, because I really was in no shape to do so. Unfortunately, we drunks never know when we're too intoxicated and incapable of operating a vehicle. In my ignorance and stupidity, I got behind the wheel to drive home. First we had to pick up Bethany at the babysitter's house. She was curled up asleep in the back of the car. Annette told me not to put her in the booster seat because she was sleeping and she didn't want me to wake her up. I headed into this intersection without looking anywhere but straight ahead. I didn't see the truck until it was too late. The old man had a heart attack and went right out of it with his foot to the floorboard. He came barrelling through a red light and broad-sided us. The back of the car fairly disappeared, with Bethany in it. She was killed instantly, but we just had minor cuts and scratches. There was so much blood, Kate," he sobbed pathetically.

"It was my fault. If my reflexes had been sharper, I would have been able to stop the car, but as it was, I was unprepared. It all happened so fast, I couldn't even think. What bothers me most is the fact that we were hardly touched, while her precious life was snuffed out without so much as a thought. It wasn't fair. Why couldn't God have taken me instead of her? Bethany had her whole life ahead of her. It's just such a waste. What kind of God would let that happen to a little girl? Annette called me a murderer and left me after that. Life has been a living hell ever since. There, you have my life story in a nutshell. It isn't very pretty is it?" he added.

Kate thought for a moment about how to best answer him. He had real problems in his life and she knew that she had to tread lightly. She said a quick prayer and began.

"Peter, I'm very sorry for your loss. I can't begin to imagine what it would be like to lose a child, so I won't even try. Although you are hurt and angry right now, I want you to know that it wasn't God who killed your little girl. And it wasn't you. It was a lot of unfortunate circumstances happening at the same time. God intercedes in some things but mostly he lets things happen in our lives. We aren't just puppets in His hands. He gave us our minds and our own free will, but it's often up to us and the choices we make, as to how our lives will turn out.

I know this won't help much, but maybe God thought Bethany was so special that He wanted her to be with Him sooner. Annette's angry response was quite natural. That was the only defense mechanism that she could draw on for strength. She wanted to blame someone else, but now that she's had some time to think about it, I'm sure she wouldn't still blame you, Peter. How could anyone have known that the old man would take ill and die at the wheel? It was a terrible accident, but you didn't kill her. Have you talked about that night, with Annette yet?" she asked timidly.

He looked at her for a moment, before he spoke. This woman seemed wise beyond her years. She fascinated him in a hard to read way. "Annette and I haven't spoken since the accident. I don't know what to say to her. I've single-handedly destroyed her life and I'm sure that whatever love we did have, has been sullied by her father. He never did like me. I don't think she could ever forgive me," he added.

"Excuse me for saying so, Peter, but first you have to be able to forgive yourself. God will forgive you, if you ask Him. And the good news is that once you've been forgiven, that's it. God forgets. He doesn't let you wallow in the pain over and over again. If you give your burdens to Him, He will bring healing to your life and a peace to your heart. Perhaps, in time, you will be reconciled with Annette. Maybe if you're willing, in the next couple of weeks, we could ask Annette to come to the Centre. You both could talk things over with Graeme Miller, our social worker, or Mike Collins, our clinic chaplain. They're both really very good. I think you'll find them kind and compassionate," she said on a positive note.

Kate reflected briefly on what she had just said. She felt an attraction to Peter. Why then had she just instigated a reconciliation with his wife, when clearly, it had been the furthest thing from his mind? She didn't understand, but felt God had a purpose for reconciling the two. Maybe their lives had to be resolved one way or the other. In her heart, Kate knew her job was done in here for the time being. It was time to move on and let Peter do some thinking on his own. God had just been using her as a tool to bring Peter out of his self-destruct mode.

She wondered again what God had in store for her. Where was she was really needed? What was she to do, now that Katya was gone? Right now she had no clear answers. Kate knew they would come in time. She would just have to bide her time and wait patiently on her Lord. Kate also knew that He wouldn't leave her high and dry. Peter interrupted her musings. She looked at him in bewilderment as if she'd forgotten he was even there.

"Maybe you're right, Kate. If Annette will come here, I sure would like to talk to her. We both need to heal and this sounds like a good place to start. If you could arrange that, I'd really appreciate it. Thanks for spending the time to talk with me. I think it helped."

Kate felt like she had been led to this Centre for just this purpose and as the love for her Lord swelled within her, she marvelled anew at how God worked in the lives of His children. He certainly was an awesome God.

CHAPTER EIGHT
KATE SEES TOM

Later that night, when Kate was relaxing at home, she sat with a cup of tea on her lap and a smile on her face. What a day this had been. She wore her favourite green terrycloth bathrobe and big floppy slippers. Tiger purred contentedly at her side. Kate reflected on the past couple of weeks. Her whole life had been altered and was still in the process of changing. Katya was gone, but Paul the waiter from the restaurant, had been brought to the Lord because of it. Peter's life had been in shambles, yet Kate had been able to have a hand in his healing process.

Twice, in as many weeks, she had seen God's written word being played out in very real ways. A familiar scripture came to her mind and she reflected on the rich words of the apostle Paul. Although it was always hard to think of any good coming from trials and tribulations, she believed with her whole heart that it was so. The phone jarred Kate from her reverie.

"Is this Kate Harmon?" the man on the other end of the line inquired.

"Yes it is. May I ask whose calling?" she asked.

"This is Detective Scott Burns from the Klindale police department. We've arrested a young man this past hour who we think is the one responsible for your friend's death."

Kate's blood ran cold as he continued.

"We would appreciate it, if you could come down to the station and see if you can identify him in a lineup. This is really important Miss Harmon. We need a positive ID before we can charge him with anything. Can we expect you first thing in the morning?" he asked.

"Yes, I guess so," she swallowed hard. "I'll be there Detective."

She hung up the phone and staggered to the bathroom. She had barely wrapped her arms around the base of the toilet before she vomited a hot clear stream of bile into the bowl. She stayed like that for several minutes. Finally she got up and washed her face and hands off with cool water. Going to the police station and facing that monster was the last thing she wanted to do. She was afraid to look at him although his face was forever etched in her mind.

The thing she feared most, was how she would react to seeing him. How would she feel when she looked at his hate-filled eyes again? Would he know she was on the other side of the glass? Would he remember what she looked like? Perhaps he would come looking for her. All these thoughts rushed through her head, and it took a long time before sleep finally overtook her.

The next morning Kate walked up the steps of the police station with feelings of absolute dread. Maybe she would be able to sleep better once she got this over with. Detective Burns met her in the waiting room, five minutes later. He led her through a door off the anteroom where the lineup had congregated, and reassured her that the men couldn't see or hear her inside this small cramped room.

The young man, second from the left, felt his heart beating furiously. He was standing with four other men. He had seen this kind of room before on television, and he never would have imagined that he would be the one on the inside. He knew, as did everyone else in the room, that the elongated mirror on the wall had someone looking through on the other side. He figured this must be how zoo animals felt. He had been arrested late yesterday afternoon and remembered with pride, doing what the officers had said he had done.

He had been fairly high that night. He and his "friends" had enjoyed a vast array of drugs on that fateful evening in question. The whole incident had been done on a dare. The semi-automatic had easily been purchased from a boy who came by the school once a week. He had been kicked out of school 2 years earlier and always carried an endless supply of weapons and drugs in his backpack. The boys had pooled their money together to make the purchase. The money had been stolen from a wide variety of purses over the last few months and he could remember the feeling of exhilaration when his hands had finally stroked the cold metal. It had given him a thrill right to the centre of his being.

They practiced shooting bottles lined up in the dirt at the back of an old warehouse. The place was scheduled for demolition and had been a great hideout for the budding gang members. He remembered how it felt the first time he had depressed the trigger. The shot had gone wild and put out a window in the small building behind the warehouse. The more times he practiced though, the easier it got. By the time he shot the woman, he was able to plug off the shots fairly rapidly and with much precision.

Watching the woman's back turn into an ever-widening red stain had given him a real blood lust. His fevered eyes had taken in the whole scene and he knew that he wanted more. Had there been time, he would have taken out the other one as well. She was staring at him in horror and he remembered laughing about it later. The boys knew they had to get out of there fast and it was with disappointment that they turned the corner and headed away from the scene. He had played the whole thing over and over in his head and still received satisfaction knowing that there was one less adult out there that could hurt him.

He wondered if it was the other woman who now judged him from behind the glass. Maybe she was going to be his downfall. He should have taken her out. He had just the hint of a smirk on his face as he imagined her blood all over the place. At that moment a voice came over the speaker telling all of them to look ahead and not speak or move.

Kate felt the hair rise on the back of her neck. She recognized him instantly and also saw the little smirk playing at the corners of his mouth. She told the detective that it was definitely the second man from the left.

"Are you sure? I can have each one of them step forward so you can get a closer look," said the detective.

"That won't be necessary," Kate replied. "I'd never forget that face in a million years. He's really not much more than a boy is he?" she added.

"That kid has been in here twice already…once for shoplifting and once for running away from home when he was only nine. He had stolen his step-father's credit cards but didn't know how to use them. I was talking to him earlier and he is hardened beyond his years. He's a teenager and now he's going to be charged with murder. It really doesn't say much for our society, does it?" he added.

Kate shook her head sadly. "What's going to happen to him now?" she added, feeling a little sick at the prospects.

"He'll be charged with first degree murder and he'll go to trial. He can't hide behind the system this time, because he turned eighteen two months ago. He'll be tried as an adult and I wouldn't be surprised if he goes to jail for a long time. His lawyer might be able to weasel it down to manslaughter or some other such thing, because he'll play up the fact that he's only a kid. Who really knows? Kids like this usually turn into adults like this. I've seen his type so many times, and I know I'll see this one again," Scott said hotly. "Because of the nature of the crime, you won't be called as a witness in the trial, for your own safety. We've registered your positive identification already and there were several other witnesses at the scene. All of them have identified the same boy. I'll let you know how things turn out. He probably won't get a trial date for at least a couple of months. He'll be in custody until then, so you can rest easy," he added.

Kate wondered if she would ever be able to rest easy. Too much had happened and she felt like the circumstances surrounding that night had scarred her beyond repair. She left the station house feeling not the release she had expected, but a feeling of dread. It was like the calm before the storm. She could feel the clouds roiling in her mind. This didn't feel like the end of something, but the beginning of something far more sinister. She shivered despite the warmth of the day.

CHAPTER NINE
LIFE GOES ON

As Kate left the police station for the safety of her home, a deep sadness filled her heart and she said a prayer for the boy. She asked God to change his heart and convict him of the error of his ways before it was too late. She guessed he was just a troubled boy who hadn't had the same opportunities in life that she had. Instead of feeling hate towards him which would have been a natural reaction, she now felt only pity and compassion.

Kate decided that a talk with Marg and Mike just might be something that would pick her spirits up. Marg was shopping while Mike was working on a sermon. He looked up and smiled as Kate walked through the doors.

"Hello, Kate! I was just thinking about you," he said with a boyish grin.

"Hi Mike! I just came from the police station. I had to identify the person who killed Katya. Mike, he was just an eighteen year old boy. I wanted to hate him but I could only feel sorry for him. I feel terrible about being the one to send him away to jail. We both know what the boy needs and prison isn't it! But what else could I do? He has to pay for his crime, doesn't he?" she asked hurriedly.

"You did the right thing, Kate. It must have been really hard for you to look at him. You were a very brave young lady to face your nightmare head on, like that," he added.

He paused for a moment as he formulated his thoughts. There was a ministry opportunity that had just come across his desk and immediately Kate had come to mind. He didn't know why he would have thought of her because she already had a good job at the Detox Centre, but he felt she would be perfect for this job as well. She seemed happy enough in her work, but he still felt he had to give her the chance to say yes or no. He cleared his throat and began the spiel he had been practicing in his mind all morning.

"Kate, I know you have a great job and everything, but a ministry opportunity has come to my attention and I thought you might like to hear about it. I'll tell you what information I have. If you're not interested by the time I'm finished, don't worry about it. You won't be hurting my feelings any," he said quickly.

Kate didn't know why, but her heart started to race just a bit in anticipation. Mike brought out a map of Canada and laid it on his desk. "In northern Manitoba, we have the Churchill River winding down from Hudson Bay."

He was drawing his finger along the lines on the map. "As we follow it along, you'll see it goes into Southern Indian Lake. On the northwest side of this lake is a small settlement called Poweetan. I only know what the climate is like in Churchill. Poweetan will be slightly warmer, but not a whole lot."

He poured a glass of juice for the two of them and continued. "In January the temperature can get as low as minus 30-40 fahrenheit but in the summer it can fluctuate between 55-85 degrees fahrenheit. Snowfall isn't overly heavy, but it tends to accumulate during the long winters and gives the impression of great abundance. A major railroad runs as far north as Lynn Lake, here," he said, pointing again to the map.

"This is approximately one hundred miles from Southern Indian Lake. The last jog you can get to by a well-used gravel road in the summer months and by small plane in the winter. The settlement is made up mostly of Me`tis, with a smattering of descendants from the original Cree, Salteau and Chipewan tribes. About three tenths of the population consists of non-aboriginals. Approximately eight hundred people live there. They have a general store where goods are flown or driven in, although it's fairly expensive by the sounds of it."

Mike took a breath and a drink and continued as Kate looked on, quite frankly puzzled. She wondered what all this had to do with her, but she quietly let him carry on.

"There's a Presbyterian church there, along with a Catholic church. There's also a dental/medical clinic. There's a doctor there named Matt Jenkins. He needs help, as the population has grown over the years since he's been there. He could use a good nurse and it was you that I thought of. The pay isn't that spectacular, but there's an apartment at the back of the clinic where all you would have to pay for would be your food and utilities. The rent is free. That was one of the terms when the clinic was built ten years ago; that the staff would get free lodging. That's because the need was so great for the residents living around the area."

Mike looked up at Kate sheepishly and continued quickly before she could interject. "The place is mostly government funded. Now I know this is a lot to think about, but I really hope you will consider it. It would be right up your alley, Kate. I thought that maybe a change would do you some good. Anyhow, I won't say any more about it for now. You go on home and look over this stuff and you can decide for yourself. Call and let me know what your answer is though. If nobody is interested in the job offer, I have to fax it on to the next church in line. They want the position filled by March. That's only four months away and a lot of arrangements will have to be made before then."

Kate took the heavy brown envelope from Mike as her eyes fairly danced with excitement. It sounded like something she may be able to sink her teeth into. A change might be just what the doctor ordered she thought to herself.

"Thanks a lot, Mike. Let me think on it for a few days and then I'll get back to you. I want to talk it over with my mom as well. See you soon," she said as she bounded lightly out the back door. Mike was already poring over some other books and just grinned and nodded to her.

Kate left the manse with a feeling akin to emotional release. All the events of the past couple of weeks were finally being pushed to the back of her mind. She felt peace and renewal replace the anguish and fear that had been so much a part of her since Katya's death. The next couple of days literally flew by. There was work of course, and grocery shopping, banking, laundry, and paying the bills that always seemed to accumulate.

During the evening, Kate sat with Tiger on her lap and scanned the pamphlets and brochures. The more she looked, the better it sounded. Time spent in prayer confirmed what she already knew in her heart. God wanted her there. It would get her away from the city for a while. It would take her mind off Peter and it would keep her safe from the boy she was helping to send to jail.

Kate had the weekend off and decided to drive the two hours it took to get to her mother's house. Betty had valuable input in Kate's life and was always there with words of encouragement. Saturday dawned clear and cold with the thermometer reaching forty- eight degrees Fahrenheit. With Tiger tucked safely away in his kennel and a valise filled with clothes, Kate left the apartment. She was surprised when her watch read 8:30 a.m. She didn't realize she had been so anxious to be off. Traffic was light at this hour of the morning and she made excellent time. As the sounds, smells and sights of the city were left far behind, Kate eased up on the accelerator to enjoy the rolling hills and the sporadic farms that dotted the countryside. Two hours on the highway might just have been a lifetime away. The temperature dipped to the freezing mark as she approached her destination. Soft white snowflakes began drifting lazily down like manna from heaven she thought. It made beautiful patterns on the window and Kate marvelled anew at the wonders of God's creation.

She waved again and again at the familiar faces of old school chums and neighbours, as they strolled down the main street or drove by in cars. The whole pace of life slowed right up in a small town. Gone was the urgency to be everywhere at once and at a specific time. The noise was minimal and the sound of car horns had been replaced by a dog barking a block away. There wasn't much chance of being anonymous in a town like this. Everybody knew their neighbours and their business. As she turned onto Ferguson Road it was like literally going back in time. It seemed that nothing had changed in the past couple of years. Everything was as she remembered it, including old Hester Cramer's pink house. Kate had always loathed the colour but Hester had continued over the past twenty years or so, to faithfully repaint it the same vile colour. She was a dear old lady who you could say was almost regal in her bearing. That was the only reason why the townspeople stifled their smirks and kept their opinions to themselves.

You would have thought the prodigal son or in her case, daughter, had just returned. She was met at the front door by her mom, sister, brother and their families. What a homecoming! The smell of turkey roasting in the oven with sage dressing made with cranberries, apples and sausage, made Kate's mouth water. How long had it been since she'd had a really good feed of turkey she wondered? Excited chatter filled the home as everyone had news they wanted to share as a family. Edward's wife Cheryl was pregnant with their third child. This baby was not planned, as their second child was already six years old.

Both were only mildly concerned that Cheryl was almost forty. She was a healthy, big boned woman who delivered easily, so their family doctor had been very encouraging. Eva and her husband Tom had opened their own law firm together above the old hardware store. They had a son, Josh, who was nine. Both had been interested in their careers, so had decided on a "smaller family unit" as they called it. Everyone talked, hugged and laughed together for the next couple of hours.

Kate revelled in the conversations and the feeling of togetherness. She hoped that one day she would have a large family and when they got together there would be plenty of children to contend with. She just loved kids. Just the thought of them brought a smile to her face. After a huge late supper or early dinner had been devoured, along with two of mom's apple pies, everyone was all talked out. By mid-afternoon, the house had quieted considerably. Eva and her family had another engagement to attend to and Edward and his kin were off visiting the neighbours. Kate had decided not to mention her news until she had a chance to run it by her mom first. She wanted Betty to be a sounding board and now was her chance.

They sat on the bed in Kate's old bedroom. Always in the past, when Kate had a problem or needed her mother's advice on a matter, they would come to Kate's bedroom. It was always quiet and cozy. She noticed that everything was just as she had left it. Kate's apartment in Klindale had been furnished, so her things were still here. There were the swimming trophies still on the shelf above the headboard and the picture taken on prom night of Kate and Jim Scott, still stuck in her mirror.

"Mom," Kate began, as she sat with her feet dangling off the side of the bed. "I have been given an opportunity for a new job."

"That's nice Kate," her mom interrupted, "but I thought you loved the job you already have."

Betty looked deeply into Kate's downcast eyes and read a story within them. Before Kate had a chance to speak, Betty calmly asked her where this new job was. She knew she didn't want to hear the answer.

"It's in Canada. The place is called Poweetan and the majority of the people there are aboriginal."

As Betty's face registered shock at the word Canada, and thought how far away from home it sounded, Kate rushed on with a torrent of words. She wanted her mom to have the benefit of all the information, before she asked her opinion. There was an uncomfortable silence for about thirty seconds, while Betty digested everything and carefully chose her words.

"Kate," she began. "You've always been a special girl to me and I will always love you no matter where you are. You have never been one to jump into things blindly. Your father used to call you "the thinker" because you were always turning ideas over in your head before you voiced them. I'm sure you've already prayed long and hard about this and I certainly won't stand in your way if it's God's will that you go there. You know that my heart will be with you Kate, wherever you go. I just hope you aren't running away from your problems. I know Katya's death was a big shock to you and I pray that you aren't trying to find an escape from your pain."

Kate had always appreciated her mother's candor. As per usual, she allayed any fears Kate may have been harbouring inside, once and for all. Kate threw her arms around her mother's neck then. They just rocked back and forth while they took turns alternately crying and laughing. Things were going to be all right, Kate thought to herself. They were both at peace with Kate's decision. Leaving the room, they walked hand in hand downstairs, sharing the great love and respect they had for each other.

She spent an enjoyable weekend with the family, catching up on all the latest happenings. Everyone agreed that Kate would be missed terribly, but no negative words were said. They loved her too much for that. As Kate returned to the city on Sunday afternoon after spending a memorable morning seeing all of the familiar faces at her old church, it was towards an unknown future that she headed. Left behind would be family, companions and the grave of a very dear friend. Only God knew what lay ahead, but she would put her life into His capable hands, trusting Him with her very soul.

CHAPTER TEN
PAUL'S STORY

The first two months following Paul's conversion, were a glorious time of learning God's Word and being with fellow believers. Mike was teaching him all about the Christian faith and he was growing in leaps and bounds. His heart was on fire for the Lord and his eyes fairly glowed with the hunger usually seen in new believers. Mike was able to get him registered into a reputable bible college although the first semester was just about finished. Enrollment was down, as less people were interested in preaching the Word of God. Nevertheless, they took him without question. Paul got himself a tutor to fill him in on the lessons he had missed.

Although he worked twice as hard to catch up, the work was completely fulfilling and challenging and he never complained. His life finally had meaning and direction. He was glad to be away from the restaurant and the rat race of downtown city life. Pioneer Bible College was on the outer limits of the city. The serenity and silence of the library and dormitories, was only broken by the sounds of pages being turned in books and the voices of those who studied out loud or in front of mirrors.

It was a temporary haven from the outside world where one could find peace of heart, mind and soul. It was a literal refuge for the whole person, where God could heal any wounds of the past, and bring forth a strengthened and empowered man or woman ready to take on Satan and his emissaries. It was to this place that Paul had come. Although he was thirty-two years old, that didn't bother him in the least. There were many students who had enrolled later in life. Change brought renewal, he reasoned.

Paul didn't want to be a waiter for the rest of his life. Perhaps he would still be able to write that book that threatened to write itself in the back of his head. There hadn't been much time to make friends while he was at school. The days were just too full of seminars, classes, daily prayer and devotional time, meals and then studying late into the night. One hour a day was set aside for athletics. The school officials realized that a person couldn't have his or her face buried in the books twenty-four hours a day. It just wasn't healthy, and enough people as it were had dropped out from the stress, pressure and burnout, which came from constantly having to think.

Paul spent the first half-hour in the weight room. He wasn't that interested in having a body-builder's physique, but just in being physically fit and healthy. He was a handsome man with naturally blond hair and a cleft chin, which seemed to drive the women crazy. His was a classical story taken right out of a Dicken's novel. He had immigrated to America with his mother and father when he was four. They had come from Australia, where his parents had done some sheep farming. There had been a terrible fire and the old homestead had been left smoldering and levelled.

The spirit and life inside his father had died with the home and never did come back. He became a very bitter man and decided to chuck it all for a better life in the United States. Nothing could have been further from the truth. They had ended up in a slum in New York when his father got work as a bouncer in a bar. His bitterness eventually changed into something more sinister. Gone was all his compassion and love. His mom had said that he wasn't the same man she had married, but she took his verbal and sometimes physical abuse in silence for the sake of her boy.

The older Paul got; the more poverty, squalor, racial tension, and hatred he witnessed. When he was fourteen, his mother died and Paul blamed his father for her death. She died in her sleep from an unknown virus the doctor had said, but Paul figured she really died of a broken heart from years of dreams that had been smothered and laughter, which had been quenched.

His father began staying away for days at a time, so Paul had to learn how to fend for himself. He learned a lot about life on the streets, when his dad finally left him for good and Paul was kicked out of the apartment because he couldn't pay the rent by himself. With his good looks, he was able to land a job as a bellboy in a fancy hotel. He roomed with the manager who offered him a job on the side to make some extra cash. Paul was desperate for money because he wanted to leave the city, so he jumped at the man's offer. An escort was needed for wealthy women who were lonely and looking for some excitement and companionship.

He was to be "obliging in all ways" the manager had said with a wink, and for his trouble he would be paid handsomely. Although only in his mid-teens, he was mature beyond his years, so nobody was ever the wiser. The women just assumed he was in his twenties and absolutely adored him. The "work" was absolutely degrading. Although he was treated like a prince, he was ashamed and humiliated to stoop to such depths of depravity. He lost all sense of pride in himself and numbly threw himself into the work. With any luck, he would be able to get out of New York for good. Paul knew that he was nothing more than a male prostitute and if his mother had been alive, she would have been mortified.

When he finally saw his way clear, he gathered his meagre belongings and headed west. For some unknown reason, he had ended up in Wisconsin and the restaurant where he had worked for the past thirteen years. He'd been able to save some money from years of tips and still maintain an apartment. When Mike told him about the college, he really wanted to go but knew he wouldn't be able to afford paying for more than one year. After the first month, Mike had recognized a great potential for learning in Paul. He was able to get the financial backing necessary to send him to school, by rallying his congregation together to sponsor him on a one year trial basis. If Paul maintained good grades, the church would back him for another year. That was the terms of the arrangement and Paul thanked God for the abundant blessings He had bestowed upon him. He was grateful for everything being done and the hope that had been given him concerning a future in the ministry.

Life was certainly full of unexpected turns, he thought wryly. And then his mind turned to thoughts of Kate. She barely knew he was alive and he had done nothing to build a relationship with her. Paul figured she still needed time to heal from her friend's sudden death and he didn't want to interfere with the process. He had been taken by surprise when she had announced at the potluck last weekend that she would be leaving Klindale for a nursing position somewhere in Canada. He couldn't believe his ears, as he looked at her with longing and desire.

This was the first time he could remember that he had actually fallen in love with someone and now she was just going to waltz right out of his life just as suddenly as she had entered it. Two and a half more months she had said. There wasn't much point in pursuing a relationship with a shadow, he thought dejectedly. He was saddened but vowed to work all the harder to compensate for love lost, or never really found. He didn't come this far to go throwing it all away on a dream, he figured. First things first! He would become an ordained minister and go wherever the Lord wanted him to go. Then maybe he would find someone to love and who would love him in return.

CHAPTER ELEVEN
POWEETAN

Dr. Matt Jenkins had worked in the Poweetan medical clinic since it had opened, ten years earlier. He shared it with Dr. Davis Westcott who had majored in dentistry. Twelve years before that, he had operated his small clinic out of a room in his own home. His wife Vira, had helped him when absolutely necessary, but she was untrained and hated the sight of blood, which was not a good thing in a community which did a lot of hunting. More than once, Matt had picked her up from the floor and gently laid her on the old couch. They were both middle-aged and prayed earnestly that God would send them a real nurse.

They had sent word of their need to the churches in the area, and they in turn had passed the information on. It was like a vast relay network. That was almost a year ago. They both knew it was Poweetan's isolation; mainly aboriginal population; hard winters and low pay that had been the big deterrent. People were afraid of the unknown. They were leery of taking chances. Matt and Vira knew exactly how they felt. They had answered the call for the need of a doctor in this remote and isolated place almost twenty-three years earlier. Their two daughters had been born and raised here.

Leah had moved away last year to go to university in Brandon. She wanted to be a social worker. Matt knew she'd be excellent in whatever field she might choose. Rachel was two years younger and at nineteen, was quite content to work the cash register in the general store or throw herself into whatever odd jobs she could find. She was an avid reader and usually could be seen with her nose stuck in a book. Rachel was not driven or hungry like Leah was and had her heart set on marrying her lifetime love, Stephen Westcott.

Mail was slow to arrive in Poweetan. It came by plane about once every two weeks in winter time, depending on the weather and once a week in the summer, as long as the road was passable. When the drone of the plane could be heard getting louder, everyone that was able would go out to meet it. This was one of the highlights of Poweetan.

Today they heard the drone and the townspeople filed away from their homes and work. No one worried about locking anything. This wasn't the city after all. They went by path through the woods and down to the edge of the lake. It had been frozen solid for months now and made a great skating rink for anyone with the desire to test it out. By skirting one corner of the lake, they came to a large area that had been cleared for a single runway. It wasn't pretty, but it did the trick.

Before the propellers had stopped, the community began to push forward in anticipation. Small faces eyed the plane with wonder as games of tag were played around the legs of their parents. Older gap-toothed men and women chattered happily away, from browned and weathered faces that had been exposed to the elements for years on end. This was not a place that thought about sunscreen and UV rays.

The sleighs were ready to be loaded with merchandise for the general store and medical supplies for the clinic. The bag that was delivered last held the mail. It would be gone through by Rachel at the store, and those with relatives outside of the settlement were eagerly waiting for some word from them. One could access Poweetan by a gravel and dirt road leading northeast from Lynn Lake, but it was passable in the summer months only. Then it would be baked hard, but it was still a rough ride by any means. Things like furniture, paint and clothing would be brought in by road during the warmer weather. There wasn't a lot of cars or need for them in the town but there were countless snowmobiles, a few trucks, and about five all-terrain vehicles.

Snow or no snow, the people would still get around. It wasn't like the old days when dog power was used and snow shoes were the footwear of choice. Although it was remote, technology had still arrived and was a welcomed commodity. On this day, after Rachel had sorted and distributed the mail, she held in her hand a letter for her father. She prayed that it would be someone to help him in the clinic. He was tired a lot, from doing almost everything himself.

Rachel trudged through the deep snow that had accumulated, to get to the clinic which was at the far end of town. The sign over the door simply read: "CLINIC". What else was needed, she thought? She kicked snow off her boots and proceeded down the hall to the first door on the right which read Matt Jenkins, MD. As she passed the door on the left, she glanced in shyly, hearing the sounds of the drill. The secretary, who was Stephen's mom, glanced up and gave Rachel a big smile.

"He's in with a patient, dear. He shouldn't be much longer. Are you going to be around for a bit?" Carol inquired.

She genuinely liked the girl and figured there would be wedding bells in the near future. Stephen couldn't do much better, she noted with admiration. Rachel was a good Christian girl with high morals and a gentle, compassionate spirit. She would be proud to call Rachel her daughter-in-law.

Stephen was twenty four and had followed in his father's footsteps. He had graduated from the school of dentistry just this past year and had become a partner with Davis. It was great to keep it in the family, she thought with a smile.

"I just came to drop off a letter for Dad," said Rachel. "Hopefully, it's good news. I'm sure you'll hear if it is," she added with a twinkle in her eye. Although her dad had the voice of a bear, everyone knew he was a gentle giant.

"Could you please tell Stephen that I'll be ready at 7 tonight? We're going to go skating on the lake tonight with a bunch of the others from our young people's group."

"Sure thing, Rachel." Carol smiled and bent back over the forms she was filling out.

"Thanks a lot Mrs. Westcott." She ducked back into the hall and then over to the medical office. Her mom worked behind the desk five hours a day. It helped her dad out a lot and if the truth be known, he just enjoyed having her nearby.

"Hi, Mom. I came to drop off a letter for Dad. It's from a church in Klindale, Wisconsin," she added hurriedly.

Vira stood up and took the proffered letter from her daughter, flipping it over once to look at the return address.

"I'll see if he's finished with Lillian yet. I'll be right back, Rachel." No sooner did she stand, when Lillian Bailey slowly walked out from one of the two back rooms. She smiled at both of them as she waited for her prescription to be written up. The woman had a widow's hump, caused from osteoporosis. The disease had really slowed her down over the years. It was no wonder, because she was the oldest resident in Poweetan, at ninety-six years of age. She was loved by all, and was an absolute joy to be around. She had a dry sense of humour and a quick tongue which usually got everyone in stitches.

Lillian was born in Poweetan and had never left it in all those years. She had birthed eleven children of which four were stillborn. Of the seven remaining, five had moved away. Only two of her sons remained in Poweetan. Lillian had twenty-two grandchildren and thirty eight great grandchildren which were strewn somewhere across Canada.

"Rachel, would you be a dear and run across the street to the garage and have my grandson, Albert come here. I'd like him to take me home now," she said as she slowly lowered herself onto a chair by the desk.

Just then, Matt stepped into the room. Both mother and daughter looked up at him expectantly. He was smiling from ear to ear.

"Well, we're finally getting ourselves a nurse. Her name is Kate Harmon and she's twenty-nine years old. A letter of recommendation was written by her friend Mike Collins who is the pastor of a church in Klindale, Wisconsin. He says she's an excellent nurse, with very good credentials. He has given a really glowing report of her. And she's a Christian to boot," he added quickly with a smile. "This letter was written about three weeks ago, which means she'll be arriving within the next four weeks. That will give us lots of time to get the back apartment polished up for her arrival. She's not married either. According to this, she just has a cat, so we can get the refrigerator filled up as well."

The relief Matt felt, was visible in his features. As the tension drained out of him, his shoulders relaxed and his brow became less furrowed. This was going to be a good arrangement, he thought to himself.

Tom Erikson was angry. The more he paced back and forth, the uglier his mood became. Six steps up and six steps back, over and over again. His own mind fuelled that anger. He couldn't see the ugly paint-chipped walls or smell the urine or body odour. All he could see was the face of that woman. She was the reason he was stuck in here. Of that, he was fairly certain. He vowed that one day he would make her pay. One day she would beg him for mercy and he would laugh in her face. He daydreamed all the time about what he would do to her.

Tom pictured her screaming but in his dream state there was no one there to hear her. They were all alone and the smell of moss and mould was overpowering. It was damp and cool and beckoned him like something alive. He felt like he'd been given a vision. The sinner must be punished he thought, as feelings of desire and excitement stirred inside his loins. She'd beg him all right, he giggled out loud. And then she would bleed.

The court had given him ten years in jail. Tom wasn't overly concerned because he was sure they'd let him off for good behaviour in probably three to five years. After all, he was just a kid, and this was the first really serious offense he had been convicted of. His lawyer had pleaded temporary insanity. He told the court that the boy had just been coerced by his friends to pull the trigger. The jury hadn't bought the story, even though Tom was a good actor. He had cried and everything, but it hadn't changed the outcome. Now he just resigned himself to staying on his best behaviour and biding his time.

"You will be delivered into my hand lady and you will suffer like I have," he mumbled under his breath. If the boy could have seen into the invisible realm, he would have been terrified by all the darkness, the cold, and the smell of sulphur. He was not alone, nor had he been, for the past five years. He was encircled by the powers of darkness. They were watching and waiting for their big move. This kid was useful in the world of the evil one, and they knew there was a big payoff coming for all their patience. Time would tell all, they cackled around him, as the pacing continued… back and forth, back and forth.

CHAPTER TWELVE
LOVE BLOSSOMS

Paul threw his book up in the air and laughed out loud with pure joy. His marks had been posted for the second quarter, and according to the stats, he was second highest in his class. He'd been beaten out by Cally Wilson. She was a bookworm, with the personality of a dead fish. Her ambition in life as she was bound to tell everyone, even if they didn't ask, was to be a professor of homiletics. Not your basic fun date, he though wryly. Oh well, right now he just wanted to celebrate.

Mike had invited him to supper and the bus would finish its last run for the day within the hour. He had to hurry or he'd be walking. Twenty minutes later, found him showered, shaved, dressed and out the door. Dinner at Mike's was always an adventure. After rough-housing with the kids before dinner, he was more than ready to sit down and relax.

"Everyone is so proud of you Paul," Mike began. "You've worked so hard and grown so much since I found you staring at the sign out front. Have you thought about what you want to do yet? I mean, do you feel like you're being led in any specific direction?"

"Hey, hey now," Paul laughed. "One question at a time, please. To answer you, I really would like to be a preacher. I feel that's where God wants me, but I'm just a little bit nervous as well. It's going to be hard for me to step out in faith with my life. Who knows where God will have me go? That's a frightening thing to face, alone. Am I wrong to feel like this?" he asked.

Over the next hour and a half, Mike reassured Paul, and told him he had nothing to be ashamed of. Mike explained how questioning sometimes leads to seeking and when we seek with all of our heart, we will find some answers. It may not be the ones we are looking for, but it will be an answer just the same.

"Faith begins with simply reaching up so God can reach down," he added. "He won't leave you on a sinking boat, as I'm sure you know already. God's ways are not our ways and he will see that you are placed where the most good for His Kingdom can be accomplished. He has a plan, Paul, and we are all players, no matter where we go or what we do. Just don't try to second guess Him. He'll usually surprise you," he said with a wink.

The rest of the evening flew by. As he was leaving, he quietly asked Mike if Kate was still going to move away.

"I'm afraid she has already left, Paul," Mike said with a knowing look.

He had been certain he wasn't reading something that wasn't there. Paul was in love with Kate and it obviously wasn't going to be a relationship that would blossom right now. Marg probably knew from day one, he thought to himself. She was always the most discerning of the two of them. Oh well, he reasoned. Paul wasn't going to have time to think about Kate over the next couple of years. He'd be too busy.

As Paul walked down the front stairs, he waved goodbye and looked at the Detox Centre across the street. The first couple of months after he'd given his heart to the Lord, Paul had gone into the chapel every Friday night. They had a sing song and Paul usually brought his guitar. Mike would play the old piano and one of the nurses from the third floor, could play a mean harmonica. Between the three of them, they ministered in music to the residents who were able to get up and about. Mike was saying tonight, that old Amos had left last week. He had made it through the cold of another winter and was back out on the streets. This year he had left with a well-worn bible though, and a big wide smile on his face.

Peter had been reunited with his wife, almost two months earlier, after weeks of counselling. A blind man could tell that Kate had been smitten with him, but had graciously not followed her heart. Instead, she had done her utmost to maintain a purely professional relationship with him. When it came to the crunch, it was Kate who instigated the reunion with Annette and brought the two of them together.

At first, their meetings had been angry and full of name calling and other nasty things. Gradually though, they had arrived at a mutual agreement where they would at least attempt to live together again. Granted, things hadn't been what you would call rosy, but they were going to give it a shot. They owed their marriage that much. Paul had admired Kate from afar. She had done nothing but encourage the two. That had taken guts, he reasoned. As he walked unhurriedly down the street he said goodbye to the centre. Paul doubted if he would be back there any time during the near future.

The college was approximately two and a half miles from Mike's house, but Paul had declined their offer of a ride. Tonight he wanted to feel the wonders of creation at work. There was a soft cool breeze blowing on his face and the sounds and smells of the city were being carried away with it. The farther he walked from the lights of the city, the more vast the sky looked. The myriad of constellations that twinkled like diamonds were more visible as the height of skyscrapers and apartments diminished in size.

Few people were out walking at nine o'clock at night, although he had seen several people enjoying bike rides after the long winter. Paul realized he'd come a long way since his days of living in the slums of New York. Gone was the fear of the future, the absolute poverty, the uncertainty and the terrors of a small boy towards an abusive father. He still didn't know what the future held for him, but he wasn't concerned either.

He was a new creature in Christ and his life was now fully in God's hands. The frightened child had grown into a man with a mission. The fire in his heart, reassured him of the Lord's presence in his life. Paul strode down the street with great purpose as a smile graced his face and his eyes glowed like well-lit wall sconces, displaying the passion he felt. Life was good, he thought, as his strong legs took him up over a steep hill with the ease of a seasoned athlete.

CHAPTER THIRTEEN
THE JOURNEY

This fine spring day in April was perfect for beginning a new adventure, Kate reasoned. She stood guard over her worldly belongings, as the large crowd was jostling to and fro. Tiger was tucked safely away in his kennel while awaiting a place in the baggage car where he'd be looked after on the long trip north. Kate clutched a rope, which she had wound through the handles of four suitcases. This would protect her things, in case somebody wanted to steal her paltry possessions.

Kate had been grateful for the cab driver who had brought her to the Klindale Train Station. She never would have been able to carry it all by herself were it not for him. She had tipped him handsomely for the kindness shown her. She had seen very little of this in her time spent in the big city. Secretly, she was glad to be leaving this aspect of her life behind. It held some happy memories, granted, but it also held some very hurtful ones. A small part of her heart had been buried with Katya, and she was still reeling over her death and the reconciliation between Peter and his wife. She had been so sure that God wanted her to be with him, which had made her feel somewhat foolish, when Peter and his wife smiled at her as they left the safety of the detox centre hand in hand.

Oh well, she thought. They had a lot of troubles to work through, but with Peter's life getting a lot less complicated, she was sure they would make out okay. Now that the booze was no longer a factor, they might stand a fighting chance of staying together. The incoming train whistle blew and startled Kate out of her reverie. People started pushing to the front so they would be able to embark first. Kate followed a baggage handler into the luggage compartment to make sure Tiger had a farewell talk and some loves before they left.

Suitcases, bags, boxes and crates were tied down onto racks built specifically to hold large ponderous items. Kate grabbed her purse and hurried to find her sleeping compartment. She'd be travelling on board for the next two days with daily stops every 6-8 hours so they could stretch their legs. The first thing Kate needed was a nap. She hadn't been able to sleep last night due to excitement and she was quickly overcome with fatigue. She wanted to be well rested for whatever lay ahead. Once again the whistle sounded as the train pulled laboriously out of the station. As it picked up speed, Kate heard a knock at the door. The porter was gathering everyone's tickets and he brought two people to share the compartment with her. One was the most strikingly beautiful black woman Kate had ever laid eyes on. She was regal in bearing and obviously had been well educated. The girl holding her hand, was obviously her daughter, as she appeared to be a small replica of the woman.

They made a striking pair and Kate smiled as she stood to introduce herself. The porter herded the two inside, all the while letting a sneer escape out of the corner of his mouth.

"I saw you carrying that black book back there in the station, and I rightly thought, "well wouldn't that little bible believer like some real special company. I think I picked out the perfect type for you and I done smacked myself on the back and said: Well Luke, you surely know how to put the trash where it belongs." He roared as he slammed the door behind him, which covered the stunned silence from within.

"I am so sorry you had to hear that," Kate began. "There goes a very angry and hurting man. Please sit down," she gestured to the long couch and berth on their right. "My name is Kate Harmon," she added quickly to cover the flame of embarrassment that was rising on her cheeks.

"I'm Theresa McArthur and this is my daughter Constance." Kate smiled knowingly.

"I was sure she was your daughter. You're a beautiful little girl, Constance. How far are the two of you going?"

"We're off to Brandon, Manitoba. My husband is a professor of antiquities at the University of Brandon. We've been visiting family," she said as they made themselves comfortable. "What about you?"

"I'm going as far north as Lynn Lake in northern Manitoba," said Kate.

"Well, I'll be so glad to get home," said Theresa. "You may think that man was one of a kind. Unfortunately, a lot of things haven't changed much since the forties and fifties. I was hoping Constance wouldn't be subjected to such ignorance by another human being though. It's really hard not to be bitter but I've learned its better just to ignore them and pray for their souls. We may be dark on the outside, but their hearts are as black as the night. You may not believe it, but the Ku Klux Klan has resurfaced in the last few years too. Although their main targets now are the Jews and other religious sects, we still aren't out of the woods. Did you know they are still burning crosses and the like? History certainly repeats itself," she added softly as a deep sadness settled itself on her features.

"May I join you for dinner tonight?" Kate asked. "I'm all alone here and would really like some company, unless you have other plans."

"Dinner would be nice," Theresa said. "Would you rather have something just brought to the room, just in case that porter is in the dining car? I wouldn't mind if you'd rather do it that way."

"I won't hear of it," Kate quickly interjected. "We have done nothing to be ashamed of and I'll be darned if I'm going to hide because someone was rude to me. We have every right to be there just like anyone else. I'm going to have a nap first though. I'm exhausted. I put in a fairly sleepless night last night. See you in a bit," she added as she drew the curtain around her like a cocoon.

Kate dropped herself onto the most luxuriant down-filled pillow she had ever felt and sleep overtook her almost instantaneously. The dream began about ten minutes into her nap. It started out harmless enough but quickly developed into a fear-filled traumatic experience. She was sitting alone by a lake. It was early morning and a mist that resembled fog was blanketing the water, so she couldn't really discern anything on it. The mournful cry of a loon and the water lapping up on the shore was the only sound which penetrated the shroud of mist.

"Why do you sound so melancholy, my friend?" she called out to the bird. Kate felt the hair bristle on her neck as if she were being watched. It wasn't a pleasant feeling. She could feel the tangible presence of evil prying its ugly way into the tendrils of her very being. She quickly turned around, but nothing could be seen except the forest which totally filled the area at her back and sides. Why had she come here alone, she wondered? Her first instinct was to scream for help but Kate knew her screams would not be heard. That's why she had come to this place so early in the morning. No one would be up yet and the solitude was so inviting after spending a few years stuck inside the mayhem and rat race of the city. The sound of a pebble rolling down the incline assaulted her senses in the stillness. Was that an animal? Was that a face peering out from behind the tree up there, she thought as panic started to seize her and her heart threatened to pound its way out of her chest. Kate could literally taste the fear rising in her throat as her imagination ran wild.

She laughed out loud at her silliness. What am I getting so worked up about? I'm just imagining things and being foolish to boot. She arose anyway and decided to get back to wherever it was she had come from. As in most dreams, many of the details were hazy in her mind. She swung left up the winding path that would take her past a deserted mine shaft. Time had not been gentle, as the mine opening attested. Rocks and the debris of broken wine bottles and discarded cigarette butts graced the whole front of the place. She figured this was probably a great haven for teenagers.

As Kate walked quickly by, the presence of evil was stronger so she started whistling a mindless tune to drive away the terror she was feeling. The dry grass made a soft rustling noise as if something or someone was slowly making its way towards her. The snap of a twig made her wheel sharply around to confront her fear head on. There in front of her stood a man. It was hard to tell his age as dirt and hatred had disfigured him and distorted his features. Somehow he looked familiar, but Kate couldn't remember where she had seen him before. Maybe if he was cleaned up, she'd know.

There was dry grass and a bit of mud stuck to his clothes, which were torn beyond recognition. Obviously he had spent some time sleeping on the ground. His hair was dirty and matted and the colour of it was anyone's guess. He wore a filthy yellow baseball cap and had a fresh scar, running from the left side of his nose, up to the corner of his left eye. A sporadic growth of fine hair on his chin was the only evidence that he was still reasonably young, whoever he was.

The early morning light glinted off the only clean thing on his person. It was a large shiny hunting knife with a deadly looking double edge to it. One side was smooth while the other side was serrated.

"Who are you, and what do you want?" she pleaded with a slight tremor in her voice. His laughter was demented and the sound of it chilled her right to the bone. As he moved towards her, a scream finally erupted from her throat. That's when she recognized him and remembered the night he had driven by her with a smoking gun in his hands. Instantly she awoke with a start.

Kate's clothes clung to her skin and her hair was plastered to her scalp. Theresa was shaking her and telling her to wake up. She could see Constance staring at her with wide eyes.

"Kate, you were having a nightmare, I would wager. Here's some water. You look like you've seen a ghost. Is there anything I can do?" she said hurriedly. Even Theresa looked visibly shaken.

"Ah, no…thank you. You were right. I just had a bad dream. I'll be okay now. Perhaps I'll go for a bit of a walk and clear my head. Would you look at me? I'm shaking like a leaf. How silly of me!"

Kate walked down the narrow corridor as the train noisily rocked its way toward an uncertain destination. She opened the door at the end of the hall and entered the space between the sleeping quarters and the dining car. It was a confined area with a small window on each side. She opened one of them and felt the stiff breeze blow against her skin.

"Who was that man in my dream, and what does it all mean?" she inquired of the Lord. "I don't understand, Father, nor do I know why I am filled with a gnawing fear that something terrible is going to happen. Are you trying to warn me?" she asked, afraid of the answer she might get, yet needing to know all the same. She felt the need to be on guard and aware of her surroundings at all times. The Lord was imploring Kate to get prayed up. She would need the full armour of God if she were to have victory over this evil spectre, dampening the excitement she had felt about this new adventure. Somehow, that eagerness had dried up inside her like a fresh flower left out in the hot sun. The exhilaration she had felt at the beginning of her journey, had been replaced with a set determination. She was assured of the victory, and right now that was good enough for Kate.

The landscape continued to flash by at a dizzying pace. Kate marvelled anew at its ability to change like a chameleon. The train rumbled steadily and relentlessly down the track. She waved out the window at two young boys sitting astride their bicycles up on a hill. They were pointing and waving back. Kate remembered when she was younger. She had gone with her friends, a few blocks to the railroad crossing. They had each put a penny on the tracks and then hidden behind some trees to await the train. Ten minutes later the familiar rumble sounded and the whistle shrilled in their ears.

They waited until the caboose had disappeared around the bend before running to the tracks to snatch up their treasures. The pennies were warm to touch and the size of quarters. Later that evening, her father had drilled a hole in the metal and made it into a necklace. She had worn it proudly around her neck until her mother had insisted she either take it off or get rid of the green tarnish ring. Kate had tucked it safely away in a shoe box beside a stack of dog-eared baseball cards, a nickel ring, some marbles, a small box of costume jewellery, a horseshoe magnet and a locket with a picture of her grandmother Ann in it.

These were childhood treasures that just couldn't be parted with through years of spring cleaning. It was still sitting dusty and forlorn on the top shelf of her closet at home. She smiled at the memory. Kate jumped as the door behind her swung open with a well-aged creak.

"Well look what I've found myself! A darky-lovin' bible thumper. Shouldn't be all alone like that. Who knows what could happen to such a pure white thing?" the porter said as he ran his tongue across a pair of thick tobacco stained lips.

"Excuse me," said Kate as she tried to push her way past the vile man before her. He grabbed her by the upper arm and his broken nails bit into the tender skin hiding there under a pale violet blouse.

"Don't be in such a rush little girl. I need myself a little feel and you'll do pretty well, I'd reckon." He was at least five feet ten inches tall and weighed about two hundred and sixty pounds.

"Please, let me go," she pleaded. "I'll be missed if I don't get back to the room in the next few minutes. They'll come looking for me."

"That's long 'nough for me, girl. C'mere."

He wrapped a large meaty hand around the back of her neck and forced her into his massive arms. The more she struggled, the tighter he squeezed. Hot fetid breath assaulted her nostrils as he forced his lips against hers. Kate's head swam as she fought suffocation and nausea. She felt his hand slip inside her blouse. Where is everyone, Lord? Help me, she petitioned silently. Just then, the train headed around a bend. The swaying and jarring was just enough to catch the man off balance and throw him against the far wall.

It gave Kate plenty of time to slip out of his grasp and through the doors. With head lowered in shame and tears running silently down her cheeks, she swiftly moved down the narrow corridor, rubbing her lips with her hand. She opened their door with the key and quickly closed it behind her, leaning heavily against it. She took several deep breaths to calm her rattled nerves before venturing an explanation to Theresa who was watching her with growing concern.

"I thought you went for a walk to calm down. You look like you're in worse shape now than you were before you left. What happened?"

"I'm not having a good day," replied Kate with a forced laugh for the sake of Constance. "I was just attacked by our mutual friend, Luke the porter. I think I will just stay locked in our room for the duration of the trip. I'm definitely going to report him to the railway officials. No one should have to be subjected to that kind of abuse."

"Would you like me to go and get someone now for you?" inquired Theresa.

"I think we should all go together," said Kate. "There's safety in numbers."

They met with a railway official in a small office near the back of the train. A written complaint had to be submitted. It turned out that Luke was already on probation for a similar incident three months earlier, which had involved another young woman. He was officially dismissed and held in custody until the police could remove him from the train at the next stop.

The rest of the trip was without incident, much to the relief of Kate, Constance, and Theresa. They shared stories and had a few laughs, as only strangers are apt to do. Unfortunately, Brandon came too quickly for the three. It was with a sad heart that Kate waved goodbye to Theresa and Constance. Kate walked back to her room, deep in thought. She wondered what was in store for her. What would her apartment look like? Who would be her new friends? Would she even be accepted? Would she ever be truly happy again and would she ever find someone to love? These questions haunted her and troubled her sleep that night.

Kate knew that if she wanted answers she was going to have to be patient. Things were done in God's own time and that was the reality of the matter. Kate's heart knew this. She just had to make her mind know it as well. Life sure could throw a person a curve ball. You never knew from one day to the next what would come your way. Two words drifted slowly into her consciousness. They were, "stand firm." As she dwelled on them, and tossed them back and forth in her brain, Kate felt a warm resolve coming over her. She was loved already, by one who wanted nothing but the best for her.

It was a love that said: "It doesn't matter what you've done or what you've said or who you've hurt. I love you in spite of everything." Kate's heart fairly burst with joy and as His peace washed over her and flooded her senses, she finally slept like a baby who's been fed and now lies safely in the arms of her mother. She felt totally secure and protected.

Rachel and Stephen walked hand in hand as the twilight turned to dusk. Any blind person could tell they were in love. Rachel's eyes betrayed the absolute trust she felt in Stephen. They sat down on a bench that was so totally carved up with the initials of past loves, that it was a wonder it was still standing. Behind them was the old town well, with the hand pump still primed and working after endless years of use. It still squeaked with an awful grating noise too. Daily, the townspeople would secretly get a laugh as they watched old Lillian apply muscle to the handle. She would set her jaw with grim determination and the veins in her neck would protrude as she struggled. It was Lillian against the world. At least that's what you could read into it. People had long ago quit asking if they could help her with the handle. She would spit a string of colourful expletives at them, no matter who it was, and vow out loud that the day she stopped being able to use the pump, would be the day they laid her in the ground.

She was such a fixture, that the people stopped worrying, and instead just listened for the daily squeak of the handle. Stephen seemed distant tonight and Rachel knew something was on his mind. He always got this way when he was thinking about things. She kept her silence, as she knew from past experience that he would talk when he had his thoughts fully formulated in his head. Stephen was not one for just talking to hear himself talk.

The silence was far from uncomfortable. It was natural and uninhibited, as the two just basked in each other's company. After a period of ten minutes or so, he finally spoke up.

"Rachel," he began..."We've known each other all our lives and I would like nothing better than to spend the rest of my life with you. Will you marry me?"

The corner of Rachel's mouth turned up in the most radiant smile he had ever seen. She had played this moment over and over in her mind for years and here it finally was at last. She took his hands and gently squeezed them.

"You don't know how long I've waited to hear you say that, Stephen. Of course I'll marry you. You've been the only man I've ever loved, and I can't wait to spend the rest of my life with you."

As the star-filled night surrounded them like a warm woollen blanket, they made plans for their future. Talk became animated, as love once again found a home on the old worn bench. A man passing by just smiled knowingly. He'd been there before. In the innocence of youth, no trial was too difficult and no situation too complicated, that love couldn't conquer it. And it was a good thing that they could feel like this now, because life could sometimes be a cruel lover that could exact a high price from a person. They would need strength to survive. If you told them that right now, they would probably just laugh it off and never think another thing about it. The knowing could only come from experiencing and that was something that had to be learned somewhere down the road. Rachel and Stephen were content to just love each other, until marriage could bring with it a deeper understanding of themselves and the intimacy and passion of a husband and wife. Both had kept themselves pure, not just because God commanded it, but because they wanted to come to the marriage bed with anticipation, mystery, and a little fear and ignorance. They wanted to explore this special gift, with joy and newness…together.

Stephen and Rachel would wait until the right time, before giving away a part of them that could never be retrieved once lost. And so they sat hand in hand, with their future lying bright and unsullied before them, like untrodden snow on a field.

As the train slowed with a shriek of brakes, Kate readied herself for the next phase of her journey. A fine rain was sprinkling down, but from the looks of the large black clouds rolling in the distance, it was only a matter of time before it turned into a deluge. She found herself unprepared for such a liberal soaking and hurried to seek shelter. A baggage handler gently placed Tiger and her belongings beside the ticket office. She was one of two people disembarking. Obviously they didn't get lots of company here. A young boy ran up to her and in a breathless voice offered to carry her bags for a dollar.

"Free enterprise has gone up in price, since I was your age," laughed Kate.

"We take whatever jobs we can," quipped the boy.

"What's your name, if you're going to be working for me?" asked Kate.

"My name's Todd. I'm ten you know. We have a farm not far from here. I get every Wednesday and Sunday off, so on Wednesdays I come here to make some extra money. On Sundays we go to church, of course," he added with a smirk.

Kate smiled to herself as Todd chattered happily away. At least he had an umbrella. Kate went to the ticket master to see if her ride had called or not. Matt and Vira Jenkins were supposed to come for her. The train had been an hour early though, which was unusual as trains go. There was no message, so Kate made herself as comfortable as possible on the hard bench. It looked more like an old church pew, but she was grateful to be sheltered from the fast approaching storm. Because he had nothing to carry right now, Todd contented himself to sit beside her and share stories from his young life and Kate was relieved to have the company. It kept her mind off whatever future lay ahead. She was nervous and the butterflies were flitting around within her belly.

She was so deep in thought that Kate jumped with a startled cry when someone said her name. She looked up and up further still. The man before her was huge, but he had a friendly smile and his eyes, although showing some fatigue, were decidedly pleasing. The woman beside him was at least a foot shorter. She was smiling as well. This looks like a great start, thought Kate.

"I'm Matt Jenkins, and this is my wife Vira," he was saying. "You have no idea how glad we are to have you join us in the clinic." Kate jumped up and took the proferred hand and gave it a firm shake, as her father had taught her.

"I'm so happy to meet you," said Kate with a huge grin plastered on her face. "I've been looking forward to this for the past couple of months and I can't wait to get settled in."

If you'd like to get in the truck, we'll get heading home" said Matt. He bent over to pick up a couple of bags, but was stopped by Kate.

"I already have someone to carry the bags," she said, as she tossed her head in the direction of Todd.

Todd grabbed the first couple of bags and although he strained from the weight, he just dug his heals in and struggled his way to the truck. Setting them by the tailgate, he ran back to get another load. Lastly, Tiger was put down in his pet carrier with a thump. Kate fished around in her purse and handed the boy five dollars.

"You deserve this, Todd. I've never seen anyone work as hard as you did," she said as she smiled down at him.

"You'd better get on home, Todd. There's a nasty storm coming. I can give you a lift if you want."

As Todd started to run away, he looked over his shoulder and said: "It's okay Dr. Jenkins. I can make it home really fast. And thanks a lot for the money, lady. I'm saving to buy a bicycle."

"I don't think we'll miss the worst of the storm. It will probably get really bumpy. There were a lot of potholes on the way in. That's what took us so long to get here. You'll get used to this though. The road doesn't get much better than this," he added with a wink shot in Vira's direction. Obviously this road was the butt end of many jokes Kate mused, as she smiled and nodded her head.

The trip to Poweetan, although extremely bone-jarring in many places, was also made delightful by the company. The Jenkins seemed like a wonderful couple and told many colourful stories about life in the small community. The picture in Kate's mind grew as details were put into place and names were put to as yet, formless faces. Kate felt sure that she would know many people just by the descriptions that had been given throughout the long afternoon drive.

CHAPTER FOURTEEN
KATE FINDS A HOME

"We're almost there," said Vira. "Just around that bend up there, close your eyes. This is a favourite for all newcomers to Poweetan."

As they turned into the last curve, Kate closed her eyes. In a moment Vira shouted out once again. "Open your eyes Kate." Kate opened her eyes slowly and gasped at the breathtaking view. There before them was Southern Indian Lake. The storm had thankfully abated about a half hour earlier. A perfect rainbow arched its way gracefully over the lake and seagulls dipped and dove in the sky. There couldn't have been a more welcome sight for Kate. She felt the strong pull of the place on her spirit and knew that she was truly home. The heartaches and disappointments of the past six months were pushed to the back of her brain in an instant. Everything Kate had gone through seemed to lead her to this place.

She thought of the very first rainbow and how it was to be a sign and a covenant from God to Noah and the generations to follow that never again would he destroy the whole world by water. What did Noah think when he saw the colours brushed across the sky as if by a giant's paintbrush. It made Kate feel small in the light of God's power and majesty. It was also a symbol for new beginnings and Kate felt humbled that God would allow her such a beacon of hope. She sent a prayer of thanks up to her Lord and began to look around more closely at her new home. She felt strange, as people stood out on front stoops and even in the street to wave to the Jenkins and their passenger. Surely they're not waving at me, she thought.

Kate didn't have long to think about it before Matt stopped the truck in front of a low white building. The sign simply read, "Clinic." For someone who had just spent a couple of years in a large city, this place was a bit of a shock to the system. It was like stepping back in time. It would definitely take some getting used to, but Kate felt up to the challenge.

People were milling around the truck now, to get a better look at the new nurse. Kate hoped the novelty would soon wear off, as the attention embarrassed her. They all stepped out of the truck and many eager hands groped for her bags as people tried to be helpful. They led her to the back apartment and opened the door with great relish as if they were children who knew a secret.

The place was quaint in a rustic sort of way and Kate could tell that everyone had worked very hard at getting it spruced up for her. There was still a faint smell of paint and cleaners. There was an air of expectance as if the people were holding their collective breath. Kate turned and gave them one of her biggest smiles.

"This place is wonderful, and I thank you all for making me feel so welcome. I'm overwhelmed by it all. I can't wait to start work next week and I hope to know many of you by name, before the month is out. Thank you again for your kindness," she said as they ushered her in and gently closed the door behind her.

Matt and Vira stayed behind for about an hour, so they could show Kate around the clinic and get to know her better. They hit it off right away and knew that they would make great team, working together. There would be lots of time for small talk, learning the ways of the clinic and meeting people. That could all wait. Like an eager child at Christmas time, Kate wanted to explore everything. An angry meow brought her back to her senses.

"I'm sorry, Tiger. I forgot all about you," she cooed as the door to the kennel was unlatched hopefully for a very long time.

Tiger immediately began to search out his new territory with eagerness. Kate laughed as she said goodbye to the Jenkins' and began to examine the place more closely. There were lots of handmade cupboards above and below the kitchen sink. There were enough dishes for six people and a well-stocked pantry and refrigerator. Kate couldn't believe her eyes. She wouldn't have to buy groceries for at least three weeks. There was even a small stack of cat food in one cupboard.

The townspeople had left nothing out. The floors were all spit and polished hardwood that you could almost see your face in. Throw rugs were scattered randomly throughout the place, which gave it all an appearance of being homey. What caught Kate's eye was the fireplace made out of large slabs of grey stone. Beside it was a healthy stack of chopped wood and an axe.

The furniture was colonial and looked like it had been handmade. The cushions that adorned the couch and chair looked big enough to jump on. Kate felt like a little girl again and simply lost herself in the joy of her new surroundings. There was a small closet by the door and a bathroom containing a toilet, a sink with a medicine chest over it and a huge clawed bathtub.

Kate couldn't wait to sink into a deep bath full of bubbles. There was a good sized closet, a dresser with a mirror, an end table with a lamp and the biggest feather bed with a charming quilt that Kate had ever seen. She flopped across it and sunk. It was a wonderful sensation and as past tensions drained away, her eyelids became heavy and sleep quickly overtook her.

Hours later, she awoke with a start and became disoriented with her surroundings. As awareness set in, Kate realized that she'd slept straight through from four o'clock until six in the morning. She began her first day in Poweetan with a long, luxurious bath and then unpacked her meagre belongings. The finishing touch was the well-thumbed bible which she placed on her coffee table. The rest of the day was spent greeting visitors. Everyone wanted a chance to talk to the new nurse and the excuses they gave were often times quite comical. Lillian Bailey's reason for visiting was that she wanted to make sure the living room furniture was suitable. Her grandson had made it fifteen years earlier and you just never knew how things would hold up.

In the late afternoon, Kate was able to slip away by herself. She decided to go down to the lake and see it close up. As she headed through the woods, something seemed vaguely familiar and gave her an unsettled feeling in the pit of her stomach. Perspiration beaded on her forehead. She laughed off her silliness and started to whistle to allay her fears. Then she remembered the dream on the train had been similar to this. There was a clearing up ahead, so Kate hurried to get her bearings.

In her haste, she tripped over an exposed root and fell headlong into the opening of an unused mine. There was debris strewn about the mouth and weeds were everywhere. The smell of moss and wet earth assaulted her nostrils, as panic rose within her like a tangible presence. The snap of a twig made her cry out in fear. As Kate cowered in the dirt, a hand reached down and grabbed her about the shoulders. She struggled blindly until a gentle voice said, "I'm sorry if I startled you. I was just coming back from the lake when I heard something fall. My name is Stephen and you must be Kate. Let me help you up," he added.

"I thought I was lost and I'm afraid I started to panic. I must look the fool! she stammered. "Yes, I am Kate. Kate Harmon."

There was no way she was going to tell him that this place had been in her dream or vision. He'd think she was crazy. Because the dream had been so graphic, Kate decided never to come this way again unless she was accompanied by someone else. Gratefully she fell in step behind Stephen who led the way out of the woods and back into town. She looked at her rescuer more closely. He was a good looking boy with a ruddy complexion. He appeared to be in his early twenties or so. He had said they would be working in the same building.

Stephen worked in the dental office and was eager to introduce her to Matt and Vira's daughter, who she hadn't had the pleasure of meeting yet. Stephen blurted out to Kate that he had proposed to Rachel and she had accepted. He was so obviously thrilled that Kate couldn't help but feel happy for him. Young love was so full of life, she mused.

CHAPTER FIFTEEN
WICKED WAYS

The next few weeks flew by as there was much work to do and lots to learn. She enjoyed the work immensely and even knew most of the locals by name. She'd found an unexpected friend in Rachel. Although the girl was younger, she was a pleasure to be around. Rachel had a great sense of humour and was very likeable. Whenever she was around, the day just seemed a little bit brighter. She was a lot like Katya. They had many similar traits. Her laughter was infectious and it was hard not to get caught up in the excitement of her wedding plans with Stephen. They were so perfectly matched, that it never failed to bring a smile to Kate's face when she thought about them together. Secretly, she longed for a similar relationship as she was sometimes lonely, but was also content to wait.

If God wanted her to be with someone, it would happen. Much time was spent in her new church home too. The Poweetan Presbyterian Church had about seven regular Sunday School children and about forty adults. Many others graced the pews for the traditional Christmas and Easter services, but felt their presence wasn't required more often than that. The old minister could often be heard mumbling to himself that God didn't take holidays, so why should they feel it was necessary to do so. But it fell on deaf ears.

Reverend James had a heart of gold and lived a very godly life, even though his sermons were quite often sleepers. Kate joined Rachel in leading the young children in their lessons and soon became a favourite amongst the congregation. The two girls would fill the walls with angelic music as they sang many duets together. Kate borrowed Rachel's books and Rachel quite often borrowed Kate's clothes.

The two were almost inseparable until Rachel's marriage to Stephen took place six months later. Then a most natural thing occurred. Rachel spent less time with Kate and more with her new husband, as was to be expected. Kate felt a sudden pang of loneliness as she now had more free nights, than busy ones. She also realized with a start that it had been over a year since Katya had died. The time had simply flown by, and she thought that was all right too.

A surprise visit from her mother over the Christmas holidays had been a welcome respite from the cold and snow and the fireplace proved to be a real blessing as it cheered up her apartment and made it cozy beyond all measure. Over the winter months, life in general slowed up to a snail's pace. About the only people who dared to venture very far were the trappers. Many in Poweetan still clung to the old ways. Old Lil was known to say that if it worked, why bother fixin' it. Unfortunately, that was the same with their religious beliefs.

Kate was saddened to see so few people who had made life-changing commitments to the Lord. It broke her heart, more so in this small community than anywhere else, because these people had become like family to Kate. They loved and protected her. Kate knew that if she wanted the spiritual darkness to be flooded with the light of revival, there had to be a real effort made to have concentrated prayer vigils. So far, there were about four to six people every Tuesday and Sunday night. But Rachel was fond of reminding everyone that where two or more gathered in the name of Jesus, there He would be in their midst.

Once Stephen started coming regularly, their little number grew to seven. One Wednesday afternoon, Kate went into the general store, a.k.a. coffee shop, a.k.a. post office. She greeted Ruby who was a permanent fixture behind the counter.

"What'll it be today Kate? I just made some fresh coffee and donuts."

She knew that donuts were Kate's weakness.

"Oh Ruby, you just had to, didn't you?" Kate laughed. "I'll have one of each please. Have you seen Rachel? She was supposed to meet me for coffee," she added.

"I saw her about an hour ago. She seemed to be in a hurry. I'm sure she won't forget about you," said Ruby.

Kate sat down to a delicious steaming mug of coffee. A sudden sense of foreboding settled on her like a living breathing thing. Now why do I feel like this, she wondered? She tried to swallow back the rising uneasiness, but it wouldn't go away. Something wasn't right. She felt a strong urge to pray, although she didn't know what to pray for or who to pray for, for that matter.

She was thankful that God's Holy Spirit was able to take her groaning before the throne, as sometimes she just didn't know how she should pray. Just then, the little bell on the door tinkled. In skipped Rachel with her new puppy struggling to keep up to her. Puppy was an unusual term to use as the animal was really a wolf cub that Stephen had found abandoned on the far side of the lake.

"Tie him outside please, Rachel. He may be cute now, but he's going to be huge. I don't want him getting too used to coming in here. Then he'll want my fresh donuts too," scolded Ruby.

"If you insist," sighed Rachel.

"Now don't you go laying a guilt trip on me," chided Ruby. "You just remember that I've changed your diapers."

Kate and Rachel both had a good laugh over that one, although Kate's sense of uneasiness didn't dissipate with the conversation. The two laughed and chatted for the next half hour. Kate couldn't help thinking about the last coffee she had shared with Katya. It was hard to believe that a year and a half had passed since that fateful night. She had kept in touch with Mike and Marg and several of the people from the old church.

She had even received a letter from Paul, although she hadn't gotten around to writing him back yet. She felt just a faint stirring of nostalgia. Kate knew in her heart that there was no going back. It wasn't healthy.

"What's up Rach? You're obviously busting a seam and have been since you skipped on in here. Out with it already! I've been patiently biting my tongue, but I can't stand it any longer. You're driving me crazy."

"I wanted to keep this quiet for a bit longer, but I simply can't Kate. You know Stephen and I have been trying to start a family, right?" she hurried on without waiting for an answer. "Well I got Stephen to pick me up a home pregnancy test the last time he was in Churchill, just in case, you know! I was two weeks late, so

I tried the test yesterday, and guess what? We're going to have a baby, Kate. Isn't that great?" she gushed excitedly.

Kate looked at the joy and love written all over her friends' face. Grasping Rachel's hands in hers, she gave them a squeeze.

"That's wonderful news, Rachel. I'm so happy for the both of you. I know you'll make great parents."

Ruby, overhearing the last line, rushed over and gave Rachel a big bear hug. "Well, I'll be darned. Isn't that the greatest news we've heard for a while."

"So much for keeping things quiet," laughed Rachel.

Unfortunately, if they had been listening to the news reports out of Klindale, they wouldn't have been so thrilled with the news. For the past three weeks, police had been searching the area for an escaped prisoner. He had supposedly "walked away" from a minimum security prison after having a supervised weekend pass. Some figured he had help. They never suspected that a young man of almost twenty years could think up such a daring escape on his own and in broad daylight to boot. He was nowhere near where they were searching. If someone had been able to read the thoughts going through his head, they would have been mortified. Surely such evil couldn't exist in such a young mind, could it?

As Kate glanced up, she noticed someone in a yellow cap walking by on the other side of the street. Kate was fairly certain she had never seen anyone with a hat like that in Poweetan. They didn't get a lot of strangers around this time of year. He or she was hunkered down against the cold. Odd that someone would walk around in this weather without proper clothing on, she thought. Kate promptly dismissed the thought as Rachel rose to leave.

"By the way Rachel, what did you decide to call your puppy?" asked Kate.

"We're calling him Hunter, because I think he'll be a good one."

Kate waved out the window as the two of them hurried down the stairs and headed off in the opposite direction from the person in the yellow cap. After finishing her drink, Kate paid Ruby and then headed back to work. Needless to say, Rachel had told Stephen and her parents about the good news. So a general buzz of excitement was humming around the office. This would be a first grandchild for both families. The baby doesn't stand a chance, Kate thought with a smile. He or she will be loved to death.

Many knitting needles would be heard over the next weeks as soon, the whole town would know about the baby. News travels fast in small towns. Too bad the townspeople hadn't pooled their information when it came to various incidents of garbage that had been routed through, small quantities of food stuffs that had been stolen and a good number of small animals that was taken from the trapper's snares. Most individuals just reckoned some animal had been prowling around for food and dismissed any thoughts about it. Had all these incidents been put together, something would have smelled rotten.

Although Kate's walkway outside her apartment door was "miraculously" shovelled each snowfall by Lillian's grandson, Albert, Kate was still sure that there had been several occurrences where it looked like someone had been prowling around outside and looking in her windows as the tracks often led up to the windows. The notion that somebody would be trying to invade her privacy in such a sneaky fashion gave Kate the willies. Not for a moment did Albert enter her mind. He was such a kind and gentle man. She knew that he wouldn't stoop to voyeurism. But in the busyness of the next few months, she had little time to dwell on it.

A nasty flu had gone through the town and many had succumbed to diarrhea, vomiting, and high fevers. Kate went with Matt for house visits almost daily. Barely a homestead was left untouched, with at least one person afflicted. Even Rachel got it. When mixed with morning sickness, she became downright ill. She lost five pounds, but with lots of care, she recovered without incident.

During that time, Kate received a disturbing letter from Mike Collins. In it he told of Tom Erikson's bold escape many months earlier and how he had fooled everyone and just vanished into thin air. He said that the police were confident that he was still in the area, but so far he had eluded all attempts at discovery. The thought that Katya's killer had escaped was cause for concern, but Kate was sure that God would watch over her. Besides, nobody would ever find her in this remote place, she reasoned. A couple of times when she'd opened the drapes in the early morning, Kate had caught a glimpse of yellow out of the corner of her eye, but passed it off as still being half asleep.

"I've got to get more sleep, Tiger. I'm starting to imagine things," she said to her cat. Tiger just looked at her with big eyes and meowed.

After a thoroughly long, but delightful winter passed, the land began to transfigure itself. The snows receded like an old-timers' hairline and tender green shoots wormed their way to the surface of the ground to greet the sunshine. The pure, fresh air assailed the senses and brought with it, a hint of renewal.

During the latter part of the winter, old Rev. James retired and left the Presbyterian Church without a pastor to shepherd the flock. Members of the small congregation had taken turns leading the worship services but were also searching for a new pastor. So far they had been unsuccessful in seeking one out, but were not overly concerned either. They had been meeting regularly every week for prayer and were confident that God would lead someone to them in His time.

Kate was eager for the ground to harden, so she could get back on her bike. She felt really out of shape. On a particularly cold day in April, as a steady drizzle fell silently to earth and a thick fog cocooned Poweetan, Kate's world began to unravel unceremoniously. She walked down the street through icy slush whistling a new song the youth group had been practicing the night before. It was Saturday afternoon and Kate looked forward to putting her feet up and doing some reading. As she rounded the right side of the clinic to head to her apartment, her eyes immediately noticed flecks of red standing out starkly against the wet sidewalk.

With rising alarm, she could see it getting heavier and more defined, the closer she got to her door. As Kate slowly turned the back corner, the saliva dried up in her throat, tears sprang to her eyes and her whole body began to shake convulsively. She slowly sank to her knees in the slush and whimpered like a small child. There in front of her was Tiger. He'd been nailed to a crude make-shift cross. His small throat had been slit and his head lolled to one side as if he were sleeping. The blood had congealed in a pool underneath him. In revulsion, Kate rose unsteadily and staggered blindly down the walkway only to smack into Matt who was checking out the strange noises coming from behind the clinic.

As she wept uncontrollably, she could only point out back. The violation of Tiger was bad enough but with a clarity brought on by grief, Kate thought about not only the cat, but whoever had done the deed. Someone out there was mentally deranged and for some unknown reason, had targeted Kate as the object of his or her anger. But why would somebody want to harm an innocent animal, she wondered? Kate had read about animals being sacrificed before, but until one actually sees the results, even the wildest imagination couldn't dream up anything that would come close to the horror she had just witnessed this afternoon. If she had known that Tiger would be just the tip of the iceberg, she probably would have fled Poweetan on the next plane out...if only she had known.

In reality it was just one more piece of the puzzle God was putting into her life. Kate's life was like a beautiful tapestry to Him. He saw the finished product and although God wasn't making these terrible things happen to her, He was using them for good. Since leaving Klindale, Kate had learned how to persevere. This had strengthened her faith and reworked her already strong character. Rather than being hardened by life's harsh realities, she was becoming even more compassionate and forgiving, if that were possible. No longer could she be called naïve. She was becoming strong in the Lord, which was good because she would need to draw on that strength all too soon.

CHAPTER SIXTEEN
PETER'S MOVE

Peter inched up to the stoplight and laid on the horn. What's holding this traffic up, he thought, miserably? I'm going to be late again. He had moved to Fulson, Manitoba to start a new life for himself. It was supposed to be a new chapter in his tarnished life, but had only helped to make him more bitter and self-serving. After the death of Bethany and subsequent reunion with Annette, Peter thought his life would finally get back on track.

He remembered leaving the clinic so full of hope. Kate had said things about her God that had really made sense to him. Unfortunately, a series of unpredictable events following his release, only served to snatch away his newly budding interest in spiritual matters. He wrongly reasoned that if you wanted something positive to happen in your life, you had to make it happen yourself. Who got anything by waiting on the Lord or anyone else for that matter? People would only let you down and hurt you. That attitude was for losers only.

Oh, things had started out all right. Annette was very supportive on his road to recovery for a change. Peter spent the first couple of months sending out resumes and going for job interviews. Unfortunately, the hospitals that he'd contacted were unwilling to take him on. Word travels fast in the professional field and for most people Peter was a risk they weren't willing to take. He had been in the papers and so had his wife.

After one particularly dejecting day of listening to feeble excuses, Peter slunk home carrying a large chip on his shoulders. What he wouldn't give for a long pull on a forty-ounce bottle of Gilbey's, he thought wryly. He entered through the back door unannounced and threw his coat on the back of an expensive cherry wood high-backed chair. If Annette were home, she'd have a fit, but thankfully she had a meeting this afternoon. He padded up the stairs in his stocking feet, pulling his shirt up over his head.

Peter stopped dead in his tracks as he heard the sound of his wife's laughter coming from the bedroom. A soft light spilled out into the hall from the door which stood slightly ajar. Quietly now, he inched forward and slowly pushed the door open. Clothes were strewn all over the floor and a strangers' naked backside was hovering above his wife. The laughter quickly died in Annette's throat and the colour drained from her cheeks as she took notice of Peter standing stock still in the doorway.

As the unwelcomed houseguest turned towards him, Peter noticed that it was Aaron Weinburger, his supposed best friend. Peter visibly seethed as the acid rose in his stomach. With a barely controlled voice, he ordered Aaron out of his house, called his wife a few choice expletives, and stormed out of the house as well.

He drowned his sorrows in an uncountable number of gin and tonics at a local bar and cried in hurt and anger in the arms of a highly painted lady who for fifty dollars, could swear undying love and allegiance to him. Peter was able to blessedly forget for a short while. He was unable to perform due to inebriation, but he didn't care. Just the fact that he was in unforbidden territory, made it all worthwhile. To hell with Annette, he thought bitterly. Over the next couple of days, he moved into a motel and methodically liquidated all his assets. He left Annette the house and cleared out the joint account at the bank. Not once did Peter give her a chance to explain. He could only look at her with revulsion and disgust.

At the end of that week, he hopped into the Porsche with a loaded suitcase and took off for good. He never looked back. Peter ended up in Fulson, one month later. He landed a job at the Fulson General Hospital. A few of his colleagues had tried unsuccessfully to break through his tough outer shell, but to no avail. He kept himself insulated from everyone and everything.

Peter's lifestyle took a decidedly unusual turn for the worse. He started doing things that would normally be reserved for those few daredevils in life who were so reckless that they challenged death for laughs. On his days off, he would go rock climbing on nearby Mount Killaloma, so named for its dangerous crevices and unpredictable atmospheric changes. Storms could blow up out of nowhere in a relatively short period of time and many a person had lost their way or their life on its steep slopes.

This had become a home for Peter's passion. He would have welcomed death with open arms, but it seemed just inches out of reach. He also tried his hand at hang gliding, bungee jumping and car racing. Although these sports could produce a wonderful rush of adrenaline and pure unadulterated fear, more often than not, Peter would go home dejected after participating in them. He would count it a failure that he had lived to see another day.

Conquering anything and everything became his main goal in life. This included sports, recreation, work, the stock markets and even women. Many a broken heart was left behind in the wake of Peter Carson. But something had to give very soon, or he was going to self-destruct. Again he cursed the traffic and shook a fist at the car in front of him.

CHAPTER SEVENTEEN
MISTAKEN IDENTITY

If one had known Tom Erikson at the time of the drive by shooting of a young woman, they certainly wouldn't know him now. Naturally, two years can change a person, but anger and pure hatred can totally rearrange a person's character. For a city bred boy to rough it in the wilds for months on end meant that something had to have happened inside his head. And happen it did. A cold spirit of dementia had totally possessed him. He was Tom the invincible, or so he thought.

Tom had been living in the back end of an abandoned mine for ages it seemed. It was equipped with an odd assortment of stolen essentials such as a chipped cup, plate, blanket, mouldy sleeping bag, and his razor sharp hunting knife with a wicked serrated edge. To help pass the time of day, he would spend an hour working out and although he ate sporadically, stealing whatever he could, his body was sinewy and muscular. Living in a world of silence only served to further his madness. Daily he played over and over in his mind the scenario of what he would do to Kate. He knew he could do it blindfolded if the need arose. He had been watching her movements for months and pretty well knew her boring routine off by heart.

Tom had even been cocky enough to show himself to her a few times, from a distance of course. He wanted her to think someone was watching. He wanted her filled with fear. But when he saw the cat, he just couldn't resist the excitement that stirred within him. It wouldn't be as great as wasting the woman, but it would calm him down a bit and help him to bide his time for the right moment.

Within a couple of weeks his goal would be accomplished and then he would get out of this god-forsaken place and head somewhere warmer. This cold weather and sickening abundance of snow was for the birds, he reasoned. He wanted to close this chapter of his life once and for all and move on to something better. Perhaps he could land a job and get a place of his own. Whatever the case, Tom was honed and ready like a well-oiled machine.

Now he just had to wait for the perfect moment, when Kate was by herself and then her life would be history. She would pay for the last two years. Yes, she would pay--big time! But for now, Tom knew he had to stay in hiding a little while longer. There was another unknown opening into the mine. Approximately three hundred feet from the main opening was a hole in the side of the hill. Tom had made sure that it was covered in brush so no one passing by would give it a second look.

He had stumbled upon it purely by chance. There had been several months when Tom had nothing to do all day but explore. Although he was almost twenty now, he was still basically a kid at heart. Therefore, searching and exploring his home held a bit of excitement and mystery for him. It was during one of these forays through the old shaft, that he came upon a tunnel he had previously overlooked. Using his flashlight like a beacon, he gingerly stepped over fallen rocks and ducked under the odd beam that had become dislodged and was hanging at haphazard angles. For obvious safety reasons he made sure that things were left untouched in case the walls or ceiling collapsed. Good thing he didn't get claustrophobia, he mused.

After Tom had gone about one hundred and fifty feet into the new tunnel he came upon a small room hewn out of the rock. It had probably been used for storage or as a lunch room as there were some weathered looking crates stacked one on top of the other in one corner, an old rusty lunch pail tossed to one side, a table covered with half an inch of dirt and grime and a couple of chairs. Cobwebs were the order of the day and Tom was thrilled as he took in the scene before him. This is where he would do her. Right there on the table. It would be perfect and nobody would ever hear her scream.

Tom felt himself getting aroused again as he pictured in his head her struggling, crying nakedness. Tom knew he had to stop fantasizing or he would be unable to contain his wild lust for her death. It wasn't time yet. As he left the room and took a sharp right, that's when he saw it. Daylight was seeping through the disturbed dust particles up ahead. One large cobweb was moving gently in the breeze from the opening and a hint of fresh air was permeating the stale tunnel where he stood. Tom worked away at the hole for about fifteen minutes, until it was large enough for him to shinny through.

Using a chair from the room behind him, he pulled himself up over the lip and found himself in the forest at the side of a hill. It took him a while to get his bearings and to find the mouth of the mine again. Once the two openings were ingrained in his head, he methodically put together a mental map of the whole area, inside and out. He played and replayed several scenarios in his head looking for glitches, just in case something was to go wrong. Tom figured that all avenues had been looked at and that no matter what happened, he would be prepared.

He also had a stolen motorcycle ditched and covered over, about three miles away. That would be his way out of this hole. Because Tom had kept himself in such good shape, he knew he could crawl out of the hole and be leaving the area on his bike in just under forty minutes. Now he just had to wait for the right timing. He planned to hit her from behind and then carry her to the mine. That way nobody would hear them. Luckily there was still icy slush and puddles everywhere. No footprints would be left behind. His cover was secure and Tom Erikson was ready. Nothing would stop him now.

Paul had just finished his second year of seminary. His marks had been excellent which was not surprising because he had put hours and hours into his studies. He loved the challenge that most of the classes had afforded him and was eager to finish off the final two years. Although he was looking forward to the summer, Paul was more interested in starting his new job. It was only for two months, but it was the location that excited him more than anything. He was going to be the student pastor at New Life Baptist Church in Fulson, Manitoba. He would also have a chance to work in the hospital there as a chaplain in training, on a part-time basis. He was flying out the next day and could barely contain his excitement.

Paul had picked that location to apply for a job because of its closeness to Poweetan. He was hoping to make time to visit Kate, if she would have him around. Not once had he forgotten her soft eyes and beautiful smile and could barely wait to see her again. Paul hoped she hadn't found someone else, but according to the letter that she'd written to Mike and Marg, she still sounded free as a bird.

Countless times Paul had started to write her another letter, only to scrunch the paper into a ball and throw in into the wastepaper basket. She had written him back once but had put nothing personal in it. It spoke only of the weather, etc. He didn't feel worthy of her love and wasn't surprised that she hadn't noticed him. He failed to take into account the fact that Kate had been traumatized when he saw her last.

She had been coming down from a roller-coaster ride of emotions and was hardly coping, let alone functioning. As Paul walked slowly to his dorm, he began to feel a heavy burden fall upon his heart for Kate. He didn't know why or what he was to pray for. All he knew was that God's Spirit was imploring Paul to pray for her. So, on that early spring morning as the buds were just beginning to come alive on the trees and the sun beat down warmly on the back of his neck, Paul prayed for the woman he loved from afar.

In the unseen realm, God was dispatching his angels to cover Kate and form a hedge of protection around her. This was due to the heartfelt prayers of one righteous man and as God beseeched him to pray, Paul in obedience stood in the gap for Kate. Had he known the future, he would have stayed under that tree until evening instead of going to his room. Paul savoured the warmth of the day and as he proceeded on his way he hummed a familiar praise song and felt his spirit rise. Hopefully he would see her very soon.

It was time. He was as ready as could be. It was raining quite heavily. It was dark and he knew the woman was at her church group. She would be leaving at eight thirty just like clockwork, so he intended to grab her down the street, where it was the darkest. His heart beat wildly inside his chest as he waited in anticipation. This was the moment he had prepared for. He glanced at the clock in the café as he quickly made his way past. Eight twenty-five and ticking… He stomped his feet in agitation and pulled his jacket tighter around his neck to stop the rain from coursing down it. A nervous chuckle escaped his cracked lips and a twitch pulled at the corner of his eye.

As the evening wound to a close, Rachel approached Kate.

"What's on your mind, Rachel?"

"Well," began Rachel, "Hunter took off this morning down by the lake and I haven't seen him all day. I think I'll scoot around by there, before I go home tonight. I just wouldn't be able to sleep if I knew he was caught in a trap or something."

"So I'll go with you. It's dark outside and maybe you shouldn't go out there by yourself. If Stephen were here tonight, you know that he would have a fit if I let you go by yourself."

"It's not necessary Kate. I've been down there thousands of times at night and I would know my way with my eyes closed. You could do me a favour though," she added sheepishly.

"Sure Rachel. What can I do?"

"Could I borrow your rain slicker? I'd only get soaked in my jacket. I'll bring it to your place on my way back home."

"Of course you can take it, Rachel. It's hanging over the back of the chair over there. Don't worry about bringing it around tonight though. I'll get it from you later. There's no rush. At least you'll stay dry until you get home. I hope you find Hunter."

Rachel grabbed Kate's slicker and pulled it around her slightly bulging abdomen. She tucked her hair inside and pulled the hood over her head. Kate laughed at the comical figure she cut.

"You look like a big yellow duck, Rachel," Kate laughed. "Watch out for any wayward puddles. They might be the death of you." The two girls bid each other goodnight and Kate smiled as Rachel slipped out the door.

Here she comes, he thought giddily. Her head was bowed under the heavy rain and she was moving quickly. Just when she should have crossed the street to where he was hiding, she instead veered off into the woods on the right side of the street. Where's she going now, he wondered? She always goes straight home. What does she think she's doing to me? The rage inside his head and heart reached a crescendo. He ran off after her, hoping his plans weren't going to be ruined for another week. He was gladdened when he saw where she was going.

Kate was heading towards the lake, all by herself. Foolish girl...she was playing right into his hand. He didn't know why, nor did he care. If he could nail her down there, he wouldn't have to carry her as far and could be assured that nobody would see them. It was the perfect scenario and he raised his arms in a silent power salute of victory.

He heard her calling out a name. What was she saying, he pondered as he strained to hear. She was yelling the name, "Hunter." How odd, that she'd be calling for the other girl's dog. Oh well, he thought. There's probably some logical explanation. He kept pace at a short distance from her. A little bit further and she'd be walking to her death all by herself. This delighted Tom. He would have her in his grasp in no time.

As Rachel stopped to listen for any answering yips, she heard a branch snap behind her. The rain wasn't as loud in the trees, so she was sure of the sound. Perhaps Hunter was coming on the run, she thought with a smile. Rachel retraced her steps until she came to the path that went by the old mine. It was a short cut and the prospects of going farther than necessary in this rain, was a thought Rachel didn't relish. She continued calling for Hunter as she made her way quickly down the weed-choked path. Although the snow was melting, the tangle of vines and brush made walking a hazard. Rachel slowed her pace so she wouldn't trip.

As she approached the mine entrance she picked up her pace. This place had always given her the creeps and it didn't help being in the dark and rain all by herself. As she opened her mouth to call again for her dog, she felt, rather than heard, something step up behind her. Before Rachel could turn around she was hit on the head from behind. With the sound of a sickening thud, Rachel mercifully felt nothing as she slipped heavily to the ground and unconsciousness quickly overtook her.

Tom bent down, grabbed her roughly and threw her over his shoulder as if she weighed no more than a bag of potatoes. Even with the rain slicker on, he could smell her perfume permeating his nostrils. It almost drove him completely mad with lust as he made his way over boulders and fallen branches to the small hidden opening at the back of the mine. He slipped once and almost dropped his prize, before regaining his footing.

When Tom reached his destination, he knelt down on one knee and set the woman on the ground beside him. In the dark, he passed a sturdy piece of rope under her stomach and tied it in a knot at her back. Quietly and quickly he slid on his belly through the opening in the ground. He was grateful that the rain would cover all tracks and smells. He gave a sharp tug on the rope and slowly she slid into view. Her jacket caught once on something but after straining his muscles, he felt the tension release as she moved freely through the opening after him. He let her fall heavily to the ground which dropped about five feet inside of the opening. He didn't care as he planned to do a lot worse to her before this night was over.

Tom dragged her as far as he could, before carrying her the rest of the way to the special room…the one he had been saving just for her. He tossed her onto the table without fanfare and stopped to catch his breath. She was heavier than he had imagined all this time. Tom lit the hurricane lamp and tied her down securely. The hunting knife was taken from its place of honour in the drawer by the woman's head, and almost reverently he began to cut away the yellow slicker. It was then that her hair tumbled out of the hood and he saw that he had grabbed not Kate, but her friend, Rachel. Tom couldn't believe his eyes, nor could he imagine how he could have been tricked again by the witch. He spewed out his venom, as he stuck the knife into the table and watched it quiver several times.

Just then, Rachel's eyes began to flicker open as a soft moan escaped from her lips and a tear silently rolled down the side of her face. As she looked around in panic, Tom could tell that her eyes were registering first pain and then confusion. Then her eyes locked on Tom's and she screamed loudly.

"Please don't hurt me," she whimpered. "My baby," she added lamely, as she glanced down at the growing mound that was her belly.

"I didn't want you," he seethed. "I wanted your friend." He hadn't talked for so long that his voice was nothing more than a croak. "Obviously I can't let you leave this place or you'll spill your guts to everyone. Then again, you're going to spill your guts anyway," he laughed without mirth.

Rachel then did something which she had never done with such urgency before. She turned deep within herself to meet her Lord with her silent plea. "Dear Father God," she prayed as her lips scarcely moved. "I come before your throne right now to give you my life and the life of my child. If this is where it ends Lord, I just pray that it would be over quickly and that I would be ushered into your Holy Presence. Please watch over Stephen, Father and help him to have peace. The same goes for my parents. Thy will be done Lord, not mine. I love you with all of my heart and all of my soul. Receive me in Jesus' name."

At the very moment she began her prayer, she knew God was with her. He had promised never to leave or forsake her and He was making good on that promise. She felt the warmth of His Holy Spirit wrapping itself around her. As if from very far away, she was also vaguely aware that a cold blade was violating her chest area, but what Rachel wasn't aware of was any pain. Whoever this man was and why he was trying to kill her was an absolute mystery to her. Rachel was grateful for this moment in time though, because she was also very in tune with her unborn child. She could feel the little boy inside her and was overwhelmed by the love that was shared between the two of them in that brief instant. It brought a smile to her face and filled her heart with joy.

CHAPTER EIGHTEEN
HIDDEN ON KILLALOMA

Tom was baffled as he stood in that dirty room with blood on his shirt front, face and hands. He had carved the word "SATAN" right across her chest above her breasts. He had done it slowly and with great relish. Tom had also drawn the picture on an upside down cross with fire coming up from it on her belly. He didn't do it deep enough to touch the child. That would come much later. Tom intended to take his time so he could enjoy every minute of it. But right now he was getting excited. It was time to have a little bit of fun with his prize, first.

What he couldn't understand was the radiant smile that shone from her face. Just what the heck was that all about, he wondered? The whole time he had been carving her up, she hadn't uttered a moan, a whimper, or anything for that matter. What was wrong with this woman? As Tom scanned his handiwork, he was startled by the sound of a dog or something making a racket outside the back entrance of the mine. It sounded more like a wolf howling and the hair rose on the back of his neck. Tom ran to see what the commotion was all about. He didn't want the animal to give away his hideout. As he neared the covered hole, he could see bits of earth floating lazily to the floor as whatever was on the other side, methodically dug away at the entrance while still howling without letup. Sensing danger, Tom ran back to the room, grabbed a few things including the bloody knife and ran out the front entrance of the cave. He would have to alter his plans somewhat but that was okay too. He was used to that.

Tom ran down the path and through the woods bordering the lake as the sounds of howling filled the night air. He could make out lights now illuminating the woods behind him, but he kept running and the sounds receded with each passing step. Eventually he came to the side of the rutted road and after backtracking for a bit, was finally able to see the soft mound off to his right. After brushing off some icy dirt and leaves, Tom pulled back a well-oiled tarp and lifted the motorcycle to a standing position.

After a few false starts, the engine roared to life like a beast that had been dormant for far too long. He swung his leg over the seat, did his jacket up, pulled on his neoprene face mask and left the area as fast as he could safely travel. Driving a motorcycle on a road full of potholes and slush was hazardous, but Tom was confident in his abilities. By the time they found the girl, he would be well on his way to his next place of refuge.

There was a large mountain range about 90 miles from here which he had scouted on his way to Poweetan. That was where he was headed. He was furious that he hadn't been able to kill the one he wanted so badly that it made his belly ache from the acidity. But he paced himself and tried not to dwell on her, but on the road ahead. Nobody would ever find him up there and when things cooled down a bit, he would go back for Kate. She was not going to get away from him that easily. He knew everything about her and she would still pay. It was not over by a long shot. Tom grimaced against the cold air, as the rain hit him like thousands of tiny needles. Stopping briefly, he donned a blue rain suit from the mouldy saddle bags. Immediately he felt much warmer, although he was soaked to the skin. There would be time to warm up later. Tom headed south towards Mount Killaloma.

He had been following a wily rabbit. Hunter didn't usually stray so far from home, but the pesky rabbit had intrigued him and it was in his nature to hunt it down. He had tracked it down to the lake and was still in pursuit when he came upon a familiar smell. It was coming from the patch of disturbed dirt and sticks over by that large rock. The smell was concentrated in just one spot. It wasn't anywhere else, but Hunter knew that smell anywhere. It was the odour of his mistress, but she wasn't anywhere to be seen. He sniffed the ground several times and then began digging and whining in earnest. The smell grew stronger, so he began to howl. Hunter saw a small scrap of yellow material sticking out of the debris. Picking it up in his mouth he turned and ran towards town.

When Rachel was two hours late from the prayer meeting, Stephen started to get concerned. He had work to do at home tonight so he hadn't been able to attend. The faucet in the bathroom had been leaking and needed to be fixed. No longer able to stop the uncomfortable feeling he had, Stephen called Kate to see if Rachel had gone over there for a visit after the meeting. Kate explained to him how Rachel had wanted to go down by the lake to look for Hunter and that she had taken Kate's rain slicker with her so she wouldn't get wet.

Stephen told her that he was going to go out and look for her, as she hadn't come home yet. He didn't want her wandering alone in the woods...not with the baby and everything. What if she had slipped or something? Kate volunteered to go with him and he agreed. He wouldn't worry anyone else until he had a reason to do that. He was dressed in less than five minutes and ran out the door. Stephen met Kate who was just coming onto the street from her apartment. Together the two of them made their way towards the path to the lake.

It was still raining slightly and they could feel the chill of the night biting through their clothes. They took turns calling out for Rachel. Stephen shone his flashlight ahead of them but in this weather it didn't cast much light. As they approached the lake, a sound pierced their very souls. It was the mournful howling of a wolf. They both took off running towards the sound, calling out Hunter's name as they went and hoping it was him and not a pack of wolves.

In no time at all, they could hear a heavy panting noise coming towards them very fast. All of a sudden, Hunter bounded into the light...a very welcome sight indeed. Stephen stooped down to scratch the wolf on the ears and noticed a small scrap of material protruding from the animal's mouth. He gently took it from the wolf and handed it to Kate. She felt the material and knew in an instant that it was part of her jacket. She told Stephen that it was her slicker that Rachel had been wearing.

Hunter looked at the two of them and then started to run away. He looked back several times to make sure they were following. When they had gone about 300 feet through the trees they came upon Hunter digging in the ground. Stephen shone his flashlight at the spot and was able to see a hole begin to take shape. He could see definite drag marks on the ground and felt sick to his stomach. He had no idea where the hole went because he had never come across it before.

One thing was fairly certain though. Something or someone had been dragged into the hole fairly recently. He shone the light into the darkness but could see nothing. From behind him, Kate called out Rachel's name. There was no answer.

"Shouldn't we go in there?" whispered Kate.

"I don't think it's a good idea. We don't know who or what is in there. I think the smartest thing to do would be to get some of the townspeople out here to help. Maybe somebody knows where this hole leads to," said Stephen with more bravado than he felt. "Let's face it," he said. "We only have a flashlight to protect us. It could be a bear or something in there."

Within half an hour, the place was swarming with worried and anxious people full of concern for Rachel. Matt and Vira were beside themselves with fear. Matt had his arm around his wife as they prayed non-stop for Rachel's safe deliverance. Dave Tenderfoot had been a trapper in these parts for about thirty-five years. He took one look at the hole and it flooded his mind with memories of childhood games of hide and seek. Right away he remembered where the hole led to.

"This is the back part of the old mine," he said. "We used to play here all the time when we were kids. You can go in through here, or you can get to it through the opening on the path to the lake. Either way, it ends up in the same place. I wouldn't have thought it was very safe in there after all these years, but obviously someone has been here. It looks like this hole was covered over with these sticks and rocks. Peering closely at the ground, he noted the heavy imprint of boots, and then the disturbed ground around it.

"The prints are too deep to be just one person. It looks like someone was carrying something and then dropped it and dragged it into the hole. I think it would be safer to go into the mine by the main entrance. Let's go," Dave said as he led them through the woods and down the hill to the entrance of the mine.

Paul had just started working in the Fulson General Hospital. He had arrived the previous week and already loved the job. His mentor, Pastor Allan Douglas was such a genuine and honest man. He was in his late fifties and had taken Paul under his wing. He was learning so much, having on-the-job training. There were things they didn't teach you in school that could only be learned from experience.

Paul was going into his third year come September and was becoming very adept at his new calling. He showed all the signs of being a good preacher and teacher. His grades had been excellent and he displayed many of the fruits of the Spirit such as patience, kindness, goodness, gentleness and self-control. In two short years he would be ordained and be able to legally perform weddings, baptisms and communion. Paul couldn't wait. His calling into the ministry was a balm to soothe his soul. It was certainly not one of those jobs where you hate to get up in the morning. There was never a dull moment.

As Paul ate his lunch in the hospital cafeteria, he was stunned to see the familiar face of Peter Carson. Now what was he doing here, he wondered? Peter was wearing hospital scrubs, so he must work here. Paul hoped against hope that Peter didn't have the same motive for being in Fulson as he did. Paul sauntered over to where Peter was eating with a sultry blond woman with legs up to her armpits. Paul wondered if Annette was still in the picture. If she was, then she had some stiff competition to contend with. Peter looked like he was getting very familiar. Paul stood uncertainly for a moment before blurting out what was on his mind.

"Excuse me, but aren't you Peter Carson?"

"Yes, I am. You're Patrick from the Centre in Klindale, aren't you?" he smiled disarmingly.

"The name is Paul. But yes, I'm from Klindale. You haven't by any chance seen Kate, the nurse that used to work there, have you?"

"I haven't seen her for two years," replied Peter.

After a stony glance from the lady at the table, Peter said that he had to hurry with lunch or he'd be late getting back to work. Paul nodded and backed away towards his table. It was all he could do not to jump for joy. He figured he still had a chance with Kate. He had seen how Peter had ogled Kate when they were in Klindale. Paul was glad Peter hadn't seen her. He wondered why he had come here of all places but decided to let it go, for now.

Paul looked forward to another productive day at work. He never knew from one day to the next what he might come up against. He would only be working in the hospital on Wednesdays and Fridays. After lunch, Paul followed Pastor Douglas out onto the surgical floor. That would be their job for today. Each room would be visited and if someone needed prayer or just somebody to talk to, they would be there for them.

Today, as they approached the nurse's station, a warning buzzer went off. That meant they were bringing someone in who needed attention quickly! Coming around the corner was a doctor, two nurses and a technician bearing a stretcher. Paul glanced down as it was wheeled quickly by. The woman on it had beautiful raven coloured hair which spilled across the white pillow but her skin was deathly pale. He could also see blood seeping through the sheet in several places.

She was visibly pregnant as well, as could be determined by the bulge under the sheet. Paul instantly began to pray for this woman, that God would intercede on her behalf and save her and the child she was carrying. Following further behind were a man and woman who were probably her parents and a man who could have been her boyfriend or husband. His eyes were red as if he had been crying. Paul prayed for them as well as he stayed with his back to the cool wall of the hallway. He felt their pain in that brief moment in time and his heart went out to them. Hearing a slight cough, he looked back at Pastor Douglas. Allan waved him into room 410 where they would be talking to a little girl who had been in a farming accident and lost her leg.

CHAPTER NINETEEN
RACHEL'S DREAM

Stephen was the first to enter the mine. He stopped just long enough to let Dave Tenderfoot scoot on ahead of him. He knew his way around much better, which was needed because the place was a wreck. There were broken bottles, fallen timbers, rocks and garbage all over the path inside the mine. After a few false turns they were finally on the right track. They could see the prints in the dirt and evidence that somebody had been living in here for some time. They plodded on as quietly as possible as they didn't know if the person or people were still here.

Just as Stephen was about to follow Dave around the next corner, he found his way barred by a big burly arm.

"You'd best stay here for a minute." he said.

"No way," said Stephen as he pushed his way past Dave and shone his flashlight on the table in the centre of what looked like an old lunch room. The sight before him made a sob catch in his throat.

There was Rachel on top of a dirt covered table. She was naked from the waist up and there were crude designs carved into her chest and belly. Blood was still seeping from the wounds. She was as white as a ghost in the dark and that's when Stephen grabbed the side of the table and began to shake. He snapped his head up when his name was called.

"Stephen! She's still breathing. We have to get her out of here right away," said Dave, as he ripped off his own jacket to wrap around her. As if she weighed nothing at all, he scooped her up gently in his massive paws and ran out of the room with Stephen in close pursuit. They almost ran headlong into a small handful of people who had come upon the room as well. Included were Kate and Lillian's grandson, Albert.

Seeing Rachel, they all followed Dave out of the mine. Only Albert stayed behind, although he didn't know why. Whether it was just morbid curiosity, he would have been unable to tell you. In the now silent room he stooped to pick up a newspaper clipping that was curled up and semi-crumpled on the floor. He pulled it open and shone his flashlight down at it. He looked at the clipping in disbelief. It was a picture of Kate. It went on to describe the night of a terrible shooting in a place called Klindale and how someone had given a positive ID on the guy who had shot her friend. Because of that witness, the boy had been sent to prison.

Albert hadn't known about Kate's background until now, but this piece of newspaper began to shed some light on who the person might be, who hurt Rachel. He didn't know why Rachel had been targeted instead of Kate, but was sure that someone had the answers. He blew out the hurricane lamp and hurried after the others with the clipping shoved away in his pocket. The man obviously had wanted Kate dead, so she might still be in grave danger. There was no sign of the man now. They all moved as fast as possible into town. It wasn't long before word spread throughout the town and worried people gathered in huddles and talked in low voices. A chopper was fired up and Rachel was loaded into it for the ride to Fulson which housed the nearest hospital. It was obvious that the Clinic wasn't equipped to handle an emergency like this. Rachel may need a place with a neonatal unit. It was unclear whether or not her baby was harmed.

Albert shook his head sadly. What kind of demented person would harm a pregnant woman like that? Only time would tell the whole story.

Tom stopped to take a rest. He was freezing cold and couldn't stop his teeth from chattering. He had to ditch the bike about a mile back because he was now going up into the mountains. It was much colder here and the harsh elements were taking its toll on his body. He was tired and extremely hungry. He knew he would have to get some food fairly soon and some dry clothes on. In the distance he could make out a light shining through the trees. It appeared to be a small cabin. He wondered who lived there. As Tom approached, a dog began to bark angrily. Tom tried to shush him, but to no avail. Within seconds, he reached the dog as it strained against its chain and growled angrily. He withdrew his hunting knife and slit the dog's throat without hesitation or preamble. All you could hear was a pathetic gurgling noise and the animal dropped quietly to the ground.

Someone yelled for the dog to shut up from inside the cabin. Tom ran up to the window and looked inside. An old man was making a fire and had his back to the window. Tom turned the door handle slowly and it opened quietly to his touch. He quickly stepped inside. The man wheeled around and faced Tom in surprise. He barely saw the knife as it sailed through the air like a small missile and struck him in the chest. The old man tried to grab at the handle of the knife as he looked at Tom in bewilderment. He was dead before he hit the floor.

Tom began to rifle through the refrigerator. He grabbed a partially eaten sandwich off a plate and a cold beer. Setting it on the table, he went to the man's room and yanked open the dresser drawers. He tore off his rain suit and wet clothes and pulled on a pair of slightly big overalls and a heavy warm sweater. He hunkered down in front of the fire and as the heat began to permeate his new clothing, he grabbed the sandwich and wolfed it down. Time was passing quickly and he still had a ways to go before he was safe. At least he was warm and fed. He grabbed a large rucksack and threw some clothes and food into it. He needed to be on his way before it got light or someone came by and noticed the dog.

Peter was called into the fourth floor operating room. There was some sort of emergency. A woman had been carved up like a Christmas turkey. She had lost quite a bit of blood and was in shock. She was also pregnant. Peter scrubbed up in the anteroom and donned a sterile gown, mask and gloves. There she lay on the table with her chest area exposed and her belly protruding slightly. There were angry red lines oozing blood all over her front. On closer look, Peter was able to make out the cross and words printed crudely there. He could barely believe his eyes. What kind of sick individual would do something like this to a pregnant woman, he wondered.

Sheila, the head nurse came in behind him and pushed a fetal heart monitor into place and hooked it up to Rachel. Within minutes, the sound of a tiny heartbeat could be heard throughout the room. It was strong and steady. Peter and Sheila looked at each other in relief.

"It looks like the baby is going to be okay," said Sheila.

Peter went to work on Rachel. She had a nasty head wound that took about 13 stitches to close. There were small pieces of bark stuck in the wound that needed to be cleaned out. One rib appeared to be fractured and many stitches would be required to close the numerous wounds on her chest and belly.

"Sheila, could you please write the information down that I dictate to you. I'm sure the police are going to question me and I need to have all the facts."

"I'll get one right away Doctor! I'll just grab a clipboard and pen."

Peter grabbed another needle and the appropriate sized floss and bent over the woman in earnest. There was much work to do.

Meanwhile, Stephen paced the corridor outside of the waiting room with anguish. Nobody seemed to know anything and Rachel had gone into surgery over two hours ago. He felt the panic tangibly. What was going on with his wife and baby? He wanted to see her desperately. Just to wrap his arms around her and tell her how much he loved her would mean the whole world to him. If only he could do that one more time, he would be happy.

Matt and Vira were still in the waiting room. They were holding hands and fervently lifting their child up to the Lord in prayer. They wouldn't stop until they heard one way or the other how Rachel had made out.

There hadn't been enough room in the helicopter for Kate to go to Fulson, although she had desperately wanted to go with them. Somebody had to stay behind and watch over the clinic until Matt returned. She sat down on a rock and cried in frustration. First Katya and now Rachel! Just what was going on, she thought angrily.

Just then, Albert ran up to her breathlessly. He was holding something in his right hand. He looked Kate in the eye as if he wanted her to understand what he was about to show her. He gently unfolded the newspaper clipping and handed it to Kate. The first thing she saw was a picture of her own face. She held it up to the large spotlight by the airstrip and as she quickly scanned the page she let out a gasp and her eyes widened in dismay.

"Where did you find this, Albert? I must know!"

"I found it on the dirt floor in that back room of the mine. I picked it up just after Stephen and Dave ran out of there. I thought you should see it. You might be in some danger, Kate. Remember when you found Tiger?"

He waited until she nodded before going on. "Perhaps that was some sort of sick warning. He's probably been around here for some time just watching and waiting. I'm not trying to scare you, but I think you should be aware of it. We should show this to the police, Kate. Come on," he added gently. "Let's get you back into town. There's nothing more you can do out here and we don't want you catching your death of pneumonia. It's really wet out here."

Kate couldn't recall hearing Albert talk so many words to her since she had arrived and tried to give him a weak smile. She took his proffered hand and stood on shaky legs. He led her back to town like one would a small child. Any other night, the walk would have been beautiful. The air was cold and smelled fresh from the rain. The ground was spongy underfoot. The piles of snow and ice still left, looked like lonely sentinels set up around the community to protect it.

Kate felt like she had a large hole left in her heart that might never be filled again. She knew that God wanted her to be here but his purpose was totally beyond her. Did He bring her here to have her be hurt all over again? Was this just some sort of test or a morbid joke? Well, it wasn't funny. Kate was tired of the pain and loneliness. She just needed someone to hold her, love her and who would tell her everything was going to be okay. But things just didn't seem to work that way. Kate knew that she was simply feeling sorry for herself but felt she had a right to feel this way. She had suffered so much loss in the past couple of years that she felt like a drowning victim going down for the third time. What she needed right now, was a life buoy. Kate needed someone to throw her the ring and save her from the water that was threatening to crest over her head at any moment.

She hoped Stephen wouldn't forget to phone her with some news about Rachel. Kate assumed correctly that there would be no sleeping tonight. This was all her fault. Albert was sure that she was the cause, by the sound of it. That made her feel even worse, if that was possible. She couldn't even pray. Her heart just wasn't in it. Kate tried to go to her apartment alone, but Albert insisted on checking out the place first.

"You don't need any unforeseen problems, Kate. It will only take a second for me to make sure your place is secure and then I'll feel better too. I hope you don't mind but I'm sure that Grandma would have a fit if I didn't go in," he said sheepishly.

"Okay, Albert. I guess that would make me feel a little bit better. You're right of course. After you," she said as she gave him a sweeping bow and held her arm out for him to go on in ahead of her.

Everything was as it should be. Albert checked all the locks and was satisfied that Kate would be safe. He insisted that she lock the door after he left. Kate thanked him, locked the door and sank down onto the couch. Staring her in the face was the music stand where she and Rachel had been singing earlier in the evening. The musical piece was a duet that the two of them were supposed to sing at church on Sunday. Kate felt ill. She didn't even know if Rachel was going to make it. There had been so much blood. Stephen had shielded Kate's eyes from the worst of it but she had seen enough…enough to know that her friend was in grave danger. Stephen and Rachel were a match made in heaven. Kate didn't really believe that God would take her so soon. Then there was the baby. Surely that small life would be allowed to take its first breath. There was no point dwelling on the "what ifs." That would serve no viable purpose and it certainly wasn't helping her any. She had to think positive. There was a clinic to run and the townspeople needed her alert and functioning. And that's how they would find her.

One thing didn't escape Kate's thoughts throughout the long dark night. It was the boy, Tom. I guess he's not really a boy anymore, she reasoned. He must be at least twenty, so that makes him a young man. Was it possible to hate someone so much that you would travel to another country to try and kill them? Kate wondered at the malevolence that must be in this guy's head and heart. Satan must be having a heyday with him, she mused. Although she abhorred the filthy act that he had done, she couldn't hate him. That was just not in her nature, even if she had just cause to feel these things. Kate only felt pity for him. Maybe he didn't have a family who loved him or cared what happened to him and maybe he just lived on the streets with his gang. The biggest thing was that he obviously didn't know Jesus.

Someone who knew and loved Jesus would never have been able to commit murder, she reasoned. They would have been convicted of their sin long before it was committed. By changing her focus from Rachel and the pain, to Tom and his salvation, Kate was finally able to pray. And pray she did…for the next two hours.

Rachel was still very far away, in a land devoid of worldly sounds and thoughts. She was strolling hand in hand with a young boy through a beautiful field full of lush wildflowers which she had never seen before. The colours were brilliant and the fragrance was amazing and wonderful. Rachel didn't know this place but it was lovely in its placidity and calmness. She imagined that this was indeed what paradise must look like. She knew that the boy had come from her own body but there was no recollection of giving birth to him. The place seemed to be deserted. They might have been the only two people alive because all they knew was each other. And knowing was more than enough for Rachel. She felt a remarkable oneness with this small piece of herself and smiled as they began to run with a gentle breeze blowing their hair back out of their eyes.

Colours had never been this vibrant and distinct before. That much she knew. She also felt the presence of another. Wherever He was, He seemed to transmit a vast store of unconditional love oozing into every pore of the two. With a tenderness Rachel couldn't begin to fathom, she felt enveloped in warmth from the top of her head to the tips of her toes. She was overjoyed and leapt like a young deer from rock to rock over a small crystalline stream that cast off a brilliant array of rainbow colours like a prism refracting the sunlight.

Each tiny droplet of water had a place here. Nothing was wasted or desecrated by evil or pollution. Until now! Rachel grabbed the child's hand a little bit tighter as a foreign sound permeated her senses. Someone was crying out to her from far away. The sound was strange and yet it was somehow familiar and comforting. She didn't feel threatened in the least. Whatever the noise was, it was welcome. She looked down into the little boy's eyes, smiled lovingly at him and nodded her head sagely. She gave his hand a gentle squeeze and bent down to make him understand. It wasn't time yet. They were to be someplace else and the Presence was telling them that it was going to be all right. They were needed elsewhere and they could come back to this place again one day. What was he saying?

"Rachel, can you hear me? Squeeze my hand, if you can hear me."

Rachel felt herself responding to the gentle persuasion of the voice and gave a slight perceptible movement of her hand. Then she could hear the glorious sound of laughter as she came closer to the sound and the light that shone beyond her eyelids.

"Matt, Vira, come quick. She's waking up. I'll go find the doctor," Stephen added happily.

Within minutes, the room held several of the nursing staff along with Peter who was the physician on call and Paul who had come by the hospital just to see Rachel. Their church had been praying for her since she was brought in several days ago. She had not regained consciousness in all that time and there was a real fear that there might be some brain damage or the baby would go into fetal distress.

Rachel's eyelids fluttered several times before finally opening and trying to focus. Stephen was by her side with tears running down his face. Her parents were standing just behind him. There was a doctor to her left and several nurses. This didn't look like home, she thought absently. Rachel tried to speak but her throat was so dry it just cracked.

"Water," she said and licked her lips.

Vira held a cup to her mouth and brought up her head a speck. She let a little of the cool water dribble down her throat. The doctor was taking her vital signs. That much Rachel knew, so she must be in a hospital for some reason. But what she couldn't figure out was why? How had she gotten here and just where was here?

"Where am I", she said as a coughing fit threatened to debilitate her.

"You're in Fulson General Hospital," began Peter. "You were brought in here about three days ago. You had an accident and we've done some surgery on you. Physically, it appears that you will recover nicely and your baby is doing fine too."

A dawning came upon her and she weakly reached down to feel her belly. The baby! She remembered the little boy and gave an angelic smile to everyone present. Her child was indeed fine. She still didn't know why she had been brought here. The doctor said that it was some kind of accident.

"What accident was I in?" asked Rachel weakly.

"Don't you remember anything Rachel?" asked Stephen.

She shook her head negatively. The doctor warned Stephen with his eyes that bringing up the subject at this time, was dangerous to her health.

"Don't worry Babe. There will be plenty of time to talk about that. Right now we just want you to concentrate on getting well. We've missed you terribly. I love you so much Rachel. I had best call Kate. I promised her I would call, the moment I heard any news. I'll be back in a few minutes," he said and left the room just bursting with joy and love.

Paul had been outside the hospital room talking to the young man Stephen, whose wife had been knifed so horribly. Before he found out if Rachel was going to be okay, he had needed some comforting, so Paul had engaged Stephen in small talk to pass the time and to take his mind off his wife and child. Just before it was Paul's time to be leaving his shift, Stephen said something which caught Paul's attention. He had mentioned where they came from and Paul could barely hide his smile when he heard him say the name, Poweetan. Now how many places could there be with that name, he wondered?

When he could contain his curiosity no longer, Paul asked Stephen if he knew a lady named Kate Harmon who had gone to live in Poweetan a couple of years ago. Stephen was speechless. What were the odds of coming to a large city and finding out that somebody knows one of your good friends. He blurted everything out in a long rush then.

He told Paul how Rachel had borrowed Kate's raincoat the night she was violated and that they were best friends. As yet, Stephen didn't know about the newspaper clipping which Albert had found. He also told how someone had cut up Kate's cat outside of her apartment. Paul was mortified. No wonder he had felt the urge to pray for her so many times recently. She still might be in danger he thought and decided right then and there that he had to see her for himself and make sure she was all right. He'd see about going Thursday night. Paul was sure that Allan would lend him the beat up old blue pickup truck. Then his mind would be at rest. Just then, Stephen had been called back into the room so there was no more time to pick his brain. Paul followed closely behind and watched as Rachel squeezed Stephen's hand and then her eyelids fluttered open. He shook his head in amazement as he digested the information that Stephen had given him. God certainly did work in mysterious ways, he thought to himself.

Killaloma was a very dangerous place to be this time of year. The snows were melting due to normal spring weather conditions and the ground was highly unstable. Snow and mud slides were not unheard of during April and May. When there had been an exceptional amount of snowfall during the winter like there had been this year, then the mountain was extremely volatile. During this time of year, the rangers were kept busy, warning the visitors and those living in the area of the dangers of the mountain. More than one inexperienced hiker had lost his or her life to the feral terrain. Wild animals were another thing one had to contend with. There were black bears just coming out of hibernation and beginning to forage for food…of any kind. Thoughtless hikers often forgot to clean up their garbage which only served to draw hungry animals closer to the human population.

It was a world all by itself. It never wanted to be known in an intimate way. Killaloma preferred to keep its secrets to itself. It was savage and beautiful; wild, yet inviting. It was a land that drew the pleasure seekers and photographers, along with the daredevils and those who had something to hide. This was a place where one could come if they didn't want to be noticed or found, for that matter.

When the warmer air hit the cold snow on the peaks, a thick blanket of fog could often be seen from below, bathing the mountain in a greyish white hue. Sometimes the fog made you feel like you were living inside of a golf ball. All sounds would be muffled and the colours of objects would be muted as if everything on earth were painted with the same pigment. The fog seemed to make people whisper. You could almost say that it was due to reverence. It was a land to be respected on all terms. Killaloma…was aptly named. Just ask anyone!

Right now, Killaloma held a secret in its hand and it wasn't about to let go of it. Someone had come here who needed the protection which the forests could afford. Someone had come here to hide. A large array of tools and weapons were spread out in front of him. He was whistling a mindless tune and somewhere along the path of his short life, he had crossed an invisible line. There was no going back now as he continued to sharpen and clean his wares.

He was not as alone as he first thought. The trees and rocks around him housed a menagerie of foul smelling beasts of all sizes and shapes. Some just sat in their positions around him with drool hanging out of their mouths, while others chattered away plotting and calculating. They were sensing that victory was almost theirs. The man had only one goal now in life and that was revenge on the woman, Kate. He had wrongly put all the blame for his incarceration on her. In his mind, she had to be stopped and he wouldn't rest until he had done just that. He was being used and manipulated like a puppet, yet he thought he was in complete control.

One day he would self-destruct and all those gathered around him tonight would scream in delight. His would be one more lost soul for their master's kingdom and they would be rewarded accordingly…perhaps a principality of their own to rule over or a little less severity in the heat blasts from the eternal inferno. Kate's witness had to be terminated. She was a threat to the Evil One's plan. She kept on telling everybody about their arch-enemy, Jesus. And they were listening to her and accepting him as their Lord and Saviour. This made Satan furious! He kept trying to get Kate to turn her back on the Lord, by eliminating her best friend and just about finishing off another one. But she kept getting stronger in her faith.

She was the one who kept persevering, just like that dreaded apostle of old… Paul. He had been a hard one to shut up too. Whatever adverse situations that Satan's minions had dealt him, they were never enough to get him to bite his tongue. Neither shipwrecks or stoning or prison terms or beatings had destroyed that man's witness! This case seemed to be very familiar. They knew that others of their kind were having the same problems with their charges as well. These filthy stinking creatures knew that all the followers of Jesus could never be stopped but with due diligence, they could snatch many unsuspecting ones out of His grasp. The easiest were the ones who just assumed that because they were good people and even went to church, they would automatically be going to heaven. Their mistake would cost them dearly and they would have eternity to pay the price for their ignorance.

That's why practicing and professing Christians were so dangerous. They had been given a power that was often left untapped. However, once they realized what they were capable of doing, they were virtually unstoppable. It was an attitude of..."Look out Satan. Here we come!" It literally sickened these emissaries of evil as they regarded their play toy much closer. Victory would be sweet and they would have it. Once again, they underestimated their adversary and gave their own powers too much credit.

By the end of the first week, Rachel was feeling well enough to get up and walk around. Her chest and belly area were still thankfully covered in bandages. Rachel didn't have the courage to look. She didn't know if she would ever be able to do that. The doctor had said that plastic surgery would eliminate the majority of the scars so at least she wouldn't have that filthy word and drawing on her body and longer. They were going to do the cosmetic surgery after Rachel had her baby. There was no point taking any risks with her unborn child because of the anaesthetic and medications.

Rachel was just glad to be alive, as she walked slowly down the hallway while absently feeling her abdomen. She had sent her parents packing, two days earlier. She was feeling much better and told them that they should go back home. Matt and Vira both needed some well-deserved rest, as they had been hovering around the hospital for days. It looked like fatigue was taking its toll and Rachel didn't want them getting sick. Besides, her dad had a clinic to run and if he didn't hurry back, Kate was going to take over his job. She smiled to herself as she pictured how that confrontation might take place.

Stephen had been an absolute pillar of support. He had poured out his love, tenderness and affection in abundance over the past week. He had truly stood by his oath that said: "For better, or for worse." Rachel knew that she could never begin to thank him for getting her out of that slime-walled mine. She understood that Albert needed to be thanked as well. He had carried her for some distance and wouldn't take a breather until she had been placed safely aboard the helicopter.

When she had finally been able to talk about her ordeal, Stephen had told her about the real hero of the day. It had been her faithful dog, Hunter. He had found the opening in the hill and had gone for help. He had run ahead of Stephen and Kate, leading them into the forest and once he had relocated the hole, he howled until they found him digging. Eventually they had found Rachel.

She couldn't wait to wrap her arms around her magnificent wolf and let him give her a big sloppy kiss. Rachel was unaware that she had been cut up as a substitute for Kate and Stephen wasn't about to tell her right now. She was anxious to have a visit from her friend. Kate was coming down tomorrow to be with her. Rachel wanted to see how Kate reacted to Paul. They'd had quite a few opportunities to talk with him and he seemed like such a super guy. Rachel couldn't help but notice that he had everything going for him. He was halfway through the ministry, was well-built, handsome, kind and compassionate. And the biggest thing of all was that to hear him talk about Kate, you could just tell the guy was truly in love with her. Kate was important to him, even if she didn't know he existed. But that would be rectified very soon. Rachel planned to do some match-making of her own.

What a wonderful couple they would make, especially because of their great love for Jesus Christ. Theirs would be a special match. Rachel was unaware of the feelings Kate had towards Peter. If she did, she would have told Kate to get a life. Obviously Paul was the only man for her but sometimes love is hard to figure out. It can pop up in the most unsuspecting places and times and between the most ill-suited people. Rachel knew that given time, Kate would see Paul as she did.

Little did she know that at that precise moment in time, Kate and Paul had just passed each other on the road to Poweetan. Kate was coming to visit Rachel at last and Paul was going to visit Kate. Their timing seemed to be destined for failure, but all things were being done in God's perfect timing and according to His plan for them. And God doesn't make mistakes!

CHAPTER TWENTY
FULSON BECKONS

After a somewhat arduous journey over every bump and into every pothole that covered the road, Kate finally arrived at Fulson General Hospital. She was given a week off by Matt and planned to stay here with Rachel. He had even let her use his truck to come because he knew how much it meant to Rachel that Kate be there. She decided to have a good visit first and then she would find a motel to stay in. She went directly to the front desk and inquired as to what room Rachel Westcott was in. After being given some brief directions and going up the elevator, Kate got off on the fourth floor. She hurriedly went to find room 408 and as she reached her destination, she pushed open the door and entered the room. Rachel was propped up against some pillows reading her bible. Kate gave her the biggest smile ever, walked over to the bed and gently took Rachel in her arms.

"I've been wondering when Dad would let you come," she said with excitement in her voice. "I've missed you so much Kate. How is everything going? Did they catch the guy who did this to me yet, or have they found out who it was?" she went on in a rush. "Do you realize you were instrumental in saving my life Kate? I don't know how I'll ever be able to repay you."

"Hold on already," laughed Kate. "Come up for air Rachel," she added as she held up her hand for Rachel to stop. "Let's go slowly, because I have a lot to tell you. First thing I want to know is how you're doing. I've been worried sick for almost a week. Does it hurt, Rachel?"

"Well, it doesn't tickle, that's for sure. But it's better than it was. I got the dressings off this morning and got a good look at what that creep did to me", she added angrily. "I couldn't believe it Kate. Luckily Stephen was with me when the doctor came in, or I don't think I would have been able to handle it. I was so ashamed, but Stephen said I was beautiful to him no matter what. I'm a real mess, but Dr. Carson says that I will heal in time and then I can have some cosmetic surgery done after the baby is born."

Startled, Kate interrupted Rachel to say, "That wouldn't be Dr. Peter Carson, would it?"

"Yes, Kate. Like I said, Peter is my doctor. He's been very professional, but sometimes I wonder about him. He seems a little arrogant to me, as if he's God's gift to women everywhere" she added quickly.

Rachel didn't like to talk about others in a negative way. She had been raised in a family that stuck to the old rule that a person shouldn't judge another, lest they be judged themselves.

"I knew a Dr. Peter Carson where I used to live. I really liked him but I found out he was married. He and his wife and little girl were in a horrible car accident one night after a party. They were hit by another vehicle and their little girl was killed. Peter tried to kill himself and ended up in the clinic where I was working. When I found out he was married, I stayed away from him." All this was said as Kate slowly sank into the armchair by the hospital bed.

"Well, I don't think this guy is married Kate. At least not the way the nurses were talking. They say he's a player and a bit of a daredevil."

Kate decided to drop the subject, although her interest had been peaked and quickly changed the conversation around to the newspaper clipping that Albert had found. She knew Rachel had a right to know that she didn't do anything wrong and that the person who had hurt her had really been after Kate.

She told Rachel to get comfortable because she had to tell her something important. She spoke about Tom Erikson and how he had killed her best friend Katya. She had told Rachel bits and pieces before, but now the whole sordid story came out in a rush. Kate had several talks with the police regarding the incident with Rachel and had been informed that Tom had escaped from a minimum security prison almost a year earlier.

There had been a largescale manhunt for Tom, but as yet, he was flying under the radar undetected. Kate refreshed Rachel's memory regarding Tiger and told her about seeing someone wearing a yellow baseball cap on several occasions around the town. There was a good chance it could have been Tom. Albert said that most likely he had been living in the mine for several months by the looks of the bones piled up by the back entrance.

"He's been stealing the trapper's food for quite some time now. They just figured it was an animal or something, but the stories have been coming fast and furious since you were hurt. People are starting to piece things together. Remember how you borrowed my rain slicker that night?" Kate asked. "Well, the one police officer thinks that Tom may have been watching my movements for months and was probably waiting for me to come out of the prayer meeting that night. When he saw you come out wearing my raincoat, he thought it was me. It was raining hard if you recall and it was already dark. He is obsessed with revenge because I was the one who gave the positive ID that was instrumental in getting him sent to prison. At least that's what the officer said. I'm so very sorry, Rachel," Kate said hurriedly as she watched the tears fall from Rachel's eyes.

"All of this was my fault, Rachel. This would never have happened to you, if I hadn't come to Poweetan."

They both gently embraced, as Kate didn't want to hurt Rachel. They rocked and cried together and then after a while, the two held hands and prayed while God cleansed their hearts of any bitterness and filled them with peace. It was a time of healing for both of them, as the day wore on and the shadows of late afternoon grew longer.

Rachel told Kate about the dream she had when she was unconscious and how she was certain that God had shown her the child that she was carrying in her womb. Kate was astounded and tenderly touched Rachel's belly. She drew her hand back in wonderment as she felt a tiny kick push up against her hand. She laughed with delight. Kate hoped that one day she would have the opportunity to have the same thing happen inside of her own body.

She was happy for Rachel of course, but inside, she longed to have a child of her own…someone who she could share her life and love with…someone who she could rock, cuddle and sing to. Her heart ached for that kind of relationship, but knew that it was in God's hands. She had prayed for years that God would place the right man in her life and trusted that He would do just that. Only God knew what was in Kate's heart and she also knew that God would meet her needs. Again, it was all a matter of His timing. Often it was hard to wait on the Lord. Like everyone else, Kate wanted things right now, but God doesn't work that way and she knew it.

In the feel-good society in which we all live, there is an innate need for instant gratification. We want what we want, when we want it and for Kate, who often struggled with this very thing, she had to learn to be patient. Her father had always called patience the "dirty P word," when she was growing up and Kate smiled now as she thought of him saying it. She would wait and see what God had in store for her, and quit worrying and dwelling on things that she had no control over.

CHAPTER TWENTY-ONE
HOW TO CHOOSE?

Feeling a little tired, Kate took leave of Rachel, assuring her that she would be back the next day. She was so absorbed in thought, that as Kate prepared to board the elevator, she ran smack dab into a surprised Peter. As he gently pushed her back from his arms, a smile broke out across his face.

"Well, look who's here! What brings you to Fulson, of all places, Kate?"

"My friend Rachel was hurt, and I came to visit her," she stammered, as her face began to turn red from embarrassment.

"Rachel is your friend? I didn't know that. What a small world we live in, eh?"

Kate smiled as her eyes ran appreciatively over his smooth shaven face. She noted that although he looked a little tired, Peter was still as handsome as ever and her heart began to flutter maddeningly. There was a hardness in his eyes that hadn't been there before and Kate determined to find out why.

"How are you and Annette getting along, Peter? It's been such a long time since I've seen the two of you." A shadow passed over his eyes momentarily and his smile quickly faded away.

"Annette is history, Kate. I caught her in bed with a supposed friend one afternoon when she thought I would be away for the day. I left her to her own sordid affairs. I couldn't endure being in the same house with her, because every time I looked at her, I was sickened. Look! Do you have a bit of time to spare? Maybe we could go to the cafeteria and talk while I have my break. I just have to get a file for another doctor and I'll be right with you. Would that be okay?"

"Sure thing, Peter," she said with a smile.

As he walked to the nurse's station, Kate was able to observe him unhindered. He still had that certain way of making her insides go to mush. Kate could feel her heart beating rapidly within her breast, and she took a couple of deep breaths to calm her jangling nerves. It had been just over two years since he had left the clinic in Klindale, and Kate noted with wonder that her longing for him had not diminished one iota. If anything, the feelings were stronger and she felt like she had stuck her finger in a light socket. Her whole body was tingling and a warm glow lit her face as Peter came back to her and offered his arm.

They stepped into the deserted elevator and Kate felt overwhelmed by his scent and closeness. The warning bells went off in her head as he pulled her closely and pressed his lips hungrily upon her own moist and slightly parted lips. Kate let out a tiny gasp as she succumbed to his passionate embrace and felt her whole body going limp against his firm chest.

"No," she cried out weakly. "You're going way too fast. You must stop, Peter." Kate pushed him away and quickly squared her shoulders. She could feel the heat emanating from her enflamed cheeks. "I think I had better be going for now," she gulped.

Kate knew she was losing control over her own body and it scared her silly. She needed time to deal with her emotions. She didn't want to gain Peter on the rebound. She wanted him to love her as much as she thought she loved him. Another thing bothered her deeply. In the whole time Peter had talked to her, not once had he mentioned his faith. Had he turned his back on God? If this was the case, then she had to proceed with caution. Kate knew that the bible warned against being yoked with an unbeliever. The odds were good that a relationship of this kind would have many trials. She may be able to lead him back to the Lord, or it could go the other way and he could lead her away from God. Kate knew in her heart that this was not an option. She loved her Lord too much to compromise her faith and beliefs for the sake of unbridled passion.

When the elevator doors quietly slid open, Kate backed out of the enclosed space and gave her apologies to Peter. But Peter was not about to let her get out of his reach this time. It had been too long. He gently grabbed her arm and forced her to look into his eyes, where he held her entranced, like a hypnotist.

"Please, Kate. I must see you again. Will you come out for dinner with me tonight? You have to eat don't you?" he shrugged disarmingly.

In that brief moment, Kate felt her resolve melting and she agreed, against her better judgment. She turned her back on him and walked away on wobbly legs, knowing that he was watching her every move. She breathed a sigh of relief when she got into the truck and sat for a moment before starting the engine. After driving around aimlessly for about ten minutes, Kate came upon a nicely landscaped Holiday Inn tucked back in from the road. It looked inviting so she drove in and got herself a room on the second floor, overlooking a covered pool and gardens that were just beginning to peek out from under the receding snow.

It may be peaceful outside, but Kate felt far from peaceful. Her mind was working overtime and her thoughts were all jumbled. What was she supposed to do about Peter? She had asked God, but He was strangely silent to her plea. Kate didn't know how she felt about divorce as she had never had a reason to consider it. She wished Katya was still around. She could always pour out her heart to Katya and could expect to get an honest opinion from her. She knew that Rachel would be a good one to talk to as well, but she had enough problems of her own to deal with. And she had made it known that she thought Peter was a player. Right now she didn't want somebody telling her that Peter was all wrong for her. She just wanted to go with the flow.

Kate plopped down on the comfortable double bed and kicked off her shoes. She called Peter and told him where she was staying. He told her he would pick her up in two hours. Before she knew it, Kate had drifted off to sleep. Exhaustion from the past hectic week finally took hold and she slept like one dead, with no dreams to impede her thoughts. She was startled awake by the harsh jangling of the telephone on the nightstand. It was the night clerk from the front desk calling.

"Miss Harmon. There's a Dr. Carson here to see you. Would you like me to send him up to your room?" the voice at the other end of the line enquired.

"No thank you. Please tell him that I shall be down in about fifteen minutes. I'm running a bit late."

She hung up the phone, quickly jumped into the shower, washed and blow-dried her hair and slipped into a pair of cream coloured slacks. She pulled a chocolate wool sweater over her head and slipped into a pair of flat brown leather shoes. Kate looked at herself in the mirror and approved of what she saw looking back at her. Grabbing her purse, she quickly ran out the door and took the elevator to the lobby.

Peter rose to greet her and his eyes showed their appreciation. He opened the door for Kate and they made their way to his car. Kate had never ridden in a sports car before and was delighted with the comfort and speed. The heady smell of Peter filled the vehicle. This was shaping up to be a truly glorious night, she thought. After parking, he hurried around the front of the car and held the door open for her. He gently took Kate's arm and walked her into a very posh restaurant. Each table was secluded inside a personal booth with candles on each table that sparkled off ice water set in crystal goblets.

Dark wainscoting adorned the lower half of the walls while a deep crimson paper finished off the tops of the walls. Rich Persian carpeting blanketed all sound from the floors. They might as well have been in their own little world. The light from the candles were reflected in Kate's eyes. When the waiter came to take their orders, Kate declined anything from the wine list, preferring instead, to have a cold glass of Perrier with a wedge of lemon.

Peter broke the ice by entertaining Kate with small talk about Fulson and the hospital where he worked. He never brought up Annette or Klindale and Kate understood that the topic was off-limits for now. Peter reached out and enclosed Kate's hand with his own. He ran his fingers lightly across the back of it, feeling the strength there as well as the softness and femininity. He could feel her trembling, as well. Peter couldn't remember the last time he had seen someone actually blush, but Kate was doing just that. He found it very appealing and refreshing. The women in Peter's life had always been more forward and predatory. Embarrassment was an unknown commodity for them. Peter marvelled anew at the unblemished innocence that Kate exuded. The waiter brought their meal and placed it before them. Soft music played in the background and romance was in the air.

"You look absolutely beautiful tonight Kate. That colour really suits you."

Once again the colour rose in her cheeks and he couldn't help but smile. Now this woman was the genuine article, he thought to himself. She was gracious, poised, compassionate, kind and intelligent. Peter knew he could go on and on extolling her virtues. He told her of the hang-gliding and mountain climbing that he had done recently on Mount Killaloma. By the end of their dinner he had just about persuaded Kate into joining him on an excursion up into the mountains.

Kate still felt the caution light on, but her interest was definitely peaked. Peter assured her that she would love the mountains. He described their beauty in such a way that Kate almost felt like she was there.

"I'll think about it Peter and I thank you for the invitation," she laughed. "But I'll wait to see how Rachel is making out before I give you an answer though."

Kate wasn't sure if she could trust herself being in a secluded place with Peter for a whole day. He was being a little too forward for her taste and she felt like he was sweeping her off her feet. She had to say "whoa" and step back for a moment until her senses returned. Kate felt herself falling hopelessly in love with this man. He was the first man who had ever made her feel like this. His strong features and charming ways were breaking down any barriers Kate had put up.

After a delicious meal of succulent roast beef with baby carrots, fresh beans and baked potatoes dripping in butter and sour cream, they sat back and talked some more. Neither of them wanted to break the spell. Finally, Peter paid the bill and left the waiter a handsome tip. They drove around for a while and Peter showed Kate the city of Fulson.

"I'm really getting tired, Peter. It's been a long day and I think I had better get back to the hotel. I promised Rachel I would stop by tomorrow," she replied around a big yawn.

"No problem," he said. "I start work at 8am. I'll be in to look at Rachel around two. If you're there, perhaps we can have lunch," he added smoothly.

"That would be nice Peter. But you had better watch out. I might get spoiled by all the attention."

They laughed together as Peter pulled into the semi-circle in front of the hotel. He leaned over and pulled Kate gently into his arms. He kissed her with a hunger he had forgotten even existed. Kate felt herself being swept away on a tide of untapped emotions. Once again she had to pull back from his fiery embrace.

"I have to go now, Peter. Thank you for a wonderful evening and the great dinner. I really enjoyed myself. I'll see you some time tomorrow afternoon then," she said as she hurriedly made good her escape.

With her heart still racing, Kate entered her room and put her purse down with a dreamy smile on her face. She had never felt like this before and couldn't wait to see him again. Before going to bed, Kate knelt beside the chair and asked God about His opinion in the whole matter with Peter.

"Lord, you know what's in my heart better than I do. Search me Father and remove any bad thoughts or ideas before they take root and bring evil into my life. I love You with all my heart and only serve to please You, Lord. If Peter doesn't know you personally, I pray that You would prepare his heart and ready him to receive Your truths. Give me the right words to say to him and give him a heart for You, Lord. If You don't want me to be with him, I pray that you would close that door and show me where you want me to be. In Jesus' name I pray. Amen!"

With that said, she gratefully fell into bed and at once she went into a deep sleep. The dream came almost instantly. Kate heard the doorbell ring, but was afraid to answer it. Her roommate had gone out for the evening and she was all alone. She didn't know where this feeling of fear was coming from but her heart began to palpitate and the saliva dried up in her throat. Her tongue felt thick in her mouth. Kate could feel the presence of evil and the hair on her neck stood on end, warning her of impending danger.

"Who is it?" she called out meekly through the door.

"I'm the new tenant from across the hall, ma'am. I wondered if I could borrow your phone for a minute. Mine isn't hooked up yet and I need to make an important call."

His voice was deep and rumbling. Kate still felt there was something terribly wrong but she couldn't put her finger on it. The man's request sounded reasonable enough, so she warily opened the door, while still keeping the chain on. Kate peered out into the hall and saw a very tall and darkly handsome man standing there. He had nothing in his hands so Kate didn't feel threatened by him. Slowly she opened the door. He only came in about a foot and slowly closed the door behind his back.

"The phone is over on the coffee table. You can help yourself. By the way, my name is Kate Harmon. I don't think I caught your name!"

"That's because I never gave it to you," he grinned disarmingly. "You can call me whatever you like, although it won't matter in a few minutes."

At once the room filled with the sickening stench of sulphur and Kate knew she had made a costly mistake which she would pay for with her life. Instantly, he was by her side and had her throat in his powerful hands. She felt the floor fall away from her as he lifted her towards the ceiling. He threw back his head and let out a bestial roar which shook the small apartment. Then she knew who he was and the knowledge turned her insides to ice. It was Satan himself, come to destroy her.

As she opened her mouth to protest, he grabbed her tongue and pulled it out with a wrenching sucking sound. Kate felt blinding white pain mixed with a numbing terror. Then all of a sudden a thought came unbidden to her mind. She was so busy fighting Satan that she had taken her focus off of Jesus.

"Help me, Jesus," she said weakly inside her mind.

At that moment, she felt a wonderful warmth envelop her. She didn't feel the knife enter her belly and spill her intestines over the floor beneath her feet or hear the maniacal laugh from the throat of the Evil One. Kate looked up and saw a hand reach down. She grabbed hold of it and her eyes filled with tears of joy. Her hand felt small inside His powerful, yet tender hand.

"Come to me, Kate. He can do you no harm now. He can destroy the body but he cannot destroy your soul. Evil may surround you, but I am within you. I have promised to never leave you nor forsake you, and I have kept my promise. Keep your eyes focused on me and I will always be here for you. You are mine Kate, and I love you, dear one."

There was no need to look back at the now crumpled body lying on the cold tiles of the floor. She was with her Lord and couldn't have been happier. Kate awoke with a start and looked around the strange hotel room. It took her a moment to realize where she was. Everything was the same as she had left it. Kate got up and turned on a light. It was 7am and as a shiver ran down her spine, she began to pray. God was warning her that there was danger around and was also telling her that He would be with her in all things if she would just focus on Him and trust Him completely. Kate felt her spirit soar as she thanked her God for who He was.

She had never felt more in touch with Him than she did at this moment and was filled with thankfulness. She wondered briefly if God was telling her to be careful because of Tom, or if it was Peter she should be worrying about.

"Lord," she started… "I ask that You would place a hedge of protection around me and keep me safe from all harm. Help me to keep my eyes focused on You. Keep me strong in my convictions. In Jesus' name I pray. Amen!"

That said, Kate felt a peace which passes all understanding wrap around her like a cocoon. Whatever lay ahead, she was certain that God would see her through and there was nothing to fear with Him on her side.

As for Peter, he knew what he wanted. High on his list was Kate. Seeing her again had stirred things that had long been hidden inside of him. He had to have her and would stop at nothing to get her. All women liked to be wined and dined he figured, so that's what he determined to do. He would literally sweep Kate off her feet. Sooner or later, the walls she had built around herself would come tumbling down and victory would taste so sweet.

She was his angel of the light. When Bethany died, Peter had lost all sense of love and it had never been retrieved. He assumed that what he felt for Kate was that missing love but in reality, it was nothing more than carnal lust. He wanted her in a way that was not befitting and spoke nothing of friendship, commitment or marriage. Long-term meant nothing to Peter anymore. He was only interested in the here and now.

Annette had shown him in a few short minutes what love was worth… nothing more than a cheap roll in the hay. He vowed that he wouldn't be hurt again by anyone. He intended to grab the best that life had to offer, whether it was his to grab or not. Peter figured the world owed him something and it was his right to be paid back. He had lost his daughter, his status, his marriage and his job. He would have this woman even if he had to take her against her will. Either way, it made no difference to him. Just thinking about it, was enough to stir the fire in his loins.

Once he got her on the mountain, there would be no escape and no more pushing him away and saying "No." He knew of a little used path that wound around the back of the mountain. An old man lived in a cabin deep in the forest there, but he would be no problem. He usually kept pretty much to himself. About a mile from his place was a secluded trout pond where Peter's destination would be. It was surrounded on all sides by lush forest and the only thing in the vicinity would be the occasional deer, fox or bear.

He had hiked up there several times and knew that it would suit his purpose fine. Nobody would be able to hear them or intrude on their privacy. He would get her up there on the pretext of showing her the caves that were in abundance and then he would have her. Of course he would have to have a picnic lunch all made up or she would suspect his less than pure motives, but that was a minor concern. He smiled to himself as he formulated a plan in his head.

Paul came back to Fulson after spending the night with the Jenkins family in Poweetan. He was disappointed that he had missed Kate. Matt said that she had gone to visit Rachel. He couldn't believe the rotten luck he seemed to have when it came to being with Kate. Some might say that it was fate, but Paul knew that if God wanted them to be together, it would happen, one way or another…with or without his interference.

The Jenkins had been very hospitable to him and had welcomed him with open arms. Rachel had told them of the numerous long talks she had with Paul and they felt bound to repay some of his kindness. And to top off the night, they had told him a lot about Kate and what she had been trying to do at the little church. They mentioned that she sang, led Sunday School and a prayer meeting every week. They told him about how invaluable she had become to the clinic and what a blessing she had been to the townspeople. By the time Paul left the tiny community, he felt like he knew Kate better than he ever had and was anxious to get together with her. It sounded like her faith in God was as strong as ever too.

Paul arrived in Fulson at two in the afternoon. He went to the hospital on the off chance that Kate might have gone to stay with Rachel. Upon entering the room, he found Rachel sitting in front of the window in a big easy chair. Sunlight poured through the open pastel drapes and the picture this scene created was one of peace and serenity. Her one hand absently rubbed her distended belly. She turned her head, looked up and smiled at him when he gently tapped on the door.

"Well, hello there, Paul. I guess you know already that you just missed Kate. She was here this morning and part of the afternoon. She left about a quarter after two."

"That's all right Rachel. I spent a really nice evening with your parents."

"How are they doing, Paul?"

"Oh, they're fine. Your mother is a great cook and you wouldn't believe how well I slept. It must be all that fresh air. I'm not used to it, Rachel," he laughed with a mischievous twinkle in his eye.

"Can I talk to you seriously for a moment, Paul?"

"Sure you can," he replied as he pulled another chair up beside hers. "You have my undivided attention."

"Well," she began. "You are in love with Kate aren't you?" She held up her hand as he started to protest. "Please, let me finish. I've seen it in your eyes when you talk about her. Kate is my very best friend and I think the two of you would be great together. You both love the Lord and are dedicated to serving him. Kate has been waiting for Mr. Right all these years. She's never even had a steady boyfriend. I know, because she has talked to me about it. But there's one small problem. It's Dr. Carson."

"What about him?" Paul said as he jumped in with just a touch of jealousy in his voice.

"Kate told me this morning that Peter took her out for dinner last night. It sounds like he's trying to win her over and Kate is revelling in the attention he is paying her. She can be a little naïve and I think she's falling for him. But I don't like it one bit. There's something about him that just doesn't sit right with me Paul. I feel like Kate is being reeled in like a big fish. I heard some of the nurses talking one afternoon when I was walking by their station. They were saying what a player he is. I tried to talk to her about him, but she seems to have closed ears. I don't think she can see what I'm seeing because she's too closely involved. I've prayed about it and I think you need to talk to her Paul, before it's too late. I don't have a good feeling about this and you're the only one who may be able to stop her."

"How can I stop her, Rachel? I don't think she'll listen to me. Kate barely knows I'm alive. The only one that can get through to Kate is God. All we might do, is drive her right into Peter's arms."

A shiver ran down Paul's spine as his mind played out all sorts of different scenarios. "Is she supposed to be coming back in here later on today?" he asked.

"Not that I know of," replied Rachel. "She mentioned they were going dancing tonight, and that he planned to take her to Mount Killaloma on Sunday, for a picnic and an afternoon of hiking. I don't like the idea very much. I think they're moving pretty fast for two people who haven't seen each other for almost two years. By the sound of it, she barely knew him when they lived in Klindale. I just don't know what sort of hold he has over her. It has me baffled."

"Do you have her number at the hotel?" asked Paul. "Then I might be able to get in touch with her. Maybe she'll have lunch with me tomorrow and we can have a serious talk. I know I have to tell her about how I feel really soon, or I'm going to bust. How about you? Have they told you when you can go home?"

"They've been a little vague, but there was mention made of going home on Tuesday. I'm feeling much better and the baby seems to be fine. They've been monitoring him daily. Stephen said that he would come here first thing Tuesday morning, so hopefully they'll let me go. The doctor just said that I have to take it easy until our baby is born. That shouldn't be a problem though, because I think I could sleep for the next month and still be tired out," she said with a grin.

After they had talked some more and spent some time in prayer, Paul took his leave. With Kate's number in hand, he walked out of the hospital whistling as he went. There was still hope and that's all that mattered at this point in time. As Paul drove down Wellington Street, he spotted a phone booth beside a dirty looking garage. A man leaned against the greasy wall with a cigarette dangling out of the side of his mouth. He eyed Paul from a face that was blackened from oil and dirt.

"What can I do for ya?" he asked as he spit a large wad of something black at his feet. "We don't get a lot of pretty boys around here!"

Paul felt the bile rise in his throat as he mumbled in passing that he just had to use the phone. The man pushed himself away from the wall and started to trail after him. Paul sensed trouble coming and quickly ducked back inside the truck and locked the doors. As the man came around the driver's side of the vehicle, Paul pushed his foot to the floor and gunned the engine while spinning gravel all over the man's ripped and faded overalls. He decided to just stop by Kate's hotel in the morning instead. He didn't need the hassle. For some reason, things just weren't right in Fulson. Paul could feel the presence of evil surrounding him but he couldn't figure out why. The ministry was going well and he hadn't made any enemies as far as he knew. People seemed to like him and he was about to ask the love of his life out for a date. Then why did he feel like a pressure cooker was building up steam and it was about to blow?

He knew what he had to do about it though. The bible told him to pray without ceasing and that was exactly what he would do. Paul started immediately, as the old truck rumbled down the road.

The doe stood motionless with ears pricked and on the alert. She had sensed something in the wind, but as yet, had been unable to figure it out. It reeked of death and things she couldn't fathom from her limited experience. She had caught the odour on several occasions over the past week or so and wondered anew at its strangeness. Ever on guard, she made her way around the small shallow pond with her nose to the wind. She had been coming here for the past three years. The grasses were lush and hikers and campers were few and far between.

The old man down the hill had never been a threat to her and it was just in the thicket to her left that she had given birth to a fawn last spring. Hunters had been banned from this side of the mountain because the deer herd had almost been depleted. As the wind shifted again, she bent her head and continued to graze in the rich tasting grasses. It had been a long winter and the new shoots were a welcome addition to her diet.

Her last rational thought before she fell, was of the sweet grass going bitter in her mouth. The hatchet whizzed through the air with deadly accuracy. She was gone before she hit the ground as the cold steel imbedded itself in the back of her head. Tom bent over her with savage glee and pulled the hatchet free with a sharp pull. He hadn't eaten since yesterday and was proud of his catch. He reached for the warm flesh and sliced off a chunk. He ate like a savage. After his fill, Tom licked his bloody fingers and mumbled incoherently to himself. He would stay in this forest until he felt sure of his own safety.

Once he gave it a couple of months, the heat would probably be off him long enough to make good his escape. He couldn't go back to Poweetan for a long time. They would still be looking for him. He longed for the day when Kate would die, but he realized that her time would come. He was learning great patience. Tom had nowhere to be and nobody to be with, so his time was his own…to waste as he saw fit.

He had decided on this place to hide out because of its seclusion. The trout pond had brought him nothing but frustration. He could see the blasted fish but was unable to catch any. And then there were the caves. Tom had stumbled upon them quite by accident when he had been climbing the other day. He had slipped on some loose dirt and fallen over an embankment. After rolling for a short distance, he finally came up short, against an opening in the rock face. There were several holes around him and he smiled at the possibilities that these caves offered.

Tom had love the darkness of the Poweetan mine and these caves would be just as special for him. After exploring the area for a while, he found what he was looking for. It was a perfect hideout. Most of the holes were nothing more than indentations, or only went in about five or six feet and stopped. But one of them was totally unique. Hidden behind some fallen vines and rocks, it was no more than a foot wide slash in the side of the mountain. Tom retrieved the flashlight from the backpack he had picked up at the old man's cabin.

Shining it into the opening, he could see nothing but darkness ahead. He turned sideways and slipped inside the mountain. It was at least twenty feet tall and went back much further than the light cast by the flashlight. It was obviously unused, as it housed nothing more than some rocks, dirt and a few bats that were stirred by the sound of his footsteps.

"Honey, I'm home!" he laughed uncontrollably as tears streamed down his dirty face.

Saturday morning began with a beautiful sunrise. The dirt and grime of winter's residue was melting rapidly and new buds were breaking through the ground in gardens everywhere. Buds were popping up all over the barren tree branches as if they were stretching their arms from a lengthy sleep. The birds and animals were busy looking for mates and love was in the air. Spring was a time for renewal and refreshment. Today was the first day of May and it held a time of promise in its grasp. People everywhere had been waiting a long time for winter to be over and the warmer weather to come. They looked forward to resuming summer sports and activities. It was to this day that Kate opened her eyes sleepily and stretched her long slender arms in the air.

What a beautiful day she thought to herself as she pulled the curtains back with a flourish. The world was just coming alive and people were off to their weekend jobs or wherever else. After quickly dressing, Kate went downstairs and enjoyed a leisurely breakfast of wheat cakes with butter and pure Canadian maple syrup. They were her favourite and she indulged herself with abandon. A large glass of frothy orange juice topped off the meal and then she sat back to look at a magazine until her breakfast settled.

The waitress interrupted Kate halfway through the second paragraph of the article she was reading.

"You have a gentleman caller at the front desk Miss Harmon. They called your room first but someone said they saw you come in here, so they called here next. What should I tell him?" she asked.

Immediately thinking it was Peter, Kate's face flushed with excitement.

"Could you please show him to my table? I still have a coffee coming."

The waitress departed and Kate was left feeling pleased with the way things were going. She kept her back to the door because she didn't want to look too eager. That wouldn't do.

Kate saw a blur of dark material out of the corner of her eye and looked up expectantly with a radiant smile on her face, but was taken aback when she noticed it wasn't Peter after all. He was very handsome and vaguely familiar. Paul could see that she didn't remember him. The last time he had seen Kate, she had been grieving deeply the loss of her friend. She had only gotten more beautiful in his eyes and he grinned with pleasure.

"You don't remember me, Kate." It was more a statement of fact than a question. "I'm Paul from Klindale. I'm working in Fulson for the summer, at New Life Baptist Church. Remember I wrote to you a couple of times?"

Kate was at a loss for words. Of course she remembered Paul writing her, but for the life of her, she couldn't remember him looking like this. Granted, she hadn't been thinking too clearly when she met him last, but surely she would have remembered a face like his. It was hardly forgettable.

"I'm sorry, Paul. I was expecting someone else and you took me by surprise, that's all. Please, have a seat. How have you been?" she added quickly to hide her embarrassment.

"I'm fine, Kate. Obviously Rachel hasn't mentioned to you that I've been at the hospital with her."

This took Kate totally by surprise and she registered her shock by the look of bewilderment on her face.

"First I find you in my life when something bad happened to my friend Katya and now I find you back in my life when something bad happens to my new friend, Rachel. How is it possible that you come into my life during two times of great stress and in two different countries? It seems to be too much of a coincidence, don't you think?" she stated in obvious confusion. Paul smiled at her and gave her a sheepish look.

"I'm afraid it isn't all that mysterious," he said shyly. "I asked to come here this summer to do part of my curriculum for school because I wanted to be as close to Poweetan as possible."

"Why would you want to do that?" Kate asked as a small light began to dawn in her head and she figured what his answer was going to be. She wanted to hear it from him though.

"I wanted to see you, Kate. I know that you barely know me", he rushed on, "but I feel like I know you very well. Mike Collins and his family are really good friends of mine now and we've had lots of meals together. Their children are great fun. You were the topic of discussion on many occasions."

Kate felt the heat rise in her cheeks and wondered what was happening to her. He went on quickly.

"I met Rachel and her family quite by accident, though. I was working in the hospital with the pastor from my church as we do twice a week. Rachel was wheeled past me on a stretcher and I started praying for her immediately. Since then, I've had some long talks with Stephen, Matt and Vira. When Rachel regained consciousness, I was able to talk with her as well. She told me all about her friendship with you and I must confess that I soaked it all up like a dry sponge. I've prayed long and hard about this Kate and I feel like God is telling me to be honest with you and tell you what I've been feeling."

Kate picked up her coffee in two hands so he wouldn't see her tremble. This was all too weird. She looked up at him and realized he was still talking to her.

"I would like to get to know you better, Kate. Rachel told me that you're going out tonight with Dr. Carson, but I was wondering if you would do me the honour of having dinner with me one night. My intentions are purely honest and I don't expect anything from you. Would you give me that chance, Kate?" he asked while looking into her eyes with all seriousness.

Kate thought about what Paul had said for just a matter of seconds before saying, "Sure! Why not! Peter and I are not together. We've only been out for dinner once. After all, I'm not going to be in town for much longer."

"What about tomorrow afternoon, Kate? We could go roller skating after church if you would like!"

"Hold on a minute, Paul," Kate laughed. She had to admit that his enthusiasm was infectious. "Peter has already invited me to go hiking with him on Mount Killaloma tomorrow afternoon. Maybe another time?" she added meekly. "I'll be spending the morning with Rachel too. I already promised her."

"That's okay, Kate. May I call you on Tuesday instead? I have some time off."

"That would be nice, Paul. I'll look forward to that."

They talked amiably for the next half hour. Paul caught Kate up on all the happenings from Klindale. She laughed when he described some of the antics that the Collins kids had pulled off in his presence. Kate could picture them too. They were so full of mischief that she smiled when she thought of them. Too soon, Paul had to excuse himself to run some errands. Kate actually felt disappointed as she turned and watched him saunter out the door. What were the odds of her coming to Fulson in the first place, let alone running into two men who obviously cared for her?

Kate had the feeling that it wasn't a coincidence so much as it was God's will. She had come to realize a long time ago that things didn't just happen by chance. There was a reason for all these strange happenings and in time she was sure that the answer would come to her. Meanwhile, she would bide her time and pray. God wouldn't leave her high and dry. He had promised her in His Word and she believed it with her whole heart and soul.

Paul left the hotel feeling like he was walking a foot off the ground. Finally he had done something that he should have done two years ago and he felt good about it. The best thing was that he and Kate seemed to hit it off. She had been a little leery of him at first, but once the ice was broken, things just seemed to fall into place like the pieces in a puzzle. He couldn't wait to tell Rachel. She would be happy too. Paul knew that she was trying to be a matchmaker between the two of them but that was okay by him. He didn't care, as long as it worked.

Something Kate had said was bothering him. She had mentioned that Peter was going to take her hiking up Mount Killaloma. Paul had heard that it could be very dangerous this time of year. Often there were mudslides because the ground was so unstable. The snow was melting quickly and there had been a lot of rainfall lately. Hopefully Peter knew what he was doing. Another thing was bothering him about the outing. Paul didn't know if it was jealousy or just fear for Kate's safety but he had a bad feeling in the pit of his stomach. Something was not sitting right and he felt the need to cover Kate with a hedge of protection from God's angels.

As he prayed, he felt an idea forming in his mind. He was being urged to follow Peter and Kate on their excursion. Now where did that idea come from, he wondered? Surely God didn't want him to be a peeping Tom because that's how he would feel. The more he prayed about it though, the clearer the thought became. He also had the feeling that Stephen should go with him and Paul knew that he had to tell him. Usually he had pretty good intuition about things and he felt this was one of those times. Paul decided to call him as soon as his errands were finished.

Stephen received a surprise call from Paul that evening around seven. Stephen listened intently as Paul described what had been happening between Peter and Kate. After getting all the details, he had to admit that something about Peter just didn't sit right with him either. He had been an excellent doctor to Rachel, so there was no complaint there but something was sending out warning signals to his spirit. Paul told Stephen about his urgings from the Lord to follow them up Mount Killaloma but unfortunately Stephen had to bow out. He had promised to help Albert put a new roof on Lillian's house. He gave Paul his deepest apologies but said that he would have a group praying for all of them.

Stephen knew just where to begin. As soon as he hung up with Paul, he made several calls to the members of the prayer group and then got together with Matt, Vira and his mom and dad. They all agreed that Kate needed their help and each of them pledged to pray for Kate, Peter and Paul, for the next few days. That done, Stephen called Rachel and found out that she would be able to go home for sure on Tuesday morning. Stephen told her that he would come on Monday and stay overnight. That way he would be able to take her home as soon as the doctor said everything was okay. In truth, it was nothing more than an excuse, as he was just anxious to be with her. He had missed Rachel terribly and couldn't wait to get back to their life together. He didn't know what she would think about the mine being so close to their home. It may just bring up some very bad memories.

He decided to go and talk to Albert. Maybe somebody could be brought in to blow the place. It was a safety hazard anyway, so he didn't think there would be a problem. He would look into that right now and put his own mind at rest.

CHAPTER TWENTY-TWO
KILLALOMA REBELS

Sunday morning rolled in with a big bang. Lightning and thunder rumbled and crashed with wild abandon as the rain came down in torrents. Mount Killaloma was awash in water as melting snow and rain made paths slick and saturated. Animals ran for whatever cover could be found and most people gave up their planned outings to stay inside where it was dry and warm.

Peter woke up, looked out and softly cursed his poor luck. There was no way Kate would go with him now. They would have to postpone and he was angered at missed opportunities. He picked up the phone and dialled her number while absently tapping his foot against the hall table.

"Hello, Kate," he said when she picked up the connection. "I guess our little hiking and picnic is out for today. Can you believe this weather?"

"It is fairly rotten out isn't it?" said Kate. "I figured it wouldn't be long until you called to cancel," Kate replied with disappointment etched in her voice.

"I have Monday off as well, Kate. Would you still be interested in going up the mountain tomorrow instead? It's alright with me. I would just like to spend some time with you before you go back to Poweetan if that's okay?"

"That would be great, Peter. Hopefully it will have stopped raining by then and we can enjoy the day. By the way…Do you remember Paul Winchester from Klindale? He used to come by the clinic and play music for the residents on Friday nights."

"As a matter of fact, I do," cut in Peter. "I ran into him in the cafeteria the other day. What about him?" he asked with suspicion nagging his thoughts.

"Well, I haven't seen him for almost two years and then out of the blue, I saw him yesterday. He has written me a couple of times since I left Klindale. We're supposed to meet on Tuesday for a visit. Isn't that a coincidence? What were the odds of seeing both of you in the same place and at the same time too?" she laughed.

But Peter wasn't laughing at all. If the truth be known, he was seething inside but there was no way he was going to let on to Kate.

"Yes, that is odd, isn't it?" he said with as much enthusiasm as he could muster on such short notice. "Well, I have to go now. I'll pick you up tomorrow at one in front of the hotel. Weather permitting, of course. Don't forget to dress warmly. It still gets fairly cold the further you get up the mountain. See you, Kate!"

"You bet, Peter. I'm really looking forward to it. Bye for now," she said as she hung up the phone.

All was not lost, Peter thought to himself. He would still get to be alone with his angel, and he was sure she would submit graciously to his attentions. All he had to do was go slowly and by tomorrow night she should be his. There would be no way she would want to be with Paul after she got a taste of him. Experience had shown him that the only difference between each of his conquests was how he treated them. Some needed gentle prodding while others liked his fast and furious approach. But in the end, they all succumbed to his persuasive romantic techniques. He had no doubt that Kate would be any different. It may just take a bit longer. Although she did seem genuinely bashful, he had felt her resolve slowly melting over the last couple of days. Oh well, tomorrow would tell.

Stephen arrived in Fulson around ten o'clock on Monday morning. He spent a couple of hours with Rachel and then went to meet with Paul, who was staying with the pastor at the manse. He had called him the day before to tell him that Peter had postponed the trip with Kate because of the weather. Paul had been ready on Sunday, to follow the two. He had gathered all the things he thought he would need to go for a hike. Stephen's eyebrows shot up in surprise, as he took in the scene before him. Stephen had grown up in the woods and it was second nature for him to go hiking. Paul had obviously been brought up in the city. You would have thought he was going away for a week by the amount of stuff he had arranged all over the floor.

"I hope you aren't planning to carry all of that by yourself are you?" he said with a barely concealed smirk.

"What's wrong with it? We're going to need all of this."

Paul was secretly relieved that Stephen would be able to accompany him after all. He had told Albert that they could do Lillian's house next week instead. Another few days wouldn't matter one way or the other and Lillian didn't mind at all. Rachel had been glad when Stephen told her that he and Paul were going to follow Kate and Peter.

"The only way you will need all that, is if you are climbing Mount Everest! Now I realize that you've gone to a lot of work getting this stuff organized Paul, but we are going hiking…not mountain climbing. Do you see what I mean? You have pitons, expansion bolts, and an ice axe for heaven's sake. All of this will just slow you down and wear you out. It's far too heavy to carry for any distance."

Paul looked at him sheepishly.

"I've never gone hiking before, as you've probably noted. I'm used to living in the city. Let me see what you brought and I'll take the same thing. Okay?"

Stephen opened his pack to show a medical kit, flashlight, cell phone, rope, clean socks, trail mix, water bottle and other items. Stephen also brought a beautiful hand-carved walking stick that Albert had made for him when he was younger. Paul ran his fingers lightly over the exquisite workmanship.

"That's an awesome walking stick, Stephen. Where did you get it?" he said admiringly.

"A friend of mine made it for me. Don't worry about taking one with you, Paul. There will be plenty of sticks and fallen branches in the forest. We'll just break one that will suit your height. It's no big deal. By the way, I hope you have a good pair of hiking boots. They are one of the most important parts of your gear. Don't forget to bring a warm pair of thick absorbent socks and a spare pair to put in your pack. If your boots are fairly new, you'll get blisters quickly."

Paul brought his boots from the foyer to show him. Stephen was pleased to see that they were well worn and looked comfortable enough. The treads were in good shape and he smiled his approval.

"Well, this ought to do it then. Let's go and grab a quick bite to eat," said Stephen as he rubbed his grumbling belly. "It was a long drive here this morning, and I didn't have much breakfast. I'm famished. Rachel told me that Peter was going to pick Kate up in front of the hotel at one o'clock. We'll wait down the street for them to drive by and then we'll follow them. Just like the movies, eh?" he said in jest, but was unable to keep the concern out of his voice.

"At least we'll be able to drive a good chunk of the way. I've been there before and there's an old rough road that runs up the back side of the mountain that the forest rangers use to patrol the area and keep open in case of fires. It stops just below a cabin where an old man lives. He's sort of a hermit. I've talked to him on many occasions and if we have time we can go and check up on him. He loves chocolate, so if it's alright with you Paul, I would like to pick up a box and take it to him."

"Sure, that sounds nice. I don't think I could live alone in the middle of nowhere. I'm not that brave."

Together, the two young men walked towards the dirty gray jeep Cherokee that was parked lopsided to the curb. They were headed towards God only knew what and before they turned the key in the ignition, they spent about five minutes in prayer. They would need God's help before this day was over. Of that, they were quite certain.

CHAPTER TWENTY-THREE
THE HIKE

Kate's face was all aglow as she waited in the lobby for Peter to pick her up. He had bought her some clothing for their hike as he knew that she had not come prepared for this type of activity. A parcel had arrived for her early this morning and she had been called down to the front desk to retrieve it. Kate could do nothing to hide her immense pleasure at receiving such a gift.

She hurried to her room and tore open the box that was wrapped in floral paper with a large gold bow. Inside was a pair of warm wool slacks with a lavender sweater to match. Thick wool socks and a pair of ladies hiking boots finished off the ensemble. Topping the pile was a single red rose and a card. Kate ripped open the envelope and quickly scanned the note.

"Dear Kate," it read. "I hope these clothes will be to your taste as I've picked them out especially to suit the colour of your eyes. See you at one o'clock. Love, Peter."

Her heart fluttered inside her breast like a bird trapped in a cage. She couldn't believe her eyes. How did he know what sizes to get, she wondered as she hurriedly stripped off her jeans to try on the new outfit. It all fit perfectly, right down to the boots. Kate clasped her hands in excitement and ran to the mirror to examine her reflection. Nobody had ever paid her this kind of attention before and she was basking in the wonderful warm feelings that were stirring inside her. This day was going to be absolutely perfect and it was about time, she thought. She was going to be thirty-two in October and wanted to settle down and have a family before she was too old.

Maybe Peter was going to ask her to go steady with him, she thought with anticipation. He did tell her that he had a secret planned for today and she felt certain that he was in love with her. The new outfit proved that and Kate felt absolutely giddy. Everything just seemed to be naturally falling into place. Why wouldn't he want her? Annette and Peter hadn't been together for a long time. If he did ask her, she knew what her answer would be. I would be a resounding "Yes!" She had fallen head over heels in love with him, or so she thought.

Just then, Paul came to her mind and she wondered how she felt about him. He was really nice too, although he wasn't as exciting as Peter. But Peter came first and he obviously loves me, she thought angrily. All of a sudden her thoughts were waging war in her head. She felt torn between the two. What was wrong with her? She had been so certain only moments before, but now that still small voice was reminding her of Paul.

For some unknown reason she was being told to slow down. She felt terrible that she had put her own desires first...ahead of God's will for her life. What had she been thinking? Kate gave her head a shake and looked at her reflection again. A frown was creased between her brows and her heart sank. "Please Lord," she pleaded. "Peter really likes me a lot and I think I love him. If this is your will, I pray you will find a way for us to be together. Thy will be done, Lord. In Jesus' name I pray." Having said that, she went to the bed and plopped down with a deep sigh. Kate vowed not to let her anxiety show and wreck their outing. She was sure that God wouldn't lead her astray. He knew what was best for her, even if she didn't.

As the clock in the lobby chimed the hour, Kate could see Peter drive up to the front. She went out the doors with a slight bounce to her step that she couldn't quite hide, yet waited demurely for him to open the door for her. Kate could remember her mother doing the same thing with her father so many years ago and it brought a smile to her face.

"Penny for your thoughts," said Peter, interrupting her reminiscing.

"Oh, I was just daydreaming," she laughed softly.

"You look marvellous, Kate. I hope you didn't mind that I took the liberty of getting you some clothes. I didn't mean any offence by it," he hurried on in a rush.

"No offence taken. I love them, and they fit perfectly. Just how did you manage that?" she asked with a twinkle in her eye.

"It's not all that mysterious. I went to Rachel and asked her to give me an honest guess. She said that the two of you often shared clothes, so I took it from there. They look great on you, if I do say so myself."

One large backpack was filled in the back seat and he had to move their walking sticks off Kate's side of the car so she could sit down. That accomplished, Peter got in and fired up the engine. Before she knew it, they were heading out of Fulson and according to the signs, they were approximately ten miles from Mount Killaloma. It stood in the distance like a proud sentinel watching over its domain. The top of the mount was encased in a heavy fog from the rains yesterday and the warming temperatures. It held a touch of mystery and intrigue in its grasp and Kate felt her heart begin to pound in exhilaration. This promised to be a day like no other and although no one would have believed it when they woke up this morning, each of the players that were about to join the drama would never be the same. Stephen, Paul, Kate and Peter had a few surprises awaiting them on Mount Killaloma.

Arriving at their destination about thirty minutes later, Peter began the steep climb up the winding dirt road. There were a few warning signs posted to alert hikers of any hidden dangers. Signs like: "Watch for fallen rocks ahead," and "Don't feed the animals," littered the side of the road. None of these was a deterrent on this Monday afternoon. They were able to go about half way up the mountain before being forced to park in a clearing due to a fallen tree. After gathering their gear, they started trudging up through the forest.

Peter bypassed the cabin because the old guy who lived there gave him the willies and he didn't feel like running into him again. They did little talking for the first leg of their journey, to reserve their energy. Kate found it hard going and was thankful for the solid boots on her feet. The paths were quite slippery from the rains and several times she had almost landed squarely on her haunches. Peter stopped and waited for her to catch up.

"Do you want to take my hand, Kate?" he inquired of her. "I can pull you up behind me."

"I'm okay, Peter. I'm just finding it a little greasy underfoot, that's all."

Kate was finding it a little hard to catch her breath and she realized just how out of shape she really was. But she tried to hide her fatigue from Peter. She didn't want him thinking less of her.

"I can't believe how beautiful it is up here. Too bad it's so foggy. I bet on a sunny day, this place has a life all of its own."

"It certainly does! It won't be much longer until we get to the lake where the caves are. You'll love it up there, Kate."

Just then, Kate felt something strange. Her feet seemed to sway for just an instant and then she felt nothing.

"Did you feel that, Peter?" she asked in fright. "It felt like the earth was moving under my feet."

"I didn't feel anything," he replied in bewilderment. And then he smirked. "You aren't supposed to feel the earth moving until later," he said with a grin. She punched the back of his arm.

"I'm not kidding, Peter. I know what I felt."

"Don't worry about it, Kate! There's probably some logical explanation. Let's keep going." She gave him a weak smile and continued after him.

Paul pulled the jeep in beside Peter's car and he and Stephen loaded up their gear and followed after them. They were about ten minutes behind because they didn't want to be seen or heard by the two. Stephen led the way until they came to a clearing in the woods. He almost fell on top of Clay Wilson's dog that was lying on the ground in a heap.

"What the heck?" he yelped as he jumped back in revulsion.

Nature had been making short work of the dog's flesh and Stephen pinched his nose to block out some of the smell. The animal had been dead for at least a week, he noted. They moved with caution towards the cabin and with much trepidation, Stephen knocked on the door. When nobody answered, he looked back at Paul, shrugged his shoulders and lifted the rusty latch.

Instantly, the smell overpowered them like a tidal wave and both had to stop and gag. Stephen pulled his shirt over his mouth and nose and quickly pushed open the door. He saw Clay lying in a black sticky pool of dried blood over by the fireplace. There was a slash right in the middle of his shirt and it looked like the blood had come from there. Stephen ran to his backpack and fumbled with his cell phone before finally being able to dial 911. The woman on the phone told him that help was on the way and asked for their location. He told her they were hiking on Timberline Road up on Mount Killaloma.

"I'm presently at Clay Wilson's cabin and it appears like someone has killed him and his dog. They've been dead for at least a week, I'd say. Please get somebody up here quickly. It's really awful."

"Please stay on the phone," the voice said in a monotone. He waited for minutes that seemed like an eternity. "I've called the ranger station over there. They're sending someone up right away. I've also called the authorities in Fulson. It's their jurisdiction, so they'll send some people as well. Try to stay calm until someone arrives. It shouldn't be too long."

Exasperated, Stephen looked over at Paul and ended the call with the push of a button.

"This is just great! We are supposed to stay here until the police come. Come on, Paul. Let's wait outside. I can't stand it in here. Poor Mr. Wilson," he said as he shook his head in disbelief. "Clay was a nice old guy. He just liked to be away from everybody because he hated the noise and the congestion of the city that he used to live in. Look what good it did him."

He felt the anger rising inside him at the injustice of it all. What a waste of human life he thought with bitterness. Whoever had done this, had to pay for his crimes. Stephen hoped the police would be able to track him down. Any trail would have been obliterated by the rains yesterday. He sat down on the porch and bowed his head into folded arms.

Paul came over to him and sat down as well. There wasn't much to say in a situation like this, so Paul silently prayed to God that the killer would be caught. There was no chance of catching up with Kate and Peter now, he thought dejectedly. He also prayed fervently that God would watch over Kate and keep her safe from harm and from Peter. Something was terribly wrong here, besides the obvious. He felt there was more at stake than the death of Mr. Wilson, and Paul vowed to stand in the gap for his friends and plead the protective blood of the Lamb over the whole situation. His brows knit together in concentration and he barely noticed the discarded box of chocolates resting alone and forgotten on the stoop. Clay wouldn't need the chocolates now.

A feeling of disquiet prevailed, as the fog thickened and swirled around in lazy patterns. All sound became muffled and clipped. Noises that sounded far away were in reality, up close. The majestic mountain was beginning to make known its sovereignty and the reason why it was the king of the castle. Mere man would never rule over her. She would see to that!

Kate could barely make out Peter, who was stopped up ahead. She was winded and slowed her step to wipe the perspiration from her brow. Her face was flushed and she undid her jacket to cool off a little.

"We made it, Kate," said Peter. "There's the pond just up ahead."

But for the life of her, she couldn't see where he was pointing.

"That blasted fog sure came up in a hurry. But I won't let it ruin our time. We have the flashlight and we were going to be inside the caves for part of the time anyway. Let's stop and rest for a bit over there on those rocks. We can have something to drink and to munch on."

Peter opened up his knapsack as Kate finally caught up with him. He was dragging things out of the pack that made Kate's eyes go wide in surprise. A lot of thought and preparation had gone into filling his bag. Out came a tightly rolled blanket that contained two champagne glasses. Next, he brought out a bottle of sparkling grape juice with a royal flourish. It still had condensation running down its sides from being chilled earlier.

Kate put her hand over her mouth to stifle the laugh that was about to burst forth with joy. He had really tried to make this day memorable. Too bad the weather hadn't been a little more cooperative. She sat down on the blanket and pulled part of it around her legs to keep out the dampness. The air did seem to hold a slight chill to it, now that they had stopped climbing.

A hiss of carbonation slid out from under the twisted bottle cap, and startled Kate. She watched Peter's every move in fascination. Gently he sat down beside her and handed her a frothy glass of juice. Sipping gratefully, she looked up to find Peter staring intently at her. She swallowed hard in discomfort and tried to lighten the mood.

"I thought maybe you were going to produce a table and chairs," she laughed easily.

He moved a bit closer and took the glass from her hand. His arm moved quickly around her shoulders and he pulled her close to him. Kate put out her hand to stop his advances.

"Slow down a bit, will you Peter? Can't we just talk for a while? We just got here."

"Yeah, sure Kate!" he said breathlessly. "I find myself getting a little carried away every time I get around you. You do something to me girl," he smiled.

"I don't know how to put this, so I'm just going to come right out with it. I've been meaning to talk to you about your walk with God," said Kate sheepishly. I haven't heard you mention Him once since I've seen you. You seemed fairly serious about religious matters when I left you in Klindale, and I wondered if you still thought that way?" Sensing his hesitation, Kate rushed on. "Jesus Christ is the Lord of my life Peter and I couldn't possibly be with you if you didn't feel the same way I do. It's very important that I know how you feel."

The silence between the two of them was a living, breathing, tangible thing. Peter felt the sourness rise in his throat. She might just as well have thrown ice water onto his lap, for his desire for her just dropped off like a lead balloon. Angrily he looked at her and in that moment, Kate knew that their romantic time together was over for good.

"Why did you have to bring that up? Your God might be the centre of your universe but He isn't a part of mine and never really was. He's brought nothing but heartache to my life. First there was the booze problem, then the death of Bethany, then I lost my job and ended up in a drunk's clinic and then I found my wife in bed with my supposed best friend. Where was your high and mighty God then, my dear?"

His words were clipped and flew from his mouth along with the spittle from his rage. "Just who do you think you are? You act so uppity and yet I've seen your passions and desires burning you like a fire. You want me just as badly as I want you and if you were honest with yourself, you would have to agree."

Peter's voice was full of malice and venom as he threw the glasses and watched in fascination as they shattered into a thousand pieces. The grape juice stained the rocks like droplets of blood. His fury found release in a resounding slap that threw Kate's head back with a snap. Her hand flew to the red mark on her cheek and tears welled up in her eyes.

"How could you have done that, Peter?" she stammered in confusion and fear. "All I did was ask you a question. I don't understand!"

At that, she broke down completely and sobbed into her hands. If the truth be known, Peter had no idea what was going on. For some reason he felt an uncontrollable anger bubbling up inside of him. He had never hit a woman before and was just as shocked as Kate. What was happening, he wondered vaguely in the dark recesses of his mind? Whatever had a hold over him, wasn't about to let him off easily. With a jolt, he realized that the slap had excited him immensely and he wanted to watch Kate beg and plead for him to stop. He felt carnal lust take over. He was decidedly bigger than she was, so overpowering her would not be a problem. If she wanted to act like the timid virgin, that was her problem. But he intended to have her for his very own. He ripped the sweater right off her back while she struggled and tried to scream. His hand clamped tightly over her mouth and all that came out was a pitiful moan. That only aroused him more. Pressing her back to the cold ground, he fumbled with his own clothing. He ignored her tears of humility and shame and continued with the task at hand. He was so in the moment, that he never heard the footsteps stealing up behind him.

When the knife plunged into his back over and over again, his mind went blank with the intense pain. He fell sideways to the ground with a heavy thud. His eyes were wide open in death as if his last breath had brought nothing but confusion for him. Those same eyes stared up at their accuser in one final act of defiance.

CHAPTER TWENTY-FOUR
HEARING GOD

Kate looked up in muted shock at the sight before her. The man had wild looking matted hair and an ugly scar ran down the side of his face. A dripping knife hung loosely at his side and his clothing was filthy and smelled horrid. Looking up into his face, Kate saw nothing that resembled a man. All she could see was dementia and quite possibly, madness. His eyes were red and glazed. There were scratches all over his face and hands and his nails were black with dirt. And in that moment, Kate knew without a doubt who stood before her and she shuddered in fear. One word came unbidden to her mind…Tom!

Kate's mind began to shut down completely as he bent over her and started dragging her towards a gap in the cliff wall. In no time at all, she was inside the belly of the mountain. There was no point screaming because she knew they were alone. There was no point struggling because she was no match for him. And there was no point trying to run away because she didn't know exactly where she was.

After tying Kate up, Tom went back outside to hide the body of the man. It wouldn't do getting caught now. Tom had heard them coming up the mountain and had watched in fascination from the safety of a large tree to see who was invading his territory. It was a man and a woman but because of the heavy fog, he was unable to make out any details. Then he heard a word that was music to his ears. It was the name—Kate! He didn't believe it was his Kate, but knew he had to check it out. What were the odds, he wondered idly? As the two of them drew within viewing range, he knew his dreams had finally come true. There she was, being hand delivered right on his doorstep.

He put a stinking hand over his mouth and giggled. God is soooo good, he chuckled mockingly. He decided to wait and see what they were going to do. The big man would be hard to take if he sensed danger, reasoned Tom.

But then the unmentionable started to happen. He slapped Kate across the face and began to methodically rip at her clothes. "NO!" he yelled in his head. It wasn't supposed to happen like this. She was his and the other one could never have her. She had been promised to him by the one who had control over his mind. A strange noise interrupted his musings. It sounded like a deep growl and simultaneously he felt the earth begin to shake under his feet. "What the heck's that?" he wondered absently as he wheeled around to look behind him.

Fast approaching, was a dark wet mass of mud coming right at him. Rocks and brush came with it, while trees toppled and fell into the oozing swirl of debris. Tom dropped Peter's body and started running haphazardly down the wet slope, stumbling and yelling as he went. His screams were swallowed up in the noise of rending earth and crashing trees. The swirling mass had just grabbed at his left heel when he went headfirst over an embankment. As his throat opened to allow a scream to issue forth, the noise was silenced immediately as his body hit the top of a small tree and was catapulted unconscious to the ground further down the hill. It rolled for several feet before finally settling under some dense foliage.

The sound of branches snapping and the wrenching noises made by the trees being pulled up, were all that could be heard for miles. All signs of the three who had been up on the mountain ten minutes earlier, were completely erased. The mud had covered up all tracks and hidden all clues as to what had occurred here this day and it wasn't about to divulge its secrets without a fight.

Further down the mountain a different scene had been played out. Paul and Stephen waited anxiously for the authorities to arrive. Before long, the first of three vehicles arrived and quickly pulled in beside Stephen's jeep. He went out to meet with the two rangers. One was a no-nonsense type who stood about six foot five, while the other was short and heavyset with a ruddy complexion. Stephen led them past the dog and onto the porch of the cabin.

"Clay's in there," he pointed. "He's over by the fireplace. If you don't mind, I'd prefer not to go back in there. It smells pretty bad."

"That's okay, son! I'll go in and have a look and then I'll be back to ask the two of you some questions, so please don't go anywhere."

The tall ranger had on a pair of rubber gloves and a mask and was closely examining the dog. He had a small jar in his hand and a pair of tweezers. After putting something into the jar, he stood up and went back to the car. Curiosity got the best of Paul, so he moved a little bit closer to the animal. When the ranger came back his way, Paul asked him what he had found.

"I was just collecting some maggots for forensics. You'll have to stay back now. This is a crime scene."

"Why do you have to collect bugs?" asked Paul.

"We can determine the exact time of death by the size and amount of the maggots present on the body. The rate of decomposition can relay to us a vast wealth of information," he said as he walked past Paul and proceeded to put up some yellow tape around the dog.

Then he headed back inside the cabin without another word. Before fifteen minutes had passed, two more vehicles arrived on the scene. The police were there, along with the county coroner and a forensics photographer. Paul and Stephen were politely asked to stay out of the way. Both were impatient to resume their climb, but realized that their hands were tied in the matter. So the two decided to do the thing which they did best…they bowed their heads in prayer and took their concerns and petitions to the Lord. He had promised to always carry their burdens if they would give them to Him and both believed in His promises.

Another ten minutes passed before a deep rumbling could be felt within the ground. The vibrations started out quite small and built in crescendo until the rangers ran out of the cabin with eyes wide and frightened. They had been around these mountains long enough to recognize the tell-tale signs of a mudslide. The tall one started barking out orders to everyone and they all started running towards the vehicles. They were only interested in their own safety now, and Clay Wilson was left alone, all but forgotten.

Nature was once again showing man who was really in control. It would never be tamed and man was foolish to think that it could. The awesome power behind disasters such as these could only point to a Creator God—One who was in full and complete control. It was by His Word that the world was first created and it would be by His Word that it would come to its summation.

The group congregated at the base of the mountain and waited for about an hour. That would give the ground time to settle. It was during this period, that Paul was able to get everyone's attention.

"My friend Stephen and I came to Killaloma for a reason this afternoon. Another friend of ours, Kate Harmon, went up the mountain ahead of us, with Dr. Peter Carson. We were about ten minutes behind them when we found Clay."

There was no way Paul was going to tell them about feeling that Kate was in some sort of danger from Peter. These men would probably not understand or appreciate that Paul and Stephen were following them.

"What I'm trying to say is that they are still up there. We have to go and find them and just pray to God that nothing has happened to them."

At that, the men began to bustle around and get things organized. One man radioed ahead to have a rescue unit brought in, while another phoned for an ambulance to be on standby. Meanwhile, the fog continued to hang heavy upon the mountain and in Fulson, late afternoon turned into early evening.

Rachel was half listening to the small television beside her bed. She wondered how Stephen and Paul were making out. She hoped everything was okay. Rachel knew that Stephen was a cautious hiker, so she put her silly fears and concerns aside. Just then, a news bulletin interrupted the station and Rachel's ears perked up to hear what was happening. She didn't catch the first part, but definitely heard enough of the rest to feel sick inside.

"There was a mudslide down the back part of Mount Killaloma around mid-afternoon today. Two male hikers have just informed the police that local resident, Dr. Peter Carson and his travelling companion, Kate Harmon are still somewhere up on the mountain. We are unsure of their whereabouts at this time but will keep you posted. A rescue team has already been dispatched and they will work until the pair have been located. We have also been told that an old man and his dog, who lived alone on the mountain, were found slain just prior to the mudslide by the two hikers. His name is being withheld pending notification of his family. Investigators on the scene have ruled the death a homicide but have been unable to complete their investigation due to the mudslide. They were forced to evacuate the area. We'll keep you abreast of the situation as the news comes in to us. You're listening to CKLZ 95 reporting live from Mount Killaloma. Now we return to our regular programming."

Rachel rightly assumed that the two male hikers were probably Stephen and Paul. But Peter and Kate were still somewhere up on the mountain. "Oh God," she pleaded. "Please let them find Kate and Peter unharmed. I pray that You would cover Kate right this minute with a hedge of protection by Your mighty angels. Keep her safe from all danger. I lift Stephen and Paul to you as well, Father and pray that You would bring them home safely. In Jesus' name I pray."

Rachel quickly called her home in Poweetan. Vira picked up the phone and Rachel asked her if she had seen the news. Her mom had just heard and promised to come right away and to tell the Westcott's what had happened. They would just close the clinic for the day. If there was an emergency, Albert had a spare key and he could fly the helicopter. Vira made one quick call to the leader of the prayer group and explained what was going on. They all promised to lift the situation up to God in unified prayer. Within minutes of hearing the television broadcast, there were sixteen people down on their collective knees petitioning God…and He was answering their fervent prayers.

Kate began to be aware of her surroundings after Tom left the cave. She wept openly for Peter who was obviously dead. She couldn't imagine what had gotten into him. Had she led him on in some way and instigated this whole sordid mess? Thinking back, all she could remember doing was taking a sip of juice. Then it came back to her! She had questioned him about his relationship with God. He had become angry and violent and then he had hit her. Her cheekbone ached. A chill ran down the back of her neck and arms and she realized that she wasn't wearing her sweater. She wrenched her hands mercilessly back and forth for about ten minutes, until she was finally able to pop one of her hands out of the rope. Her extremities tingled as the feeling started coming back in them.

Rubbing her hands slowly over her sides and front, she noted that her skin had been cut and scraped in several places. One cut felt fairly deep and she winced in pain. Her fingers came away wet and sticky. Then reality sunk in. Tom had killed Peter and he was going to come back and kill her too. She had no idea where he had gone but looked frantically around for a place to escape. Glancing behind her, she found the blanket, backpacks and sweater that Tom had obviously brought in here. They were lying beside a small fire that was more smoke than flame.

She hurried over to the fire and tried to get warm. Kate thrust her arms into the ripped sweater and was grateful for the warmth it provided. She quickly searched Peter's backpack to find anything that might be of use to her. She extricated a flashlight and closed up the bag. Kate looked around and saw only one opening. She was afraid to rush out too quickly in case Tom was waiting for her. Her hesitation saved her life.

At that moment, Kate heard a scraping and rending noise that was muffled by the cave. The walls began to vibrate and a fine dusting of dirt floated lazily down upon her head. She covered her mouth to stop from choking and jumped up, ignoring her numerous aches. Kate ran to the entrance of the cave and had just started to put her leg through the opening when she felt a relentless pressure pushing her leg back inside. Her leg felt wet and she didn't have the vaguest idea what was happening. The flashlight flew out of her hand and hit a rock. She screamed for help as the light disappeared completely and she was left in darkness that was complete except for the faint light cast by the fire.

The pungent smell of cold wet earth was almost overpowering. That was when the panic began. Nobody would be able to find her. Only Tom knew exactly where she was. That produced a shiver that had nothing to do with the cold. Mud was slowly oozing in through the entrance. She picked up the hiking gear and moved further into the cave, going by feel more than anything else. She grabbed a branch from the fire that had a small ember on the tip. She blew on it. The light produced was weak at best, but it was better than nothing.

The cave went back about twenty feet. There was a ledge jutting out about three feet wide by six feet long. Kate stood on her tiptoes but her fingers didn't quite reach it. Letting her eyes roam over the floor, they stopped at a large rock sitting up against one wall. Kate put all her weight against it and rolled the rock under the ledge. By standing on it, she was able to swing her leg up and over the ledge. With some effort, Kate pulled herself up and lay winded on the cold stone. She held the stick in shaking hands until the weak light finally went out. And then the darkness was complete.

Kate's world turned upside down and her imagination started to run rampant. This cave felt like the inside of a large coffin, or so she thought. It was pitch black and smelled like dust and earth. Kate felt a momentary panic rising in her throat but swallowed hard and tried to slow the heartbeat that was threatening to burst out of her chest. She needed to change her focus. Just then, the dream from the hotel came unbidden to her mind. She remembered struggling against the devil and losing. The Lord spoke softly to her then. "Though the devil might be able to destroy your body, he cannot destroy your soul. That is mine and one day we will be together for eternity. Be patient my dear one. You are not alone."

Kate wept silently. "Why am I here Lord? Nobody will ever find me in here. Is this how it ends? What about my family?" she rushed on in a torrent of words.

"Just be still and know that I am God."

Kate hung her head in shame and begged the Lord's forgiveness. "I'm sorry, Father. My life is in Your hands and I trust You with all my heart. Please look after my mom and give her a deep sense of Your peace. And Lord, forgive me for getting so carried away with Peter. I really wasn't thinking straight or looking at the possible consequences of my actions. Because of my carelessness, I just about lost a part of me that I've been keeping pure for my husband one day. Thank you for interceding on my behalf, Lord. But there's something I'd like to know. When I lived in Klindale, I thought you were leading me in the direction of Peter. I felt like we were meant to be together. I don't understand."

"Kate, you were instrumental in bringing about a second chance for Peter. But he made the choice to turn his back on me, willingly. He paid a heavy price for that choice. What you didn't know, is that Annette has come to know me personally. When Peter left the house, Annette was forced to face her indiscretions head-on. A time of healing and cleansing came about because of that time of great pain and heartache. If the two had never been reunited, she would never have felt driven to cheat on him. This is where you came in, Kate. You brought the two of them back together and my plan for Annette bore fruit. She is now my child, just like you are."

A light finally began to dawn in Kate's head. The Lord had always been working in her life. She had never been alone.

"Why did Katya have to die, Father?" Kate asked.

"Her death brought her sooner to my side, while leading Paul to me as well. He will be instrumental in leading many more to me. So you see Kate? Things may look very dark and bleak but I can make good come of it."

"And I guess you allowed Rachel to be hurt but not killed, so I would come to be with her in Fulson and meet up with Peter and Paul again?"

"You're learning, my beloved. You have a future to look forward to, outside of this cave, but you'll find that out soon enough. Go to sleep, Kate."

And then there was total silence, but Kate was no longer afraid. She was in good hands and was at peace with herself and with her God.

CHAPTER TWENTY-FIVE
HOMEWARD BOUND

The steady thump of whirring helicopter blades could be heard coming through the trees. It sped past the onlookers at the base of the mountain and headed towards the summit. Within fifteen minutes it returned and slowly lowered itself to the ground. The pilot jumped out and ran to converse with the rangers and police. Head nodding, he got back in and took off. The rangers in turn spoke with the men and women from the rescue unit. Within moments, they were driving as quickly as possible up the mountain. Time was of the utmost importance when lives were possibly at stake.

When it appeared that nobody was going to come and talk with them, Stephen finally went up and tapped one of the rangers on the shoulder.

"I would like to know what's going on, if you don't mind. That's my best friend up there and I am very concerned for her safety."

"Well, I just talked with the pilot who flew over the scene. He says that the slide was not very large, as slides go. It seemed to come from above the cliff face where the caves are. It filled up the lake and then went over the side. The mud seems to have stopped when it hit the flats by old man Wilson's place. We're going to head up there now. They're going to send a dozer up, so we can get some of the debris cleared out and then maybe we'll be able to locate your friends. Hang tough, guys! We won't stop until we find them."

Paul put his arm out and stopped the ranger from leaving. "Please, sir. Can we go with you? We won't be in your way and maybe we could help out. We could do some digging or something. Waiting around is driving us crazy."

The man eyed Paul and then gave a barely perceptible nod of his head. "I guess we could us a couple of extra hands. Come on and ride with me."

He led the way to his truck while the two young men followed gratefully behind. Before too long, they arrived back at the cabin. The mud could be clearly seen glistening through the trees. The police were quite relieved that their crime scene had not been contaminated in any way and got back to work gathering information. The rest of the team went to the edge of the mud and looked at the destruction in awe. Trees and branches rested at haphazard angles in the mire.

Where to begin, thought Paul in anguish. There was no way Kate could have survived this devastation. In frustration, Paul wearily turned away with a heart that felt like it was breaking in two. He hadn't felt such loss since the death of his mother and he struggled to keep his emotions in check. Kate was Stephen's friend too and he would need someone who could give him strength, not bring him down. As darkness began to fall, the rumbling sound of a bulldozer could be heard coming up the road. It had two large floodlights mounted on top and soon the area was lit up like a B-rated movie set.

The hours dragged on as the heavy machine laboured tirelessly, dragging away tons of mud and debris. Members of the rescue unit had long poles which they were pushing into the mud to see if they could locate the bodies of the two hikers. Before long, one of the workers yelled out that he had felt something in the mud that had some give in it.

Stephen and Paul looked where the man was pointing. All they could see was some dark hair in the thick mud. Paul assumed it was Kate and felt sick. Two men grabbed hold of the head and began to gently dig around the body, until the mud let go of its catch with an obscene sucking sound. It was a male and when the mud was wiped away from the face, Paul let out a deep sigh of relief. It wasn't Kate, but it was really hard to tell if it was Peter or not. It was highly possible. What a way to go, Paul thought with revulsion. Mud had entered every orifice on the man's face. His eyes, nose, ears and mouth were all full of the rich dark brown paste. Whoever it was had died a horrible death and Paul prayed to God that Kate hadn't met with the same fate.

Further up the side of the mountain, the going was a little bit tougher. One of the rescue workers had to be rescued himself when he sank into the mud and quickly disappeared up to his neck. It was determined that he had fallen into a pond or some such thing that had been filled up with the mud. It was fairly shallow as ponds go, and as the dozer did its work, evidence began to appear of the life that it once housed. Dead fish popped up here and there in the soupy quagmire.

By eight o'clock, all the workers were famished, so two hampers of sandwiches and thermoses of hot tea and coffee were brought up and consumed greedily by all. After being satiated, the men resumed their tiresome and filthy work. By ten o'clock, they had still found no sign of Kate. The search continued in earnest, although the men and women were now showing some signs of fatigue. Another crew was due to relieve them within the hour. The night dragged on for all those involved in the search. Kate was nowhere to be found.

Two of the rangers were talking quietly together. Stephen's curiosity was peaked, so he moved a little closer so he could overhear what they were saying. The taller of the two looked exhausted with his shoulders slumped and mud caked all over his clothing and boots.

"Do you think we're going to find the woman?" he asked the other man who was just as dirty.

"I really don't know. It's hard to tell what this area looked like, what with all the mud and everything. But there's a bunch of caves around here somewhere. Maybe she was lucky and jumped into one of them."

Stephen jumped in then. "That's right! Sorry guys, but I just overheard you talking about caves. I remember now! Rachel told me that Kate and Peter were going to go exploring some caves. But surely they would have gone together? It doesn't make much sense," he added.

"All I know is that we've been looking around here for hours and we haven't found one thing that resembles the girl or any of her belongings. They probably both had backpacks too, so where are they? I have a gut feeling that when we find those packs, we'll also find the girl. Over by that cliff face," he said pointing, "are the caves. Excuse me for minute guys!"

Walking towards the bulldozer, he started barking out orders. "Go over to that cliff and start hauling away the crud," he yelled with his hand cupped to his mouth. "There are several caves under that mess that we need to check out before we go any further. Let's move it people."

Everyone hustled over to the area of the caves with renewed strength and energy. Paul and Stephen held their collective breaths and prayed with fervour.

"I found one," a man said excitedly.

After clearing out some of the mud, they were disappointed to note that it only went in about four feet and stopped.

"Let's keep looking, folks! There are more around here," commented another person who had his jacket off and his sleeves rolled up to his elbows.

Everyone was covered in the cold grime and it was hard to walk with all the mud caked on everything from boots to skin. Morning dawned gray and lifeless on the mountain. The fog had lifted, which only served to show the mass devastation which had been caused by the mudslide. Destruction was vast and it would be years before this area ever looked the same as it had been. Last night's rescue units had been replaced by two different groups. Stephen and Paul caught a couple of hours sleep in the jeep. They didn't want to stray too far from the area.

Stephen's parents came by to give moral support, while Rachel's parents went to stay with her. She was worried sick and hadn't heard any news since yesterday afternoon. All visible caves were checked out by mid-morning and unfortunately all of them turned up empty. The mud had been moved and sorted and carted away to be piled in one main area. There had been no visible signs of Kate and by now, everyone had all but given up hope of finding her alive. The dozer drove slowly back down the mountain…its job completed.

The rescue team was just about to join it when one of the men tripped on a rock and fell headfirst into a tangle of wet and muddy vines. They pulled away from the wall easily and behind them a wide crack in the rock was revealed. "Hey, would somebody throw me a flashlight, quickly! I think I hear something." The packed mud had seeped into the crack and had to be dug out by hand.

"Tony!" the man yelled over his shoulder. "You don't have as much meat on you as I do. See if you can squeeze through this crack, will you?"

The man named Tony, put down the tools he was using and rushed over to the opening. He eased his slender frame through the rock and disappeared from view. Minutes passed slowly, before a leg came out through the hole wearing wool slacks, followed by the welcome sight of a scared, dirty and battered looking woman. Kate shielded her eyes from the hazy light. The blackness had been so complete that any bit of light was painful to contend with.

She heard claps and cheers from all the people around her. Then she heard a familiar voice and looked in that direction. Stephen and Paul were hurrying towards her, as fast as the mud allowed. Paul got to her first and swept her into his arms with joy. He laughed and cried as he hugged her unabashedly. Next in line was Stephen who held her warmly and welcomed her home.

"We had just about given up hope of finding you, Kate," said Stephen who looked like he hadn't slept in a couple of days. He gave his arm a mighty flourish to encompass all of the people gathered on the mountainside. "These wonderful people have worked around the clock to find you, Kate. You have no idea how good you look right now to us. We found Peter's body yesterday and figured you were lost to us."

Kate looked at the men and women around her. Then she lowered her voice so only Stephen and Paul could here.

"I've been through a terrible time, but I'm so thankful to be alive right now. Tom killed Peter. Peter was trying to attack me and Tom came up behind him and knifed him in the back. It was awful," she said as a tear squeezed its way out from under an eyelid.

He fell and then Tom dragged me into the cave and tied me up. I don't remember too much because he hit me in the face and I think I was in shock at seeing him. Where's Tom now? Have they found him yet?" she said as a shiver took hold of her and she started to panic.

A Fulson police officer who had been listening to Kate's story interrupted her as a female officer wrapped a blanket around Kate's shoulders.

"Who's this Tom guy you were talking about? Nobody mentioned anyone by that name that was missing. It would make our job a lot easier if we had all the information." Kate looked at him and yawned.

"I'm sorry officer, but I'm starving, cold and exhausted. Could we talk about this somewhere warmer? It's a long story."

The man shrugged his shoulders and waved her on to the waiting medic. He looked at the female officer and gave her a barely perceptible nod.

"You'd better go with her. When she's feeling up to it, I want you to question her. I want to know who Tom is!"

The rescue team searched for another two hours but found no sign of anyone else. Except for the forensics team that was working over Peter, Clay and his dog, the rest were pulled from the mountain. They made their way to the base of Mount Killaloma in exhaustion. It had been a long couple of days and they were bone weary.

CHAPTER TWENTY-SIX
NEW BEGINNINGS

Kate took Albert's hand as she got out of the helicopter, followed closely by Paul and Stephen. I think we have a lot to talk about," she said to Paul. He smiled back at her. "I know Kate…I know." Together they walked as far down as the cabin and were greeted en masse by many smiling faces. There was Vira, Matt, Carol and Davis. Kate strode towards them with her arms outstretched. These people were family and she welcomed them graciously.

As the parents parted, Kate's face lit up in pleasant surprise. Standing before her and looking more beautiful than ever, was Rachel. Kate laughed and ran to her. The two hugged and cried as they both realized that they had been survivors of Tom and his madness. And the best thing of all, was that it was finally over. Tom was probably buried under tons of mud and may never be found. What had begun over two years earlier in Klindale, U.S.A., had just ended on a wild mountain top in the north country of Canada.

Between the shooting and several stabbings, God had taken these horrible events and used them for his glory. Many who might never have accepted Him under normal circumstances, had now given their hearts fully to Him. Included in the ranks were Albert, Lillian and Ruby, who had begun to attend church regularly. They still kept their native ways and lore. The difference was that they now personally knew the Creator God of the universe.

...3 Months Later...

Kate had been back in Poweetan for the past two months. She had taken a month off and gone back home to stay with her mother for a while. She needed a time to rest, think and heal. Kate made it back just before Rachel gave birth to a beautiful healthy baby boy. She named him Caleb and he looked like a miniature Stephen. The boy would grow up knowing all about love, because he was adored by everyone in Poweetan. A love of the Lord was ingrained in his heart as well.

Paul went back to Klindale to finish up his studies. He visited the Collin's family regularly and spent a good deal of time on the phone with Kate. When he had boarded the train at the Fulson station, he had waved out the window at his fiancée. Kate wore his engagement ring on her finger and she smiled and blew kisses to him. They had agreed that Paul would finish school and then come back to live in Poweetan. The town's people had also agreed that Paul would stand in the pulpit of the old church as soon as he was ready.

In the meantime, they would just keep doing their own services like they had been doing. As the months continued to creep slowly by, God looked down on His people and smiled with tenderness. Each day brought them closer to the day when He would gather them all to His breast and they would spend eternity with Him in the New Jerusalem. Time was of no importance to the Lord. All He required was that the people, in return for His love and mercy, would give Him their obedience and devotion. That's all He had ever asked for!

None of them ever knew that the night following their ride down Killaloma, some twigs could be heard snapping off and a slow shuffling noise sounded as if something was being dragged through the brush. And out of the complete darkness could be heard the sound of guttural laughter.

CHAPTER TWENTY-SEVEN
A STIRRING OF UNEASE

The woman dabbed at her forehead with a starched white handkerchief and smiled lovingly at the man carrying her bags beside her. She had been making this run monthly, for almost fifteen years, from this same little airfield. Today was no different except for the intense summer heat refracting off the tarmac and the strange man she had seen working on a small sea plane just off to the right of them. As they boarded the plane, the woman glanced over her shoulder to see the man leaning against the side of a ladder. She was shocked to find him staring right back at her. She felt the hair begin to rise on the back of her neck and a slight shiver ran down the length of her spine, in spite of the heat.

"Paul," she whispered. "That man over there is staring right at us. I've never seen him before. Have you?"

As Paul reached over and took Kate's hand, he glanced to where she had been pointing. There was no one there.

"I heard Luke say that he hired a new guy named Jim Adams, about three weeks ago Kate, but I haven't seen him yet. He told me that Jim is great with plane engines and the guy must be a hard worker because Luke also said that he stays behind and works after everyone else has gone home for the night. I would like to see more people like him around. Wouldn't you?"

Kate shrugged her shoulders and moved aside as Paul closed the door to the plane. She sat down beside a window and looked out one more time. The man was back beside the ladder again. Judging by his appearance, Kate figured that he was probably in his forties. He had dirty blond hair that came down past his shoulders and a full beard. He wore dark mirrored sunglasses, so his black eyes were thankfully hidden from view. As she watched, he turned around and walked slowly away. She immediately noticed that the man had a noticeable limp. He must have been hurt, she thought absently to herself.

CHAPTER TWENTY-EIGHT
LOST IN REFLECTIONS

Kate reflected on her life as she sat back to enjoy the twenty minute ride. She and Paul had been flying to the remote northern community of Hawksburg for years now. Once a month she would bring medicine from the Poweetan Clinic where she worked and help out wherever she was needed. Paul was a pastor in the Poweetan Presbyterian Church and he would join Kate on each excursion north, to minister to the aboriginal people.

She looked fondly at her husband and smiled to herself. They had been married for eighteen wonderful years and Kate's love for him grew, day by day. He was a gentle man who gave generously of himself. At fifty-four, he was still ruggedly handsome with only a little grey peeking through his blond hair. He had a mustache which only added to his good looks.

They had been blessed with two beautiful children. Her eldest was a son, Jacob, who rebelled at every turn. At seventeen, he had caused them no end of grief and many a sleepless hour had been spent lifting him up in prayer to God. He was dearly loved, but for some unknown reason he had it in his head that nobody understood him. He had a bitter spirit and seemed bent on self-destruction. Already, Jacob had been expelled numerous times from the small school they attended and had been arrested once for shoplifting in an expensive clothing store in Fulson. He had spent the night in jail until she and Paul had walked into the police station in shame, to bail their son out.

Jacob seemed to mock their Christianity and went out of his way to make life generally unbearable for them all. Jacob had long black hair which he wore in a ponytail and piercing dark brown eyes. He had a tattoo of a dragon emblazoned on his left shoulder blade and his fingers bore the stains of smoking too much. Kate was sure that she had even smelled marijuana several times on his clothing when he had returned from some party or another.

Kate and Paul had agreed to pray continuously for Jacob and had determined not to sever the lifeline between themselves and their son. He had been raised to be a good boy and they were confident that given time, he would come full circle. He had to find out everything the hard way and no amount of pleading or lashing out in anger was going to change that. Kate just hoped that he wouldn't hurt himself or someone else in the meantime.

Unfortunately, he seemed to be teaching Rachel's son Jonah some of his bad tricks. Paul was looking for a job for Jacob who was too shiftless to get out and look for one himself. He had finally finished his grade twelve and was quite content to let mom and dad look after him. But Kate knew that he had to learn some responsibility. Just today, Paul had put in an application at the airfield in Clarkson. Hopefully, he would be accepted. Luke had known Jacob since he was a baby and would be an excellent mentor. He was about six foot five and weighed in at two hundred and fifty pounds of pure muscle. He was a no-nonsense guy who wouldn't take any guff from anybody. He told Paul that he would let them know within the week. After all, he had just hired Jim.

Kate and Paul's daughter Sarah was a whole new ballgame. At fifteen, she was a beautiful girl with long black hair cascading down the middle of her back. She had a deep love for her Lord and had a quiet gentle spirit. She kept good grades and sang in the church choir with Kate. During the summer months she loved to tag along with her parents when they went to Hawksburg. There she would read to the younger children and play baseball with the older kids. Sarah was very popular and had found a place in the heart of Rachel and Stephen Westcott's eldest son Caleb, who was eighteen. Any fool could see that they were very much in love but being the sensible girl she was, Sarah determined to go to Fulson and get her teaching certificate before she would consider a serious relationship.

Caleb had been away for the past four months with the group, "Youth for Christ." These young people travelled around the world distributing bibles, sharing God's Word and working with the members of each community they visited. He had been faithfully sending Sarah postcards from each place. In September, he would be going to seminary in Brandon which was about three hundred and fifty miles away. He vowed that when he returned, he would be asking for Sarah's hand in marriage. Only time would tell though. Nobody could plan for four years away. Just too many things could happen in the interim.

Rachel and Stephen were very proud of their children. Although they were having some problems with Jonah, they still had faith that God would speak to their middle son in His time. They had been faithfully covering Jonah and Jacob in prayer for years and trusted that God would do a great work in both boys.

It was obvious to both parents that Caleb was not going to follow in his father's footsteps. He had no interest in dentistry whatsoever and that was all right. Rachel had been given a vision early in her pregnancy that Caleb was destined for serving the Lord. She had gone through an unspeakable assault on her body and spirit when, in a case of mistaken identity, she had been grabbed, knocked unconscious and carved up with a knife. Her pet wolf, Hunter, had caught her scent just in time and interrupted an incensed killer.

Tom Erikson had wanted Kate dead because she had been instrumental in sending him to prison for killing her best friend Katya, in a drive-by shooting. During a heavy downpour, he had grabbed Rachel instead of Kate because they had traded coats. When he noticed his error, he had been filled with an uncontrollable rage towards the woman who had caused him so much grief. After being found out, he had hidden away on Mount Killaloma outside of Fulson, Manitoba. In a final confrontation, he had killed two more people and hidden Kate away in a cave. A terrible mudslide came erupting down the mountain and Tom disappeared from sight for good. His body was never found.

Months later and three operations for skin grafts, had all but erased the words that Tom had carved on Rachel's chest. It would be several years later before the nightmares would go away though. During that time of deep healing, both physical and spiritual, Stephen faithfully surrounded his wife with all the love a man could give his woman. Her children were also instrumental in helping her to get on with her life. She was never bitter towards Kate as some might have been. She knew it was nobody's fault but Tom's that the young man had turned out bad. That was a personal choice that he had made. She only felt an extreme sadness that before he met his eternal destiny, he had not known God.

His torment now would be unparalleled. In her heart, she had forgiven the one who had caused her so much pain and anguish.

She had poured her life into raising her two sons and caring for her husband. Four years after the birth of Jonah, Rachel and everyone else had been very surprised and delighted to find out she was pregnant again. They were blessed with another son and named him Mark. And so, life went on and things changed in the small community of Poweetan. The old mine no longer existed. Albert and a stick of dynamite had seen to that, after Rachel had been held there. With the passing of years, the ground had been beautifully transformed with long grasses, wildflowers and many trees. The path still wound through the area and down to the edge of the crystalline lake. The mournful cry of the loon could often be heard floating up from the lake.

By mutual consent, the townspeople had decided not to build any houses around the lake. They wanted it left untouched by man. In a world that was rapidly changing, this one place would remain a sanctuary of peace and a haven for those looking for an escape. The population had risen to almost two thousand people. The main dirt road had been paved and there were now some street lights in place. The old clinic\dental office had burned to the ground almost ten years earlier and a larger structure had been built in its place. A new sign now adorned the front of the second story. It read, "Dental Surgeon--Dr. Stephen Westcott; Dentist--"Dr. Davis Westcott, and General Practitioners—Dr. Tyler Verstegan M.D. and Dr. Samuel Fulbrook, M.D. Dr. Matt Jenkins had retired almost eight years earlier and had built a new home behind the café.

Ruby still ran the cafe as she had for the past twenty-five years and still made the best coffee and pastries in town. She was loved by everyone, even if she was a bit of a softy towards "her kids," as she called all of the town's children. About six months after Rachel had been hurt, Ruby had married long-time resident Albert Bailey.

Albert had helped to rescue Rachel that terrible night so long ago. He was a skilled carpenter and at sixty, had started to pass some of his duties down to their son, Jimmy, who was the same age as Jacob.

One thing left unchanged by the passing of time was the old town square. It still displayed the large oak tree with all the initials carved around its base—a testimony to love gained and love lost. The gnarled bench that used to adorn the square had long since fallen into disrepair and had been replaced by a fine new one. The town water pump was now rusty with disuse and sported a shiny plaque, dedicated to the memory of Lillian Bailey. Lillian used to use the pump daily, even when everyone else had discarded it as being old fashioned and out of date. Now she watched it daily from her home on top of the hill beside the church where she had gone to after turning her life over to Jesus.

She had been put to rest two days after her 103rd birthday. She still had all of her faculties and was a stubborn woman right up until the end. But she had passed away with the most radiant smile upon her face and her eyes glowed. Whatever she had been seeing, it had been a private viewing to which no one was privy to. Nobody, except the host of cheering and praising angels whose job it was to escort this fine woman to her beautiful new home. And she had discarded her frail and weathered body for a glorious new one. If a person could have seen into the heavenly realm, they would have heard the sounds of the saints praising God and singing, "Holy, Holy, Holy is the Lord God Almighty." If only they could have seen!

All of these things were sifted and sorted through Kate's mind as she languished in the seat with her eyes closed. Soaking in the steady drone of the plane and the gentle rocking was like a balm to her soul. Kate was startled from her reverie by Paul's hand upon her shoulder.

"We're home Kate. Here, let me take your bag. You look really tired today."

As she gazed lovingly at the concern shown on his face, she handed her bag to him and took his proffered arm to steady herself. Together they walked down the stairs and waved at Lester Hobson who owned and operated the tiny airstrip in Poweetan. This is where Albert kept his helicopter. There wasn't enough business to warrant hiring anyone else, so Lester was sort of a jack of all trades and very proud of it. He monitored everything that passed through.

Lester often told anyone who would listen that no guns or drugs or such would ever pass by under his nose, unnoticed. He obviously was unaware of the changing times and the ingenious methods used to hide contraband of any kind. If he knew what really got through, he would have been truly mortified. But that would all come to light in due time.

CHAPTER TWENTY-NINE
THE CHAMELEON

Jim Adams had been working at the airstrip in Clarkson for about a month. It had proven to be a very lucrative business. The pay was menial, but his extracurricular activities paid very well. It was sweltering for this early in July and Jim wiped his forehead with an oil stained rag that he kept tucked away in his front pocket. It wasn't the heat alone that had Jim so agitated. In less than ten hours, he was expecting another special shipment to come in from South America. His boss Luke was such a deadbeat, he thought to himself. The guy was so trusting that he left a spare set of keys to the hangar with Jim, so that he could "work" a little while longer. And Jim made sure that he always did more that his fair share of work, so that he would never come under suspicion. He didn't need that kind of hassle. Absently he rubbed at the long faded scar that ran from the corner of his left eye to the left side of his nose. Even after all these years, it still got itchy when he got overheated.

He had grown a beard a long time ago, to hide the disfiguration and to stop the constant stares. Unfortunately he had been unable to hide his lame leg. Yes, he had a past just like everybody else, but he wasn't about to disclose it. He had started this little side business when he had been working in Brazil almost eight years ago. Quite by accident, he had stumbled upon a covert drug and gun smuggling operation. The men in charge had beaten him senseless until they were all in agreement that he knew nothing of what was going on. His life had been spared when he had blurted out that with a pilot's license and all, he could probably be a big help to them. The work was not hard for someone who was used to being secretive. All he had to do was fly from point A to point B; stay approximately twenty minutes and then head back again…all without saying a word of course. After a successful mission was flown, he would pocket about eight thousand dollars. Not bad, considering it only took about two to five hours at most.

When he moved back to northern Canada, he became the go between for other incoming pilots. There was a lot less pressure, but the take was also smaller. About four thousand dollars exchanged hands after each of these operations, but he was now much happier. He had lived just south of this area a long time ago and being back had stirred some dormant desires and had sparked that old fire in the pit of his stomach. He still thought about that shadowy woman who had messed up his life and made it into a living hell. She was to blame for all of his hurts. He couldn't forget and he'd never forgive.

Jim took a swig of warm coke, swished it around his mouth for a moment and spat it out on the ground. He crumpled up the can, gave it a rim shot into the large waste receptacle and sauntered away. There was still some work to do until the drop. He had to maintain the façade that he was really busy. That was easily accomplished. He had lived his life doing as little as possible.

Jim was not a bad looking guy. However, his furtive glances, secretive manner and aggressive behaviour towards women had all but quashed any serious relationships. There had been one girl a few years ago whom he had dated for about two months but she had left him when she found out about his volatile nature. He hadn't seen her since. Jim had stopped seeking them out. When he got those uncontrollable urges now, he would go into the city and just cruise the streets and highways, looking for the three H's as he fondly called them—homeless kids, hitchhikers or hookers. He would use them unmercifully and then discard them like an old worn out pair of shoes. Usually they had been so high on crack that they were unaware for the most part about what was happening to them.

Now that he thought about it, there had been that one young boy and that teenage girl. The boy had gotten away from him and had headed into the bush. Unfortunately, his speed was no match for Jim and after a short struggle, Jim had slit his throat. It was his own fault, Jim reasoned. If he had been quiet and stayed where he was, he would probably still be alive. They had found the kid's body about two months later, but by then, the coyotes and decomposition had erased any signs of foul play. There just wasn't enough of him left. He made short work of the girl as well.

Then there had been that other girl. Her name had been Suzie, or that's what she said, anyway. She said she was eighteen, but if she was thirteen, he would have been surprised. She had been standing by the bus terminal with a skirt on that barely covered her buttocks and a plunging neckline that hinted of small hidden delicacies. He had been instantly aroused and had stopped the car and rolled the window down.

The makeup made her look tough and weathered but she had fine legs that didn't quit. That more than made up for her other flaws. She had leaned in through the window and given him a forced grownup smile. It didn't mask the vulnerability he saw in her eyes. She climbed in and they rode around for a little while. Before she knew it they were heading out into the country. He showed her some money from his back pocket to appease her and gave her some story about wanting to show her to his mom because the old bat had been bugging him to settle down. Being naïve, the girl had fallen for it, hook, line and sinker.

He drove up in front of an old house that was in a sorry state with the shutters hanging lopsided and the yellow paint coming off in big strips. The house looked decidedly abandoned and Suzie had started to ask some pointed questions. She was beginning to show the first signs of fear. He had latched onto her arm with an unbreakable grip and hauled her inside where she was viciously assaulted in unspeakable ways for a day and a half. He did like the leather straps and the hunting knife best. That had always been his favourite.

Suzie had died slowly from exsanguination, among other gruesome things. He had dug a hole in the back yard and thrown her body in, like a broken rag doll. Odd, how young she looked now! He smiled as the last vestiges of dirt cascaded down into the hole and smoothed the surface. Some leaves and a couple of dead branches helped to mask any wrong doing. He had used this property many times before and knew from past experience that nobody lived there. It had all the earmarks of being forgotten for life. That had been some time ago. He was about due for another foray any time now.

Jim glanced at the scratched digital watch on his arm and noted with surprise that it was closing time already. Time surely passes when you're thinking happy thoughts, he smirked. He spotted Luke Wilson walking towards him.

"Jimbo, its closing time. Are you planning on staying around for a while or shall I lock up behind you?"

God, he hated being called Jimbo. If he didn't need this job, he would have done something about it from the beginning. He put on his best game face and said: "I'd like to go now but I would also really like to finish this engine for Senator Wilcox. He's only here on business and is eager to get back home before the end of the week. It shouldn't take too long to get it greased up and put on a new blade. I'll probably be finished up by eight. You go on ahead Luke, and I'll close up and see you tomorrow."

Luke gave him a slap on the back.

"I sure struck gold by hiring you, Jim. See you in the morning."

He started to walk away and then turned back for a second.

"Oh, by the way, I almost forgot to tell you. There's a minister and his wife who come through here once a month to look after the people of Clarkson. They have a son who I just hired as a favour to them. His name is Jacob Winchester and by the sounds of it, he has gotten a little wild. Paul says he wants him to learn some kind of responsibility and a trade of some kind. I'm sure we can find something to keep his nose clean, eh? I know that his mom Kate is at her wits end with the boy."

At the sound of her name, Jim's ears perked up.

"She used to work for Dr. Jenkins who's been a friend of mine for almost thirty years. I had better be heading. My wife has a royal fit when I get home late for supper."

With that, he turned on his heel and headed across the tarmac. Jim turned his head because he could no longer hide the smile which had spread across his features.

Nico d'Arva had been running drugs, cigarettes and guns from South America to various drop off spots in the U.S. and Canada for the past three years. It was a lucrative little operation he had going for himself. The people he worked with were very dangerous men, but he always managed to keep his mouth shut and turn a blind eye to the more shady things going on, while missing nothing. Nico was Brazilian by birth. At 31, he still had the arrogance of a teenager but the wisdom to know when to be discreet. He stood about five foot ten, but his stature was more than a little compensated by his muscular build. He sported a bushy black mustache and long straight hair.

He was known by those in the trade to be an army surplus junkie. He wore standard army green fatigues and always carried on his person a vast assortment of knives and a gun that had seen plenty of action. As he checked the gauges in the cockpit, he glanced down at the watch on his arm. Should be there any minute, he thought. This was a new place for him to come to, but the guy he was meeting wasn't new. He had done business with him many times before and the guy gave him the creeps. There was something not right about him that he couldn't put his finger on. It wasn't the fact that he had probably iced a few people that made him weird, but something deeper and less visible. He went by the name Jim, but Nico was sure that it was just an alias. Guys like him rarely used their real names.

As the small, poorly lit airstrip came into view, Nico started to bank the plane and head on down. Within minutes, he was taxiing down the runway towards the hangar at the far end. He brought the plane to a rolling stop and stood up to stretch his cramped muscles. He opened the door and climbed on down. All of a sudden, Jim stood behind him, although for the life of him, he hadn't heard a sound.

"Where did you vaporize from, man? You scared the crap out of me!"

Before he could say another word, Jim interrupted him in a voice which was devoid of any human warmth.

"You're five minutes late," he said in a monotone. "Let's get this job done. I want to be out of here in twenty minutes."

With that said he went over to his car and drove it up to the side of the plane. He opened the trunk and a blast of some foul smell assaulted Nico's nostrils. Jim didn't seem to notice, although Nico gagged a few times and had to rub his watery eyes. Whatever, or whoever he had kept in there, had not come to a happy end.

"Give me a hand here and quit standing there gawking," grumbled Jim.

Nico shook his head to clear it and walked over to the plane. He grabbed several boxes containing bags of good quality black ice. Most of the longer boxes had stacks of assorted weapons in them. He was not interested in their destiny. They would probably end up in a sleazy little part of some city. They always did. Business was improving as the world got more violent and uncertain. That's what it was like when people had no hope for anything better than what they already had. Except of course, for those crazy people who went to church and thought they had first dibs on a so-called heaven. They were only fooling themselves, he thought bitterly. This world was as good as it was going to get and if you wanted something, you had to just take it, whether it was yours to take or not. If you lost out, it was your own fault.

Nico intended to do just that. He had been putting his money away in a safe spot and would enjoy it when he got a little bit older. There was no way he was going to be somebody's lackey the rest of his life! He had big plans. An elbow in the ribs snapped him out of his reverie with a sharp gasp of pain.

"Hey, what's your problem, man? I don't have to help you unload this stuff. All I was told to do was fly the bloody plane, so just lay off or I'll see that you don't get any goods again."

His words sounded braver than he felt inside but he squared his shoulders and assumed a tough guy stance. He glared at Jim for only a split second before having to turn his face away. Once again, he had been cowed by this guy and was embarrassed by his own timidity. He had stared into the eyes of death many times, but this time he had envisioned his own. Rubbing at the goose bumps that were crawling over his skin like a thousand tiny insects, he quickly picked up the last load of boxes and stuffed them into Jim's car. He tried to act calm as he patiently waited for some money to exchange hands.

Jim went to the front of his car, grabbed something from out of the glove compartment and came back to where Nico was standing. He handed him a soiled, thick manila envelope, turned his back and got into the car. In minutes he was gone, leaving Nico standing there sweating profusely despite the cooler night air.

"Well, I'll be damned," he said to nobody in particular, and actually thought he might be. He had to get away from here fast. Nico looked down at his hands and were surprised to see them shaking uncontrollably. He gave a half-hearted laugh and climbed back up into the pilot's seat. He had enough fuel to get him to his next destination and decided to just get the heck out of here. It was getting harder and harder to make a buck these days. As he thought back on the last half hour or so he reasoned that perhaps he had read too many things into the stop. Surely the guy hadn't had "dead" eyes and the smell in the car could just mean that Jim was a hunter. He liked that picture much better than the one he had envisioned earlier. Again he chuckled to himself and relaxed as the engine purred to life and the plane slowly picked up speed as it headed back down the runway. In moments he had all but forgotten his fear, as the plane soared and he thought of how he was going to spend his money. Maybe it was time to consider a different line of work.

By 3:45 in the morning, Jim had made connections with his top dealer in Fulson and three quarters of the stash had been rerouted to some major cities across Canada. By the time the sun crept above the horizon, the distributions would be complete and the minor players would be hawking their wares to the drug addicts. Included in the numbers would be some leading business people, gang members of all ages and drug dependant mothers or fathers. All in all, it was a very productive night's work.

Jim fell exhausted into bed around a quarter to seven in the morning. He placed a quick call into work and told Luke that he had a touch of the flu. It was his first sick day so he was sure that Luke wouldn't care much. As he quickly drifted off to sleep, he remembered what Luke had said before he left. He had hired a new kid. What was his name? Jake, or some such thing. He wondered if it could possibly be Kate Harmon who the guy had been speaking about. She had worked for a doctor many years ago, but Jim couldn't remember the guy's name. The woman at the airport had looked really familiar. Surely it couldn't be a coincidence. As his eyes closed wearily in submission to the fatigue, he thought about Kate Harmon. What that woman did to him!

CHAPTER THIRTY
FREE SPIRITS

Jacob dreaded this, of all days. His father got him a job at that nondescript airfield in Clarkson. Talk about a bore. His friends would laugh him out of Poweetan if they found out. Most of them were going to work in Fulson where the pay was better and the girls were plentiful. So far, he had kept this news hidden from them although it was only a matter of time before they found out. Some of the guys were heading into Fulson this morning and Jacob intended to go with them. He would call in sick on the way and make Luke believe his lie.

Jacob got word from a couple of college kids, Chris Holton and Cass Birwell, that a major shipment of drugs would be hitting the streets in the next couple of days and he planned to be there with his hands out. His mom and dad would have a hairy fit if they knew he took drugs but at this point he didn't really care a whole lot. Jacob had been dabbling in quite a few things recently. He felt like he needed to erase the goody-two-shoes image he had because his father was the pastor of the local church. He had been teased about it for years and he was sick of it. Maybe if he did bad things, the other guys would begin to respect him because of who he was, not because of who his father was.

Jacob loved his parents and his sister, but he needed to have his own space. He had begun to rebel in earnest about four years ago and was getting to be a master at it. Once he had heard his mother crying about how he was going to go to hell if he didn't straighten out soon. Jacob didn't think that would ever happen. He had answered an altar call when he was a boy and figured he was now free to live his life the way he wanted. His dad had tried to make him understand that a personal relationship with Christ didn't work that way but he had closed his ears and his heart to his father's pleas. There was lots of time to make a serious decision, he thought irrationally. He would do it later, but for now he wanted to have some fun. He figured you could still be a Christian and have fun.

He grabbed the lunch his mother handed him, gave her a half-hearted hug and ran out the door. "Goodbye Mom. Don't forget that I'll be staying over at Chris's house tonight after work. I'll see you tomorrow night and tell you all about how the new job went. I'm really looking forward to it." He waved as he turned his back to her.

Kate assumed that Chris was going to drop him off at work, or that's what he told her anyway. For just a moment, Kate wondered if her son was telling her the truth but she shook off the rotten feeling that she was experiencing. She had to learn to trust him sometime, and now was as good a time as any.

Once he rounded the corner of the garage down the street he spotted the guys waiting and ready in Cass Birwell's rust speckled black pickup truck. He jumped in to the sound of popping beer caps and sank back into the seat with a big grin on his face. Life just couldn't get much better than this, he thought. They burned rubber heading out of town and the sound of their laughter floated on the wind.

One hour and forty-five minutes later found them slightly inebriated and just entering the city limits of Fulson. Chris roared with laughter when he almost ran over a hitchhiker.

"The boys are on the town today," he guffawed. "Let's find ourselves a motel and ditch our stuff. Then we can go and score a connection and grab some more beers."

Jacob felt a momentary stab of guilt but quickly shook it off. Another fifteen minutes found them in a rundown part of the city where old brownstones lined the streets and kids played hide and seek behind the garbage cans.

Groups of wayward teens huddled in stairwells and swapped raunchy jokes and secrets. Approaching one of these groups, Chris asked where Blade could be found. A mulatto youth pointed a few doors down with a bored expression on his face.

"You better have some money man, or Blade's gonna cut out your liver and feed it to you, while you die!"

The others laughed uproariously, as if it was expected of them. Jacob suddenly felt very sober and with this, the first stirrings of fear assaulted him and he wondered just what he was doing here. He was supposed to have started a new job today and he had blown it…again. If his parents ever found out, he was going to be grounded for life. There wasn't much point in dwelling on this train of thought though. He couldn't do anything about it now. He might just as well forget about it and focus on having a great time. He looked down and saw Chris's arm holding him back.

"You had better stay right here guys. I'll be back in a few minutes. Blade expects me to come alone. That was part of the agreement."

Jacob and Cass let out a collective sigh of relief. That was fine and dandy with them. In no time at all, Chris came sauntering up to them with a big smile pasted across his face. He never said a word until they were back in the truck and driving down the street. Then he let out a whoop and held up a small bag containing white powder.

"What time is it?" he yelled out.

"It's party time!" the other two added in unison. Like homing pigeons, they were drawn to the beer store and purchased two cases. It wouldn't do to run out. They were all in agreement that it was time to find themselves some dates for the evening. Might as well start early! As they went on the grand tour, thoughts about his mom and dad evaporated like smoke.

Sarah was a chip off her parent's block when it came to good looks. Her father was an extremely handsome man and her mother, while not exactly stunning, was a fine looking woman. Her true beauty glowed from within and in that way, Sarah and her mom were duplicates. At fifteen, Sarah was going to break more than a few hearts before she found her niche in life. She wore her long black hair in a single braid down the middle of her back and had no need to wear makeup. Her natural features were beautiful enough without having to paint them up cheaply. At least that's what her dad and Caleb always told her.

Sarah and her brother were like night and day or two different sides of a coin. She had an unwavering love of God and had gone to the front of the church for the altar call, just before Jacob did. But where Jacob had gone up on head knowledge alone, Sarah had been prompted by God's Spirit deep within her heart. Her salvation was real, while his was only imagined. She loved her brother deeply and was burdened often in the middle of the night with the need to cover him in prayer. She knew the word of God to be true and believed it fully.

On this particular night, Sarah was awakened from a deep sleep around four thirty in the morning. Something wasn't sitting right in her spirit so she immediately fell down on her knees and began to petition God. Within moments, she had the feeling that Jacob was in some kind of trouble. Sarah prayed and prayed until she finally felt a peace come upon her. Whatever happened, things were going to be okay.

Sarah padded softly into her parent's bedroom and gently shook her mother awake. "Mom, can you come into the kitchen for a minute? We need to talk," she whispered in her ear.

Rubbing the sleep from her eyes, Kate quickly rose and followed her daughter out of the room, grabbing her bathrobe as she went. Shielding her eyes from the glare of the overhead light, Kate sat down across from Sarah.

"What is it dear?" For just an instant, Kate feared the answer.

"It's Jacob, Mom. I think he's in some kind of trouble. I was just awakened and felt the stirrings to pray for him. I think everything's going to be all right though. I had that assurance."

Kate looked at her daughter and sighed. Why couldn't Jacob be more like Sarah, she thought to herself? Life would be so much easier. But then again, nobody ever said that the Christian life would be easy. She knew in her heart that without the trials and hardships in life, a Christian could never expect to grow. It was while being tested that one learned to persevere and perseverance produced character and character produced hope.

"Chris was supposed to take Jacob to work yesterday and then pick him up to stay overnight at his house. I think that as soon as it gets light out, I'm going to call Cyndy and see if they're even there. I hope your brother didn't miss his first day of work. Luke was just doing us a favour by hiring him."

There was no way Kate was going to get back to sleep now, so she got up and started to make some hot chocolate. "Why don't you go back to bed Sarah and see if you can get some more sleep. I'm just going to stay up a little while longer." Sarah knew better. There was no way her mom would be sleeping again this night. She gave her mom a kiss.

"Goodnight Mom. See you in a couple of hours."

"Goodnight dear. Thanks for telling me. I appreciate it. Don't worry yourself, Sarah. We'll get everything straightened out in the morning." With that said Sarah let out a big yawn and sleepily went back to bed. Jacob was in God's hands now. It would be a very long time before things would ever be straightened out though. First thing in the morning, Paul phoned Cyndy's house and asked to speak with Jacob.

"Jacob's not here, Paul. I haven't even seen him for a couple of days. I thought maybe Chris was with him at your house. That's where he told me he would be staying last night."

Paul could read the worry in her voice and understood completely. Cyndy was a single mom who tried to raise her son in the best way she knew how. Although she worked a lot of hours at the diner to put food on their meagre table, she still tried to make time with her only son. Once he got into high school though, things had changed drastically. He was not the loving boy he had once been and was more often than not, rude and belligerent to her. She had found drugs in his bedroom before, but when questioned, he had said that he was storing it for somebody else. Many times she had seen new clothes in his room and wondered where he got the money to purchase such things because he didn't make much pumping gas at Freedman's Garage. He always had a good answer, but in her heart Cyndy knew that her son was getting to be a very adept liar.

As a parent, she wanted to blame his intolerable behaviour on the friends he was hanging around with. Maybe they were a bad influence on her poor boy. But Cyndy knew better. Chris was a leader, not a follower. She wondered where she had gone wrong. Maybe if the boy had a father to emulate, he would have turned out differently.

"Have you tried calling Cass Birwell's house yet, Paul? Sometimes they hang out together and maybe he'll know where they are," Cyndy suggested.

"That's a good idea, Cyndy. I'll let you know if I find out anything. Talk to you later."

A phone call later confirmed their suspicions. Cass hadn't come home last night either. The three of them were probably together. Next, Paul gave Luke a call and asked if Jacob had shown up for work the day before and if he was there now.

"I haven't seen hide nor hair of him, Paul," said Luke, who sounded more than a little perturbed. "I thought he wanted this job. He called in sick yesterday. You tell him that unless I see him bright and early tomorrow, he can find himself another job. I'm not mad at you Paul. I realize that the kid has to learn responsibility on his own, but he's not going to be doing it on my time," said Luke.

Paul could feel the colour rise in his cheeks as he hung up the phone. He was ashamed and embarrassed because of something his son had done, or rather not done and he didn't like the feeling much. He had tried discipline but that hadn't worked. He had tried just loving him, but Jacob seemed to push his love away as if it were nothing at all. The best thing he could do for him now was to pray for his soul. His son didn't have a personal relationship with the Lord and that scared Paul more than anything else could. What if he were to be killed today? Did he know where he was heading? If he did, he wouldn't be carrying on like this, he reasoned.

Paul felt that there were some mighty black clouds rolling their way and they were going to be tested like never before. He prayed that they would be up for the challenge. If he knew just how bad things would get, he would have fallen to his knees on the spot and wept in anguish to his God. Some things were better off not known in advance.

CHAPTER THIRTY-ONE
THE PRODIGAL SON

All throughout the day, Rachel Westcott stayed by Kate's side, sitting patiently while Kate poured out her frustrations and quietly praying when her friend was deep in thought. They had been through hard times before and would probably go through lots more before it was all over. Rachel and Kate had been the best of friends for about twenty years. Kate had come to Poweetan to work as a nurse for Rachel's father, Matt Jenkins.

A lot of things had changed since then. She remembered the moment when she had fallen in love with Stephen and how he had nursed her back to health, both physically and spiritually after that man had hurt her inside the mine. The details of that time had been blessedly removed from her mind. All she could remember was being pregnant and getting a vision from God of the unborn child in her womb. She had no recollection of how her chest had been mutilated or what the guy even looked like. Rachel had an unsettled sense of foreboding in the pit of her stomach. All was not right. She felt that troubled times lay ahead. So she continued to pray…for all of them. Somehow she knew that Sarah would not be exempt from whatever pain lay ahead for this family.

She was startled out of her musings by the loud jangle of the phone around five o'clock that night. It was Cyndy calling to tell them that Chris had just stumbled in, high on something and that Jacob was passed out in the back of his truck. Cass wasn't with them though. Kate had barely set down the phone before she was heading for the door.

"I have to go get him, Rachel. Thanks for sitting with me. I shouldn't be too long. You're welcome to wait here."

"That's okay, Kate. I'll just go home and get dinner ready for the gang. I hope Jacob will be okay," she smiled at her friend.

"I'm going with you," said Sarah as she grabbed the door behind her mom.

Kate went by the church and hauled Paul out of his study. In minutes they were at Cyndy's house and staring down into the barely recognizable face of Jacob. From the smell that was emanating from him, he had wet himself. The palms of his hands were scraped and his knuckles were raw and covered with coagulating blood. His one eye was swollen and blackened and he had a nasty looking cut above the bridge of his nose.

Kate felt a sob escape from her mouth as she jumped into the back of the truck and pulled her son to her breast. He flinched noticeably in her arms and mumbled something incoherent. A solitary tear squeezed its way out of his good eye. Rational as ever, Kate got them all moving.

"Paul, you had better go and get the car. We can't very well carry him home like this."

He hurried down the street while she sent Sarah to get Dr. Verstegan. She could see that he had been in a fight and he was obviously drunk, but she wanted to make sure that there were no broken bones or more serious injuries. That was one good thing about living in a small town. Doctors still made house calls. Paul returned in less than five minutes and gently picked his son up and slid him into the back seat of their car. He drove them home. By the time they got Jacob into the house, Dr. Verstegan was walking up the front steps with Sarah.

A cursory examination showed no physical problems besides cuts and a lot of bruising. He would heal completely although one of his teeth had been chipped and the cut on his nose took four stitches to close.

"I'd say he got off pretty lucky," said Dr. Verstegan as he tied off the knot. "A bath will get the rest of him clean but his belly will probably be churning for a day or two. He's had more than his fair share of alcohol and there's a trace of what looks like coke inside his one nostril, but I can't be sure without having it tested. His vitals are all good though, so my guess is that he'll sleep like the dead unless he starts to vomit. In that case, you have your work cut out for you."

Tyler gathered up the tools of his trade and put them back into the black leather case on the table. "If you need me at all Kate, don't be afraid to call. I'll be working late tonight as usual. If you feel like you can't make it in to work tomorrow, don't worry about it. Wednesdays are usually fairly quiet as you well know." With that said he sauntered to the door and let himself out.

Obviously Jacob wasn't going to be waking up for a while so Kate let out the bath water and filled a basin with warm water and a bar of soap instead. Carrying it down the hall, she grabbed a towel from the cupboard and went to minister to her son. Sending Sarah on some trivial errand, she and Paul stripped their boy and looked with horror at his black and blue torso and the swollen bruises on his shins and thighs. He had surely been kicked or punched repeatedly while on the ground.

As gently as possible, Kate washed and cleaned Jacob's body while Paul turned him over so the other side could be done as well. That accomplished, Paul dressed him in clean pajamas and covered him with a soft blanket. Both parents then held hands and prayed like they had never prayed before. And the peace of God which transcended all understanding filled them with love and healed their hurting hearts.

The next day found the Winchester family looking decidedly haggard. Sleep had been a luxury that neither Kate nor Paul had been afforded. Jacob had cried out continuously in his sleep. Whatever demons had been chasing him seemed to dissipate with the coming dawn. Around ten o'clock he started to stir and Kate was there, stroking his forehead. Paul looked down expectantly and smiled as his son began to focus on him with his good eye.

"Welcome home, Jacob. We were afraid that we had lost you son…" his voice broke off in a choked whisper as tears ran gently down his face. Kate squeezed his hand for reassurance and sat down on the side of the bed.

"How are you feeling, Jacob? Dr. Verstegan was here last night and he said that you're going to be all right. Your body just needs to heal from the cuts and bruises."

"I feel like somebody ran over me with a bus and cleaned my teeth with the toilet brush. Other than that, I guess I'll live. How did I get here? The last thing I remember was this really big guy taking a pipe to my guts."

Kate had to bite her tongue. Now was not the time to be chewing him out. That would come later.

"We talked to Luke this morning and he has agreed to let this week go, but under no circumstances are you to miss next Monday morning or any day after that." Paul tried very hard to keep the shame and disgust out of his voice as he remembered having to grovel on his son's behalf. He wasn't entirely successful.

"Look, I'm really sorry Dad…Mom. What I did was wrong. Please forgive me? I promise I'll never do it again. I've learned my lesson."

Paul turned away then from Jacob's simpering tone. Somehow he doubted his son's sincerity. He might feel remorse now while he was feeling under the weather but once he started feeling better, Paul knew that he would go back and do it all over again. The boy seemed bent on self-destruction and there was only one thing that would stop his downward swing. As always, he would have to learn his lessons the hard way. One nagging question had yet to be answered.

"Where did the cocaine come from, Jacob? Tyler said you had been snorting coke." Jacob looked like the proverbial cat with the canary in his mouth. "And I would like to hear the truth for a change."

Jacob could tell by the tone of Paul's voice that he meant business. "We bought it from a kid in Fulson. It was the first time I ever tried it and that's probably what made me so sick."

It was a wonder the kid could say that with a straight face because both parents could see that he was lying through his teeth. The look that passed between Kate and Paul told volumes. They would let things rest for now. When he was better, they would be demanding some answers and if they didn't get some satisfactory ones, perhaps it was time that Jacob started looking for a place of his own. It would grieve them terribly but they couldn't live with uncertainty like this either. It was far too taxing on their nerves. It was like walking into a room full of eggshells.

As the workday ended and the airport in Clarkson prepared to close down for the night, Jim sauntered up to Luke as he was locking the office doors.

"I was meaning to ask you something, Luke. I thought you were hiring a kid to help out around here. Wasn't he to start work yesterday? I haven't seen him yet."

"He was supposed to start yesterday but the little bugger decided to go on a bender instead of coming to work. He'll be coming in on Monday instead and if he doesn't show, he's out of a job before it even starts. I can tell you one thing though. I'm gonna knock that irresponsibility right out of his system. I can't stand it when someone says they're gonna be somewhere or do something and they back out at the last minute."

With the worst of his frustrations vented, Luke pushed the door open and turned his back to leave.

"See you in the morning, Jimbo. Hopefully this heatwave will break. We're due for some cooler weather. Goodnight!"

"Goodnight Luke."

Jim absently rubbed a dirty hand across his nostrils. That sure is good coke, he thought to himself. Maybe he should get that Winchester kid hooked on the stuff. That would be the ultimate hoot if the little brat turned out to be related to the Kate that he used to know. What beautiful revenge he would be able to exact on him. If it was the same woman and she had married a preacher, well that was even better. Jim hated anybody who acted like they were better than him, whether it was real or imagined. He looked forward to Monday morning with relish. He intended to drill the kid for information. First he would befriend him and then see what took place. Jake might also be able to help him with the shipments coming in next month. Jim needed someone who was afraid of him that he could blackmail. That could work to his benefit. He rubbed his hands together in anticipation and limped towards his car. Life was good and Jim was happy. Things were finally coming together for him and it was about time. Jim had wasted a lot of years trying to make it big but nothing had ever come from it. He wanted to make people squirm when they were in his presence. He was determined that never again would he be a little fish in a big pond.

Jim had painfully learned that lesson long ago in a deserted forest. If there had been an inkling of compassion or love left in his body, it had surely died the moment when he fought a life and death struggle for his very soul and lost it all. He now served an unforgiving master and would eventually pay dearly for that service. Jim would regret the day he sold his soul to the devil.

Most people in the town of Poweetan were blissfully unaware of the spiritual battle going on in the midst of them. Only a handful of faithful followers knew that they were battling the dark forces of evil. But the telltale signs were blatantly being witnessed everywhere, if only the people would open their eyes and their hearts to see. Three Aboriginal and two Caucasian teenagers had committed suicide in the past four years. Those were big numbers for such a small community.

Paul had been meeting with Reverend Thomas Gerrety from the United Church, Father William Pietro from the Catholic Church and William Jessup from the Aboriginal community, for the past six months. These four had joined forces to set up a youth centre in the old fishery building. Fresh paint and a lot of scrubbing from numerous volunteers had erased any unwanted odours from years of neglect. They had completed several fundraisers to get the money for a good used cd player, a small kitchenette where they kept a well-stocked fridge full of pop and some cupboards for snacks.

A couple of ladies had made some curtains to dress the place up a bit and some beautiful new throw rugs had been made. Several tables, chairs, a couple of old couches and games completed the ensemble. They opened up on Wednesday and Friday nights from seven until ten o'clock pm. with volunteer adults chaperoning. The first night had seen only a handful of nervous giggling kids who were trying to act like they didn't have any cares in the world and the centre was no big deal. Their main mission had been to check the place out and report back to their friends. They figured that the centre would be a big joke but were pleasantly surprised to find it to their liking.

Three weeks later, there had been about twelve teens and two nights ago, about eighteen youths had played games, laughed and listened to tunes until closing time when audible groans could be heard from all of them. To have a little fun in this hick town of theirs, they were more than willing to listen to the opening and closing ten minutes when one of the ministers would talk about God and would pray with them. It was a small price to pay so they listened politely and then did their own thing.

For Paul, the youth centre had been a blessing in disguise. He knew that the Word of God never came back empty-handed and so he prayed that the teens would be touched in a very real way. Several came from pathetic backgrounds where there had been alcohol and substance abuse. A couple of the kids would walk through the doors sporting black eyes or other such bruises.

Poweetan didn't have a lot of jobs to go around. A new leather factory was going to be opening soon but it was too little too late. Many families had gone under and lost either their homes or their life savings in the interim. All in all, it was the perfect breeding ground for evil to abound. Behind the newly restored main street and the brightly painted store fronts, lurked something foul. Locked doors and closed windows couldn't always contain the hurled insults, cries of pain and angry outbursts. That was why the four spiritual leaders of Poweetan had joined forces in the first place. They had to have a common starting point and they might as well begin with the kids. If they could be reached with the Good News, then perhaps the parents would soon follow.

Many in the Aboriginal community weren't too sure about the "Jesus thing" as they put it. But they did note that there were many similarities in their beliefs.

Both groups believed in a supreme being who created everything. Both believed that they had to be good stewards of the land and all that was in it. And both respected their elders and heeded their counsel. And so these four men put aside their differences to make a concerted effort to better their community.

Paul knew that the kids who came to the youth centre needed guidance. They needed to hear that there was someone who loved them unconditionally and that He had died for them and taken their sins upon his own back on the cross. He had obtained victory over death so that they too could have eternal life with Him. All they had to do was believe and then ask Him to come into their hearts as their personal Lord and Saviour.

This place that Paul called home was his own personal mission field as he liked to call it. There was a myriad of lost sheep looking for a shepherd and Paul knew where He could be found. All he needed to do was introduce them to each other and let God's Spirit do the rest. Unfortunately his own son fit into the same category and as yet, Jacob hadn't graced the steps of the centre. As long as Paul drew breath, he would always open his arms of forgiveness to his prodigal son, just like his Heavenly Father had opened His arms to a hopelessly lost and wounded young man named Paul, so many years ago.

Paul remembered what God's grace was all about because he could still vaguely recall his own bittersweet memories of a childhood full of sadness, hardship and hate. His mother had been the one bright light in his young life but she had died of a broken heart when he was still a boy. His own father had abandoned him and left Paul to fend for himself in a large and hostile city. He had been forced to take on any menial task that would fill his ever empty belly, finally crossing an invisible line to where he sold his own body for money.

Yes, Paul knew what these teenagers were feeling because he had been in their shoes himself. He also knew there was a way out of the downward spiral and he vowed that they would know where the right path to freedom could be found. He prayed that the Lord would keep a lamp shining on Jacob's path as well. The boy was straying afar and was going to go over the edge if he wasn't careful.

So, as the darkness tried to gain a foothold in Poweetan, Paul and many others in the community met two times a week to pray. They covered the people, the buildings and the town around them with prayer and their tiny flame grew brighter and began to illuminate the darkness from within. And so the battle raged on…each side vying for victory but knowing that only one could ever succeed.

CHAPTER THIRTY-TWO
DANGEROUS LIAISON

Monday morning came too early for Jacob. He grudgingly floored the foot pedal and sped towards his new job. For just the briefest of moments, he contemplated turning around and driving to the city instead. He was sick to death of living in a hick town and wanted more from life than it could offer him. Unfortunately, that meant that he would have to work. That was not something that Jacob relished. He wanted the big bucks but he didn't want to spend the required time working for it. He knew that his parents wanted him to go to a respectable college or university but he wasn't willing to go that route either…at least not for now. He had done his time in school and now wanted to have some fun. Jacob knew that if he didn't show up for work today then he might just as well keep on driving down the road because he wouldn't have a house to go back to. He also knew that his dad wouldn't back down this time. He had been pushed too far already.

At the last possible minute, Jacob pulled hard on the wheel and squealed the tires as he fishtailed into the airport parking lot. At this time of day there were only three other vehicles. Slamming the car door, he sauntered into the office as if he owned the place and was doing everyone a big favour by being there. Luke took one look at him and could see the arrogance written all over the boy's face. He had grown into a good looking young man and obviously knew it.

"You're ten minutes late, Winchester. And you can't be around the engines and stuff with your long hair hanging out. You have to either wear it in a ponytail like Jim does, or cut it off. It's your decision but do something about it now. Put your lunch in the fridge over there and then follow me. There's work to be done and I want to introduce you to the guy who you'll be working under."

Jacob raised his eyebrows in surprise as he watched Luke's back exiting the office. He had known this man since he was little but this was the first time he had spoken to him like this and Jacob took an instant disliking to Luke. He may be his boss but he didn't have to be bossy. Who did he think he was anyway? Jacob grabbed an elastic band that was sitting on the counter and bitterly pulled back his hair. He went out the door and looked around. Luke was nowhere to be seen. What was he supposed to do now?

He walked across the tarmac to the hangar where he could hear the sound of an acetylene torch being used. Jacob called out to the man using it.

"Heh! Have you seen Luke? I was supposed to follow him out here but he took off."

The man pulled the face guard up onto his head and blankly regarded Jacob with a look that could have meant anything.

"You must be Jake. I'm Jim Adams and I'm supposed to show you the ropes around here. I'll just finish this piece up and be right with you."

Jacob could tell that the man was not used to talking a lot. He probably would have been more comfortable just grunting his answer. As if Jim could read his thoughts, he turned around and stared up at Jacob. Jacob could feel a tiny flutter in his chest as the man regarded him. He couldn't quite put his finger on what he was feeling but the closest thing he could associate Jim with, was that of a predator. Instantly he could sense that this man who knelt before him was dangerous. He would have to keep his eye on him and see what the guy was up to. Something just wasn't right.

Jim was staring for a very good reason. He had never seen the kid before but immediately he recognized him. His face looked like a slightly different version of his mother. This boy was surely Kate's offspring. It was just too much of a coincidence. He resisted the urge to just come right out and ask him if his mother's maiden name had been Harmon. There would be a better opportunity later. First he had to make the boy comfortable around him so he would open up on his own with minimal prodding. Jake mustn't know the reason for Jim's obsession with his mother.

The rest of the morning flew by as Jim filled Jacob's head with more information than he could possibly take in on his first day. By lunchtime, Jacob was ready to put his feet up. Sitting quietly in the shade of a tree, he ate while looking around at his new job site. Maybe things were going to be okay after all. Perhaps he had misjudged Jim. The guy seemed to be going out of his way to be nice to him and he thought it would be a good idea to give him the benefit of the doubt. He jumped and let out a shout of surprise when he felt a large hand clamp down on his shoulder.

"Thought you might like some company," a deep voice sounded from behind him.

"Yeah, sure," swallowed Jacob thickly as he just about choked on his sandwich.

Actually he wasn't sure at all, but he was darned if he was going to let on to this man. The next thirty minutes found Jacob pouring out his life story to a virtual stranger while finding out literally nothing about him. Jim seemed to know what he was going through and was very sympathetic. He laughed at Jacob's stories about partying, drinking and girls. He really had it all together. That afternoon went very well as Jacob became drawn to Jim like a large magnet and Jim just strung him along and reeled him in like an unsuspecting fish. Then Jim took him totally by surprise when the whistle blew for the end of the day.

"I have a nice little two bedroom winterized cottage about twelve miles from here. If you decide you'd like to get out from under your parent's thumb, I'd be glad to have you move in with me. I don't spend an awful lot of time at home, but you'd be more than welcome. I could use a buddy to talk to once in a while."

As planned, Jacob was flattered beyond measure that an older guy would want to be his friend and Jim could see the wheels turning as he took time to mull things over in his head.

"You don't have to give me an answer right now, Jake. Just think about it. Here's my number," he said as he handed Jacob a small slip of crumpled paper. "If you get yourself in trouble again, just give me a call. I've got a lot of friends in the city who could help you out."

As the weeks progressed, Jacob became more sullen and harder to reach. Kate was at her wits end with him and even Sarah had given up trying to get a conversation out of him. He couldn't even be civil to her and they used to be so close. Paul cornered him one Friday night after Jacob had come home from work.

"Your mother found this in your bedroom this morning son, while she was cleaning." He held up an offensive magazine, full of nude women being degraded in unmentionable ways. "What are you doing reading this trash? You've been brought up better than this. Magazines like these are demoralizing to women and cheapen what God meant to be a beautiful thing," said Paul in a rush.

By this time, Paul had raised his voice in anger and had drawn his wife and daughter out of the kitchen and into the living room by his surprisingly harsh words. Usually Paul was soft spoken and gentle, but the sight of this magazine had reminded him of his own sordid past and he was sickened to think that his own flesh and blood would follow in his footsteps after all that he had taught him.

Jacob gave him a crooked grin and then did something that would have been unthinkable only two months earlier. He gave him a lurid wink that was pregnant with meaning.

"Perhaps you wanted to see it first, Dad? Where are my manners?"

It took only a second for Paul to cover the distance between himself and his son. His hand went up in an arc that left Kate speechless and had Sarah covering the gasp that escaped her lips. Just as his arm descended, he felt a powerful grasp stay his hand in mid-air.

"Don't ever raise a hand to me again if you know what's good for you," yelled his son. The words were spat out with such venom that Paul shook his head in confusion. This young man in front of him was a stranger and Paul felt the first prickling of fear in the pit of his stomach. He was just as shocked at his own angry response. He hadn't felt like hitting someone since his dad had hit his mother so many years earlier.

Jacob stormed out of the house and Paul literally sank to his knees and started to weep for the loss of innocence in his son. Kate ran to him then and wrapped her arms protectively around her husband. Together they rocked and cried and held each other closely. Hearing a choked sob, Kate looked up and saw Sarah still standing in the same place in bewilderment. She got up off the floor and gently pulled her daughter into her arms.

"I'm so sorry you had to witness that, Sarah," she said apologetically.

"Mom, what just happened here?" she cried. "I've never seen daddy raise his hand to anybody and I've never seen Jacob like that before. He was scary. What's wrong with him, Mom?"

Kate felt an ache deep inside, which she doubted would ever go away until Jacob straightened up. "I don't know, dear. I just don't know!"

Tires spewed gravel as they gained purchase and sped down the road. The three family members then held hands in silence and prayed for Jacob's soul. Only God's intervention could change him now, so they begged God to convict Jacob's heart of his need for repentance and that Jacob would turn from his self-destructive ways.

While his family prayed, Jacob could feel the anger and the hate building to a crescendo. Things are going to change around here right now, he thought to himself. "I'll be eighteen years old in less than two months and I shouldn't have to put up with nagging parents who want to keep me under lock and key until I'm eighty," he fumed under his breath. Maybe he would just take Jim up on his offer. Granted, the guy was a little weird for his taste but he also had a place far away from any of the watching eyes here and that suited him just fine. He was sick to death of being told what to do and he wanted everyone to see that Jacob Winchester was his own man. He didn't want to be known only as the preacher's boy.

The resolve that had been growing inside him finally came to a head and a decision had been reached. He drove over to the Holton's house to share his good news with Chris.

"Chris is over at the garage, Jacob. How have you been doing?" asked Cyndy.

"Never better!" he grinned smugly.

Cyndy watched him go down the front steps and rubbed her arms to get the goose bumps to settle down. For some unknown reason, this was not the Jacob she knew. Something wasn't right with the boy and she hoped that he would keep on driving and not see Chris today.

Chris looked up in time to jump out of the way before Jacob almost ran him over. "Hey, watch where you're going, man! You just about nailed me. What's wrong with your head?" Chris yelled out.

He tried to maintain his cool guy image but it was next to impossible to do. He really had been scared but he wouldn't let Jacob know that.

"I just came over to talk. Have you got a minute?" he asked while smiling like he had a big secret to share.

"It's just about break time anyway, so let's go over to the square and sit down for a bit. You look like the cat that just ate the bird. What's up?" inquired Chris, whose interest had now been peaked.

"I'm moving out," said Jacob, nonchalantly.

"You're kidding, aren't you? There's no way your parents would let you leave home yet. They'd have a fit," Chris said with excitement in his voice as he mulled over the numerous possibilities that a place of their own would bring. They could party until the cows came home and nobody would be any the wiser. "And I suppose you're looking for a class "A" roommate, right?" Chris added with a smirk.

He was more than a little surprised when Jacob adamantly shook his head in the negative.

"Not this time, buddy!" I'll be moving in with the guy I work with. You remember me talking about Jim, don't you? Well, he said he has this great two bedroom cottage and he said if I ever have problems at home, I can move in with him," he went on in a rush.

"Are you joking? You barely know anything about the guy. I thought you said he was creepy. Why don't we go together on a place if you want to leave home? I wouldn't mind leaving either. It would be a lot of fun and at least we've known each other for years." Chris knew in his heart that all the persuading in the world would never change Jacob's mind. He looked too determined for that.

"Sorry, Chris, but I've already made up my mind. I'm going to talk to Jim about it in the morning and hopefully by tomorrow night I'll be out of here." With that said he slapped his friend on the back and waltzed on back to his car.

"Take care, buddy. I'll be seeing you. We can still get together and go into the city on the weekends," he called back over his shoulder.

Chris watched him pull out of the parking lot in a cloud of dust and shook his head again. That just left Cass to hang around with. He wondered about Jacob's changed behaviour. He used to be a great party animal to hang around with. But there was definitely something different about him. He couldn't quite put his finger on it but the word that came unbidden to his mind was…sinister. Jacob was turning really cold and he was sort of glad that they wouldn't be staying together. Maybe it was for the best after all. Cass wasn't really a bad sort.

Sarah met with Amy Cutler in the church sanctuary. Amy was the head of the prayer chain and had agreed to meet with Sarah this morning to pray for Jacob and their community. This was a long standing ritual for the two young women. Every Thursday at lunchtime, they would leave the school down the street and make their way to the church to join together in prayer. On this day, they would fast and then storm the gates of heaven with their petitions. They lifted Jacob up and laid him at the foot of the Lord's cross. That was one burden they didn't need to carry alone. Unaware of the spiritual battle being fought in the heavenly realm, the girls asked that the angels would do battle on their behalf and that the chains of darkness that had their town in its grasp would be loosed.

Within thirty-five minutes, they had the calm assurance that their prayers had been heard and answered. Cleansing tears of peace rolled gently down Sarah's face and she gave her friend a sisterly hug.

"Things are going to work themselves out now, aren't they? I don't know why I continue to worry when I know in my heart that God has everything in the palm of His hand and that everything is under His control. It's sometimes easy to forget and I want to solve all the world's problems in my own strength and knowledge."

Amy smiled then and threw Sarah's own words back in her face.

"We're human and we've been taught repeatedly that we are to be full of self-control, be self-fulfilled, be self-sufficient, be self-employed, and self-secure but that is just being selfish. We're so busy worrying about ourselves that we forget what Jesus said. We are to be servants to all and love others more than ourselves."

The two girls laughed as they walked back to school, unaware that they had been watched leaving the church. Jacob watched them head down the street and then made his way around to the back door of the church. Entering quietly in the dark, he made his way to the altar. One of the grade eleven students had given him a frog he had dissected in biology class. Jacob placed it on the communion cloth. It had been opened up and its entrails were slowly oozing out of the open belly. Its little legs had been stretched out and pinned to a piece of cardboard as if it had been crucified. Jacob laughed at the irony of it all. His dad would freak when he saw this and nobody would figure out that he had done it, because he was leaving home today.

He left early with Luke's permission after telling him he had an appointment with the eye specialist in Fulson. Jim had been very happy when Jacob told him that he would be moving that night. Unfortunately, he forgot that this was the day his parents always flew in and out of Clarkson and as Jacob was leaving his treasure at the front of the sanctuary, Paul and Kate were questioning Luke as to why their son wasn't at work.

"Why don't you go and ask Jim," Luke suggested. "He's been spending a lot of time with Jake. Maybe he knows where he is."

Walking towards the single hangar, they came upon a man who had his head buried in the body of a small four-seater Piper Comanche.

"Excuse me," Paul began. "Luke said that you might know where Jacob went today. We're his parents and we're looking for him." Without lifting his head, Jim grunted out something unintelligible.

"I'm sorry, but I didn't get that," called Paul who was getting a little exasperated that the guy couldn't even look at them when he was being spoken to.

"I said that I am not the kid's keeper. What he does is of no concern to me. I haven't seen him since yesterday."

His words fairly dripped with hate-filled venom and Kate was appalled by their harshness. The pair quickly exited the hangar and glanced sharply at each other. Again Paul had the distinct feeling that something was terribly wrong but as yet, he couldn't put his finger on it.

Kate was very quiet as a hundred thoughts went through her head. The main one seemed to be screaming at her. The man's voice had sounded vaguely familiar and that familiarity caused her to fear and she didn't know why. Shaking the sinking feeling that had come over her, Kate grasped Paul's hand and let him lead her back to the plane. They could do no more here. Somebody had to have some answers and they were determined to get them.

CHAPTER THIRTY-THREE
RANSACKED

Sarah beat her mom and dad home as usual, when they went to Clarkson. Coming through the door of the house she stopped dead in her tracks. The furniture had been overturned, books from the bookcase were strewn everywhere and her father's family bible was sitting open in the middle of the debris. Unable to shake the fear she felt, Sarah called out meekly.

"Is someone here? Come out right now," she added with false bravado.

The only thing that greeted her ears was silence. Stepping gingerly over the upturned coffee table, she was drawn to the open page of the bible. She could see that something had been angrily circled in red marker and her curiosity got the best of her. It was circled at Exodus 8:13. She started to read the passage out loud.

"And the Lord did as Moses asked. The frogs died in the houses, in the yards and in the fields. The Egyptians put them in piles and the whole country began to stink." The word "houses," had been stroked out and the word "church" had replaced it. Sarah's eyebrows knotted in a frown. She clearly had no understanding what this was supposed to mean but felt that given time, they would all become painfully aware of its meaning. If this was somebody's idea of a joke, they were indeed sick and needed some help. Sarah was glad that today of all days, she was the first one home. She threw her books on the floor and got to work.

She was afraid to look in the other rooms. Luckily Jacob was at work. At least this couldn't be pinned on him. They didn't have a lot of stuff worth stealing, so she wondered if the person had been looking for something in particular or whether this was just some random act of vandalism. The phone jarred her out of her reverie. She hunted around, trying to follow the sound of the jangling. Finally, buried deep under a pile of books, she retrieved the pesky instrument. Holding the receiver to her ear, she recognized the voice and Sarah's eyes lit up like a Christmas tree.

"Caleb!" she exclaimed in delight. "Where are you calling from? I've missed you so much. How have you been?" she ran on breathlessly. Laughing, Caleb broke into the one sided conversation.

"Hold on, will you? Give me a chance," Caleb laughed.

Sheepishly, Sarah grinned to herself. She was surprised at the intensity of longing she had for him. Until now, she was unaware of its existence and it took her completely off guard.

"I'm at the Fulson airport, Sarah. My plane just arrived. I'll be home now until I go to school in September. Sorry I didn't tell everyone sooner that I was coming home but I thought we still had a couple of weeks. I phoned home to get a ride from the airport but mom and dad aren't answering and I don't have enough money to get home any other way. Do you think your parents would mind helping me out somehow?"

Sarah thought for just a moment and then was struck by a great idea. "Mom and Dad aren't home from Clarkson yet and your dad went to Bakersfield for a dental conference. Your mom went to keep him company. They'll be back late tonight. I'll bet I can get Albert to go and get you. He can take the plane and be there in a quarter of the time it would take to drive there. One way or the other, I'll see that someone comes for you Caleb. Just hang tight! Okay?" she added quickly.

"All right Sarah. I can't wait to see you."

Turning to set the phone down in its usual place, she was brought back to reality. In the excitement of the moment she had forgotten the mess that lay around her. First things first, she thought to herself. She dialled the number for Albert and spoke briefly with him. It took no persuading on her part, as Albert and Ruby were such good friends of her parents and the Westcott's. The next number she called was the police station. Sarah recognized Sergeant Cal Davie's voice immediately.

"Sergeant Davies, this is Sarah Winchester calling. I need you to come over to the house. Mom and dad are still away and somebody has broken into our home. It was vandalized and I'd like you to have a look at it before I clean up any more. I should have called when I first noticed the mess but I wasn't thinking too clearly."

"Don't touch anything else Sarah. I'll be right there."

Hanging up, she surveyed the room sadly. She knew there would be no keeping this from her parents. They would be here within the hour and would find their house in shambles. Sarah opened the front door and sat down on the couch swing that sat along the one side of the veranda. Slowly she rocked back and forth and was comforted by the gentle rhythmic motion.

It wasn't until Cal's heavy boots hit the first step that she was even aware of his presence. Startled from her thoughts, Sarah jumped right out of the seat.

"You scared me, Sergeant! I guess I was daydreaming and didn't hear you. Come on in and have a look."

Walking in through the front door, Cal gave a low whistle. Seldom had he seen so much damage in Poweetan. Oh sure, sometimes people threw things when they got mad but this was on a whole new level.

"Do you know if anything is missing, Sarah? That would be a good place to start."

Slowly they walked through room after room while Sarah kept a mental inventory of things they had. Thirty minutes later, she shook her head in the negative.

"I can't see anything of value that's missing but did you notice Jacob's room? Although it's messy too, there seems to be quite a bit of clothes missing. It's like somebody took some of it. Now that's kind of strange, don't you think?"

"Where is your brother, Sarah? Has he been home today?"

"No sir. At least not that I know of! I was at school for most of the day and at the church during lunchtime, with Amy. We meet there every week for prayer as you know. Jacob has been working with Luke Wilson at the Clarkson airport for almost two months now. He should be home from work soon. He usually comes in around six o'clock. Do you want to talk to him?"

"I may want to talk to him later. Don't worry, Sarah. He's not a suspect or anything. I can't think of any reason why someone would have a grudge against your family. A person doesn't just go wrecking a place for the sheer pleasure of it. Tell your mom and dad I'll talk to them later. I have a report to write up. I'm going to send someone over here to check for any prints. They'll be here soon and then you can clean up if you want. See you later, Sarah!"

About twenty minutes later, Kate and Paul drove up to the front of the house. Sarah could tell that her mother looked tired and dreaded letting her see the inside of the house without preparing her. Running onto the porch she waved and called out to them.

"Can I talk to the both of you for a second? It's really important."

Thinking it was probably some school problem, Kate yawned and asked her if it could wait until they went inside.

"No it can't, Mom!" Sitting down on either side of her, Paul and Kate listened as Sarah described the devastation within. Moments later, Paul jumped up and ran inside. He stopped at the door and surveyed the damage. Kate followed closely behind. Letting out a small cry of despair, she moved into her domain and looked around in obvious shock.

"Who could have done such a thing?" she asked in dismay.

"I have no idea, but I intend to get to the bottom of it," said Paul angrily. Sarah showed him the bible then and he read the passage in bewilderment. "What's this supposed to mean?" he asked nobody in particular. At his daughter's prompting, he followed her into Jacob's bedroom.

"What's the matter, Sarah? It looks the same as the other rooms to me."

"A lot of his clothes seem to missing, Dad. I can't find his jean jacket or his leather jacket and a lot of his shirts, pants and boots are missing as well."

Turning to look at his girl, he was almost afraid to ask the question that popped unbidden into his mind.

"What are you getting at, Sarah? If you know something, you'd better tell me all about it."

"I've had some time to think dad and I wonder if maybe Jacob had something to do with this? I know we have to give him the benefit of the doubt but he has been acting very strange lately. I know it's a long shot, but do you think he might have taken off and wrecked the place on his way out?"

"Don't even think that, dear! Your brother may be having some problems but I can almost guarantee that he wouldn't willfully destroy our property. He's mad at me but not mad enough to do something like this. But that does remind me. When your mom and I were in Clarkson today we looked for your brother at work but supposedly he took off early with some lame excuse about seeing an optometrist, in Fulson. Of course we knew that wasn't true and your mom and I think he's gone out to the city again. There's no other logical explanation. I guess we'll just have to wait until he gets home."

"Wait until who gets home?" asked Kate as she came into the room. Paul told her what Sarah had said about Jacob.

"Oh, surely you don't think Jacob did this? It's unthinkable!"

Together, the family discussed the days' events while they rearranged furniture and put their household items back in their accustomed places. In all the busyness, Sarah forgot all about Caleb. A knock at the door sent Kate scrambling to answer. She flung it open, hoping to hear Cal say he had caught the guy. The shock of recognition barely registered for a minute.

"Caleb?" Smiling then, she went to embrace her best friend's son.

"We didn't even know you were coming home. It's been such a long time. Welcome back, dear. I bet your mom was surprised to see you." Caleb held up his hand.

"Sarah told me that mom and dad are away for the day. They don't even know I'm home yet. Sarah sent Albert to come and get me. By the way," he said with a twinkle in his eye, "where is that girl of yours? I can't wait to see her."

Shaking his hand warmly, Paul led him into the house and called out for Sarah.

"What happened in here?" Caleb asked with obvious confusion. "It looks like a tornado went through the place."

Kate and Paul looked at each other and sighed.

"It's a long story," they said in unison. "Sarah can tell you all about it," said Kate.

Just then, Sarah wandered into the room with an armful of dirty clothes. She surveyed the room for only a moment before her eyes found Caleb's and lit up like the fourth of July. Dropping the clothes she ran right into his arms. Then realizing where she was, she stepped back shyly and smiled up into his handsome tanned face.

"I've missed you so much," she said demurely. "Do you mind if we go for a short walk, Dad?"

"Of course not, dear. You two run along. We'll have lots of time to talk, later." Laughing, Sarah grabbed Caleb's hand and pulled him out the front door. The two made their way down to the lake. Sitting on the shore, both looked out over the calm water while stealing glances at each other every once in a while. Finally Caleb broke the silence.

"You look more beautiful than I could even imagine. I've tried to memorize every aspect of your features so I would never forget you while I was away, but I have to admit that I didn't do you justice. I've missed you terribly. We were kept pretty busy but in the quiet times I would picture us sitting right here in our favourite place, just watching the water and each other."

Sarah was unable to hide the blush that was working its way up her face. Caleb had never talked like this before and she wondered just what had gotten into him.

"You've been reading too many magazines, Caleb. I think it's gone to your head," she laughed lightly.

"Be serious for a minute. I mean what I'm saying."

"I know you do Caleb and that's what scares me so. I haven't changed my mind about going away to college. You know how I feel about the importance of getting a good education. But seriously, if you're willing to wait for me, we'll have plenty of time to be together when I'm finished. You know I love you and probably always have."

He smiled sadly then, reached over and pulled her into his strong arms.

"I'll wait for as long as it takes, Sarah. We belong together."

And as his lips pressed firmly up against hers, she felt her resolve melting. Her soft moist lips parted in eagerness and his strong hands stroked her shiny black hair. Temptation was not something which either one was willing to succumb to, so Sarah was secretly relieved when Caleb pushed her gently away.

"We shouldn't do this, Sarah. I don't know how long I can keep pushing you away but I also know that neither one of us wants to cheapen a beautiful relationship. We'll wait for this as well. Come on!" he said while pulling her gently to her feet. "Mom and Dad should be home soon and I want to be there when they arrive. I can't wait to see the surprised look on their faces. And I haven't seen my brothers in ages. I'll bet they're a foot taller than when I left."

And although they had been sharing adult feelings only moments before, the young person hidden within each of them was soon very apparent, as Caleb chased Sarah down the path while she giggled like the schoolgirl that she was.

CHAPTER THIRTY-FOUR
EVIL COMES STALKING

Nico paced the room nervously. The only word that would adequately describe the room would be opulent. There was a large chandelier glittering in the sunshine pouring in from enormous oak patio doors bejewelled with at least a hundred tiny panes of glass. Sleek leather furniture was positioned with care around a large plush oriental rug. A dark mahogany desk with the latest in computer technology was against one wall. Another wall was made up entirely of a massive fireplace done in grey fieldstone and the skin of a polar bear, complete with head, adorned the opposite wall. A fountain finished off the scene with water pouring into a trough from a statue of a small naked boy. It was definitely a man's room which spoke of power and influence.

Nico had been summoned to the home of his boss almost thirty minutes earlier. He was probably making him wait to stew in his own juices and as each minute passed, Nico became more and more nervous. Sweat ran slowly down his back even though the room was air conditioned. He had methodically picked the skin off the sides of each thumb. He had no idea why he was here. As far as Nico knew, he had been doing his job flawlessly. He was startled almost out of his skin when a voice sounded behind him. Nico didn't even hear the panel slide softly open.

"We have ourselves a little problem Nico and I don't care for problems. Word has it we have a volatile firecracker waiting to erupt at our Clarkson drop-off point.

If he ever decided to talk, we could be finished. I know the guy used to work a little closer to home and we were better able to keep tabs on him. What is your impression of Jim Adams? You've seen him recently."

It took Nico a moment to realize his boss didn't want to chew him out. He gave a visible sigh of relief.

"You heard correctly. The guy is a walking freak of nature. When I saw him last month I couldn't get away fast enough. He snuck up on me and just about gave me a heart attack. He was rude and belligerent and expected me to do all of the work by myself. And I did it too because I felt that if I hadn't, he would have killed me. Oh yeah," he went on breathlessly. "When he opened up his trunk, the odour that came out of it almost made me heave. It smelled like he kept dead bodies in it."

Nico wiped the perspiration out of his eyes and would have gone on, had he not been interrupted.

"It sounds to me like this Jim could be better put to use in plain sight of us. We can really use a guy who isn't afraid to die. And if he "accidently" takes a bullet while on a deal, he wouldn't be missed," the man said, with what Nico could only assume was an attempt at a smile.

"You'll be heading back to Canada in about two weeks. I want you to persuade Jim to come back with you. Give him a couple of hours to put things in order and then I want him on that plane with you. I don't need a renegade drug dealer botching up my business." Walking over to the desk, he reached inside a drawer and pulled out a thick manila envelope.

"All you have to do is give this to him. If the money inside here isn't incentive enough, show him your gun. That ought to work. Come back when you've completed your task and bring the guy with you. We need to talk."

Nodding his head in dismissal he started working away at his desk. Realizing he was needed no more, Nico quietly backed out of the room, thankful that he had come away with his life. He didn't relish the idea of being on a plane with Jim, but his boss was not one to second guess. There must be a good reason for him wanting that creep to be here but Nico rather liked the idea of offing him. No strain, no pain! He would enjoy watching him squirm and die. That would be one less wacko in the world. This might be a good assignment after all, he thought to himself.

Life with Jim was certainly not what Jacob expected it would be like. This was the first time Jacob had been on his own and he was willing to do anything to prove he could make it without his parent's help. He had been able to buy an old Volkswagen Rabbit. It was kind of rusty and was an ugly brown colour but it got him from A to B, and it didn't use much gas. Jim wasn't much of a roommate. He would go out late at night and sometimes not come home at all. He would always be at work on time but Jacob wondered where he went.

Curiosity finally got the best of him one Saturday evening. He decided to follow Jim at a safe distance and see what he was up to. He almost lost him once on the way, before finally noticing the sign to Fulson pass by on his right. Stopping on the shoulder of the road to look around, he spotted Jim at the gas station up ahead on the left. He was talking to a girl. He couldn't tell what she looked like from here. Moving up for a closer look, he was distressed to see the girl get into the car and Jim turn the car around. He was coming right at him. Surely he would notice Jacob, or at least recognize the car.

Quickly, Jacob pulled into the nearest driveway and held his breath while he tried to still his wildly beating heart. Glancing in the rear view mirror, he saw Jim drive by. He appeared to be looking the other way. Breathing a sigh of relief, Jacob backed the car out of the driveway and continued following the car up ahead. But this time he made sure to keep well back. He didn't want to get caught.

They had driven many miles before Jacob saw Jim's left tail light blinking on and off. Slowing noticeably, Jim turned onto a dirt road, oblivious to the fact that he had company. Another three or four miles down the road he turned right onto something that resembled a cow path or old logging road. Jacob lost sight of the tail lights. He was afraid to turn on his own head lights for fear of being spotted. Taking a chance, Jacob pulled up under a large chestnut tree, stopped the car and quietly got out. He hoped that his car was out of sight.

He followed the tracks up ahead until he could see the faint flow of muffled light escaping from underneath a door and around some darkened curtains. He quietly moved forward, darting from tree to tree. As Jacob approached the light, he heard a scream that was quickly cut off, chilling him to the bone. Jacob wasn't sure he wanted to know what was going on inside. He slowly tested his weight on the steps and was mortified when he heard them creak audibly. He looked from right to left but gratefully didn't see anything. The old rotting porch curved around two sides of the building. Jacob pulled close to one of the windows that had a tiny gap in the drapery. Pressing his face to the glass, he ventured a look inside.

There was an old gray Formica table and four metal chairs. Some of the leather had ripped in places and dirty fluff was sticking out of the holes like little mushroom clouds. There was a wood stove in one corner with a pile of wood thrown haphazardly beside it. He could see part of a bed through a partially opened door to a room which he assumed was the bedroom. There was a light on inside but Jacob couldn't see anything. Moving along the wall with his hands, he tried to find out where Jim and the girl had gone.

All of a sudden he sensed, rather than heard, someone behind him. Whirling in surprise, he squinted as the light from a flashlight pinned him to the wall.

"I figured it was probably you. I saw you following me on the way to Fulson. There's not much point standing out here, boy. You might as well come in and share in the action," he said as he turned and walked into the house.

"Maybe I should just go, Jim," he stammered. "I shouldn't have followed you but I was curious to find out where you go all the time. I didn't realize that you just had a date. I'll see you back at the house," he said as he started to walk the other way.

The sound of a gun being cocked made him freeze in his tracks.

"I asked you to join us…Now!"

His tone held no room for second guessing. Trying unsuccessfully to mask his fear, Jacob mechanically stepped inside. As he was led to the bedroom, he felt like his feet were made of lead. He didn't want to see what was on the other side of the door.

Just then, Jim stepped aside and Jacob was looking down at the bed with his mouth hanging open stupidly. The girl was gagged and her clothes were in shreds. Her limbs were splayed to the four corners of the bed and tied with course rope. Jacob could see that it was cutting into the flesh of her wrists. She wasn't very old and had sandy brown hair which was fanned across the dirty pillow. Jacob thought the girl was pretty, but she was obviously in pain. He stole a quick glance at Jim and saw him staring right back at him. The hollow look in his dark eyes was hard to read but what passed for a smile made the hair on Jacob's neck stand on end.

"She's pretty inviting, isn't she lad? Let's go out to the kitchen for a little while. I've got some good stuff that I think you will like. The chick can wait."

Thirty minutes later, Jacob was floating pleasantly along in a drug-induced wonderland. He giggled at hidden jokes and smiled non-stop whenever Jim spoke. Taking him by the shoulders, Jim led him back into the bedroom. This time Jacob was eager to have some action. He went quickly to the side of the bed and looked at the girl. Her makeup was smudged where she had been crying. He looked at Jim for approval.

"Can I...?" he asked with a daft grin pasted across his features.

"Of course my friend," said Jim with a wave of his arm as if he were bored.

Jacob reached out to stroke her hair and she flinched from his touch which made him angry. He slapped her hard and was satisfied to see her eyes go large and round in surprise.

Jim left his hunting knife on the nightstand and turned his head to muffle the chuckle that was seeking to erupt from his lips.

He slowly walked out of the bedroom and closed the door. The boy was his now. There was no way he would ever talk about what went on in here and Jim laughed softly at the rightness of it all. If he couldn't have the woman of his dreams and nightmares, then he would have her child. This was just getting better and better.

Once again Sarah was awakened from a deep sleep. This time she went straight to her parent's room. "Mom, Dad," she called softly, but insistently. Kate rolled over and was startled to see her daughter standing beside the bed.

"What's wrong, Sarah?" Kate asked around a yawn.

"I'm feeling the leading of the Spirit again, to pray for Jacob. God's telling me that he's in big trouble. We have to pray for him right away!"

Kate and Paul quickly threw the covers back and got out of bed. Pulling a housecoat around her shoulders, Kate followed Paul out into the kitchen. The small family joined hands around the table and prayed again for the soul of Jacob. They knew that a spiritual battle was being waged. About thirty minutes later Kate made some cocoa and they had a talk.

"Have you found out where Jacob is yet, Dad?" asked Sarah.

"I was talking to Cass last night. He didn't want to talk to me, so I had to convince him that we were only thinking of Jacob's welfare. Reluctantly he told me that Jacob has been staying with Jim, all along. And the guy wouldn't even tell us when we questioned him. Jacob went to the city with Cass and Chris a couple of weekends ago. He told me that Jacob has changed and that I probably wouldn't recognize him anymore. He also said that Jacob has been talking about weird things that are very unlike him. I couldn't get him to tell me anything else. So I think you have good reason to worry about your brother, Sarah. It sounds like Jacob is in big trouble."

Husband and wife looked at each other knowingly. They both loved their son and knew that he would have a home to come back to whenever he decided. But until that time, he needed help. He obviously wouldn't listen to them but maybe he would listen to his sister and Caleb. They had always been able to talk sense into him before.

"Do you think Caleb would take you over to Jim's house to talk to Jacob?" asked Paul. You could take my car. Maybe he'll listen to you two because he sure won't give us the time of day."

A smile broke out across Sarah's face then.

"That's a great idea, Dad! If he won't talk to me, he'll talk to Caleb for sure. He hasn't seen him since he came home and they always got along so well. I think Jacob really admires Caleb but won't admit it. It sounds like a great idea. Before we go rushing into anything though, I think we should pray about his situation for a few days. We need the cover and we don't want him to think that we're spying on him. It needs to look like it was a spur of the moment thing."

Nodding his head in approval, Paul looked in admiration at his beautiful young daughter. She was wise beyond her years.

"I'll phone Luke in the morning and see if he'll give me Jim's address," he said to nobody in particular.

With that decided, the threesome enjoyed each other's company for the remaining hour before they went their separate ways for the day. Rachel and Kate met for coffee at Ruby's.

"I don't know what's gotten into him Rachel," Kate was saying. "In the last six months he's changed into somebody I don't even know. Where did we go wrong? I just don't understand it. We raised him in a loving Christian home and he never lacked for anything."

Wearily, she looked down at her coffee as she absently swirled the cold liquid with a spoon. Rachel looked across the table at her dearest friend. She could feel Kate's pain as if it were her own. She'd been having enough trouble with Jonah. Luckily he wasn't as hard to handle as Jacob was.

"You haven't done anything wrong Kate, and you know it. You've showered Jacob with love from the very beginning and have given him a great Christian upbringing. He knows the difference between right and wrong but still has choices to make in life. You can't make those choices for him although I know you would rather he didn't have to go through the pain of wrong choices and their consequences. All you can do is pray that one day God will convict his spirit and that he'll turn from his present ways. You've laid a healthy foundation and now you have to let go and let God build upon that foundation."

That said, she took her friend's hand in hers and looked into her eyes. "Your faith is so strong, Kate. God hasn't forgotten your family. I realize that you know all this but sometimes when we're going through some really bad times, it's nice to be reminded."

Kate gave Rachel a smile that lit up her countenance.

"You're right as always, Rachel. I guess I just needed to hear it from a friend. Thanks a lot."

She signalled to Ruby for coffee refills. Both women smiled as they watched her bustling around. Ruby always seemed to be in a hurry no matter what she did. Kate wondered how Albert was able to keep up with her because he was totally the opposite. He was so laid back that nothing seemed to bother him. If he didn't get things done today, well who really cared. There was always tomorrow.

Filling the two cups with steaming liquid, Ruby smiled her approval. "You look like the weight of the world has been lifted from your shoulder's Kate. Was it my good coffee?" she winked mischievously.

"Of course it was," Rachel laughed. "It worked its magic just like it always does.

"Well, I'm glad to have satisfied customers. Especially when it's you two," she said as she turned to answer the call from another table along the back wall. Ruby had become a really stalwart believer since Rachel had been hurt, all those years ago. She was in the position to witness to people daily and never shirked that blessed duty. The Lord had found a tireless worker in Ruby.

The two women continued to sip at their coffee, blissfully unaware of the events that were waiting to unfold around them. Poweetan was going to be rocked to its very core and lives would be changed forever. Evil might prevail for a season, but in the end, the light would always pierce through the dense, cold darkness in victory...just like it had for countless millennia.

CHAPTER THIRTY-FIVE
A DISTURBING FIND

Jacob tried his best to focus on the work at hand, but he was having great difficulty. He was finding out that his body was requiring more and more drugs and alcohol to sustain him for any length of time and that scared the crap out of him. No longer was he just "partying" on the weekends. Every night was spent sampling Jim's vast storehouse of goods. He was such a good buddy to Jacob that he wasn't even charging him for most of the stuff. Jacob felt very lucky to have Jim as a friend. He had even shown him how to shoot up. Now that was a buzz and a half.

Jacob was enjoying his new lifestyle away from the ever-present eyes of his parents. He could come and go as he pleased, say whatever he thought and do whatever he wanted. Luke had spoken to him this morning, though. He figured Jacob wasn't giving his all to the job and his work was suffering. If he didn't smarten up soon, Luke was going to can him. He asked Jacob if everything was going okay and if he wanted him to phone his mom and dad. Jacob just about went ballistic. He had raged at Luke that what he did on his own time was his own business and nobody else's. Luke had conceded for the time being and had walked slowly away. Jacob wondered if perhaps it was time to find a new job where no one would keep tabs on him.

He couldn't seem to get rid of the dreams that kept invading his thoughts and there were large segments missing from many of his evenings. Normally this would have really bothered him, but given his deteriorating mental faculties, he just chalked it up to blacking out occasionally from the booze. Surely that happened to everybody once in a while, he reasoned. His eyes were red-rimmed from lack of sleep and substance abuse. He kept a small bottle of Visine in his back pocket so nobody would ask questions at work. Jacob was a ticking time bomb just waiting to go off. Unfortunately, he was totally unaware of the dark side that was taking over his psyche.

His god had become a tall glass of rum and coke. That's where he got his warm fuzzies from now. Slowly, he was losing a very vital part of himself... his conscience. And that meant he was treading into very unstable territory. A person's conscience was the stabilizer that told the difference between right and wrong, good and bad. If you could no longer see a distinction between the two, then you were following in Satan's footsteps...down a well-trodden path to a well-documented ending. But although Jacob was sinking in a quagmire of degradation, there was still a tiny flame burning within his heart. Once ignited, it would pull him back from the pit. All it needed was to be fanned a little and that's exactly what Jacob's family and true friends were doing for him every day as they lifted him up in prayer.

Jacob glanced down at his hands and noted that once again he had some rusty brown dirt under his nails. He wondered where he kept picking it up from. Maybe the car! He would have to check it out later. There had also been some brownish red spots on his shoes which he couldn't account for. If he didn't know better, he would think it was blood. But that was just crazy. He hadn't cut himself. He was sure of that. Maybe he would ask Jim about it. He might know how it got there.

Jacob had been to Jim's other place several times over the past couple of weeks. He never remembered much about what happened there but he could vaguely recall seeing two different girls there. It was funny, but he could never remember them leaving. Jim must have driven them home after he went to sleep. They always went to the other place under the cover of darkness. Perhaps he would go over by himself and scout the place out in the daylight. He really didn't know what all was over there. Maybe there was a river or something that he could do some fishing in. That's one thing he really missed about Poweetan. He missed fishing out in the middle of the lake. He and the boys would grab one or more of the old canoes that were permanent fixtures on the beach. They would usually take a couple of six packs and some sandwiches and make a day of it.

Jacob figured the town had probably been built around those old dinosaurs. It was a wonder they still floated, but mysteriously they seemed to be invincible. His mom had told him that the husband of old Lillian Bailey had made them by hand from guidelines that had been handed down from generation to generation. Nobody made them anymore, though. It was easier and cheaper just to buy one. You could get a pretty good fiberglass one for about $200.

Jacob could remember the hours spent together with friends. Caleb, Jonah and Mark had usually joined him. After lunch they would usually go exploring as kids were apt to do. Sometimes they found the neatest places.

One day while digging a tunnel out in the bushes, they had broken through the ground and into a real tunnel. A lot of wood and rock had fallen into it but after weeks of persistent labour on their part, they were able to clear out a couple of rooms that had remained intact. They had sworn an oath of secrecy and kept the tunnel opening covered and camouflaged.

Caleb told them that something bad had happened out in the woods to his mother before he was born but his dad wouldn't talk about it. That only added an air of mystery to the place and the tunnels had remained under wraps for the past seven years. For some reason, Jacob felt that his parents would be really upset if they found out, so they kept their mouths closed about their exciting find. As they got older, the place didn't have the same magic, so they eventually quit going.

Childhood adventures were slowly being replaced by real life teenage problems. Jacob stopped in his musings and vaguely wondered what he was supposed to be doing. For some reason, his thinking was becoming more and more disjointed. Oh yeah! Now he remembered. He was going to go over to the other place and have a look around. Jim said when he left this morning that he was going to Fulson on business and would be gone most of the day. Jacob wondered absently what business Jim could possibly be up to. It's not like the guy had a hobby or a job on the side. That was one more mystery about Jim that Jacob intended to unravel.

Pulling his keys out of his back pocket, he looked around to see if Luke had gone. He got into his old clunker of a car and sped away from the airport. He couldn't possibly work when he had so much stuff going on in his head. He irrationally figured that Luke wouldn't mind him leaving like this. He and his dad were friends after all. It looked like a perfect day to do some exploring, he thought to himself. A sneaky grin found its way into his features…and nobody would be any the wiser.

Paul sat in his office at the church and caught up on some correspondence that he had been slow in answering. He still found it difficult to go into the sanctuary since it had been desecrated in such a foul way. Cal Davies thought it was nothing more than a rotten prank pulled off by one or more kids. It looked like something used in a biology class. He had laughed it off and said something like, "crazy kids…" Paul had been quick to point out to him that the passage circled in his bible could very likely have been done by the same person who cut up the frog. It was too similar to be a coincidence. Reluctantly, Cal had agreed that it was a possibility.

Paul didn't like it one bit. Not only had his home been breached but he felt as if his own person and family had been violated as well. They were victims of a crime and a person didn't get over that quickly. It made you think twice about getting into the shower, or going into the closet or getting wood out of the basement. Paul found himself looking over his shoulder continuously to see if he was being watched. Walking past the windows made him wonder if someone was peering inside. He knew he was being foolish but a little part of him couldn't help it. He had tried to keep his feelings to himself so he didn't upset Kate and Sarah. Kate had confided in him that she felt the same way.

The house and the sanctuary had both been dusted for prints but whoever had done the damage must have been wearing gloves. They were obviously well thought out acts of contempt which were directed at the Winchester family, not some random incident. Somebody was trying to get their attention in a big way but Paul was unable to comprehend who would be upset with any of them. He couldn't stop his thoughts from returning to his wayward son again and again. Maybe Jacob had done something to anger somebody. It's not like it would be the first time he had ticked someone off.

Maybe he should try to talk to his son again. Paul felt inadequate for the job. Every time he tried to talk calmly to him, he only ended up getting exasperated. The boy could be so maddening. More often than not, Jacob would display his rebellious attitude and terrible mood swings. He was becoming a different person. Paul and Kate had finally gotten a chance to talk with him for a bit on their trip to Clarkson this past week. He had been openly hostile towards them.

He had cut Kate to the quick with his harsh words and disgusting outbursts of foul language. He had not been provoked into such a display and Paul had been at a loss for words. What could he possibly say to someone who seemed to hate him with so much malice?

Jacob's eyes had been dark and hooded and his hair which had always been clean and shiny was now stringy and oily looking. He still kept it in a ponytail which only accentuated the fact that he had lost a substantial amount of weight. His clothes hung on his abnormally lean frame and his pallor could only be described as sickly.

"Good Lord, what's happened to you, Jacob?" Kate had cried out in dismay. "You look ill, son. Please come home with your dad and I," she pleaded with him.

Jacob's response had appalled both of them. "You're not a part of my life anymore, so get off my case! I'm doing quite well on my own and certainly don't need babysitting anymore. Just leave me alone," he had yelled into his mother's face.

Kate had been shocked into silence. Paul had felt his anger rise inside him like a beast of prey. Nobody had the right to speak to his wife like that and that included his son. He would have slapped him across the face had he not turned on his heels then and strolled away with an arrogant swagger to his walk.

"I'm not finished talking to you, Jacob!" he yelled at the boy's receding back.

"Maybe not Dad, but I'm finished listening."

"You come back here right this minute."

His words came back empty as Jacob hopped into his car and roared off in a cloud of dust. The sound of his laughter drifted on the wind as the taillights disappeared in the distance. Paul and Kate hugged then and tears of grief had washed silently down Kate's face. Paul had no words to give her comfort and that hurt him more than anything. He could say nothing that would change the fact that the boy they once had known and loved no longer existed. Instead, he had just stroked Kate's back gently while she cried.

Shaking his head and rubbing a hand wearily across his forehead, Paul looked down at the workload in front of him that was vying for his attention. He picked up the pen and with a set jaw got back to the task at hand.

Jacob almost missed the cut off from the main road. Pulling a hard right on the steering wheel, he angled the car just enough to catch the corner of the road. It was a wonder he had ever driven this road in the dark. It was nothing more than a few barely discernable plots of dirt that was overgrown with tall weeds and wildflowers. Getting out of the car, he decided to walk the rest of the way. Coming upon the clearing, he was mortified to see what the place really looked like. The porch was a dilapidated roller coaster with slats of wood missing here and there along the length of it, giving it the look of an evil grin with teeth missing. Jacob shuddered at the pictures being conjured up in his mind. How could he have ever found this place to be fun and amusing? There was something really wrong about it. There seemed to be a black presence oozing out of every crack and broken window.

Slowly, Jacob made his way around the perimeter. Against the back corner wall was a tangle of bushes that didn't belong there. Pulling back the thick branches, he was more than a little surprised to see four chipped stone steps leading down to a small door. As he took a closer look, Jacob could see that although the door looked old, it still sported a shiny new padlock. He gingerly picked up the handle and tried to shove on it. It wouldn't budge.

He would have to ask Jim about this place. He didn't know there was another floor here and curiosity was once again getting the best of him. Putting the bushes back in their original place, he continued out into the back. There was not a lot of open space as the tree line had almost come to meet the house. It was mostly moss, dirt and rock with a bit of grass thrown in for good measure. Little to no care whatsoever had been given this property. It had never seen a lawnmower or a gardening tool. It was kind of dark under the thick canopy of foliage and Jacob had to squint in places to really see.

Walking a little bit further, he shouted out in pain as his foot caught on a root and he pitched forward on his face, scraping up his hands in the process. He sat up and looked around while licking the scrape to stop the bleeding. The rock he had fallen over had been moved to that place. He could see chunks of dirt and grass clinging to the topside of it as if it had been pulled up from somewhere else and deposited here. Moving on hands and knees, he pulled the rock away. There was nothing there but more dirt. He raked his fingers across it and was surprised to feel the cool earth moving easily under his fingertips. Beginning to scoop in earnest, he had only dug down about six inches before he noticed some hair sticking out of the opening he had made.

Pulling his hand back in revulsion, Jacob jumped up and stared down into the small hole. The first thing that came to mind was that he had stumbled upon some old grave. Who could possibly be buried here, he wondered? It had obviously been dug fairly recently and Jacob shuddered involuntarily. Moving the dirt back to its previous place with the side of his boot, he tapped it down and put the rock back on top of it.

Jacob wasn't sure he wanted to know who lay deep under his feet. Wiping a dirty hand across his slick forehead he moved quickly away from the offensive spot. If nothing else, his one question had been answered. There was no sparkling lake waiting invitingly in the back of the house. All there appeared to be were trees, trees and more trees.

Walking around to the front of the house he climbed the rickety stairs and tried the front door. It was also locked which didn't surprise him in the least. Turning the corner he tried to raise the first window but it wouldn't move. Looking closer, he could see where someone had driven nails deep into the frame. He had to laugh to himself. This was not exactly a burglar's paradise so he wondered at all the locks. A thought came quickly to his mind and made him come up short. Was Jim trying to keep somebody out or was it something more sinister? Was he trying to keep somebody in?

Giving his head a quick shake, he tried the next window and the next. They were all in the same shape. Reluctantly he started to head back to his car. It wouldn't do to go breaking a window or anything. Jim would know…he always did. He glanced over his shoulder once and could feel the old place laughing back at him. Hurrying his steps, he reached the car and gave a big sigh of relief. Peering into the rearview mirror he backed up as quickly as possible. He had to get out of here and the sooner, the better. He didn't belong here. Maybe he didn't belong anywhere for that matter. Running his tongue across dry lips, he concentrated on the road ahead.

CHAPTER THIRTY-SIX
SEEDS OF BETRAYAL

Caleb grabbed hold of Sarah's hand as they left the theatre. "That was quite the show, eh? I've never seen a tornado before, except on television. They are totally awesome," said Sarah. Putting on his most serious face, Caleb looked down at his favourite girl.

"It just shows me how awesome our God is, Sarah! We can look at how powerful a tornado is and know that God is more powerful. All I can say about that movie is WOW!"

The two had come to Fulson for dinner and a movie. Normally they were more frugal with their money but tonight was special for the young couple. It was their two year anniversary since they had started seriously dating. Walking leisurely down the street, they took in the sights and sounds of the big city. The pace was so much faster than they were used to and Sarah felt like a real tourist.

"I might as well be wearing a sandwich board that says, "I'm a hick! Just lend me a camera," she laughed.

Gently squeezing her hand he smiled down at her.

"Surely we're not that bad? As long as we don't do the oooh's and awww's too loudly, I think we'll make it out of here without someone calling us hayseeds."

Caleb could see the restaurant of their choice across the street about half a block up. A simple wooden sign read, "THE GALLEY". Caleb had eaten there on several occasions and vowed that the food could not be beaten. He wanted to share this place with Sarah.

Crossing with the lights they started up the other side of the street. In what seemed like no time at all, Caleb steered Sarah into the restaurant. It took a few seconds for them to adjust their eyes. The place looked like an ancient Spanish galleon. Oils lamps on the tables invited guests to join in on the mystery of the high seas. Heavy nets and ropes hung from the ceiling and every corner of the place had displays in them, complete with pirates, old guns, treasure chests and maps. A man dressed in the typical garb of a pirate escorted them to a table about three quarters of the way back.

The menu resembled a treasure map and contained such delicacies as seafood, meat platters and a vast assortment of delicious sounding pasta dishes.

"It all looks positively delightful, Caleb. I don't think I can make up my mind," Sarah smiled.

"Let me order for you then, just like in the movies."

With a flourish, he signalled to the waiter that they were ready to order. While they were waiting, they sipped on large glasses of pop filled to the brim with ice.

"This place is wonderful. Wherever did you find it?" asked Sarah with mock coyness. "I suppose you took your other dates here as well?" She couldn't maintain the act for long and started laughing.

"I used to come here with a couple of guys from Youth for Christ. It was recommended to us by our leader. Now don't you look at me like that! I'm telling the truth," he grinned.

She looked at him with loving eyes and smiled back. Every time he smiled, his dimples would crease both of his cheeks. He could be a male model, she thought to herself. And the most wonderful thing of all was the fact that he was as beautiful on the inside as he was on the outside and Sarah felt truly blessed to have him as a boyfriend.

The rest of the evening passed quickly as they hungrily devoured Caesar salads and shrimp linguine in garlic sauce. Just before the waiter brought the check he came to their table and handed Sarah a bunch of lovely red roses. "For me?" she asked shyly.

Handing them to her, he just bowed deeply and quietly left them in her arms. She pulled the card from them and read aloud. "To-Sarah. These flowers represent the love that has blossomed in my heart for you for a very long time. Their beauty is only exceeded by your own sweet face. Love forever, Caleb." Sarah looked up from her reading with shining eyes.

"They're beautiful, Caleb," she said softly. "How did you know they were my favourites?"

"I asked your mother of course. She was more than willing to spill the beans," he said with a boyish smirk.

"You mean she knew about this all along and never said anything? Wait until I see her," Sarah laughed.

They talked for several more minutes, paid the bill and then left the restaurant. Dusk had turned into darkness as they found Paul's car and Caleb got behind the wheel. "Another two months and you can drive me around. You are going to try for your licence as soon as you have your birthday aren't you?" he asked.

"You bet I am. I won't need it much, but it would be nice to have in case of an emergency. You never know when you'll have to get somewhere fast. I hate asking mom and dad for a ride every time I have to go someplace," she added. That said, the two settled in for the long drive home.

As they neared Poweetan, Caleb had an idea. "What if we just keep going and see if we can talk some sense into Jacob?"

"It would be past my curfew by the time I got home, Caleb. It's already ten o'clock".

"Maybe you're right Sarah. Tomorrow is Saturday and I don't have anything planned, how about you?" he asked.

"I've got nothing planned either but I'll have to check with mom and dad first. Call me in the morning and I'll let you know. I think dad would like us to go and see him pretty soon. He said that Jacob has really changed. I know he'll listen to you Caleb. He always has."

Pulling into the Winchester driveway, Caleb stopped the car and walked Sarah to the front door. Since the break-in, they were all overly cautious when entering the house. He pulled her into his arms, careful not to crush her flowers. Inclining his face toward hers, he gently kissed her on the lips.

"Thank you for a wonderful evening, Sarah. I'll talk to you in the morning".

"Goodnight Caleb. Thanks for everything. It was a perfect night," she added. Glancing demurely over her shoulder as he waited for her, she opened the door and gently closed it behind her.

Resting her back against the door she kicked off her shoes and prepared herself to give her parents the play by play of all that went on that night. Her mother would be most eager to hear all the romantic details, she thought to herself with a smile.

Jacob went over to Jim in the kitchen a few days after he had come across his grisly find in the backyard of the other place. Building up his nerve had been difficult but Jacob knew he would have no peace of mind until he found out who was buried in the grave.

"Jim," he began. "I've got a bit of a problem, man. I had never seen the other place in the daylight, so I decided to go over there and have a look around. You know…curiosity and all that? Well, I went out to the backyard it was kind of dark in the trees and I tripped over a rock. I could tell that it had been moved there from someplace else, so I picked it up and started digging."

"You had no business going over there without me," Jim fairly screeched at him. His eyes took on a crazed look and for the first time, Jacob felt real fear from this man. Jim jumped out of the chair, latched onto Jacob's shirt collar and pulled him to within inches of his face. "I thought I could trust you boy, but maybe I was wrong".

"I'm sorry Jim," he stammered uncertainly. "I was just curious, that's all. I didn't mean any harm, honest". His words spewed from him in a rush of anxiety. He wondered what Jim was going to do to him.

Relaxing his hold a little, Jim looked down into his face. "What did you find, Jake? And I want the truth because I'll know if you're lying."

Swallowing hard, Jacob told him what he had found. "I only saw some hair, Jim. I don't know if the person was a male or female because as soon as I saw it, I covered it up again and ran."

Jim looked into his eyes for a moment and smiled then.

"Boy, you must have been scared. It was just the carcass of a deer I hit the other day when I pulled into the place. I took part of the meat for the freezer over there and buried the rest of it out back. That's what you found. It wasn't a human body!" he laughed.

Trying to look like he believed him, Jacob forced a laugh as well.

"God, you must think I'm a fool. Sorry again, man. I won't go over there without you anymore. You can trust me."

He smiled then, while inwardly he was shaking all over. He knew that his first impressions were correct. There was no way he uncovered the fur from a deer. It had been human hair and now he was more determined than ever to find out who lay there. If Jim had really killed someone, Jacob wanted to find out for sure, because he felt that his own life may just depend on that knowledge.

Jim wrapped a large arm around his shoulders and led him to the table. "Come and try the new stuff that I bought in Fulson the other day. It will give you a buzz that's guaranteed to keep you sailing on a cloud for the next two days."

As he waved the powerful drug under his nose, Jacob felt his resolve melting and he smiled up into the face of his mentor like a lamb being led to the slaughter.

Later that day, Jim phoned Luke and told him that he and Jacob would not be coming back in to work.

"What are you talking about Jim?" he asked. "You can't just up and quit on me without some kind of warning or something! How can I replace the two of you on such short notice? Does Jacob's family know about this yet?"

Jim cut into the one-sided conversation with a condescending retort. "Sorry for not telling you sooner Luke but we were both offered a job that's a lot closer to home and we couldn't turn it down. Jacob's not here right now or I'd let you talk to him too but you have to trust me when I say that he's finished as well. We've both talked it over a lot. Do you think you could mail our last cheques to my house? You have the address," he added smoothly.

Luke had been unable to change Jim's mind no matter how hard he tried. Finally, in anger, he told Jim to go to hell and hung up on him part way through his verbal tirade.

Once again Jim smiled to himself. Everything was going along right on schedule. He was sure Jacob would be thrilled not to go to work anymore. He hated it anyway and Jim would gladly make it worth his while to stay at home. The kid was costing him a small fortune in drugs and booze alone but it was going to pay off in the long run. He had stashed away quite a handsome amount of money over the last few years.

What Jacob didn't know, was that Jim was only renting this house under an assumed name and the address Luke had, was only a post office box number. There was no way that they could trace him here. He couldn't help but grin at his own personal cleverness. The other place had been purchased by an old acquaintance of Jim's about fifteen years earlier. Unfortunately, he had come upon an untimely death. Shovels could be real hazards to your health if you weren't careful. He laughed aloud at his own wit. Jim had continued to pay taxes on the place as the mortgage was paid off. He just forged his friend's signature. It was really his place but nobody could trace it to him. Everybody just thought of him as Jim Adams and he was more than willing to keep up the charade. Jacob would lose his lunch if he found out any differently. It would all come to light in time though, he thought to himself as he ran his finger lightly across the scar on his face. For now, Jim would keep the mask on and bide his time. Things would work out in his favour if he just had a little patience and patience was something he had plenty of. He hadn't waited for twenty years for nothing. He would taste the sweet victory he had missed out on all those many years ago. They would all pay dearly for making him wait.

Nico had made the long trek to Canada in record time. Flying low over the Clarkson airport, he waited for the sign that would inform him that it was safe to land. After the third circle he was getting more and more frustrated. Where was that fool? Surely he didn't forget the drop off that night. It was the same time each month so there was no reason for him not to show up. Finally he saw the flashlight wink on and off twice. It's about time he thought. Lowering the landing gear, he swung the plane at a tidy angle and headed in. Within moments he was taxiing down the runway, while keeping the light in his line of vision. Coming to a halt, he waited for Jim to come to him. There would be no buying or selling tonight. He had his orders and Mr. High and Mighty had better well jump or he was in for a very long, uninterrupted sleep.

Always expecting the worse, Nico pulled the gun from the other seat and stuck it in his belt. He pulled his jacket around it and smoothed back his hair. He would be able to grab and fire it in an instant if needed. Climbing out of the cockpit, he reached over and opened the latch. The door swung up and out leaving Nico staring face to face with Jim. Silently he handed over the manila envelope and waited for Jim to read through the letter and count the money. Nico could see from where he was that there was a substantial amount of cash. The temptation to just grab it and run was almost overwhelming. Finally Jim looked up at him with an expression that made Nico's blood run cold.

"You had better hope this is some kind of joke because if it's not, you can go right back and tell your boss that I'm going nowhere. I have a very lucrative business happening here and I'm not leaving it behind," said Jim.

"I don't think you got the message clearly," Nico said. "He's not asking you, man. He's telling you and if I were you, I would do as he says because I don't think you'll care for the alternative."

Sticking his hand under his jacket, he stroked the cold metal and smiled in confidence.

"You don't seem to understand," said Jim. "I meant what I said. Nobody's going to make me go somewhere that I don't want to be. Now I suggest you get back into that plane and bring out the goods. I haven't got all night. I've got places to be and people to see, before this night is over."

Tracking Nico's movements like a hawk eyeing up its prey, Jim felt his muscles tense as he calmly waited for Nico to go for the gun that he knew was underneath the khaki jacket.

In the flash of an eye, Jim saw the reflection of light off metal. It only took him a split second to react. Grabbing his knife from the sheath resting in the small of his back, Jim flung out his arm and let fly with deadly accuracy. An astonished look of disbelief crossed Nico's features before his eyes glazed over in a final shudder of death. The knife quivered once in the left side of his chest and then stopped. Clicking his tongue in disgust, Jim pocketed the money and stuck the knife back in its special place, after wiping it clean on Nico's pants.

"People will never learn," he mumbled to himself. "Everybody wants to be a hero!"

Now he had to do something about the plane. It wasn't something that could just be hidden away, so he would have to fix it so nobody would know who else had been here. He could accomplish that goal easily enough. He went to his car and pulled out two bags of cocaine worth thousands of dollars on the street. It was a small enough price to pay to get the cartel off his back. He stashed them under the pilot's seat with just a bit of the bag showing. It wouldn't do to have the cops bypass his clues. Next, he pulled Nico back into the cockpit and sat him upright in the seat. He placed his fingers around the steering mechanism so he would stay that way when rigor set in. Eyeing up the morbid scene in front of him, Jim laughed at his own ingenuity. Everyone would just think that a drug deal had gone sour.

Because he had quit his job last week, nobody would ever suspect that he had been here tonight. And he intended to keep it that way. Things were starting to heat up quickly and it was just about time to move into phase two of his plan. Within the week, he was planning to move out of the house he had been renting and move into the other place permanently. No one would be able to find him there even if they did begin to suspect him. And Jim had made sure that there was no way they could trace him there. He was going to become a faceless, nameless entity and that was okay too. It wouldn't be the first time he had gone underground, only to pop up in another place as a different person.

He also intended to take Jacob with him. The kid was just like a puppet anyway. Jim knew which strings to pull and what bait to dangle in front of him. Mechanically, Jake would follow whatever path the drugs went on. He was addicted. Jim had managed successfully to talk him out of visiting his parent many times. He had been thrilled about not going back to work as Jim knew he would be. The boy was playing into his hand blindly and hopefully he would remain ignorant until Jim's brilliant plan bore fruit, but only time would tell…

CHAPTER THIRTY-SEVEN
THE MOVE

Rachel and Kate met again for coffee on Friday morning.

"It's really not like him, Rachel. He's such a different boy since you saw him last. Thanks for letting Caleb go with Sarah tomorrow to see him. He can drive our car if it's all right with you and Stephen."

"That's okay with me, Kate. I'll talk to Stephen tonight and let you know in the morning. What time is Sarah expecting Caleb to come by? He had promised to speak at the youth center in the morning, but I know he's free later in the afternoon."

"That would be fine, Rachel. I only pray that Caleb and Sarah will be able to talk some sense into him. He's got to come back home. I'm sure he's sick and needs some help. He's got to talk to somebody before he ends up hurting himself."

Pushing back her chair, Kate rose to leave. Cal had come by again to ask them some questions. Kate could tell that he suspected Jacob of doing the vandalism in their home and in the church. Although Kate and Paul had been unwilling to believe that their own son could be so wilfully destructive, they were beginning to suspect him as well. Nobody else had such easy access to both buildings. Cal told them that he wanted to talk to Jacob as soon as possible and that he was sorry for putting them through this.

"I'd better be getting back," said Kate. "Please keep us in your prayers over the next few days. I'm feeling rather anxious about something and I don't know what it is. And that scares me. You know what I mean, don't you? I know how much faith you put into women's intuition, or should I call it the prompting of the Holy Spirit?"

The two women looked into each other's eyes and knew a bond that no one, besides two close friends could ever have.

"Yes, Kate. I know what you mean. I've been feeling it too. Never fear though. Our children have been lifted up in prayer every day for weeks now. They are all in the palm of God's hands and I have the assurance that His good and perfect Will shall be played out through the lives of them. Only He knows for sure what the future holds and we just have to have faith that He will keep our children safe from all harm."

Nodding back at her friend, Kate put the money down on the table for two coffees and together they left the café. "See you later, Rachel," said Kate, as she broke off in another direction to head home.

"Goodbye, Kate."

Kate pulled her sweater closer to her body. A faint chill could be felt in the air as the afternoon wore on. Fall was just around the corner. Caleb would be leaving next week to go back to college and Sarah would be going into grade 11. She wondered where the time had gone. Sarah was not a little girl anymore. She had grown into a lovely young woman. Many people thought she looked a lot like Kate did when she was younger. The only difference was her hair colour. Where Kate's hair had been a mousy brown, Sarah's was black. But the face was very similar. She still talked about being a teacher when she finished school. She would make a fine one too, thought Kate.

Plodding up her walkway, she absently kicked at the leaves that had fallen there since breakfast. Yep, winter was on the way. It wouldn't be long before the chill of early fall gave way to the deep freeze that would grip this town in its icy clutches for many months to come. That's the one thing that had taken Kate a long time to adjust to. She had come from a city in the states. When she lived there, she thought there was plenty of snow. They should try living here. Everything slowed right down as most people were content to stay inside around wood stoves and fireplaces. Of course it was different for the kids.

She could remember the first winter after she came to Poweetan. As soon as the lake froze up, the skates and hockey nets had come out in abundance. The kids here didn't need big arenas to have fun in. The sounds of their laughter would ride on the winds by the hour. Not much work got done but that didn't seem to matter. There was a time and a place for everything and tomorrow was another day. Why worry about rushing things. She had grown to love this town and the people in it, very deeply.

They may have a diverse mixture of cultures but they complimented each other. Out here, prejudice wasn't an issue. People had learned to need and support each other because that's all they had. Moving into the kitchen, Kate began to prepare the evening meal.

Early the next morning, Sarah rose early to pray and do her devotions. She would need the Lord's strength before this day was finished. She ate a quiet breakfast with her mom and dad and then hurried over to the school. It didn't matter that it was a Saturday morning. The teachers would be handing out the sheets today so the kids would know which classes they were going to get for the coming year. Receiving hers, she glanced quickly through it. She was taking full classes at an advanced level. There would be no slouching this year, she thought happily. Sarah loved school with a passion. Ever ready to face a challenge head on, she eagerly anticipated going into grade 11.

But today she had other things on her mind as well. Sarah had a secret that she hadn't told anybody. The local driving instructor was coming by her house this morning as soon as her mom left for the clinic. He would take her through the paces of getting her driver's license in his own car. Only in a small town, she thought to herself. Watching her house from down the street, Sarah saw her dad heading towards the church. A few moments later, Kate made her way across the street to the clinic. She was home free. Hurrying from behind a large tree she made her way back home. She had only waited fifteen minutes before Ted Lange drove up. As he got out of the car, he waved and smiled.

"Are you ready for this, Sarah?" he asked mischievously. "You can always back out, you know?"

"Not a chance, Mr. Lange," she added brightly. "I've been waiting for this forever."

Getting into the driver's seat she reached out and took the proffered keys. They made three laps of the town. Ted made her parallel park twice. The first time she bumped lightly into the curb and the second time she was wholly successful. That had been her biggest fear. She didn't like parallel parking one bit. After fifteen nerve wracking minutes, she pulled back into their driveway, turned the car off and waited nervously for the verdict.

"Well Sarah," Ted began slowly. He was going to play it out for all it was worth. Sarah tapped her foot impatiently. "Your parallel parking is not the greatest in the world but I don't know too many people who are really good at it. The rest of your test was flawless and yes, you've passed! Congratulations."

"Yahoo," Sarah yelled out excitedly. "Wait until I tell mom and dad. They won't believe it. I've been keeping it a secret so I could surprise them. Thanks so much Mr. Lange. You don't know how happy you've made me."

"If you come by the office in about an hour, I'll have your temporary licence printed off for you. It will take a couple of weeks for the permanent one to be mailed. We can take your photo then. See you in a bit," he said as Sarah jumped out of the car and he slid across the seat and took up position behind the wheel. Slowly he backed into the street and headed towards the office.

Sarah was elated. She could finally drive. Wait until Caleb found out. He would be so proud of her. Running across the street, Sarah rushed breathlessly into the clinic to share her good news. Today is such a great day, she thought with pleasure. Nothing was going to put a damper on her good mood.

Jacob grabbed the last of the boxes and shoved them into his car. He had made several trips to the other place and was getting a little tired. Jim had told him that this would be the last time he would have to come back here and he was glad. It seemed like such a waste of money to keep paying for two places although Jacob was only pitching in a little for groceries. Now Jim would have more money to buy drugs. Never once did it dawn on Jacob that he was being kept. He just blindly accepted all the handouts as if it were his due. He just assumed that Jim really liked him and that he needed the company.

He didn't really want to live at the other place but there wasn't much choice. Jim had told him that the landlord was selling this house, so they would have to leave. The other house still gave him the willies but he figured that he would get over it soon enough. Maybe he and Jim could do a little painting and maybe fix the porch. He would have to ask when he got back there with this last load. Hopefully Jim would have put most of the stuff away by then. Jacob had been surprised at the expensive looking things that he had helped to box up.

"Where did you get all this stuff?" he had asked innocently.

"I've always been a hard worker," Jim said with a forced smile.

After driving for about thirty minutes he turned back onto the weed choked path that served as a driveway to their new home. He picked up three boxes and carefully made his way up the rickety steps. He pulled up short when he noticed Jim just standing there watching him.

"I'm back," he said timidly. "There's only four or five boxes left in the car. I'll have them unloaded in no time," he added as he pulled the door open with his foot and inched his way through and into the kitchen. He looked around in dismay at all of the unpacked boxes. What had Jim been doing all this time, he thought angrily? Jacob had been doing all of the work for nothing. He felt like he was just being used. Hearing a step fall behind him, he whirled around in surprise.

"Geez, you scared me. I didn't hear you come in. You can't keep sneaking up on people."

Seeing Jim's face up close only reminded Jacob of who he was dealing with. This man was not someone to second guess or get mad at. He exuded too much power for that.

"I have to go back to the other place this afternoon. I'm going to hand in the keys and get my deposit back. Better in my pocket than his," he smiled with a wink.

There was something about Jim smiling that made Jacob shudder. It never quite seemed to reach his eyes. They remained forever black and unreadable. After a quick lunch was consumed, Jim left Jacob to unpack the boxes.

"Get this place cleaned up kid and I'll make sure you won't be feeling any pain tonight."

That was all the incentive Jacob needed. A night of promised bliss was worth more to him than unpacking a few pesky boxes. Quickly he got busy. At least it was cooler out now so he kept the door open and played some tunes on the radio while he worked.

Meanwhile, an ongoing investigation was being conducted at the Clarkson airport. Luke had gone in to work, only to come across a plane that didn't belong. He had no idea how it had shown up there as they didn't often get incoming flights during the night. He was confused about another issue as well. How did the plane land with no runway lights on? Surely whoever had flown in would have ended up in the trees which stood tall and proud at the end of the runway. It had to have been directed in by somebody or something.

Luke had called the police before going near the plane. Two officers arrived within the hour and after only a cursory examination were on the phone to their chief. He in turn forwarded their message to the R.C.M.P. They were called in on drug related incidents. By the end of the morning, the place had been swarming with law officers. A large bag of crack had been found under the front seat. One detective was sure it had been a plant. The body of the man had been found in an obviously staged position in the cockpit. The county coroner had been able to pinpoint his death at about 12:30 the previous night. Luke was questioned about who had access to the airport during the night and if the gate was usually kept locked. They wondered if the runway lights were on a timer, or if there was a security system in place. Luke answered the questions to the best of his ability. He told them how two of his workers had just up and quit the past week but he was sure they didn't have a key to the lock on the gate. He only had a mailing address for them because he was supposed to send their last cheques there. The officers were certain that would be enough to track them down and ask them some questions. They were very interested in talking to them and finding out what they might know.

The guy in the cockpit was another story altogether. There was no identification whatsoever on his person. Nothing in the plane gave them any clues as to where the man and his plane had come from. The forensics team got to work on those minute details. Pictures were snapped from every possible direction and sent to police stations across the country via the web. Within days, they would have their answer and then things would really start to heat up.

Paul received a surprise phone call the day after the grisly find at the airport. The man identified himself as Lieutenant Tim Donaldson of the R.C.M.P. Immediately, Paul's fatherly ears perked up.

"Are my children okay?" he asked nervously. He was almost afraid to hear the answer but the lieutenant was quickly able to ease his mind.

"That's not why I'm calling, Rev. Winchester. There was a murder over at the airport yesterday and we're just following up on some leads. We are interested in talking to Jim Adams about his whereabouts last night. We understand your son lives with him? We don't have an address for them so we were wondering if you could tell us."

Something wasn't sitting right with Paul and then it dawned on him.

"Why don't you just ask them yourself? They work right at the airport during the week," he told him with confusion evident in his voice.

"I gather you don't know that both of them quit their jobs last week. When was the last time you saw your son, if I might ask?"

"It's been about three weeks since I last saw him. We haven't been getting along very well," he added lamely. "And I don't know exactly where he is staying. He told me to stay away from the place. It's been really hard on our family. We're at our wits end with the boy. Jacob has a friend named Cass Birwell. He picked Jacob up one night when they went to Fulson. He could probably tell you how to get there."

After giving the officer Cass's phone number, the lieutenant thanked Paul and promised to let him know if he found out anything.

"Try not to worry yourself, Reverend. It's probably got nothing to do with them. We just have to follow up on all the leads. I'm sure you understand."

The tone of his voice belied the fact that he probably didn't care whether or not Paul understood. He just had a job to do.

Paul absently tapped a pencil on top of his bible. He wondered if he should worry Kate about the phone call but realized that if their roles were reversed, he would want to know. Dreading upsetting her needlessly, he grabbed his jacket off the back of the chair and headed out the door. On his way to the clinic he stopped off at the Birwell residence. He had barely lifted his arm to rap on the door, when it was opened by an anxious Cass. He had just received a call from the police and was visibly shaken.

"Please don't be mad at me Rev. Winchester, but I had to give them Jacob's address. I didn't have any choice, did I?" he went on in a rush.

"Now Cass, don't you go worrying about anything. I'm sure they just want to question Jim. That's what they told me. I was looking for Jacob's address as well. I know you went over there once and I think it's time one of us went over there too, whether he likes it or not."

"Come on in for a second while I find a piece of paper. I'm sorry I didn't tell you sooner but he swore me to secrecy. He said Jim would kill him if he found out he had told anybody where he lived. Supposedly he needs his privacy."

Stuffing the slip of paper into his back pocket, Paul thanked the boy and headed on down the street. He was feeling better about things now. He would go and see Jacob himself. Maybe they could come to some kind of understanding and he may be able to talk him into coming home. Kate would like that.

Caleb talked to Cass as well. "Sarah got permission from her mom to go over to Jacob's place. We're leaving soon. I still have a couple of errands to run. Did you want to come along for the drive?" he asked.

"There's no way my mom will let me go. Not after the cops phoned and then Rev. Winchester came by."

"What are you talking about, Cass? I haven't heard anything about the police. We were just going for a visit and to try talking to Jacob."

Cass filled him in and told him about the murder at the airport the night before. Kate mustn't know about it or she wouldn't have let them go.

"I'll tell Sarah what you just said but she pretty well has her mind made up that she's going. It might be hard to talk her out of it."

Half an hour later, Caleb walked up the driveway of the Winchester home. Sarah was waiting anxiously on the front step. Jumping up quickly, she hurried to the car.

"I'm so excited Caleb. I haven't seen Jacob for almost a month and a half."

Caleb held up his hand and interrupted her.

"Sorry to burst your bubble Sarah but maybe we should wait for a better time. There's been some trouble over at the airport and the police are going to question your brother and that guy he lives with."

After thinking for a moment, Sarah's face brightened measurably.

"Then maybe he needs us more than ever. Mom said we could go and I really think that's where I have to be. Or maybe you would like me to drive by myself," she added with a twinkle in her eye.

"No way," Caleb laughed then. He opened her father's car door with a flourish and ushered her inside with a big grin. "After you, Madam!"

"Thank you kind sir," she said demurely. "And would you throw your jacket across a mud puddle for me so I won't get wet?" she mocked.

"Not a chance, lady. I just bought this jacket."

They carried on their silly bantering until they had left Poweetan far behind. Both settled in for the thirty minute drive that would place them at Jacob's apartment just before nightfall. You could tell it was getting closer to winter because the days were getting shorter.

By mid-afternoon, the police had found Jim's apartment, only to discover that it had been vacated recently. The landlord let them in, after saying how glad he was to be rid of the two.

"The younger one liked to party. He was a loud drunk. It's a wonder he could even drive sometimes when he'd leave here late at night. He'd go staggering past my window with a glass or a bottle of beer in his hand. The other one was just plain scary. There was something about him that made my skin crawl. He's been living here for some time. He's always been a quiet sort, so I can't really put my finger on what bothers me about him. All I know is that he frightens me. I'm glad they're gone. So what's this all about anyway? Have they done something wrong?" he asked.

"They haven't done anything that we're aware of yet. We just wanted to ask them some questions. Has somebody else moved in yet?" the officer inquired.

"Nah!" the man drawled. "I'm going to have to give it a fresh coat of paint. It's filthy inside. They probably never cleaned the place."

"I don't suppose they left a forwarding address with you, did they?" the officer asked hopefully.

"If they had, I would have mailed them a bill for repair costs," said the man angrily.

"Do you mind if we take a look around, sir?"

"Be my guest," the man replied as he stepped aside to let the two men pass. Leaving him outside, the officers entered the apartment and quickly got to work. They checked the garbage receptacles but they had already been emptied out. Next, they dusted for prints. They were able to find lots of latent prints. Hopefully, they would pan out. Other than that, the place had been straightened up. It smelled of stale smoke and the curtains looks wilted.

One of the police officers had left briefly and returned with a police dog named Lucky. She was adept at sniffing out contraband drugs of any kind. Taking her slowly through the rooms, they weren't surprised in the least to see her whining and sitting down in many different places around the apartment. Finally, in the bathroom they hit pay dirt as she started digging away at the carpet by the toilet. Bending down, the officer scraped some white residue off the base of the toilet where it had stuck to the condensation. Somebody had tried to flush the drugs but some had fallen unnoticed. Hopefully they could match it up to the batch found on the plane.

Going over the place with a fine tooth comb, they were unable to find any more incriminating evidence against the two. They shut the door behind them and headed back to the car.

"Keep this apartment free until we give you the okay," one of the men said to the landlord. "We may need to come back and have another look around."

"I'll do whatever you say, officers. I just want to do my civic duty."

Both of the uniformed men looked at each other and rolled their eyes. Each wondered if this guy could be for real or not. They knew they had their work cut out for them. This assignment wasn't going to be an open and shut case.

Paul had a few things to do at the church before he went home. When he got there, his car was gone. Going into the house, he was surprised to see Kate all alone. "Where's Sarah, Kate? I noticed the car was gone."

"I told them they could go and visit Jacob this afternoon. They were really looking forward to it," Kate added with a smile.

Paul felt like he had been kicked in the stomach. He should have called Kate earlier and told her what the police had said. Now Sarah and Caleb might be heading into danger. If Jim had killed the man at the airport, then he certainly didn't want his children being around him. He wondered if Jacob was all right.

"Are you okay?" asked Kate with concern in her voice. "You don't look very well all of a sudden," she added.

Then Paul told her the whole story.

"Do you think the kids will be fine Paul, or should we go over there too and just kind of check up on them? Surely they wouldn't mind once we told them everything. They'd just think we were being concerned parents," she said lamely.

Nodding his head in agreement, Paul went over to the phone. "I wish the kids had taken Rachel's car instead of mine."

"It's my fault," said Kate. "I told them that you wouldn't mind. I didn't think we'd need it."

"It's not often we've had a need for two vehicles around here but what I wouldn't give right now to have another car. I'll give Stephen a call. I'm sure we can use one of their cars."

As he dialled the number, Kate felt her tense muscles begin to relax. She was starting to feel much better now that they were going to be doing something constructive. And she needed to see how Jacob was doing. It had been far too long.

CHAPTER THIRTY-EIGHT
LOVE LOST

Caleb stopped by a place called the Pizza Factory on the way to Jacob's. Maybe some food would appease his old friend. There was nothing like a shared pizza to get somebody to loosen up a bit. "What's his favourite kind?" asked Caleb.

"He loves Hawaiian pizza, the same as me," Sarah replied.

"We'll have a large Hawaiian pizza to go please," Caleb said to the girl behind the counter. Carrying the box back to the car, Sarah smiled up at him in satisfaction.

"You're right, Caleb. This was a great idea. Jacob will love it."

Cass's map was not the most legible thing in the world and Caleb had to stop twice for more directions. By the time they made their way to the apartment, it was dusk. Getting out of the car, the two looked quickly around. There wasn't much to see. Both walked up the front stairs and knocked. Nobody answered. The landlord had left for the evening, but the two didn't know that. Then they walked around to the back of the house. There was another apartment back there. It was completely dark inside. Caleb could hear Sarah's audible sigh and knew she was terribly disappointed. They knocked a couple of times but got no answer.

"Let me take a look around the side for a second, Sarah. Maybe there's a light on somewhere. Just stay here. I'll be right back."

He gave her a quick squeeze before he rounded the corner of the building. She would always remember that squeeze as it would remind her in the years to come of the final moments she shared with her one true love.

Jim had gone back to the apartment late in the afternoon. He had spotted the cruiser parked in the driveway while he was half a block away. He turned slowly into an alley, stopped the car and got out. He approached his place by the back way. Nobody would be able to see him as the light was quickly fading. He ducked behind some hedges and then inched his way down the length of two fences. Before Jim knew it, he had circled behind the back of his apartment. Watching from behind some shrubbery, he noted the police dog coming out of the door. The officer with him was carrying a small plastic bag. He had obviously found something which he was carrying between his gloved thumb and finger. He couldn't hear much of what was being said to the landlord from this distance. He could just make out bits and pieces.

Jim had to wait for three quarters of an hour for the police to finally leave. He had told Jacob that he was going to take the key back, while in reality he was going to dig up a stash of drugs that he had buried in the back yard many months ago. It had been a wise precautionary measure on his part. Finally the coast was clear and it was time to make his move. Walking stealthily from behind the fence, Jim quickly went around the corner of the building and began to dig. Within minutes he had retrieved a large brown canvas bag with a rope tie. He was just covering up the hole when he heard a car pulling into the driveway on the other side of the apartment. He flattened out against the wall, lifted the pick axe and strained to see who was invading his property now. Jim couldn't let the cops find him with the drugs.

He could hear muffled voices and then someone started to walk towards him. The man was looking through the side window. He moved a little closer, until he was standing only inches away from Jim. The man thought he was alone. That mistake would cost him dearly. And then the unthinkable happened. Caleb finally discerned the shape of a person standing in front of him and a cry of surprise started to escape his lips.

His cry was cut short as Jim brought the pick down in a hard swinging arch and embedded it in the side of Caleb's head. The only sound that could be heard was a grunt and a thud as his body slid to the ground in slow motion like a marionette with its strings cut.

Jim pulled him back out of the way and waited for a moment. Sure enough, before too many minutes had passed, he heard a girl's voice softly calling out to her fallen friend.

"Caleb, where are you? Is Jacob home?"

She looked around quizzically, expecting to see Caleb any minute. If he was pulling a prank on her, she wasn't amused.

"You come out here right this minute buddy or you're not going to get any pizza."

Hearing nothing, she started to get really frightened.

"Caleb, come here please," she whispered. "You're scaring me. Let's just go home and tell mom and dad that he wasn't here," she said meekly.

That was all that Jim needed to hear. This had to be Jacob's sister and Kate's daughter. Phase three of his plan had just been handed to him on a silver platter and he could feel his loins heating up with each passing second. Two steps further and she was his. A quick chop to the neck felled the girl like a young sapling in a windstorm. He pulled her close to him and breathed in deeply the scent of her hair and stroked the smooth skin on her throat. There would be lots of time for this later. First he had to get the two of them back to the other place without Jacob finding out. Hopefully he would be too drunk to hear him come home.

He wrapped his jacket around Caleb's head to staunch the flow of blood. Lifting him like a sack of potatoes, Jim carried him back to Paul's car and put him into the trunk while keeping his eyes peeled on the surrounding area. Then he went back for the girl and carried her to the car. She weighed nothing compared to that other dead weight. He laid her down in the trunk beside her friend. He found a scarf in the glove box and gagged her with it. Jim went to his car in the alley and took out some rope. He tied her hands and feet. Jim slammed the lid with a feeling of absolute elation.

He got behind the wheel and slowly backed out of the driveway. He didn't need to get a speeding ticket tonight of all nights. The smell of pizza inside the car was overwhelming. He reached into the back seat, snaked his fingers under the lid and pulled a steaming piece from the box. He hadn't realized just how hungry he was, until now. Licking his fingers in delight, he savoured the food and his good fortune. Things were finally going to go his way for a change. Driving down the road in Paul's car, Jim ate to his heart's content.

Paul and Kate finally arrived at Jim's apartment about 8 o'clock that same night. They knocked several times and called out to Jacob through the door. The place was dark. As they walked back to the car, a man approached them from the front of the building.

"Can I help you? I'm the landlord here."

"I'm Reverend Paul Winchester," Paul said as he extended his hand.

The man shook it and looked confused for a second. "I'm afraid I don't understand. How can I help you, Reverend?" he asked.

"I'm looking for my son, Jacob Winchester. I believe he lives in the back apartment. Do you now if he's home or not?" Paul inquired.

"I'm sorry to tell you this but your son moved out his belongings over the last couple of days. The police were here this afternoon looking for something. It must be pretty big because they even brought in the police dog."

Paul looked at Kate with resignation. Jacob could be in trouble and they didn't even know how to get hold of him. He could have gone anywhere.

"I don't suppose you happen to know where he went, do you?" asked Kate hopefully.

"Nah, I'm sorry ma'am but I didn't even talk much to him. He just moved the boxes and the other one did the business end of it," he added. Kate asked one more question before they left.

"I don't suppose you noticed a teenaged boy and girl here tonight, did you? They were supposed to be coming by for a visit."

"Sorry! I was away earlier this evening. I just got home a short time ago," he said. I did see the headlights of a car driving down the road but I didn't see who was behind the wheel or what kind of car it was. I had no reason to look," he said apologetically.

"Thank you for your time. You've been most helpful," Paul said with a brief smile. Grudgingly, the two made their way back to the car. They drove around for a little while, but were unable to see Paul's car. The kids had probably found the place empty just like they had, and headed for home. Paul reluctantly decided to do the same.

They arrived home later, only to find it empty as well. Kate gave Rachel a call to see if the kids had gone over to their place, but Rachel said she hadn't seen them yet.

"It's only ten o'clock Kate. Maybe they went out somewhere first. I'm sure Caleb will bring Sarah home soon. Don't worry love. Your daughter is in good hands," she said with laughter apparent in her voice.

"You're right of course, Rachel. I'll talk to you later. Bye," she said sheepishly and hung up the phone. She looked over at her husband and smiled at him. "Tell me I'm being a worry-wart for nothing."

He smiled as he went over and took her in his strong arms. "A parent can never worry too much about their children, I think. It's just human nature that we want to protect them from harm. Maybe we should say a little prayer for their safety."

Nodding in agreement, Kate and Paul held hands right where they stood and lifted Sarah, Jacob and Caleb up to God in prayer. They were blissfully unaware that more prayers would be raised before this long night would be over.

Sarah began to regain consciousness in bits and spurts. Her brain was foggy and she found it difficult to register where she was or why she was here. She attempted to call out to her mother but something was pinching her lips tightly together. Thinking her mouth only sticky, she stuck her tongue out and endeavoured to rub it over her dry lips but they wouldn't part. It was a strange sensation that she was unable to come to terms with as of yet. Sarah strained unsuccessfully to move her stiff and sore limbs but they seemed to be immobile as well. She tried rolling over to her other side to get rid of some of the discomfort but she was wedged into place by something pressing up against her.

She could detect the faint smell of pizza and also caught a whiff of Caleb's cologne. Breathing deeply of the familiar odour she smelled something else that she recognized instantly from being around the clinic all of her young life. It was the coppery smell of blood, thick and pungent. A wave of nausea washed over her and before she could do anything to help herself, she had mercifully blacked out once again.

And in that blackness, Sarah felt a comforting presence with her. She could see herself reaching out to someone. A man's arm came into view and took her small hand in His large one. Sarah looked to be no bigger than a child and she knew in an instant that the other person was her heavenly Father. He was supporting her like an earthly father would protect his own child. And in that brief union, Sarah felt an overwhelming love fill her to the point of bursting. She wasn't alone now and never had been. And with that knowledge, came peace.

Sarah watched in fascination as her Lord released His hold on her hand. She felt a brief moment of disappointment as she watched His receding back, only to note with surprise that someone else was hanging onto His other hand and walking slowly beside Him. Curiosity forced her to stare at the other person's back. That walk looked so familiar. Sarah couldn't believe her eyes when the person turned his head briefly to look back at her. It was Caleb and the beautiful smile on his face would be remembered by her for the rest of her natural life. He was literally glowing with health and his countenance shone like the morning sun. He inclined his head towards her once and called back in a voice that sounded like water trickling softly over stones in a brook.

"Don't grieve for me, Sarah. How could anyone deny me this?" he waved expansively. "We'll be together soon enough. I love you."

And with that said, the image of the two faded from her line of vision and once again she knew only blackness. But the calm and assurance that filled her heart would never leave Sarah again.

Jacob thought he heard a car drive in but he must have been mistaken because Jim never came in. He looked out the front door after about fifteen minutes had passed but nobody was there. It must have been his imagination. About an hour later, Jim arrived on the front porch unannounced. By that time, it was about eleven o'clock and Jacob was well on his way to being totally inebriated.

"Where did you come from, man?" he slurred as he stood on shaky legs and wobbled to the front door. "I thought I heard you come home earlier but I must have been wrong. I didn't hear your car pull up," he added.

"I'm surprised you could hear anything with the music turned up so loud," Jim yelled at him as he went over to the stereo system and turned it down an octave or four. "It's a wonder you have any eardrums left," he said angrily.

Jacob vaguely noted through bleary eyes that Jim had dirt all over him. "What happened to you? Did you get in a fight or something?"

"My car overheated and I had to leave it when I was taking the keys back to the landlord. I had to walk quite a way before hitching a ride with some old coot, who didn't know how to drive anything except fifteen kilometres under the speed limit," he spit out vehemently. "You had better grab a coffee bud, because I want you to drive me back to the apartment so I can get my wheels. I don't want to leave it there overnight. You never can be too sure. That stupid landlord was some ticked with us for leaving without a proper notice. He's liable to call the cops and have the car towed away."

Jacob bought his story hook, line and sinker. He would have preferred taking a beer with him, but Jim was adamant. They could party as soon as he brought the car back. "We have all night," Jim smiled smoothly as he held up a small bag filled with white powder. "We'll be back in no time at all. Don't you worry."

His look resembled that of a fox offering to sit on the eggs in the henhouse but Jacob was totally oblivious.

The night proved to be totally distressing for the Winchester and Westcott families. When the two kids hadn't returned home by one o'clock, Kate started to come unglued at the seams. Paul was unable to bring much reassurance to her as he was upset as well. They sat by the telephone and drank cup after cup of coffee. Rachel and Stephen were doing the same thing, further down the street. They prayed for travel mercies for Sarah and Caleb and talked quietly together about everything under the sun that might be able to take their minds off the situation. This was not like Caleb, or Sarah for that matter. They were reliable and would have called if they were going to be late.

As the first streams of dawn began peeking through the curtains, they were both startled awake by the jangling of the telephone. It was Stephen, wondering if they had heard any word yet. Paul had to say no, and it was the hardest thing he had ever done. He was worried sick. Maybe they had been in a car accident or something but surely somebody would have called them by now.

"I'm going to go over and talk to Cal as soon as I get dressed, Stephen. Do you want to join me?" he asked.

"I'll meet you there in half an hour. My kids will be fine here, so I'll send Rachel over to your house to be with Kate. Neither of them should be alone right now. I know Rachel's been pacing the floor most of the night."

Paul hung up the phone and felt better knowing that at least they were doing something. Kate had her head buried in her hands and she was crying softly.

"Something's happened to them, Paul. I can just sense it. It's not like them at all. They would have called or something, if they could have. You know that," she looked up at him with pleading tear-filled eyes.

"I know," he said with resignation. "Stephen and I are going to talk to Cal in a few minutes. Rachel's going to come over here."

No more words were needed. The two held each other briefly and then Paul left the room to get dressed. He didn't know what to expect from this day, so he petitioned God to give him the strength to cope with whatever lay ahead.

Jim had driven Jacob's car back to the old apartment. He pulled into the alley, grabbed the keys out of his pocket and started to walk to his car. Jacob watched him in confusion. Leaning out the open window he called out to Jim.

"I thought you said the car was at the apartment. What's it doing parked over here?"

"It overheated back there and I just pulled it in here to keep it safe. Now stop asking so many stupid questions that don't really concern you," he admonished.

Jacob pulled out of the alley and Jim followed closely behind. In the back of his slightly befuddled mind, Jacob wondered why Jim hadn't taken any water to fill up his rad if it overheated again. Oh well, he must know what he's doing. He just wanted to get home. He had to cross his eyes several times on the drive home, just to make the two lines in his double vision go back into one line. Luckily, he wasn't stopped and they made it back to his new "home" safely.

CHAPTER THIRTY-NINE
THE CELLAR

Earlier that night, Jim had indeed come home before Jacob saw him. The kid was such a fool, sometimes. Jim had driven into the driveway and coasted past the house and around to the back. He couldn't risk having the headlights seen, so he shone a flashlight ahead of him from an arm extended through the window. He headed deep into the brush and trees. Branches scraped loudly against the sides and undercarriage of the car, but still he continued on. After driving a short distance he turned on the lights. There was no way Jacob would be able to see him through the trees. He drove another twenty feet before his way was blocked by a large pine tree. Going any further was impossible. Getting out of the car was impossible as well. A branch was blocking him in so he climbed out the window on the passenger side. Going around to the back of the car, he opened up the trunk and shone the light around.

The girl appeared to be unconscious still and that was good. Pulling the boy up and over the side of the trunk was difficult but once he was free, the rest was routine. Jim dragged Caleb into the bush and set him down with a thud. Walking quickly to the back of the house, he picked up a shovel, went back to the body and started digging a deep hole. He was getting quite adept at this chore. Going back to the car, he grabbed the girl and laid her on the ground. She had begun to moan softly. He broke some tree branches off with his bare hands and laid them across the hood, roof and trunk of the car. There was no way anybody would be able to find this vehicle unless they actually stumbled upon it and that was highly unlikely. Luckily it was dark blue in colour and not canary yellow or something equally stupid, he thought.

Jim was sweating profusely now and wiped the perspiration out of his eyes. Picking up the girl, his muscles strained from the exertion. He laid her down once again behind a tree by the house. Going back to the car, he picked up a large branch and started dragging it behind him in a side to side motion erasing his tracks from sight. Discarding the thick limb, Jim lifted the girl again and carried her to the bush at the corner of the house. He let her drop to the ground. His whole body was protesting the punishing workout he had just put it through.

Drawing the bush back ever so quietly, he went down the four crumbling steps to a small door. He reached into his pocket and extracted a small silver key. It fit snugly into the shiny new lock and turned effortlessly. Hearing a tiny audible click, Jim pulled the lock down and it separated easily. Slipping it out of the loop with one hand, he pushed firmly against the recently oiled door. It only made a small noise as the base stuck briefly.

He went back for the girl. Setting his heavy burden down, he felt around blindly until his fingers wrapped around the string hanging from a single bare bulb covered in dust. He looked around in satisfaction at the girl's new home… at least for a little while.

There were two windows set high in one wall. You couldn't see anything out of them because the porch had been built over them. The small dirty room remained forever dark and forgotten. The floor was just hard packed dirt with new pieces of plywood set on top of it in places. Jim had been scavenging items and sticking them down here for some time now. A couple of dirty blankets were bunched up in one corner with a small pillow. Spiders and mice had found themselves a haven in the mouldering mound. A rusty pail sat alone and discarded amongst some newer store bought items such as a shiny new chain, four lengths of rope and a couple rolls of silver duct tape. These items would remain dormant no longer.

Momentarily forgotten, the large bundle on the floor started squirming around. Jim went over to his prize and looked down at her in the dim light. Even in the dusty haze, he could see the resemblance between this girl and her mother.

Jim shivered in delight. He took off the faded yellow baseball cap which he had had for years and squatted in front of the girl.

"You have no idea how long I've waited for this," he rasped hoarsely.

He pulled her hair out from under the scarf and marvelled at the long black strands. She was truly beautiful he thought as he wound his fingers around the luxurious halo framing her innocent looking face.

Sarah pulled her head back as if she had been stung. Her eyes grew wide in alarm as the man before her continued to stroke her face, hair and arms. She tried to cry out but could do nothing more than make a mewling sound. It was no use. He was big and definitely had the advantage over her. Sarah looked down in dismay at the hunting knife stuck in a pouch at his side and felt her blood run cold. What this madman wanted with her was getting more and more apparent by the minute. She wondered how she had gotten here and where Caleb was. Then she remembered the dream and for the first time realized the significance of that dream. Fresh tears of grief washed down her dirty face as she knew in her heart that she would never see Caleb again.

Sarah felt like a dagger had been plunged deep into her soul and that the pain would never go away. She gave her head a slight shake and tried to concentrate on the here and now. Her life depended upon being alert and prepared. She would look for opportunities to escape although she didn't know where she was. Sarah decided to worry about that later. Right now, the best thing was to submit to this man's foul touch and not to get him upset.

She looked up at the small windows and wondered what she could stand on to reach them. All the time she was taking note of her surroundings, Jim was fondling her roughly. All of a sudden she saw the glint of steel as he held the knife to her throat. Her heart beat inside her chest like a baby bird trying to take flight but she remained absolutely still. He untied the scarf and she gasped for air, albeit ever so dusty. He forced her back to the floor with her hands tied awkwardly behind her. She started to cry out in pain but it was cut short by his lips mashing hard against hers. His blond beard was smothering her and Sarah tried to lash out with her legs but to no avail. He snaked his tongue in through her clenched teeth and to the back of her throat. Gagging uncontrollably, she bit down with what little strength she had left.

He stifled a yell and slapped her brutally across the face and head several times. Shocked into submission, Sarah's head lolled to one side and silent tears washed clean streaks down her otherwise dirty face. In anger, he replaced the scarf with a strip of duct tape and ran a chain through the ropes on her ankles and the rusty ring embedded into the wall. He placed the old bucket within reach although she wouldn't be allowed to use it on her own until she had succumbed to his absolute authority. That would come in due time he reasoned.

But first she needed to be broken and he was going to enjoy doing just that. Looking smugly down at his handiwork, he gave her thighs a few swift kicks and walked away. Jim pulled down hard on the string attached to the light and the room was cast into utter blackness.

"Enjoy your tomb my little one," he muttered under his breath. "Enjoy it like your boyfriend is," he chuckled, as he closed the wooden door behind him.

Luckily for Sarah, she had been unable to catch what he was saying for the loud strains of music floating down through the thick flooring. Jim had strapped fiberglass bunting to the ceiling but it was insufficient to mask the music. If she could hear the music then maybe someone could hear her too. She stored the information into the back of her mind for future perusal and smiled despite her grim situation. Sarah had just received her first faint ray of hope and she was going to hang on to it for dear life, no matter what.

Cal looked up from the work on his desk as the bell tinkled at the front of the station. He was surprised to see Stephen and Paul looking so serious and obviously upset.

"Don't tell me someone broke into your house again?" he asked in dismay.

"I'm afraid it's worse than that," said Paul unhappily. "Sarah went with Caleb to visit Jacob yesterday afternoon at his apartment. They left with Kate's permission in my car before I had a chance to talk to them about what the police had said. Kate and I followed about an hour later but we missed them. Their landlord told us that Jacob and Jim had finished moving out yesterday morning and that they had left no forwarding address. The police wanted to talk to both of them about the airport murder. We think Caleb and Sarah showed up at the apartment because the landlord saw somebody driving down the road around the time they would have gotten there. The problem is that they haven't come home yet. You know them Cal and this is not like them at all," he hurried on. "We want to report them missing and we want somebody to go and find our kids.

"You know we can't do a missing person's report until they've been gone over 24 hours," Cal said with disgust. He looked at the tired men before him who were his good friends. "Ah, let's just skip the paperwork," he sighed. "I'll radio in a couple of favours from some of the uniforms in Fulson. It shouldn't take too long. Sit down and have yourselves a coffee and I'll get back to you shortly. I'll put out an APB for your car Paul and see if we can get a trace on Jacob. I'm sure somebody has seen him. Do you think you could get me a recent photo of the kids?" he asked hurriedly. "If Sarah and Caleb don't show up by lunchtime, I'll fax the pictures over to the guys in Fulson. They can put them around a lot quicker than I can from this little office," he added.

That said, Cal got to work immediately and virtually ignored the two men. Paul phoned home and told Kate everything Cal had said. He asked the women to find a good picture of the teens and to send them to the station with Jonah or Mark. He hung up and looked at his friend sadly. They were sharing a parent's worst nightmare.

A short time later, Cal got up from his desk and came to stand before them.

"I didn't get a chance to talk to you earlier Paul, but when they do find Jacob, I'll want to talk to him about the break-in at your house and the church. I'm now fully convinced that Jacob was involved, if not acting alone. I understand you don't want to hear any more bad news right now but I thought you would want to know. I'm sorry, Paul," he said as he shook his head sadly.

"That's okay, Cal. It's not your fault. Jacob has to be responsible for his own actions, however wrong they are. He's been making some bad choices lately and they're now coming back to haunt him. I'm worried sick about my son, but right now it's my daughter and her boyfriend that I am more concerned about. Please find the kids, Cal!" said Paul through reddened eyes.

"I'll get Fred to man the phones while I go out myself and have a look for them. Give me the address of the apartment and I'll go over there as well. I'm sure the police over there can use an extra pair of eyes. I can talk to the landlord and question the neighbours. That's about all I can do for now. I know this won't help much but for now you might as well just stick close to the phone at home. I'll call as soon as I hear anything. I promise," he added with false bravado.

Reluctantly, Paul and Stephen left the station and headed back home. They wanted nothing more than to bring their wives some hopeful news but there was nothing to do now, but wait.

By the fourth day, the headlines emblazoned on newspapers across the country all screamed out the same message. "DRUG DEALER'S DEATH POINTS TO SOUTH AMERICAN DRUG CARTEL!" Relegated to page three in the local papers was another article…less flashy but still bearing a frightening message for those involved. "THREE POWEETAN TEENS DISAPPEAR WITHOUT A TRACE!" The story went on to say how Caleb Westcott and Sarah Winchester had gone to visit the girl's brother Jacob Winchester. None had been seen since. The writer asked that if anyone had any information regarding their disappearance or had seen the three in the last five days, would they please contact their local police station immediately. It went on to say that Jacob was also being sought for questioning in another matter as well as his roommate, Jim Adams. A photo taken five months earlier, showed the three kids posing with big smiles for the camera in front of the new youth center.

The forensics team was able to identify Nico d'Arva by his dental records and the lizard tattoo on his chest. Thanks to a computer generated photo sent out on the web, they were able to pinpoint his birthplace to Brazil. Brazilian authorities recognized him right away. He was a well-known drug dealer who worked for some shadowy drug lord. They had been looking for him for over a year. His whereabouts had remained hidden until his body had finally been located in the remote Clarkson airport in Canada. The coke found in the cockpit of the plane had been a high quality grade which was traceable to South America. Nico's family was notified and his file was closed for good.

The plane was impounded until the investigation could be completed. They flew it into the Fulson airport and from there it was moved to a large compound surrounded by a high fence topped with barbed wire. Specialists would take it apart piece by piece in the hopes of tracing it back to its original owner.

Kate took a leave of absence from the clinic. She lost about five pounds due to lack of appetite. She had no idea where either of her children were and was frightened to death. The police had been unable to find Jacob or Jim either. It was as if they had all fallen off the face of the earth.

Kate tried to keep every moment of every day occupied. She and Rachel had posters made up with the pictures of their children and drove around the neighbouring villages, towns, and cities. They plastered them on store fronts; in banks and grocery stores; on hydro poles; street lights and trees. She even got them a spot on the W.F.Y. television station in Fulson. They made their appeal to whoever had taken their kids to please return them to their families, unharmed. Stephen put a second mortgage down on his dental business and offered a twenty thousand dollar reward for the safe return of Caleb, Jacob and Sarah.

School resumed in Poweetan as usual except for the flag that continued to fly at half-mast to remember the missing kids. Things were not the same as students talked in hushed tones amongst themselves. All three had been popular with the students and teachers alike. No one wanted to envision what would happen if they turned up dead. It was too unthinkable.

Cass was full of guilt for giving Jacob's address to Caleb. He felt partly responsible for their disappearance and nobody could talk him out of it. He stayed pretty much to himself and had stopped hanging around with Chris. He even went so far as to flush his bag of marijuana down the toilet. There would be no more drugs purchased by him in the future as he had seen firsthand just what damage they could do in a person's life.

September was fast fading when Willis James, the landlord from Jacob's old apartment turned up the first solid clue that hinted at foul play. He decided that the old building needed some new parging around the foundation. He was digging down into the ground around the places that needed new cement the most. He didn't often go around the far side of the building because there were too many trees. The blackflies and mosquitos loved the moist and shady environment. On this day however, there was no problem as the bugs were pretty well finished for the season. It was getting too cool for them.

Digging under some dead leaves and wilted grass, Willis stopped to wipe the sweat from his brow. He sat down for a minute to catch his breath and grabbed a sip of water from the plastic bottle on the ground beside him. Enjoying the cool breeze on his face, he randomly pulled up grass with his hand for something to do. All of a sudden, the grass felt strange and he looked down at his hand. The dirt was a different colour than what he had been digging up earlier. It looked dark and spongy. Rubbing it between his thumb and finger he brought it to his nose. It had a faint odour of copper and looked a little like blood. On closer scrutiny he noticed some pieces of hair and threw the lump from his hand in disgust.

Willis got up as quickly as his old bones would move and hurried into his apartment. Phoning 911 he breathlessly told the woman on the other end of the line that he had found some hair and blood in the grass of his yard. The lady told him to stay on the line until someone came to his place. Within ten minutes a cruiser pulled into the driveway and a lanky uniformed man got out and followed Willis around the other side of the building. He set a plastic kit on the ground and opened the lid. Reaching in, he grabbed a pair of latex gloves and pulled them on. He gingerly picked up the patch of grass and looked at the underside. The officer took some samples and put them into plastic vials which he labelled and put back into the box. To one sample he added some fluid from another vial and gave the mixture a slight shake. It looked reddish pink in colour.

He pulled a walkie-talkie from the side of his belt and called dispatch for backup. Quickly he stood up and gathered his things.

"You had better come with me Mr. James. We need to keep this area clear until the investigators can take a look at this. They won't want things any more disturbed than they already are. Within the hour the place was swarming with police and someone had leaked the news of a possible clue in the disappearance of the three missing teenagers to the media. Already there were two trucks parked across the street and people were milling around getting their boom mikes and cameras ready.

The forensics team quickly put a tent up over the area where the blood had been found. They didn't want wind or rain tampering with the evidence and it would also keep nosy people from seeing things they shouldn't. Pictures were taken and more samples were gathered. There was a lot of blood here. This wasn't just an accident. Someone had bled out. They found more strands of hair with bits of tissue attached. A couple of maggots remained behind and they were gathered up as well.

The news people got snippets of information from one of the newer officers who had the job of putting up the police tape to keep everyone back. Within the hour, the airwaves carried breaking news that foul play may now be expected in the case of the missing teens. They didn't have many details but told their audience they would stay until they had more news to offer. One news team drove quickly away. They decided to travel to Poweetan to interview the families and get a human interest story.

The blood turned out to be human and matched Caleb's blood type. The search was stepped up from a missing person's report to a possible homicide and abduction. Police began a door to door search in a two mile radius around the site, while Cal was given the heartbreaking task of telling the Winchester and Westcott families what had been discovered. He dreaded taking away their hope but things were not looking good for the kids. Back in the office he slowly went over to the coat rack and slipped his arms into his official police jacket and hat. Professionalism would be needed today. He wouldn't be going on a neighbourly visit to see friends but rather to a serious encounter that could possibly shatter two families forever.

Pulling into Stephen's driveway at lunchtime, Cal stepped up to the front door and tried unsuccessfully to smooth out the wrinkles in his pants. He rang the doorbell and wasn't surprised in the least to see faces watching him from pulled back curtains all around Stephen's house. The only noise that could be heard came from a lone dog barking somewhere down the street and a banging sound coming from the garage. It was as if the whole town was holding its collective breath and bracing itself for the worst.

Rachel finally opened the door only to be confronted by Cal looking all business-like and serious. She noticed a news van coming down the street and felt her knees begin to tremble and go weak. "Come on in, Cal," she said while dreading whatever he had come here to tell them.

"Is Stephen at home Rachel? I need to talk to him as well."

Fighting the tears that had welled up in her eyes, Rachel walked with dignity to the back door and called for Stephen. He ran into the house and stopped short when he saw his wife's white face and Cal standing by the door with his hat in his hand. It took him only a second to read the situation and he went over to Rachel and held her in his arms.

"The landlord at Jacob's old apartment was fixing the foundation when he found a lot of blood buried beneath the leaves and grass at the side of his place," he began.

Stephen could feel Rachel shaking as his own vision started to blur. Neither one moved or said a thing.

"The police are trying to keep some of the details from the media but they did find a tiny scrap of blue poly/cotton blend material at the scene. They determined the blood to be human and the same type as Caleb's.

A guttural howl of pain escaped then from Rachel's mouth as she sank unconscious to the floor. Running to help he looked helplessly at Stephen.

"I'm so sorry to bring you this news. You know that don't you?"

"It's not your fault, Cal. Give me a hand getting Rachel to the couch, will you? Lifting the limp woman, the two men gently laid her on the couch and Stephen put a pillow under her head. While he went for a glass of water and a damp cloth for her forehead Cal followed him into the kitchen.

"We don't know anything for sure, you realize?" he added. "Until we have more information, we can conclude that the blood could be anyone's."

Stephen looked blankly at his old friend. "You don't remember, do you Cal? Caleb was wearing a blue T-shirt when he went missing. You just about told us outright that somebody killed our son," he said in a choked whisper.

Cal felt the colour rise in his cheeks. He had never been involved in a missing person case, let alone a murder investigation. This was a very small town, after all. In his haste and ignorance he had divulged too much information without checking his initial reports first. Had he done so, he would have noted what Caleb was wearing when he went missing and he could have saved these good people some unnecessary grief. He just remembered seeing all the pictures of the three kids together that were plastered everywhere. He was wearing a jean jacket in those pictures. Feeling ashamed and foolish, Cal told Stephen that as soon as he heard anything, he would get back to them immediately.

Rachel looked up at him with questioning eyes. Stephen made her take a drink of water and sat beside her and stroked her hair. Bowing quickly out the door, Cal walked back to his car. He had to wait before he could start the car up because he was shaking so badly. Nothing in his job training could have prepared him for this and he wished for just a brief moment that he had chosen another profession. He called for backup to keep people away from the Westcott house and then he said a quick prayer while he slowly made his way up the street to the Winchester home. He would be more careful this time with what he said. So far there was no proof that Jacob or Sarah had been harmed. They were still simply missing. There was still hope.

CHAPTER FORTY
A HEART GIVEN OVER

Word travels fast in a small town and before long, there were many timid knocks on the door of Stephen's home. Some people brought casseroles and desserts. One lady offered to keep Rachel's boys for a few days but Rachel wanted them closer than ever. Businesses were shut down for the day as if the whole place was in mourning. The only place that remained open was Ruby's café. She was swamped as people milled around drinking coffee and just looking for someone to talk to. News people came and went, trying to interview anyone who might have been close to the teens.

Just then a sound interrupted conversations throughout the town. It was the steeple bell ringing rich and clear in the cool autumn air. Back and forth it swung, peeling out its mournful yet melodious tune. People stopped what they were doing and left their homes, the school and the chores to stand in the streets facing the old Presbyterian Church. The front doors were swung wide open, inviting one and all to come in and taste of the ministering goodness of God. As one, they slowly made their way to the church and marched up the steps.

Religious barriers were broken down and the townsfolk joined together in silence. Paul came through a door that was recessed in the wall behind the pulpit. He was dressed in jeans and a cotton shirt. People were even lining the steps and sidewalk outside of the church to hear what he had to say. In a voice made louder by the speaker system, Paul told them what Cal had said. Rumours were flying fast and furious and needed to be nipped in the bud. Looking out at the sea of familiar faces he couldn't help but wish the pews were filled like this every Sunday.

"I have called you here today to pray collectively for the safety of Caleb, Sarah and Jacob. As you have heard, they have been missing for over a month now. I want to petition God that our children would be found quickly and that His perfect will would be done in their lives. Only God knows and sees the whole picture while the bible says we see things like we're looking through a hazy glass."

"We sometimes don't understand why God allows bad things to happen to His people but we have to trust that He is working all things out for our own good, even if it doesn't make sense by our human reasoning. Right now I can stand before you in confidence and say that whatever has happened to the physical bodies of our children, I know without a doubt that they are in God's care. Naturally we just want to have them home safe and sound but if that isn't the case, we have to be able to come to terms with that as well."

"And no, I can't say this in my own strength alone. Only God can get us through however many days we'll have to wait for some answers. He can give us the same strength and peace that he's giving the kids right this minute, wherever they may be. What I fear most, is for the soul of my son, Jacob. He doesn't yet know Jesus as his personal Lord and Saviour. If he were to be taken now, I dread where he would end up."

Looking down at his friends and into the loving face of his wife, he could see many heads nodding in agreement. A lot knew what he was talking about and could understand his deep pain.

"Let us now lift our voices in praise to our God and trust in our children's deliverance from the evil one," said Paul as his voice rose to a crescendo. He could feel the power of God washing over him as the presence of God's Holy Spirit made Himself known to one and all throughout the small sanctuary. Tears of joy poured from young and old faces alike as the Lord ministered to His people.

Almost two weeks after Jim and Jacob had moved, they were sitting in a dingy bar with some very rough looking guys. A female stripper was making obscene gestures to the men in the audience while they yelled out cat calls and obscenities right back at her. Jacob was feeling fairly mellow and it was only seven o'clock. Happy hour had been a great success in his books. One of the men with them had arms like tree trunks and was dressed from head to toe in black leather. He had a couple of gold capped teeth and wore a substantial amount of heavy jewellery around his neck. Another was covered in tattoos and had a nose, tongue, lip and eyebrow piercing. His hair was spiked on top and had been streaked purple. His T-shirt was a couple of sizes too small to accentuate his bulging biceps and he wore hip huggers adorned with large shiny brass buttons. Nothing like advertising, mused Jacob to himself.

The third guy looked absolutely normal and that in itself was frightening because why would a guy like that hang around with these two freaks. There must be something wrong with him. Jacob wasn't thinking in terms of what strange men they were because they had been buying the drinks. That automatically relegated them to a higher place of standing in his foggy mind. Perfect strangers had become best friends within a matter of two hours and wasn't that usually the way with alcoholics or addicts? They could befriend strangers yet alienate their loved ones. Maybe it was because strangers were more willing to put up with unacceptable and offensive behaviour because they didn't have to see it too often or see what it was doing to a person physically, socially, mentally and spiritually. They were also more than willing to laugh when you made a fool of yourself instead of making you feel humiliated, embarrassed and ashamed. The increased bravado could make the person feel more important and braver than they normally would have felt. They could say and do things that they usually wouldn't have had the guts to do sober.

Substance abuse changed a person for the worst in everyone's eyes but their own. And wasn't that just another one of life's little ironies? When Jim drank he became quiet and reflective. His eyes took on a calculating look that told someone watching that there was more going on in his head than first impressions dictated. Jacob was totally opposite. He was loud, immature and wanting to be the centre of attention all the time. He told corny jokes which impressed no one and tried to be the big man when all it did was make him look even younger than he was.

Thankfully on this night, he hadn't been asked to show the fake I.D. that Jim had got for him. That would have been humiliating. Jacob had listened to the men talking about something he couldn't understand for only a short while before becoming bored with the whole conversation and evening in general. He decided to go outside for a bit and see if he could drum up a little more excitement for himself. Surely there had to be some decent girls around here.

Pushing back his chair, he rose unsteadily to his feet and excused himself. "I'll be back in an hour or so," he slurred happily. "I'm going to see if anything's happening down the street."

He wove between the tables and headed out the door. He went up one side of the street and down the other but nobody caught his interest. He knew they should have gone to the city instead of this stupid hick town but Jim had some business to conduct as he liked to put it. Who was he to argue? Those simple drug transactions were keeping him a happy young man. Jacob wondered sometimes why Jim wanted to spend so much money on him without asking for anything in return but he always came back to the same conclusion. Jim was just trying to buy his friendship. He must have been really lonely before Jacob came into his life.

Sauntering back to the front of the tavern Jacob leaned against his car and lit up a smoke. He drew deeply and exhaled, blowing smoke rings to pass the time. Vaguely he looked at his surroundings. There seemed to be a lot of papers plastered to the poles and buildings. Actually, they seemed to be everywhere and it piqued Jacob's curiosity. He waked lazily over to one pole and held his lighter up to the picture on it. It took only a moment before it registered that he was looking at Caleb, Sarah and himself. It was the photo his dad had taken of them in front of the youth center. But what was it doing on a poster, he wondered with growing concern gnawing at his belly?

He looked around but saw nobody watching so he ripped the poster from the pole. He quickly walked back to the car with his head clearing by the minute. He sat down inside and turned on the interior light. The bold letters across the top of the poster chilled him to the bone. All it said was "MISSING." He noted that a description was given for each of them. He went on to read that Caleb and Sarah had disappeared about ten days earlier while going to visit Sarah's brother. It went on to state that the authorities were looking for Jacob Winchester as well. There had been a murder at the Clarkson airport. If anybody had information regarding Caleb and Sarah or had seen Jacob with his friend Jim Adams, would they please call the police right away? It went on to give a description of Jim in chilling detail.

Jacob couldn't believe his eyes. He felt a deep fear settle in on him as reality finally sunk in. His sister and best friend were missing. That was bad enough. He wondered where they were and if they were still alive. What must his mother and father be thinking? For the first time in months, Jacob felt some of the ice begin to melt from his heart and a sense of guilt and remorse started to take hold of him as he began to think of someone else besides himself.

Then something else caught his attention. He was wanted for questioning in a murder investigation. Jacob hadn't even heard about anybody being killed at the airport. He hadn't seen a television in months. There was also a description of their vehicles. Jacob got scared then and started to feel paranoid like everyone was watching him. He got quickly out of the car and ran to the front door of the tavern. Squinting in the darkness, Jacob gave his eyes a chance to adjust before making his way to the back tables.

Jim looked up in time to watch Jacob coming back to the table. The kid wasn't gone very long he thought to himself. He could read the distress in the boy's eyes and excused himself from the table. Having closed the deal already, Jim shook hands all around, thanked them for doing business and went to meet Jacob halfway. Putting his arm around the younger man's shoulders he steered him back towards the front door. As they stepped out into the cool night air Jim breathed deeply.

"What's going on boy? You look like you just saw a ghost," he laughed deeply.

He could see the kid had something rolled up in his hand and gently extracted it from his closed fingers. Seeing the picture put him instantly on the alert. Then he noticed that descriptions had been given for himself and his car too. That wouldn't do, he thought angrily. He had tried to cover up his tracks as much as possible but somewhere he must have slipped up. Jacob was getting to be a liability as well as the girl. He obviously couldn't be seen again anywhere in the vicinity. If there were pictures in this little one horse town, then he had to assume they had been distributed in many other places as well.

As if reading his mind, Jacob pointed to the storefronts, poles and stop lights. He could see what the kid meant. The mass produced posters were everywhere. They had to get out of here quickly before somebody put two and two together. Pulling his cap down low he told Jacob to slide across the seat and jumped into the driver's seat. He pulled away from the curb and headed back home. He would have to change the way he looked or they wouldn't even be able to buy supplies. And he couldn't be seen driving these cars anymore. They would have to change the colour. It would be so much easier if he could just knock Jacob out of the picture but he wasn't willing to force his hand yet. Jacob could still be used as a pawn to get at the one he was really after. Within forty minutes they were driving back up the path to their house.

"I thought I told you to leave the porch light on when we left. How am I supposed to see the lock now?" he asked angrily.

Taken aback for a moment, Jacob grabbed the keys out of the ignition and walked towards the porch. He slipped on the stairs and just about fell flat on his duff. Cursing under his breath he put the key into the lock by feel and gave it a quick turn. The door opened easily and the two went in. Jacob could stand the pressure no longer.

"Why do you think they want to question you and me about some murder at the airport? I haven't heard a thing about it. Have you?" he asked in confusion.

Jim just gave him an odd look that silently told him to mind his own business. The warning bells were starting to go off in Jacob's head but he felt like his hands were tied. What could he do but comply with Jim's wishes? If he phoned his mom or dad they were likely to turn him over to the authorities themselves. And who could really blame them anyway? He had been so rotten to them in the last six months.

There was a war raging inside of Jacob. He wanted to do the right thing for a change but he was afraid of what might happen. Although he was sure of his innocence, somebody wanted him punished. He figured he was being framed for something he never did. For the first time in months Jacob felt unsure of himself. How could he have trashed his own home when his family had only tried their hardest to bring him up in the best way they knew how? He began to feel sick inside but had no idea how to get out of the mess he had made for himself. He knew what his dad would say if he were here.

"Everybody has choices to make son and they have to live with those choices whether they're wise or not." He could almost picture him standing in front of him saying that and he shrugged sadly and went to his room to change.

A scraping noise caught Jacob's attention. The sound seemed to be coming from the floorboards. He had just stooped down to hear, when the music went on in the living room. He changed into something more comfortable and shuffled into the other room wearing big wool socks. He noticed that it was getting colder out. They would have to start building fires in the old wood stove before too long. Winter was fast approaching and it looked like it was going to be a long haul this year if they couldn't go anywhere.

"I heard some noises in my bedroom. It sounded like it was coming from underneath the floor. Have you heard anything before, Jim? We may have rats or something?"

Jim's eyes became hooded and he looked slyly at Jacob.

"Don't tell me you're afraid of a few mice and squirrels are you? And here I thought you were a big man!" he mocked. Shamed and feeling foolish, Jacob glanced up at him with a smirk.

"I knew that," he lied smoothly. "I was just joking," he added.

Jim knew better and decided to punish the girl for her foolish mistake. He would show her who the boss was and make her pay for her stupidity.

Jacob got back to thinking about the problem at hand. Maybe it was time to move on. He was facing a big dilemma. Should he just pack up and run far away where nobody knew him or should he do the right thing by turning himself into the police? He was innocent, after all. Jacob could feel a tiny flicker growing within his heart. He knew in an instant what he would do. He wondered when he had prayed last as he got to his knees beside his bed and poured out the blackness that had taken root within his heart. That heart had to be completely broken before God could enter in and as His Holy Spirit worked on him Jacob wept cleansing tears.

"Lord," he said. "I've really made a mess of things. I can't make it on my own anymore. I need you in my life. The rest of my family are so content and at peace with You, but I've chosen to turn my back on You for years now. I wanted to be independent and not have to rely on anyone but myself. I was so wrong," he cried out in earnest. "I give you my life Father and ask if you will forgive me for all the bad things I've done. Come into my heart and use me Lord. In Jesus' name I pray. Amen."

Saying that, he felt his heart fairly burst with peace. He wondered why he had been so determined to hurt his family. He would go to the police one way or another. And he would go out and become one with the streets if he had to until he found out who had taken his sister and friend. Feeling better than he had in years, Jacob found it hard to get the brilliant smile off his face. He now felt like he was in danger. His earlier intuitions about Jim had been correct. He was obviously hiding something and Jacob was determined to find out just what that was. All he knew was that the man out in the other room was not who he was letting on to be.

He had only opened the door a speck before overhearing Jim talking on his cell phone. The noise from the stereo almost drowned him out completely, but he stopped dead in his tracks when he heard Jim laughing hysterically at some hidden joke.

"My friends call me Jim…" he was saying mischievously, "but you can call me Tom." He laughed again. Jacob looked at him strangely and wondered who

Tom was. It just didn't make any sense to him. He would have to ask Jim about it sometime. He couldn't ask now because then Jim would know he had been listening in on his private conversation. Opening his door all the way, Jacob started talking away about something totally irrelevant and feigned surprise to find Jim on the phone.

CHAPTER FORTY-ONE
COPING WITH IT ALL

The Fulson newspapers headlined a bizarre accident in their weekend report. There had been a large explosion at the police compound where many vehicles including an airplane were being housed pending further investigation. By the time the fire department had been able to respond to the call, the whole place was a raging inferno. It took many hours to put the fire out and one fireman was injured when a gas tank exploded, embedding a shaft of metal in his thigh.

Nothing was left of the place except a pile of twisted metal and burned out wrecks. The authorities had no cause for the fire as of yet but they had good reason to believe arson was the culprit. The magnitude of the blast hinted that some sort of bomb or detonating device had been used. They would keep the public informed as soon as they had more information.

About a week after the posters went up around the towns, the police received a phone call from a disturbed girl. She told the officer on the phone that she worked at the Pizza Factory and that she had seen the girl and boy that were missing on all of those posters. The man took her name and told her to stay where she was. He would send somebody right over.

Half an hour later, the girl recounted what she knew. She had been working alone that night when the two had come in to order a pizza. "I think they were getting it for somebody else because the boy asked the girl what his favourite kind of pizza was. She said something like "he likes Hawaiian pizza, just like me." "That's about all I know," she said shyly.

"How do you know what they ordered?" said the officer with some derision in his voice. "Surely you get lots of people coming through the store every day."

The girl knew he was mocking her but was determined to get her point across. "I only work on weekends, sir, so I don't see lots of people," she added. "The reason I listened to what they were saying was because they were such a good looking couple together. He was really handsome," she said blushing, "so I couldn't help but notice him. I smiled but he only had eyes for her. And she was pretty. I remember wondering why all the good ones are always taken," she said quietly.

"I don't suppose you noticed what they were wearing, did you?" the officer inquired. The girl shook her head in the negative. I don't remember what she was wearing but he had on a blue T-shirt." She shrugged then. "He had abs. Who wouldn't look? It's hard not to notice someone like that when you haven't had a date in over three months," she said quickly.

The officer looked up from his notepad and smiled at her. "You have no idea how helpful you've been. By the sound of your description, you may have been one of the last people to see those kids before they disappeared."

A chill ran up the girl's spine and she moaned softly. "Thanks a lot. That's just what I needed to hear."

The officer rose from his seat, thanked her profusely and hurried back to the cruiser. Another important clue had just been unearthed. Now they would be able to say for sure that the two kids had made it here safely. So they must have disappeared shortly after. At least they had a starting point for their search. If the two had ordered a pizza for someone then they probably weren't going far or the thing would have gotten cold.

As the days of September drew to a close, the police were no closer to finding Caleb and Sarah then they had been in the beginning. Someone thought they recognized Jacob's car but by the time the police arrived on the scene, it was long gone. They could find no records of either Jacob or Jim having bank accounts. The license bureau only had the old address so it was of no help to them. They were unable to trace any credit cards to either of the men. They probably paid for everything with cash.

The longer the Winchester's and the Westcott's waited for news, the harder it became. They received a lot of support from the community as everyone rallied around them but it just wasn't enough. Nobody could know what they were going through unless they had lost a child. Kate tried to describe exactly how she felt to Paul on one of the many nights that they spent alone.

"I feel like someone has ripped part of my own body apart and discarded it. Why would someone want to bring harm to our children, Honey? Sarah and Caleb are such good kids and Jacob just needs some help. He's still a good boy. You know he hasn't always been this way. I find myself questioning God, Paul," she said from a heart full of pain. "I keep asking myself how He could have allowed both of our children to be taken from us when He gave them to us in the first place. I know it's wrong to doubt God's love and mercy but I can't stop these things from coming into my head."

Putting his arm around her shoulders, Paul hugged her close to him.

"I know you are hurt and angry Kate, but you know in your heart that God doesn't work that way. I don't know why He's allowed this terrible thing to happen, but I do know that He'll make sure something good, will come of it. We just have to believe that!" he said with passion.

Nodding her head in resignation, Kate looked into her husband's eyes and she loved him more than ever. God had given her a good man and she just had to trust Him that He would bring her children back to her. It would be easier on them all if they knew one way or the other if the kids were dead or alive. At least they could get some closure. This way was so uncertain. One moment you could be full of hope and with a word in the newspaper or bulletin on the television, that hope could be shattered in an instant. But Kate felt in her heart that her children and Caleb were still alive. She thought she would know if that were not the case.

Poor Jonah and Mark had been devastated. Rachel and Stephen knew that it would be so easy to put them on the back burner while they concentrated their energy on finding Caleb, so they made an effort to surround the kids with lots of love. Stephen encouraged the boys to tell him how they were really feeling so he could help them through their own grieving process. The whole family became closer than ever and talked about everything under the sun.

Jonah, who had become more and more rebellious over the past six months, had settled right down. He was pouring his heart into his schoolwork and being more careful about what he said when his mother was around. Since Caleb had gone missing, he had taken on the role of "big brother, mother's helper and loving son." With that role came a maturity which extended far beyond his years. Jonah was finally growing up. He didn't say much to his mom and dad about God, but he found himself praying all the time for Caleb.

Jacob was finding it hard to get used to Jim's new look. He had shaved his beard off and cut his hair up to his shoulders. The scar on his face which had been hidden by the beard was now very visible. He looked like a whole new person. Jacob asked him how he got the scar but he never did get a satisfactory answer. Jim had mumbled something under his breath and Jacob was unwilling to press him for details. Jacob had tried to use Jim's cell phone on several occasions but Jim always seemed to materialize every time he picked the phone up. It's as if he somehow knew what Jacob was thinking.

Both cars had been pulled around the other side of the house for the past two weeks and Jim had taken to driving an old motorcycle around. One day Jacob had attempted to drive his car out of the driveway. Before he had made it to the end of the path he was startled almost out of his skin when Jim stepped out from behind a tree to stand in the middle of the path to prevent him from leaving. For an instant, Jacob was tempted to just keep driving, but reason finally took over.

He knew at that very moment that he was no longer just a resident of this house but rather its prisoner. For some reason unknown to Jacob, Jim was not about to let him leave. From that day on, their relationship became very strained. Jacob tried one more time to leave about five days later but when he went to get into the car he noticed that all four tires had been ripped savagely to shreds. He didn't even bother to question Jim about it because he had the feeling that his very life may depend upon how quiet and unobtrusive he could remain. Another day found the cell phone snapped in two with the face cracked beyond repair.

Jim passed the time listening constantly to the police band radio that he had purchased on one of his forays to town. Jacob had no idea what he was hoping to hear but it was really annoying listening to static for hours at a time. Something else was really bothering Jacob as well. Jim spent a lot of time in the cellar. Jacob had watched him pull the bushes back and vanish from sight, many times. The door had remained locked and although Jacob had tried to jimmy the stupid thing, he had been unable to open it. He had checked Jim's room to see if he could find a key but he came to the conclusion that Jim must keep it on him.

One night he finally got up enough nerve to ask him what he did down in the cellar all the time. Jim just stood there and laughed at him.

"Isn't a man entitled to have a hobby?" he said sarcastically. "I've been doing some reconstruction of sorts. It's of no concern to you kid!" he went on. "Perhaps when I'm finished, you can see the results of my handiwork," he said smugly with a strange look in his eye. Jacob wasn't sure he really wanted to know what was down there.

To pass the days, Jacob took to spending at least an hour or so in prayer. He wished he had a bible but he certainly wasn't going to ask Jim to get him one. All he wanted to do was go home. He wanted to hug his mom and dad, hold his sister in his arms and tell them all how much he had missed them and how sorry he was for causing them such grief. He prayed for an opportunity to get away so Jim wouldn't be able to find him. If he didn't do it soon, the snow was going to fly and then he'd be stuck until spring. He didn't relish that prospect and determined to keep trying.

Sarah wrapped her arms about herself for warmth. The thin blankets did nothing to keep the cold out and she knew that it was only going to get worse. By her estimations, she had been down in this hole for at least five or six weeks. She had lost track a long time ago. The only natural light she saw was when the man opened the door to come and go.

For the first little while, she had feared that he was going to rape her or even worse and prayed fervently to God that He would intervene on her behalf and keep her safe from harm. But for some reason, he had not violated her and she had remained pure. She spent the long days and nights in prayer and thinking about all the fond memories she had of her family and friends. Caleb was never far from her thoughts and she mourned deeply for him. He had been taken from her before their love really had a chance to blossom. The only thing that gave her any peace was the fact that she knew where he was. He was in heaven with his Lord and although she missed him terribly, she knew that one day they would have a glorious reunion. That was the only thing that kept her from going insane. She would play games in her head by trying to remember all the bible verses she knew off by heart, or try to name all the kids in her school by order of grades.

Sarah had no idea what she looked like. Her jeans were definitely looser around the hips and waist and she still had the same shirt on. She had long since gotten used to her own smell and the feel of long stringy hair. She kept it tied back because she couldn't stand the touch of it. Sometimes when she was feeling really low and depressed Sarah wished he would just end it for her. She couldn't understand why he was keeping her alive. He must have some purpose for her. Maybe he was blackmailing her parents or holding her until a ransom could be paid. Whatever the case, she was beginning to get a taste of the bone chilling cold that would soon fill this place and hoped that something would happen pretty soon before she froze to death.

The man allowed her to have her hands free but kept her chained to the wall. The duct tape had come off a few weeks ago. Sarah had learned some fairly hard lessons before she was allowed the small bit of freedom she now treasured. For the first week the man had kept her tied up completely. He would come to the cellar four times a day and hold her over top of the bucket to do her business. In humiliation, she had learned to submit to him in silence. He had taken off her mouth covering but in her eagerness to escape she had yelled out for help. Unfortunately, he had been close by and when he came down the steps he beat her unmercifully. She never made the same mistake again.

About a week later he had tried her again but this time Sarah made no sound. Smiling in satisfaction he had untied the ropes on her arms as well.

"Now you can go to the john by yourself," he muttered to her. "Just don't try anything stupid. I'm only right above you and if you make a sound, I'll be down here so fast your head will spin."

Grateful to have some privacy granted her, she made a vow of silence. He didn't bring her very much food but she had learned to get by with less. When her belly growled now, she was able to quietly hum a song and take her mind off it. She seemed to get tired much quicker than normal but that was okay too. It made the time go faster. Smiling to herself, she closed her eyes and rocked herself back to sleep just like her mother used to do when she was little.

And the Lord looked down upon his little angel with an unconditional love that could never be surpassed. As she slept, He brought peace and rest to her bone weary soul.

Investigations into the explosion at the Fulson police compound found a startling discovery. It was revealed that C-4 had been detonated. Human remains had also been discovered underneath the burnt hulk of the airplane. It turned out to be the body of Nico d'Arva which had been taken from the morgue where he was being stored until his family was able to claim his body. The police had kept that news under wraps until some detectives could dig up any information that would help them with their case. They felt foolish enough, having lost an already dead body. They didn't want the media to have a heyday at their expense.

It was obviously no coincidence that both the plane and the pilot had been blown to smithereens. Someone had wanted to leave no loose ends and had gone to a lot of trouble to accomplish their goal. It was a professional job done with boldness and the authorities could only guess that the drug lords had taken care of their own.

The second week of October saw the first light snow flurries falling softly to blanket the earth with the cold and silence of winter. The people could still hope for one or two weeks of Indian summer, but it wouldn't stop the inevitable. Kate walked down to the lake by herself. It had been a very long time before she had been able to come down here alone.

After Rachel had been hurt at the old mine, Kate had dealt with night after night of frightening and cruelly graphic dreams involving the crazed Tom Erikson who had killed Katya. She was haunted by visions of him still. Just before he had thrown her into that cave on Mount Killaloma, she had gotten a real good look at his face. She would never forget that dirty blond hair and seeing that yellow baseball cap wherever she turned. He had been stalking her for months wearing that cap but she had been totally oblivious. Two more things would be forever etched in her memory. One was the scar that had run from the corner of his left eye all the way down to his nose, and the other was the shiny hunting knife that he had carried with him everywhere.

Years of living with a kind and loving husband who adored her and two wonderful children had thankfully dulled Kate's memories until she was finally able to put the past where it belonged…in the past. God had brought healing to her but it had been a long haul back. Sitting on one of the many benches built around the lake, Kate looked out across the water as she had been doing for years while seeking solace and comfort from her heavenly Father.

She prayed again as she did every day for the safety of the three kids. All she wanted was some kind of answer. Should she keep on blindly hoping for something that was never going to happen or should she put this part of her life to rest and get on with living. What to do…hope or grieve.

"Please Lord," she called out to the bleak looking skies. "I need your direction. Help me Father," she cried as the tears once again washed down her face.

Feeling renewed and refreshed she slowly headed towards the path which would take her back to town. When she got to the fork in the path she felt indecision taking hold of her. Ever since the incident at the mine, she always took the path to the right which totally avoided the old site. For some reason, she felt drawn to the other path. It had been such a long time since she had been there but her steps followed the barely discernable path with inbred familiarity. Kate's step slowed as a large overgrown hill came into her line of vision.

Grass, weeds and wildflowers had quite obviously flourished on the mound. But now the vegetation just lay wilted and dying as the snow fell lightly to blanket and disguise its once ugly face. Looking around in relief, Kate noted that the place no longer held any threat for her. She was no fool and knew in her heart that the town's children still played around here. It was just a sixth sense that most mothers could attest to. Like children from the beginning of time, when told not to do something or not to go near a place, they were more apt to be drawn to that thing like sand to a magnet, than ever before.

Slowly Kate climbed up the hill and headed towards a place where a gnarled tree stood with its back bending in the wind that was gradually picking up. She rested her hand against the now leafless spectre to catch her breath. There was a time not so long ago when a short hike like that wouldn't have left her winded. She whistled to mask the fear that was attempting to make itself known once again. Stiffly, Kate got down on her hands and knees and started brushing the snow and leaves away.

Although the landscape had changed drastically since the mine had been blown, she would never forget this tree. It forever marked the place where she and Stephen had found Hunter digging and howling. Brushing some leaves away, she saw that five boards had been laid across the hole. Brown grass was hanging limply from each and the ground made a sucking noise as she pulled up on them. Kate peered down into an opening which had been made larger by one or more industrious children.

Smiling despite herself, she pulled up a homemade ladder made from pieces cut from an old broom handle and some thick fraying rope. So this was the secret place where the kids had spent so much time. It hadn't been used for a long time by the look of the ladder and that was all the better. Some things were best left alone.

Replacing the boards where she had found them, Kate stood and rubbed her stiffened knees. She had no idea why she had come here but was glad that her fears had been licked once and for all. Perhaps this place had come full circle. It had started as a hill, been destroyed by man and was now a hill again. That was like everything in life. A person was formed from the dust of the earth. He or she would exist for a small time and go back to the dust of the earth. There was a time for everything and everything had its own season. There was a seeming rightness to her musings that Kate was drawing strength from and she felt a deep sense of peace wash over here.

All of a sudden she remembered a vow she had taken long ago when her children were infants. One warm summer night she and Paul had taken Jacob out under the stars and lifted him high up in the air. They had offered God their baby son and dedicated him right then and there. They had thanked God for blessing them and promised to nurture and look after Jacob until God called him home as His own. Two years later, they had repeated the process with their baby girl, Sarah. In her anguish, Kate had all but forgotten about those incidents but she was being reminded of them now.

Finally she understood. All this time she had been angry at God for letting someone take HER children when in reality she had given God the custody of them a long time ago. They were His children not hers and who better to look after them then a loving heavenly Father. Wherever they were at this precise moment in time, it didn't really matter because God was watching over His own precious babies that had been dedicated to Him at birth. Kate found herself understanding and began to praise her God. Her weary soul had found rest and her heart cried out in thankfulness. Making her way down the hill, Kate felt her step lighten. She couldn't wait to get home and share her findings with Paul.

CHAPTER FORTY-TWO
THE FIND

Jacob was just about at the end of his tether. He didn't have access to a phone. He couldn't drive his car anymore and he certainly couldn't walk out of this bleak area. If he walked to the left he would eventually come to the main road but Jim never strayed too far. He hadn't seen other places either although he was sure they existed somewhere hidden amongst the trees. He was afraid that if he took off running down the road, Jim would catch him. No! That wouldn't work at all. He would have to make a run for it through the woods. Maybe if he could take a fairly straight route, he would eventually find a road. It would all be a matter of timing. Jim never seemed to be gone longer than an hour or two even when he brought back groceries.

Jacob had been trying desperately to wean himself from the booze and drugs without Jim becoming too suspicious but it was so hard. Sometimes during the night he would wake up with the shakes and find himself stifling a scream from horrifying nightmares. He would hear voices coming out of the floor and get the distinct impression that he was having the life smothered out of him. Jacob knew that these were only the results of withdrawal but it didn't make things any easier for him. How he wished that he could run into his parents room and find comfort in their arms but that was not to be…at least not until he made things right?

Many times he had faked being drunk so Jim wouldn't suspect that he was up to something. On this particular evening, Jacob kept getting them some more beers, although in reality, he was nursing the same one. He wanted Jim to loosen up a bit. Then maybe he would tell Jacob what he was up to and why he was keeping him here against his will. Jacob knew that he hadn't killed that guy at the airport but he was more than a little certain that Jim had. He could read it in the guy's eyes. He wanted to know why? It just didn't make any sense.

"How did you get that limp?" asked Jacob with feigned interest. "Have you always had it?"

"Nah! I got caught in a mudslide many years ago," he shrugged drunkenly. I would have lost my life if I hadn't gone over an embankment head first and rolled under some thick brush. My leg got pretty mangled in the fall. There was nobody else around at the time so I had to pull myself off that mountain with the sucker hanging behind me. Unfortunately, by the time I was able to get to a doctor, it was too late to set it properly. So now I walk around with this god-forsaken limp. Why did you want to know?" he added testily.

"No reason," said Jacob. "I was just curious, that's all," he said hastily.

A little while later, Jim started to question him about his home town. He wanted to know about the people there.

"I spent a little time in Poweetan once," Jim bragged.

He began to recite details that had Jacob looking at him in amazement. The more he talked, the more agitated he became. He told Jacob that he had followed some chick there all the way from the United States.

"You must have really loved her to follow her halfway across the country," said Jacob with a wink. "She must have been hot, man!"

Jim looked at him strangely and then gave a lopsided grin that bunched the scar up on his face.

"Oh she was hot all right and I would have had her for my own pleasure if it hadn't been for her meddling friends. Maybe one day I'll go back and look her up again. A reunion would certainly be sweet and I can just imagine how surprised she would be," he added with a laugh.

"What was her name?" asked Jacob. "Perhaps I know her or have heard of her. My mom has lived there for about twenty years and she knows everybody."

"It doesn't matter kid," he mumbled under his breath. "That's old news and doesn't concern you."

Jacob shrugged and got Jim another brew. When he got back to the couch he could see Jim slouched down and running his finger absently around the rim of the beer bottle. He was mumbling incoherently, or was he? Straining eagerly to hear the one-sided conversation Jacob waited a little behind and off to the side of the couch.

"Damn mountain would have killed me too…she should have died…stupid to grab the wrong girl…but she'll cry and beg before I'm done with her…she took away my youth, but now I'm taking hers." He chuckled to himself, leaned forward a little and promptly passed out.

Seeing his chance to escape, Jacob went to his room, grabbed his knapsack and started throwing in a few essentials. It was getting really cold out there and Jacob didn't have any proper clothing. His boots were still at home, as were his warm sweaters. Luckily he had brought a jacket with him. He would need it before this little adventure was over. Jacob had no idea how long it would take to get to the highway but Jim would no doubt be unconscious for several hours. He would never get a better opportunity. He could feel his heart racing and sent up a silent prayer for deliverance.

He grabbed his things, took some money from Jim's wallet and quietly exited the front door and closed it softly behind him. There hadn't been much in the way of snow accumulation as of yet. He looked down and noted with dismay that Jim would be able to follow his tracks if it didn't snow a little harder than it was right now. He had just started running past his car when a thought pulled him up short. If he hurried, he could break into the cellar and find out what was keeping Jim occupied for hours on end. He smiled in satisfaction.

Pulling his keys from inside his jacket pocket, Jacob opened up his trunk and extracted a crowbar. He raced over to the corner of the house and pulled back the bushes. He gingerly stepped down the icy stairs so as not to fall. Jacob turned on his flashlight and drove the bar in under the lock. Exerting pressure produced the results he was looking for. He heard an audible ripping sound as the screws pulled away from splintered wood. He was sure that with the wind picking up, Jim would be unable to hear him, but he still held his breath for a few moments until he felt sure that it was safe to proceed. Jacob shone the flashlight around the room quickly. The place was a dump from what he could see. There was a table with some tools on it, a pile of rags or blankets piled up against the wall and a rusty bucket sitting in the middle of the room that just about took his breath away. It smelled like human waste.

Swallowing his rising gorge, Jacob stepped all the way into the room. He saw a string hanging and pulled it down. Immediately the room was bathed in dull light as dust floated lazily through the foul air. Jacob took in the surroundings with astonishment. There was a large metal ring attached to the wall with a chain going through it. It ended under the pile of rags. He just about jumped out of his skin when the rags started to move. Maybe I've startled a rat or something he thought with dismay. Then he heard the soft moan. That was no rat! Picking up the fallen bar, he carefully walked over to the pile of rags and looked down in horror. There was a person lying under them and he could see where the chain was wrapped around a too small ankle.

Quickly he grabbed a handful of the offensive material and threw it back. There was the form of a male or female curled up in the fetal position and cowering in the light. The face was so filthy that it was barely discernable. But it was the long black matted hair that made Jacob gasp in recognition.

Assuming that the person before her sleep-filled eyes was Jim, Sarah scurried back against the wall like a frightened animal. She whined like a kitten expecting to be beaten for some real or imagined offense. Her whole body shook from the cold and she couldn't stop her teeth from chattering. She vaguely wondered what he wanted now and if he would hurt her again. She heard him get down on all fours beside her and tensed up for whatever lay ahead. She stared into his face and frowned in confusion. This wasn't the man. It was somebody different, and then she heard a soft voice speaking to her.

There was infinite love in his words and she recognized the voice right away. What was Jacob doing here she thought hazily? Did he know the man who had kept her locked up down here? She tried to speak but could do nothing more than croak. Sarah felt Jacob stroke her dirty hair and felt tears of relief flow down her face. She thanked God that Jacob was okay.

"Sarah," Jacob said in a choked voice. "My God, what has he done to you?" He took her gently into his arms and hugged her to his breast. He kissed her face and hands. She weighed no more than a doll he noted with dismay. "Jim's passed out upstairs, Sarah. We don't have much time. We have to get far away from here before he wakes up!"

He looked into her large round eyes and realized his mistake in an instant. There was no way he could take her with him out in that cold. She would perish before they got a mile away. He was torn. If he carried her outside, she would likely die from exposure. There just wasn't enough left of her to sustain her body for long. And if she stayed behind while he went for help, Jim would probably kill her anyway. He felt absolutely torn inside. Could he kill the man who had hurt his sister like this?

His face had only begun to harden when Sarah noticed and weakly held up her hand. She had been reading Jim's face for weeks and was getting fairly good at it. She looked up into Jacob's face with eyes pleading. Sarah only had enough energy to get one word out. "Don't!" was all she said, but that one word spoke volumes and Jacob understood. His newly found Christianity was taking hold of his life. No, he couldn't kill, even in righteous anger. Only God had the right to take a life. His head might be saying one thing but his heart was saying something different altogether. He had to go and get the police. That would be the only thing that would maybe keep his sister alive. Her life would depend upon how quickly he could get out of here. Although her touch was light as a feather she looked into his face and smiled.

"Go Jacob!" she whispered. He wasn't even sure he had heard anything. Kissing her sweet face again, he gently lowered her back onto the floor. He wanted to go and get her some more blankets from the house but he couldn't risk it. Running out to the car he pulled the fake fur seat cover from the front and ran back with it. It was filthy too but at least it would be warmer. He wrapped it around her and looked down on her with love.

"I'll be back soon for you Sarah. Just hang in there if you can. I love you!" he added in a voice charged with emotion. Turning his back on her, he went up the steps and ran off into the frigid night.

In his haste, Jacob left the flashlight behind but there was no way he was going to go back for it. He would just have to manage without it. He ran and ran, driven on by the knowledge that his sister might not be alive by morning when Jim found out what he had done. He stumbled blindly time and time again but just kept getting up and charging ahead. After a while he stopped by some bushes to catch his ragged breath. Even in the cold night air, the perspiration was flowing freely down from his hairline. His lungs were burning from the exertion and he coughed several times. Too bad he hadn't given up the cigarettes too.

It was very hard to see in these woods although the moon was making its way through some of the foliage in places. Jacob called on God again for direction. He started walking quickly for a distance to give his wildly beating heart a break. He was feeling quite lost by this point in time. Looking around for some signs of a house or road he fell over some fallen branches. And in that instant the moonlight revealed a car. What a stupid place to put a car, he thought. On closer inspection, Jacob felt his blood run cold. It wasn't just any car. It was his father's car. There was no doubt about it. He pulled the branches away from the vehicle and realized that he couldn't open the driver's door. He ran to the other side and opened up the passenger door. I can never get a break, he thought grimly. There were no keys in the ignition. It figured. He could see a large pizza box sitting on the backseat. Then it hit him like a two by four.

The posters had described his dad's car that Caleb and Sarah had been driving. If the car was here and Sarah was in the cellar, then where was Caleb? Things weren't looking too good for him if Jim had been involved. The guy was capable of doing almost anything. For some reason, he doubted if he would ever see his friend alive again. And then he thought of something more gruesome still. What if he had buried Caleb in a grave like he had found behind the house? There was no point sticking around here wasting precious time. He had to get some help right away because time was fast running out for Sarah. Glancing back only once, he resumed his punishing run.

Morning came late for Jim. He rubbed his reddened eyes and tasted with disgust the fur coating his tongue. His head was pounding like somebody had taken a sledgehammer to it. He looked around and noted that Jacob wasn't around. He must still be sleeping it off. He hadn't been plastered like that for a good long time and knew why. There was nothing worse than a self-induced hangover. He bypassed Jacob's room and headed straight for the bathroom. Opening the medicine chest, he grabbed a large bottle of aspirin and chewed about four of them all at once. He grabbed some water in his cupped hand and swallowed. Looking in the mirror he barely recognized himself.

Losing the beard and long hair had really made a difference. He still wasn't used to it. He rubbed his hand across the stubble on his chin and decided to do without a shave for today. His guts felt too rough. It was awfully quiet in here. At least when the kid was awake, he had somebody to talk to. Going back to Jacob's room, he opened the door and walked over to the bed. He was just about ready to scare him awake when he went suddenly on the alert. The bed was empty and cold to the touch. Jim looked around the room taking note of everything as his eyes quickly scanned the contents. Maybe the kid had just gone out for some fresh air. He ran his fingers through his tousled hair and moved quickly to the front door, stopping only briefly to grab a coat before heading out. He could see the two cars still behind the house where he had left them. He laughed smugly. He kept the keys to the cars, cellar and motorcycle in a margarine container in the freezer. Jacob didn't know they were there and he intended to keep it that way. He knew the boy had searched the house for them and was pleased with his own cleverness.

It had stopped snowing sometime during the night and morning was crisp yet pleasant. Immediately he took in the jumbled footprints running helter-skelter all over the backyard. "My, my! Someone's been having some fun," he smiled. Then he noticed that a couple sets of tracks led up to the bushes beside the house. Quickly he ran back to the house and went to the freezer. The keys to the cellar were still in the container and he grabbed them and ran outside again. Pulling back the bushes angrily, he saw that although the door had been pulled closed, the lock was hanging from splintered wood.

Cursing loudly, he threw the door open and pulled the string to the light. Looking over at the pile of blankets on the floor, he noted that a seat cover had been added to the heap. He yanked them down and nodded in satisfaction that his prize was still chained to the wall. He woke her from a fitful sleep and Sarah tried to shield her eyes from the light.

"So, you had some company this morning, did you?" he said as he felt an insane rage take hold of his mind. "That big brother of yours sure showed you how much he cares if he just left you behind! That's love," he laughed hysterically.

Looking up into the crazed man's eyes, Sarah felt real fear. This guy's temper was volatile at the best of times. Now he'd been provoked and Sarah didn't figure she had much time left on this earth. She had to make him think that they didn't get along, and maybe then he wouldn't care as much that Jacob was gone.

"He never did like me!" she croaked from a throat made sore by lack of use. "He thinks I'm my mother's pet," she added weakly.

Jim huffed and threw the blanket back on her. "What time was he in here?" he shouted in her face.

"About two hours ago," she lied.

"I still might be able to catch him before he gets too far. The fool left his tracks all over the place. I know those woods like the back of my hand. He doesn't stand a chance." Going over to the table, he picked up an axe and smiled wickedly at Sarah. "When I find him, I think I'll give him a part for his hair."

He hurried out the door leaving Sarah to breathe a huge sigh of relief. Jacob had at least a ten hour head start. She didn't know how many miles he would have to travel before he found some help but she prayed that he would make it to safety soon.

Jim didn't need a bloodhound to follow the trail of footprints. The fool might just as well have lit flares and put arrows on the trees. They were as clear as mud and Jim was able to follow behind very quickly. It didn't take long before he noticed the large branches all over the place and the car standing like a sentinel, guarding the forest. So, the brat has made it this far. Looking beyond the car he saw that the tracks continued deep into the woods. Further on he knew that something was wrong. Paying closer attention to detail he discovered what had bothered him. He had just made a circuit with his footprints. The kid was no fool after all. He had doubled back and gone in a complete circle to slow him down. That meant that if he had time to play games, then the girl had probably lied to him. He had to have left much earlier than she had indicated. Jim felt a momentary hint of panic. Maybe Jacob had made it to the road already and was on his was back with help. That didn't leave him much time to high tail it out of here.

He would have to leave the girl but that was okay too. She didn't have a lot of life left in her and he had done what he'd set out to do. He had gotten back at Kate in a way that would hurt her more than anything he could have done to her physically and he felt a thrill despite his circumstances. He had finally made that witch pay just like he always said he would do. The only problem was that if he took off now and left the country for good, he would never be able to find complete rest. He wanted…no, that was the wrong terminology…he NEEDED to see the look on her face when the girl was found. She wasn't far from death now and he had to watch the woman crumble. It would be epic.

In his twisted mind, Kate had been the cause behind all of the problems in his life. His youth had been destroyed by spending time in a minimum security prison for a couple of years. He would have been there a lot longer had he not escaped and made his way north into Canada. It was Kate who had identified him in a police line-up and he had been charged with murder and put away for shooting her friend. Jim had just been having a little fun with his buddies and she had wrecked everything. He had traced her to Poweetan through a member of her old church and had stalked her for months in that bloody awful frostbitten town. She had tricked him once and gotten out of his grasp but he had finally nabbed her on Mount Killaloma.

He threw her into a cave and would have tortured her slowly, if that mudslide hadn't destroyed his chance once and for all. A long time had passed since then and he would see his patience rewarded or die trying. He'd come too far to be cheated now.

CHAPTER FORTY-THREE
JIM'S IDENTITY REVEALED

Jim Adams was finished with the deceptions of the past. It was time to become Tom Erikson again. He hated the name Jim anyway. Tom's bitterness had begun long before Kate ever came into the picture. He was an angry young boy who had grown into a violent and hate-filled man. His mother, Valerie Erikson had sacrificed plenty to keep her only son by a previous marriage clothed and fed.

Tom's father had been a cruel and cold-hearted man. She had met Allen in New York and they had fallen in love almost at once. He had told her in one of his more lucid moments that he had been married about ten years earlier, but his wife had died in childbirth along with their only child. She felt like she had to nurture him with maternal love and he played her like a fiddle. All he had to do was pout or whine and she would wait on him hand and foot. Valerie was nothing more to him than a live-in maid who kept him fed and serviced.

He treated her horribly, always calling her ignorant names and seemed to enjoy belittling her in front of her friends. He didn't seem to have any of his own, although he was forever explaining his frequent absences by telling her that he was out with his buddies or working on some job or another. Valerie worked two and sometime three jobs a week. She worked in a factory on the midnight shift and took in babysitting during the afternoons. On weekends she would do sewing for her neighbours. And her husband let her do it too! He was too busy drinking away her hard earned money to pay her much attention.

It was hard for some of her friends to understand why she stayed with him but she had her own motives. Valerie wasn't getting any younger and she wanted to have a family while she still could. She hadn't had any other luck in the romance department, so she stayed with her husband and put up with his numerous faults, one of which included beating her regularly and being verbally abusive. But he claimed to love her and she clung to those words when she infrequently heard them. What else did she really have? Her family couldn't stand the guy and invitations home became less and less until they stopped coming altogether.

About four years after their marriage, that thing which she desired most, finally happened. Valerie became pregnant. For some reason her husband got extremely agitated when he found out she was pregnant. She just assumed it was because he had lost his first wife and child, so she determined to love him all the more but he never made it easy. He continued to push her around throughout her pregnancy until finally she went into premature labour. In her heart of hearts, she knew that he didn't really want this child but Valerie didn't care anymore.

She had to call an ambulance herself because he had taken off somewhere earlier. When the attendants arrived on the scene, Valerie was found on the bathroom floor haemorrhaging profusely. Their quick actions saved her and the life of her baby but it was a long haul for the child. Both he and his mother required blood transfusions and the baby needed to stay in a neonatal unit for two months. The blood for the boy had been a slight issue. It was recorded as being type O-. Her son could donate blood to anyone but only someone with O- blood could give him a transfusion and they didn't have any on hand. She was asked what blood type her husband had but she was unable to give them an answer to something that she didn't even know.

"You'll have to go looking for him" she had said to the doctor while giving him a list of watering holes. The police had been able to locate him and his blood had been a match. He reluctantly gave them his blood, only because that's what everyone was expecting him to do. The boy that he didn't want in the first place had just been saved by him. In a rage he had gone back to their house and trashed the nursery before packing up his belongings and taking off for good. By the time

Valerie returned home from the hospital she was minus a husband and that was okay with her, even if it did cut her to the quick.

She vowed never to give the boy his father's name so as not to taint him unnecessarily. So Valerie just called her wee baby, Thomas. Many years would pass before the boy would learn his real name but by then it wouldn't matter much to him. All he knew was that his mother got very upset every time he brought the subject of his father up. Sometimes Tom wished he could meet Allan for just ten minutes and beat the crap out of the guy for hurting his mom but what would be the point. It was water under the bridge. When Tom was three years old, Valerie remarried. Con Erikson tried to be a good father to Tom, at least until the boy was about eleven and then the unthinkable happened. Con sexually abused the boy he had claimed to love. Nobody knew what set Tom off but in fear and shame, he picked up the gun that Con kept in the hall drawer, went to his dad's room and shot him while he slept. His mom had been working the night shift so he wiped the gun clean and placed it in his father's hand. He washed and got into a clean pair of pajamas and then called 911. Con was rushed to the hospital but died before he reached the surgical floor.

"Man Dies of Self-Inflicted Gunshot Wound," was what the papers said. And Cal Erikson was laid to rest without Valerie being any the wiser.

Val was devastated by his death and took to drinking her evenings away. She still provided for him but he couldn't care less. He became a rebel and started running away from home but was always returned fighting mad. When he turned fifteen he ran away for the last time. He ended up in Klindale, Wisconsin. So Thomas became Thomas Erikson who became Jim Adams and the rest was history.

Most psychologists would have a person believe that it was natural for a son like Tom to follow in his father's footsteps because the inherent gene was being passed on down the line genetically. They would say that the badness found in the child could also be found in the parent. And so on and so on. But in reality, each person is given a free will and they have choices to make. The path they follow will depend upon whether or not they made wise choices or foolish ones. Those who choose foolishly will pay dearly for their mistakes. Tom's deviant behaviour could be blamed on nobody but himself. He had been his own worst enemy!

That cool Sunday morning found the small church in Poweetan packed with people as they had been since early September. They were trying desperately to make some sense out of the disappearance of the three kids. But nothing Paul said could take away their fears completely. They worried about their own children too. Were any of them safe?

On this particular morning, Paul was telling them about forgiveness. It had been an old sermon that he was recycling because he was having trouble staying focused on the tasks at hand. The congregation was listening intently as he spoke with authority.

"If you forgive others for their sins, your Father in heaven will also forgive you for your sins," he was saying. "But if you don't forgive others, your Father in heaven will not forgive your sins. Jesus gave us an alarming warning about forgiveness. If we refuse to forgive others then he will refuse to forgive us. Why? Because when we don't or can't forgive, we deny the fact that we are all sinners in need of God's forgiveness."

"It's so easy to ask God for forgiveness when we mess up but very difficult to forgive someone when they have done something to bring hurt upon us or our loved ones. What we should be asking ourselves this morning is this: Have I forgiven the people who have wronged me?"

Little did Paul know, that over the next few days his faith would be sorely put to the test and those words which he now spoke would come back to haunt him.

CHAPTER FORTY-FOUR
A REUNION MARRED

Jacob was fast losing his strength. The long night of cold had seeped into his bones and he felt his steps faltering. It was getting lighter and it took him a moment to figure out why. He was leaving the forest behind and coming upon a clearing. Picking up his stride he stepped gingerly down and out of a small drainage ditch and up onto a gravel road. Somehow he must have gotten turned around and ended back on the road that ran in front of Jim's place and not the highway he had been hoping for. He would have to be very careful that Jim didn't catch him. He'd gone too far to blow it now. Hobbling down the side of the road, his eyes scanned every which way as he attempted to avoid detection. And then he heard it! A vehicle was coming around the bend and would be upon him within seconds. He threw himself into the ditch with a grunt and barely poked his head up so he could see who it was. An old pickup truck was making its way towards him.

Sending up a quick prayer, Jacob jumped up and started to flag the truck down. It drove on past and left him choking on a mouthful of cold slush. Then he heard the sound of tires sliding on the gravel as the decrepit vehicle slowed to a stop. Jacob limped over to the truck and smiled tiredly at the gnarled man that was sitting behind the wheel. He seemed to be in as bad a shape as the truck but he was a welcome sight to Jacob.

"Well don't you look like a sight there boy!" he drawled.

Jacob smiled as best he could and tried unsuccessfully to straighten his ripped and soiled clothes.

"Sir," he began hurriedly. "I'm in big trouble and I have to get to the police right away. A crazy man has my sister locked in a cellar and she's going to die unless I can get her some help. Please, can you take me to the nearest station?" he rushed on.

The old man looked at him sceptically for only a moment before finally waving him to the other side of the truck. Wearily, Jacob opened up the door and climbed in. The man kept up a steady line of conversation while Jacob just leaned his head back and heaved a great sigh of relief. He had made it this far. Now he just had to pray that Sarah would make it as well. He wouldn't let her down if he could help it. The old man touched his arm and he practically jumped out of his shoes. He was saying something and expecting an answer. Looking over at him, Jacob apologized for not hearing what he had said.

"I said that you look terrible. Are you hungry? I have a chocolate bar here that you're welcome to."

Jacob gratefully took the proffered bar and ate it with relish. "How much further is it?" he said with obvious impatience. "I'm really worried for my sister."

"We'll be there before you know it, son. About another ten minutes," he added heartily. "I don't mean to stare at you boy, but you look sort of familiar to me. I don't suppose we've met somewhere before?" he questioned.

"Not that I know of," Jacob said discreetly while not wanting to remind the man of the tons of posters he had seen around the different towns.

What he didn't know wouldn't hurt him. The elderly man was not a speed freak by any stretch of the imagination. He drove well under the speed limit and Jacob had to bite his tongue to stop from saying something insulting. After all, this guy had saved his life. He owed him something.

Fifteen minutes passed before they finally pulled up in front of the police station in Jackson. Jacob thanked the man sincerely and offered him ten dollars of Jim's money for driving him but the old fellow just smiled and shook his head in the negative.

"You don't owe me anything. I just hope you are able to find your sister. Godspeed, son!" he grinned with a countenance that literally brightened up his whole face.

If Jacob ever saw an angel, then this old man fit the bill to a tee. He felt like he had just been watched over by someone or something much greater than he and he felt truly touched by God. Thanking the man again, Jacob jumped out of the truck and hurried into the station. He glanced back briefly to wave goodbye but was startled to see nobody there. The truck had simply vanished from sight. Jacob gave his head a shake and walked through the front doors.

The church service had just broken up and people were milling around talking to each other. Paul walked down the centre aisle to join his wife who was talking to Albert. As they were nearing the front doors they heard the sound of a siren and glanced at each other in dread. All conversations had just dropped off into silence as if the people were holding their collective breath.

Kate and Paul hurried out the doors to see Cal getting out of the cruiser. He was in his uniform so everyone knew he was on duty. Rachel moved closer to Stephen and Paul took Kate's hand in his. Together they stood, gaining much needed strength from each other. The crowd parted like the Red Sea and Cal walked up the front sidewalk to where the expectant parents were standing.

"Well folks," he said to the two families. "I have some news for you. Do you want to go and talk in private?" he asked. Stephen shook his head.

"We've all been together throughout this whole ordeal. I suppose you'd better just speak your peace Cal and get it over with." Rachel and Kate nodded their agreement as well. People huddled together in fear.

"I just this minute got a call from Jackson. It seems that Jacob just turned himself in to police headquarters of his own free will. He claims that he's seen Sarah and she's still alive. The bad news is that she was being held captive in a cellar for the past month and is very sickly. The police are gathering together a team to go after her as we speak. Supposedly, the guy who's got her is the one that Jacob was living with but he says that the guy is crazy and very dangerous. That's about all we know at this time. They promised to keep me informed as soon as they hear anything. I suppose you will want to get to the police station as quickly as possible, so I wrote down the address for you."

Kate had collapsed against Paul's chest and was sobbing uncontrollably. A month and a half of emotional ups and downs had finally taken their toll on all of them. The crowd remained hushed as Rachel stood her ground and looked down at Cal.

"What aren't you telling us Cal?" said Rachel with determination. "Did Jacob say anything about Caleb?" she questioned.

"I'm sorry Rachel and Stephen," he said as he shook his head. "Jacob never said a word about Caleb. I'm sure we'll know more when the police go over to Jim's place. I wish I could tell you more," he added lamely.

Paul went up to Cal with Stephen close on his heels. "I need to go to that place, Cal. My little girl is there and possibly Caleb too and I have to be there when they bring her out. She's been away from her family long enough," he said with tears glistening in his eyes. Shamelessly, he let them pour down his face and did nothing to wipe them away.

"I agree with Paul. You have to get some directions to that house for us Cal. We need to be there."

Both wives came forward then and stood beside their husbands and then Jonah and Mark came out of the crowd to stand there also. Slowly at first, and then with swelling force, the townspeople began to praise the Lord for finding the children safe. Everyone just assumed that Caleb would be included in the list. Nobody thought differently except perhaps his mother. Deep in her heart she already knew. She was just waiting for it to be confirmed so they could lay their beautiful son to rest, once and for all. Her other boys needed her and she would have to be strong for them all.

"Come on with me," said Cal with some resignation.

He knew there would be no talking these two men out of going and he couldn't blame them. He would want to do the same thing. Following close behind, the neighbours waved goodbye to their friends as they got into Stephen's car. From there they would drive the forty minute distance to Jackson. They would get there before two o'clock.

Paul looked back at Kate, Rachel and the boys. We'll let you know as soon as we find out anything. I don't think you should come with us right now. We just don't know what we're dealing with yet. If they get the kids to the hospital, then Albert can bring the rest of you much faster." With a quick glance back at everyone, the two drove away.

While a police swat team was organized, Jacob began to pour out his story to a shocked sergeant.

"You mean to tell me you dug up a grave behind the house?" said the officer.

"I'm telling you the truth, sir. I tripped over a rock and fell flat on my face. When I looked back at the rock I saw that it had grass stuck to the top of it. I picked it up and noticed the earth underneath was soft. I had only dug down about six inches when I pulled on some human hair. Jim said he had buried a deer out back and that I had just grabbed some of the fur but I knew he was lying," he ran on non-stop.

Jacob had been carrying around a lot of unnecessary baggage for a long time and as God started to fill his heart, Jacob started to unload that baggage, one incident after another. And as he did, he felt the peace of God wash over him. Jacob went on to talk of finding his sister and his father's car that he had found in the woods. He told him about the drinking and the drug abuse.

And then he went on to tell him about that murder at the Clarkson Airport and how he had nothing to do with it but he was sure Jim knew all about that as well. The officer just kept taking notes and stared in amazement at the boy. His honesty was refreshing, if not altogether unusual. Then the kid surprised him even further by admitting to putting a dissected frog on the altar of their church at home and trashing his parent's house before he left.

The man smiled in disbelief and glanced at his partner who had been eavesdropping. He shrugged his shoulders and raised his eyebrows at the boy.

"Are you just about through admitting to every offense ever committed by a kid?" he laughed despite the seriousness of the crimes.

Jacob looked sheepish for only a moment before saying, "I'm serious, officer. All of that stuff really happened. I was there, so I should know," he replied indignantly. The officer just kept writing.

When the task force had been put together, the police cars tore out of the parking lot with siren's blaring. The media caught wind of a fast breaking story. Like vultures descending upon a carcass they hovered around the station until the police headed out and followed fast on their trail. If something big was going down, they intended to be a part of it. Perhaps this would be the story that would send them to the summit of their careers and they were hungry for any kind of news.

Reason finally set in for Tom as he ran back from Paul's car in the bush. Although he wanted to stick around and watch the faces of whoever the kid brought with him, he didn't have the desire to end up back in prison. He would rather die first then get locked up again. Listening intently on his police band radio, Tom threw some things together in a bag. Taking a look around the place one last time, he shook his head in anger and disgust. Why did that kid have to go and spoil things for him? He had given Jacob everything that he wanted and still he had been deceived by the brat. He'd filled the boy's head with lies, got him hooked on alcohol and drugs and he had the brass to be ungrateful.

Tom turned off his radio, locked the door to the house and headed off towards his motorcycle. The girl could rot for all he cared. He had gone to say goodbye earlier but she hadn't said a word. She'd be lucky to last another day he thought wryly. Hopping astride his bike, he jumped down and nodded in satisfaction when the engine purred to life. It may be old, but it still had juice. Pulling his jacket tight around his throat, Tom carefully rode up the path and headed in the opposite direction from where Jacob had gone. He was sure the kid had probably found help by now. He'd been gone for too long, not to have succeeded rousing someone.

Picking his way carefully along the gravel road, he came to a barely noticeable crossroad. Hanging a quick right, he headed north using back roads and shutdown railway lines which he was very familiar with. Tom let out a whoop as he felt free and alone, with the stiff, cool wind blowing in his face. He refused to wear a helmet. They'd have to catch him first. It didn't get much better than this, he thought. When he had left the house he was unsure of where he was going but he noted with pleasure that his bike seemed to have a mind of its own. He was heading straight towards the place where he had been totally humiliated by that woman. She had cheated him once but he had finally made her pay. He would go back to the place where it had all begun for him. If he could only see her one more time! Of course he had seen her at the airport but he wanted her to look into his eyes and recognize him for who he really was. He wanted her to feel real fear.

Kate had been waiting on pins and needles for what seemed like hours. She and Rachel had talked and prayed. By four o'clock they were practically at their wits end.

"What's taking so long?" asked Kate to nobody in particular. "They should have some news by now. Why don't they call?" she said as she nervously drank another cup of lukewarm coffee.

Paul had promised to phone as soon as they found Sarah. Was her daughter going to make it or not? The waiting was driving her crazy. Rachel seemed to be much calmer than she was. She sat wearily in the big arm chair, rocking and praying. Kate had seen tears streaming down her face on several occasions throughout the difficult afternoon. She ached inside for her friend.

"Rachel, I'm sorry for being so selfish. I haven't been thinking rationally. You haven't even heard anything about Caleb to grasp on to and I've been rambling on about my own children. Please forgive me for being so thoughtless?" she said unevenly. "I can't even begin to imagine how you must be feeling," she added.

Going to her friend then, Kate knelt down in front of her and took Rachel's hands in hers. They were still sitting that way when a few minutes later, the ringing phone startled them. Fearfully they looked at each other as Kate got up to answer it. She would rather be anywhere else than right here at this moment in time. Picking up the receiver with trembling hands she listened carefully as Paul talked excitedly on the other end. He told her that he was calling from a phone in the back of a cruiser. Sarah had been found and yes, she was alive. He had been left alone with her for a few minutes and in that brief time he had told her how much he loved her.

"What kind of shape is she in, Paul?" Kate asked, unable to hold it in any longer. "Is she okay?"

"Sarah's in pretty rough shape, Kate. She's lost a substantial amount of weight and is badly dehydrated. The bast…the creep starved her and it looks like she's been beaten a lot," he bit out angrily. "She just left in the ambulance a few minutes ago. The attendant said that there's not much I can do for her until they get her set up with an I.V. and do some tests. He told me to wait for an hour or two so I'm going to stay here with Stephen," he said. "And Kate honey, it doesn't appear that she was sexually assaulted. She was able to tell me that he didn't touch her in that way although she was sure that he had wanted to. Sarah just said that something or someone seemed to be holding him back."

Kate smiled knowingly then. God hadn't left her little girl alone.

"I'll talk to you soon, Kate!" said Paul. Sarah's going to Fulson General. You can meet us here as soon as Albert can get you here."

"What about Jacob? Have you seen him yet, Paul?" asked Kate.

"He's on his way here as we speak. He was finishing up filling out the police reports about half an hour ago. He should be here soon. Somebody said that his quick actions and thinking probably saved his sister's life. Hard to imagine, isn't it? At least considering the way he's been," he added quickly.

Paul was just about ready to hang up when Kate stopped him. "Have they found Caleb yet? Rachel's here with me and she's really eaten up."

Paul thought for a moment before speaking.

"Sarah told me the man killed Caleb. She was stuffed into the trunk of my car and said that Caleb was behind her. She recognized his cologne, Kate. But nobody has been able to find him yet. Maybe he's just being held captive somewhere else?" he added hopefully. "And maybe Jacob will be able to shed some light on his whereabouts. I'm afraid I can't tell you anything else," said Paul.

"Oh, and one more thing Kate," he added reluctantly. "They didn't find Jim Adams. Supposedly he had a motorcycle but they haven't been able to locate it either. I'm just telling you because I want you to be careful. Don't go anywhere alone until they catch the guy. Okay?"

"Yes, Paul. Whatever you say! When you talk to Jacob please be gentle. I know we've had trouble with him but he did save his sister's life. Keep that in mind, will you?" she said with a heart full of love for her wayward son.

Meanwhile, Sarah was carrying on the biggest battle of her young life. As the nurse slid the I.V. needle under her skin, she barely flinched. Worse things had been done to her over the past month and a half. She felt dirty and broken. The doctor had been so kind and gentle that Sarah had wept with gratitude. The nurse's name was Karen Palmer and she smiled down on Sarah with what could only be described as pity.

"You poor sweet dear," she said with compassion. "What horrible things you must have gone through." Sarah could only nod in agreement. "You are very weak and are to be on complete bedrest until you get stronger. I would like to give you a sponge bath, wash your hair and get you cleaned up if that's okay with you."

Sarah smiled then at her angel in white. "It's been a long time since I was clean," she croaked.

As the nurse ministered to her, Sarah felt herself getting pleasantly sleepy. She had been given something for pain and as her ordeal finally came to an end, Sarah surrendered to the best sleep she had had in ages. And for once, it was a totally dreamless sleep.

Jacob nervously fidgeted with his fingers in the backseat of the police car. They were just about at the house and he was anxious. The officer had told him that his father was there and he didn't want to blow it with his dad again. He had caused his family so much pain and heartache already. Jacob had so much he wanted to tell his father. He wanted to share with him about his newly found faith in God and how much he loved his family and wanted to come back home. But first he just wanted to hug him and tell him how very sorry he was and ask him for forgiveness.

Pulling into the driveway, the car bounced up and down over uneven ground. In minutes Jacob saw his dad standing on the porch waiting for him. He felt a momentary panic seize him but swallowed hard and said a quick prayer. He asked God to give him the right words to say and to give him the strength to say them.

The officer opened the door for him as there were no handles on the inside of the car in the back. Climbing out, he slowly made his way towards his father but he had no need to worry because his dad came flying off the porch in record time and gathered his son into his arms. Tears of joy poured down his face as he gave him a manly bear hug.

"I'm so glad you're safe, Jacob. Your mother and I have missed you so much," he started until Jacob cut him off by pulling back and looking into his face.

"Dad, please let me talk. I'm so sorry for hurting you and mom. I was really messed up and I know that now. I want you to know that I dedicated my life to God two weeks ago. I'm not the same person I was when I left home. I just wanted you to know that," he said with the most beautiful smile Paul had ever seen.

Paul grabbed him again and held him close. "That's one of the best things I've heard today. Welcome home, son!" he said with joy.

"I hear they already took Sarah to the hospital. I'm so glad they got to her in time. That Jim is a real nut case. He had her locked up under me for ages and I didn't even know. I feel like I'm to blame, dad. Maybe if I'd paid more attention to what was going on or if I hadn't been in a drunken stupor most of the time, I would have heard her. I'll never be able to forgive myself for that. And I was the one who brought Jim into the picture in the first place. If I hadn't gone to live with him, then Sarah and Caleb wouldn't have gone to visit me that night."

Paul looked at his broken son and prayed for wisdom. Wrapping his arm gently around his shoulders he led him to the stairs and sat down.

"If it wasn't for you Jacob, your sister wouldn't be alive right now. You saved her life and your mom and I will be forever in your debt for that. I don't know why this terrible thing had to happen but I do know that God worked good out of the bad. You came to know Him because of it and that's the most wonderful news we could have received. Even if Sarah hadn't made it out alive she would have gone to be with her heavenly Father. It was you that we feared for most because we didn't know where your heart was. Satan tries to snatch people out of God's grasp but you've proven that if one fights hard enough, they can reject his temptations and choose right over wrong." Paul smiled at his son with pride.

"You did the right thing Jacob. You went to the police of your own free will and confessed to your crimes knowing that you could be punished for them. You've grown up considerably since you left home. I'm very proud of you Jacob and am thankful you are my son."

Paul squeezed his hand and nodded to the officer coming around the corner of the house. Others were going through the house with fingerprint kits and cameras.

"Let's go and see if they've found any trace of Caleb yet," said Paul rising from the stairs.

Going around the side of the building, they could see several people coming in and out of the cellar. A cadaver dog jumped out of the back of a van with his handler. One man coming out of the cellar held a handkerchief over his nose and mouth to quell the awful stench.

Paul looked away in grief for he couldn't even imagine what hell that man must have put his daughter through. What kind of animal would do such a thing and better still, what had his family ever done to him that he would take such pleasure in hurting both of his children? It just didn't make any sense. He hoped they would find the guy before he hurt someone else. Jacob and Paul walked as far as the yellow tape and stood beside Stephen who looked a million miles away. Paul put his arm around his friend's shoulders and gave a gentle squeeze. His heart ached for Stephen. At least his children were alive. They didn't know if Caleb was.

Jacob started talking to one of the officers who seemed to be in charge. He was pointing at something that Paul couldn't see. Moving a little closer to the boy he listened in horror.

"It was right under that big rock over there. I only had to dig down about six inches before pulling on some human hair," he was saying in obvious disgust.

The officer was walking over to the rock when the dog started whining. His handler quickly donned a white Tyvek suit, booties and gloves. He grabbed a bag of small flags out of the van and went back to the dog. Letting the dog go ahead on a lead, he followed a short distance behind. The dog sat down by the rock and began to howl. The handler quickly placed some flags in a large square around an indentation in the ground where the vegetation and soil had been disturbed.

He spoke softly to the dog and praised him. Within moments of placing the flags, the dog started to whine again and got up and ran to another spot about ten feet away. Once again he sat down and started to howl. The handler looked back at the officer and raised his shoulders as if to say it looked like there might be more than one body out here. As the dog continued to whine and howl and the handler continued to place flags into the ground, the officer had the wisdom to call for backup and started barking out orders. One officer began to cordon off the area leading to the woods with crime scene tape. Two other officers were posted on guard so that nobody could get past without clearance. Several phone calls were placed to the county coroner in Fulson; the crime scene investigators and techs; the forensic pathologist and the medical examiner.

The pathologist in turn, called the forensic entomologist who knew firsthand, the life cycle of flies such as eggs, maggots, pupa and adults. A crime scene work van was sent which contained drawers full of anything the specialists may need for a field death recovery. There were special cameras; high powered lights and poles; white Tyvek suits; booties to go over shoes; masks; goggles and glasses; shovels, tweezers and brushes; body bags, white sheets and wooden backer boards; metal detectors; sample containers; brown bags and heavy duty tape; soil sifters; sketch pads and pencils; tents and poles; rope bundles of different sizes; clean water for drinking and cleaning items; and a couple of small refrigerators to store samples.

Nothing more was to be touched until the specialists arrived on the scene so that evidence wouldn't be destroyed or misplaced due to ignorance and thoughtlessness.

One officer led Paul, Jacob and Stephen away from the tape. He took them around to the front of the house where they sat on the steps.

"There's nothing you can do here for now," he said to them. "It looks like this is going to take some time. We won't know anything until the area has been safely cleared. It looks like there may be more than one body out there. I know this must be awful for you but you might as well go home. We'll let you know as soon as the forensic pathologist releases the body. I'm sorry I can't help you more than that."

Another perimeter was being placed well back from the house to keep the media and the curious away from the area.

Stephen wondered how Rachel was coping but knew that he was in no condition to talk to her right now. He would only upset her more. With his shoulders hunched in defeat, he followed Paul and Jacob to his car and was grateful when Paul asked for his keys and got behind the wheel. They slowly wended their way through the traffic that was now lining the old road and headed home to wait.

CHAPTER FORTY-FIVE
CALEB FOUND

Stephen had barely left the car before Rachel came running out of Paul's house and threw her arms around her husband.

"Have they found Caleb yet? Is he hurt? Did they take him to the hospital too?" Looking up into her husband's face, she stopped talking for a minute. "Is he dead, Stephen?" He leaned against a tree and just hugged his wife.

"We won't know anything for quite a while," he said as he placed a soft kiss upon the top of Rachel's head.

He then told her what he had seen and heard. Rachel cried then and clung to Stephen tightly. Their two other boys ran out of the house and wrapped their arms around their mom and dad. They held each other and cried.

Kate held Jacob's hand, while he told them what had happened over the past couple of months. Ruby had made a big casserole for everyone to eat but Rachel and her family politely backed out and said they needed to be alone for a while. Albert was willing to take them to the hospital in the morning. Kate would have preferred to go immediately to see her daughter but when they called the hospital, they were told that Sarah would sleep through the night and part of the next day. Kate had to be content knowing that one of her children was home.

Jacob had lost weight and was filthy and scratched up. After a quick shower and a good meal, Jacob told his mom about his conversion experience. They all sat together, talked, cried and prayed for Caleb and Sarah. Kate could tell that her son was exhausted both mentally and physically so she took him by the hand and led him back to his bedroom that had been cleaned up and painted. He glanced at her with gratitude and climbed gratefully under the warm comforter on his bed. As she stroked the hair back from his forehead she heard him begin to snore softly. She looked back at Paul standing in the doorway and smiled. Their prodigal son had come back home.

The Westcott home was more subdued. The family ate some grilled cheese sandwiches and some soup left by a neighbour. Stephen barely said a word about what he had seen at that old dilapidated house. He didn't want to scare his sons but he knew he had to tell Rachel before the night was over. She kept looking into his eyes and he felt like a charlatan. He was letting on he was brave and unafraid when he really felt sick at heart. They spoke long into the night after the children had been put to bed. They prayed that their son would be found quickly as both knew in their hearts that Caleb was no longer alive. They went to bed and just held each other closely, until they fell into an exhausted and fitful sleep.

As Paul had done earlier, Stephen wondered what would lead a person like Jim to commit such atrocities. He braced himself for the bad news that was sure to come. He figured it was only a matter of time before they called them in to identify their son's remains. Stephen didn't know if he would have the strength to do that but he was thankful for one thing. He thanked God that Rachel hadn't been there to see the circus that was taking place on that horrid property! It would push her right over the deep end.

The television played repeated video clips that showed spotlights in the woods and tents set up. People in white were coming and going while the police were guarding the perimeter. News reporters spoke respectfully as camera crews panned the area looking for the next fast breaking story.

Sandwiches and beverages were brought in to feed the hungry men and women. The first grisly find had already been transported to the county morgue for proper identification and an autopsy. Dental records would be sent to the forensic odontologist for positive identification. They would match the teeth of the deceased with known dental records.

Tom ditched the bike and covered it over with wet mouldy leaves. This was the same place he had hidden his bike so many years ago. He walked a few miles through the bush until he came upon a large grassy mound where the old mine used to be. What have they done to my favourite place he wondered angrily? They had no business wrecking it! It was his place! Pulling his thick lethal blade from the sheath at his side, he flung it in rage and watched in fascination as it stuck in the gnarled old tree and vibrated back and forth wildly. He laughed aloud in delight. He was back!

Kicking away at the fallen leaves and snow around him, he was very pleased to find the back entrance to the mine still intact. He pulled up the ladder and looked at the childish handiwork for only a moment before throwing his leg over the side and disappearing from sight.

Rachel tried not to feel bitter towards Kate and Paul. Kate had found both of her children alive and Rachel was sure that Caleb would never again see the light of day. If he hadn't gone with Sarah that day, he would still be here with her. Rachel didn't like the negative feelings that were assaulting her thoughts but she couldn't seem to help it right now. Maybe given time, she would find peace for her soul. Rachel decided to go up to Ruby's for a bit. She walked slowly while contemplating her life. She thought that all the evil had passed away when she escaped that mine. Now her world was tumbling down around her ears and there wasn't a thing she could do about it.

Rachel remembered the vision that God had given her when she was pregnant with Caleb. He had told her that he would be a special child who would follow the ways of righteousness. She had assumed that he was destined for great things. Perhaps he would be a preacher or a missionary? But now he was probably gone. The magnitude of her loss threatened to overwhelm her at any moment. Ruby left her to her thoughts with a steaming cup of coffee and a gentle squeeze on her shoulder. As Rachel swirled the liquid around the cup with her spoon, she tried to imagine life without her precious son. And then it hit her between the eyes and she felt great shame.

Wasn't that exactly what God had done for her? He had given up His own Son so that she could have eternal life. He had freely given the world this wonderful gift and all they had to do was accept Him or reject Him. Kate had been right all along.

Caleb had been dedicated to the Lord when he was a youngster and God had just called him home a little bit sooner. He loved Caleb more than she ever could. And because of what God's Son had already done, Rachel would be reunited with her precious boy. Surely she could live with that! Rachel felt God working on her heart and knew that she wasn't alone. Smiling despite her grief, she vowed to revel in Kate and Paul's happiness. She should be pleased with their good news even if hers wasn't going to be. Rachel felt like she owed them that much. And her son was in the best possible hands after all. She couldn't deny him that joy. Straightening her shoulders a bit and holding her head high, Rachel determined to ask her friend for forgiveness.

Stephen drove back to the old house. He needed to be here if they found Caleb but he was finding it harder to cope as each minute dragged on for what seemed like an eternity. The police still hadn't found Jim. Stephen spoke to Rachel before he left and told her to be on guard at all times until he was picked up. He also told her to watch over the boys.

Jacob drove Paul and Kate to the hospital in his own car. The tires had been replaced and Paul's car was still in the woods. Paul had offered to go and wait with Stephen after he had seen Sarah but his friend told him that he just wanted to be alone for a while.

"You need to be with your family right now, Paul. They need you and this could go on for some time. If I hear any news, I'll call you," said Stephen grimly.

As day two drew to a close, three more bodies were unearthed and sent to the morgue. A grid line had been laid on the ground, mapping the area. Several more squares containing flags had yet to be uncovered. Around one o'clock in the morning, word came back to the dwindling crowd that another grave had just been found. It appeared to be fresher as the ground under the thin layer of snow hadn't begun to settle yet. Stephen felt his muscles stiffen in anguish. His fingers and toes ached from the cold. As he blew into his cupped hands, he overheard two officers talking.

"The others were female but this one is definitely a male!" he was saying.

Stephen ducked under the tape and quietly ran towards the trees. He made his way to the spot where they were just starting to erect another tent. One of the officers yelled out a warning and tried to pull him back but gave up after seeing Stephen's set jaw and determination.

Looking down he recognized the blue T-shirt right away. It was his son! One man reached down and extracted a wallet that was sticking out of the front pocket of the boy's jeans. Stephen grabbed it with shaking hands. Inside were pictures of Stephen's family in various poses and places. There was Caleb smiling in his high school graduation photo. That's when he collapsed to the ground with his treasure held close to his heart and wept uncontrollably for the son he would never get to hold again. His grief was a heavy suffocating thing that had a life of its own. A man in white put his arm gently around Stephen's shoulders and helped him to his feet.

"You have to leave now, sir. We'll take really good care of your son and you can see him when we get back to town and get him cleaned up. I promise we'll be gentle. Go and be with your wife."

By this time everyone had heard about the boy named Caleb who was missing. The forensic tech led him slowly back to the perimeter tape and handed him off to Paul who had come back to be with his friend. Paul wrapped his arm around Stephen and spoke soft reassuring words to him. Both felt numb with shock and disbelief. Although they had suspected that Caleb had been the victim of foul play, it was still hard to take when that suspicion became a reality. Caleb had just wanted to be a good friend to Jacob and had paid for that friendship with his life.

"Let's go home Stephen. Rachel and the boys need you," he said as he led his broken friend towards the car.

Jacob had dropped him off here and then had gone back to the hospital to be with Kate and Sarah. Jacob may be going home a new person in Christ, but the lives of others close to him had been shattered forever. God had forgiven him and so had his father but it would be a very long time before Jacob would ever be able to forgive himself.

Jonah and Mark were upstairs sleeping peacefully when they arrived back in Poweetan. Rachel was drifting in and out of sleep when she heard the car pull up in the driveway. Looking over at the clock radio she noted the time and etched it in her memory. It read 4:10 a.m. Stephen was getting slowly out of the car. He looked beaten down. His shoulders were rounded and he was taking his time coming up the steps. Rachel took a deep breath and hurried down the stairs, careful not to wake up the boys.

"Did they find him, Stephen?" she asked simply.

"They just found him a little while ago Rachel. He was buried in the backyard with at least four other bodies. They keep turning up more and more. I saw his blue T-shirt and they let me take his wallet," he said as he handed it to Rachel. "I couldn't see his face. This guy was sicker than anyone could have imagined," he said with a catch in his voice. "The coroner told me that he has to do an autopsy to determine the cause of death. I told him to go ahead if that's okay with you?" he said tiredly. "There was nothing I could do, so they told me to go home. When they're finished with their findings, they are going to send our son home to us. I love you Rachel! I'm so sorry I couldn't have brought back some good news," he added as they embraced and cried.

Rachel felt like a huge weight had been lifted from her shoulders. Her son was resting in God's loving embrace and now they could get on with living. They had been waiting in limbo for far too long. She decided not to wake the boys yet. They would need their mother to be strong and she would be there for them. As Stephen crawled wearily into bed, Rachel went into Caleb's bedroom and sat on the edge of his bed. She looked around the familiar room at the accumulation of items he had hoarded since he was a child. There was the baseball trophy he had won for hitting the most home runs in a season. There was a framed page where all his swimming levels had been obtained, from a tadpole to a lifeguard. A picture of Sarah was stuck into the side of the mirror on his dresser. Rachel picked up his pillow and breathed deeply of her son's scent. She hugged the pillow to her breast and rocked quietly back and forth.

Paul got on the elevator and pressed the button for the second floor. A kindly nurse looked up from her paperwork as the man approached her desk.

"Good morning Rev. Winchester. Sarah is getting stronger by the day. Your wife and son have been with her all night. I let them sleep in the visitor's lounge with a pillow and blanket."

Smiling with compassion, the nurse got up and led the way down the hall to room 214. Opening the door, she peeked inside and looked at the sleeping figure on the bed.

"She's sleeping again. The poor child has had quite the ordeal," she said quietly and left the room.

Paul made his way to the side of the bed. Although Sarah had been cleaned up remarkably well, she was still barely recognizable. Her eyes were swollen and yellow from healing bruises. Her lip was split and there was bruising around her throat. Three ribs had been broken and were bandaged tightly. Numerous scratches and cuts were in various degrees of healing. Her hip had been dislocated when Jim had taken the boots to her. But the most dramatic evidence of abuse and torture was her weight.

Paul couldn't get over how tiny she looked. Sarah had been a robust and healthy girl. Now she looked like nothing more than a sickly child. Going over the chart at the end of her bed he saw that she weighed ninety eight pounds and he felt a primordial rage welling inside him against the person who had done this to his daughter. If he could only be alone with him for ten minutes! That's all it would take, he reasoned. He was sure that given the chance, he could kill the guy.

Tom spent the next few days roaming around his old stomping ground. Some things were so familiar while others were totally new. The roads had been paved and many new homes and stores had been built since he had been here last. Even in the dark, he could enjoy some of the memories he had of this place. The clinic may have a new building but behind the old one was where he had killed Kate's cat. Of course she hadn't been married back then. And over there was where he had grabbed that other girl, thinking she was Kate. He wandered from place to place, deep in thought.

He wondered where Kate lived now. Did he dare to stop somebody and ask for directions? Wouldn't that be a hoot he thought with joy? Or perhaps he should just pick up a phone and give her a call. That ought to really freak her out. Tom smiled to himself as he played all these scenarios through in his mind. Under cover of darkness, Tom made his way up and down the few streets looking in windows to see if he could find the object of his desire but she continued to elude him. As dawn began to spread its tendrils over Poweetan, Tom made his way back to his place of refuge. He was a patient man. The woman could wait.

Paul's car was towed out of the woods later the next day. Fingerprints were lifted from all over the dashboard and off the trunk lid. They got a positive hit in AFIS, the automated fingerprint identification system. It belonged to Tom Erikson, who had been incarcerated for murder and then had escaped without a trace, until now. Blood samples were removed from the bottom of the trunk and it was determined that Caleb had been in there. A piece of ripped blue material was also found lying in the bottom. The pizza box also proved that the girl at the pizzeria had been telling the truth. After meticulously going over it and finding out all they could, they sent it to the garage to have the side hammered back out and the window repaired. They told Paul he could pick up his car in a few days, but kept the fingerprint ID to themselves until they had more information.

Sarah had wakened fully. She looked up at her father in confusion wondering where she was. Paul reached out his hand and touched her lightly on the arm but she felt herself pull away from him. She could see the pain it caused her dad and didn't know why she had done it. It was her dad after all and not that crazy man.

"Where am I?" she asked weakly.

"You're in the hospital, Sarah. They brought you in several days ago. You were in that cellar, remember?" Paul added while trying to jar her memory. Sarah moaned as that truth finally registered in her subconscious. She looked around fearfully but the man was nowhere to be seen.

Paul looked down upon his daughter with a broken heart as he watched her curl into the fetal position. At that moment, the doctor walked in and noted her position. He looked at the girl's father and felt badly for him. He didn't know how he would feel if he were in that guy's shoes.

"It's going to take some time to rehabilitate Sarah, Rev. Winchester. Her body and spirit have been traumatized terribly but we feel that she will make a complete recovery, given time. Her ribs will set nicely but she may walk with a limp for the rest of her life. Her hip was badly dislocated and is slightly out of alignment. There's not much we can do about that, short of reconstructive surgery and we like to wait until they're a bit older to do that. But that's the least of her problems right now. As you can see, she's drawing comfort from her childhood. She's clinging to those good thoughts that used to make her happy," said the doctor as he took her vital signs and recorded them on the chart.

"The best thing you can do for Sarah now is to love her. She needs to feel nurtured and cared for," he continued. "We can only guess where her mind wandered when she was left to her own thoughts. That's all I can tell you for now. She's going to need some kind of therapy so she can deal with what's happened to her. I understand that her friend was killed. Is that true?" he asked.

"Yes, they found his body," said Paul sadly.

"Well, that's going to make matters harder for her. She will have to deal with questions like why she was spared when her friend wasn't. There might be bouts of depression and guilt as well. I'm just telling you this because it's something you should be prepared for," he added.

"You fix her body and God will heal her soul and spirit," said Paul softly, yet with complete faith. The doctor just shrugged his shoulders and smiled at him.

"Whatever works for you," he said as he quietly exited the door. Paul took his daughter's hand in his as Jacob and Kate entered the room.

"Dear Father God," he began. "I lift Sarah up to You and lay her at the foot of Your throne. I pray that you would bring healing to her body and to her mind. Meet Sarah at her greatest point of need and touch her with your love and healing hands. In Jesus' name I pray." Looking at her with eyes shining, he smiled and moved towards the door.

"She might not be able to hear but God surely can," he said with conviction as he gathered his wife and son to his side.

CHAPTER FORTY-SIX
THE HEALING BEGINS

It was a bittersweet time for Stephen and Rachel. No words were necessary. It was just them and their grief. The boys made a special effort to be quiet around their parents. They knew the loss their mom and dad were feeling. Caleb had been a loving and good brother to them and they were going to miss him deeply. Rachel seemed to be mechanical as she phoned the funeral home and made plans to have her son laid to rest. Stephen told her they could wait until Caleb came home but she was insistent upon getting their affairs in order as she put it. Caleb's grandparents were a great comfort to the family and the townspeople were wonderful as well. Cards and flowers, gifts for the boys and food filled their house with abundance.

A floral wreath was set up outside of the school and before the week was up, the area would be laden with carnations, red roses, candles under glass and teddy bears wrapped in plastic. The snow that had been threatening to fall for days, finally dumped upon the town and the whole area was enveloped in a cold blanket of white. Poweetan would cope with its devastating loss. It always did.

Kate worried about Sarah. She was so frail and thin. Her skin was pale and translucent. Kate knew she would never be the same girl after this ordeal. She had lost much more than Caleb and Kate's heart just about broke in two as she bore Sarah's pain within herself. She started to quietly hum Sarah's favourite hymn, "Just As I Am." She had only begun the second verse when she felt Sarah squeeze her hand back in response and tears of joy filled her eyes. She noticed the barely discernable nod of Sarah's head and knew in her mother's heart that her daughter was going to be okay. It would be a long haul for her but she would make it back to them as a whole person. Kate was confident that given time, God would work His miraculous powers on her girl. She was a fighter but most importantly she had a very strong faith. And that would be more than enough to see her through this time of trial. Kate continued to hum as her husband and son came in and stood by her side. Together they held hands and prayed as a family, just like they used to do when the children were small. They were now a strand of four that could not be easily broken.

By the end of the day it was snowing quite heavily. The Winchester's took a motel room so they would be close to the hospital. They phoned Stephen and talked for a while with him.

"Doc Verstegan gave Rachel a sedative a little while ago and she's finally sleeping. She's been making funeral arrangements and everything. I don't know if she's come to terms with Caleb's death but she is dealing with her grief in her own way," said Stephen from a voice filled with pain and loss. "It's been a nightmare for us all as you can well attest to. It's just going to take some time and a lot of love and patience. We would like to have the service in three days, Paul. And of course we want you to take the service if that's okay?" he added.

"I would be honoured, Stephen," he said.

After talking a little while longer, Paul hung up. Tonight they were together with their son and intended to make up for lost time and Jacob who had been starved for their affection by his own choosing, relished their attention.

Tom wondered where Jacob and his family had gotten to. Of course the girl wouldn't be coming home for any family picnics for some time, if ever, he thought with satisfaction. No one in Poweetan knew him from squat so he was able to move about quite freely. It helped that he had changed his appearance. He was a wanted man and the posters that were plastered all over the place had a drawn facsimile of him with dirty beard and ponytail. Tom wore a wool cap pulled low on his forehead and a heavy work jacket with a hood but he couldn't disguise the limp.

He had stayed away from the Westcott's place. He didn't want to run into Rachel just in case something clicked and she remembered what he had done to her almost twenty years earlier. He had walked over to the school and looked around at the various floral arrangements left in memory of Caleb. Oh isn't that sweet, he smiled smugly. The poor boy must have had a bad accident.

He wandered over to the cafe and ordered some lunch. Luckily, he still had quite a stash of money hidden away.

"Can I take your order?" asked Ruby. "We don't get many strangers around here. Are you going to be in town for long?" she inquired.

"It depends on how successful my business goes," he said with a forced smile. Ruby felt an instant dislike for the man before her and went on the alert.

"I'm staying at the Silverline Motel for a while. And I understand that you have the best food in town," he added with a wink.

Ruby felt the hair go up on the back of her neck. She wondered what this guy was really up to and decided to ask Cal if he would keep his eye out for anything strange going on.

"I hope you enjoy your stay then, sir," said Ruby mechanically as she swung quickly away from the table.

The next couple of days went quickly as Kate and Paul saw a remarkable change in their daughter's condition. Although she was still on an I.V. to pump fluids into her badly dehydrated body, she was much more lucid. She had awakened from the drug induced sleep to smile at her parents and brother. They were all together and Sarah was content. Her chest ached from the binding of her ribs and her hip felt terrible. As long as she could feel pain then she was on the right track. It would be a long time before the nightmares went away but she felt certain that a complete recovery was possible.

Paul told her he was taking Caleb's funeral the next day and she really wanted to be there.

"Couldn't I get moved to the clinic back home, dad?" she pleaded. "I don't want to miss Caleb's service. In fact, I feel like I need to be there. Pleeeaaassseee?" she smiled weakly.

"I'll have to talk to the doctor first and see what he says."

He left Kate with her and went to find the doctor. The nurse had him paged and within minutes, Paul saw him sauntering up the hall.

"You wanted to see me?" the doctor asked.

"Sarah's boyfriend is being buried tomorrow in Poweetan and she would really like to attend. She's been here for almost a week now. I was wondering if she could be moved to our clinic at home. You know Drs.Verstegan and Fulbrook I'm sure and I think they are very competent. Kate works there as a nurse as well, so I know she would get the best possible care. That doesn't mean she hasn't been given excellent care here!" he added quickly. "So I was wondering if you would consider letting her leave?"

"Normally I would have said no, considering the trauma your daughter went through. I have to tell you that seeing her three days ago I wondered if she would even make it. I've never held much store in prayer, but whatever's been happening to her can only be attributed to divine intervention in my personal opinion. Sarah's made an astonishing recovery of her mental abilities and that's the most surprising thing of all. I've seen this kind of trauma before and it takes months of therapy to bring a person back around. If your God has done this miracle, then I think I want to know more about him," he smiled. "I don't see why Sarah can't be moved tomorrow morning," he said. "She may be in a wheelchair for a while until she's strong enough for physio on her hip. I'll send a prescription home with you to last for at least a month but I would like to see her back here in two weeks for a complete checkup."

"Thanks a lot Doctor. You have no idea how much we appreciate this! And we'll take excellent care of her. I give you my word."

Paul turned around and walked lightly to the end of the hall to tell his family the good news. He hadn't felt this content in ages. Paul had to remind himself that he still had a funeral to prepare for. And it would be one of the hardest he had ever done in his career as a minister. This one was hitting a little too close to home. Caleb had been like a son to him. But the healing process had to begin somewhere and laying Caleb's body to rest would be a start. There had been far too much tension and uncertainty already. Now it was time to start living again.

A total of six bodies were eventually found around Jim's house. It had taken almost a week, but they were finally tagged and identified by their dental records. Caleb had at least been identified on the spot by his father. One other male was nothing more than a skeleton. He was the original owner of the house. Jim had still been using his name when the mortgage was paid off two years earlier.

The four female bodies turned out to be that of young women who had gone missing over the past five years. All were runaways from surrounding areas who had taken to the streets of Fulson and sold themselves to live. When eventually notified, their parents were relieved to finally have closure and the police were able to close four cold cases. No one had ever missed the man who owned the house. He was never reported. A sketch artist and forensic anthropologist would reconstruct a replica of what he may have looked like. This was shown on television newscasts. If anyone recognized him, they weren't talking. He remained unidentified and was finally buried with a grave marker that simply read: JOHN DOE #217.

Thousands of man-hours had been logged while looking for the girls. Volunteers had scoured the area on foot but were never able to find any clues into the disappearances. People who supposedly had information were questioned but later released when their reports seemed to be unsubstantiated. So it was with much relief that the news was received that the girls had finally been found. The only bad news was that Jim Adams was still on the loose. The picture that had been circulating still showed him with long hair and a beard. No one thought to ask Jacob if that picture was accurate and he never thought to tell them that Jim had cut his hair and shaved off his beard. It would be six days later that Jacob would come across a wanted picture on the side of a building and realize the error. He would report it immediately but would that information come before Jim killed again?

Tom watched from a distance as a black hearse drove into the small community. People gathered in morbid curiosity as a coffin was drawn out of the back of the vehicle. Stephen and Rachel, Kate and Paul, Jonah, Mark and Jacob were among the bystanders. Kate stood behind a wheelchair carrying Sarah wrapped up in several blankets and a hat. Two men in dark blue suits slowly made their way up the walkway to the front of the church with the casket on a trolley with wheels. They were helped up the steps by six men from the community, including Albert. They slowly made their way up the aisle of the church to the front where the visitation and service would take place.

The Westcott family walked up to the front and stopped in front of the casket.

They put Caleb's graduation picture on top and shared some private words of grief. Hugging as a family, they had a quiet time of prayer and shared their love with each other. Then they turned to face the community who had all come out to show their support. After visiting with the family, the pews started filling up quickly. Before thirty minutes had passed, the church was filled to capacity and the rest of the townspeople huddled together outside where speakers had been set up for the overflow. Included in the numbers was Tom, who had dyed his hair black at the motel the other day. Three days growth had left him with a goatee and the beginnings of a mustache.

Ruby and the owner of the motel were the only ones to recognize him as the man who had come to town before but he had changed his story when he realized that Ruby wasn't buying his charade. He told them he was really an actor from the theatre in Brandon and that he would be going home soon to be in a new play which was taking place in November. The motel manager had bought the story, but Ruby was another thing altogether. She could still see that his eye colour had been changed with contacts but that did nothing to hide the evil in them. Ruby hadn't had time to talk to Cal yet, but determined to do so as soon as the funeral was over.

The crowd outside parted as Kate, Jacob and Sarah made their way into the church. The whole place hushed as they watched the wheelchair being pushed down the centre aisle. The people could barely recognize Sarah but could read the deep pain in her eyes. Fresh tears were shed for what that madman had done to her as well. Kate took her to the front where Rachel was standing. Rachel bent down and knelt in front of Sarah. She placed her hands gently on Sarah's shoulders.

"I'm so glad you could make it Sarah," she whispered as the tears fell from her eyes. "You poor child! Caleb's hurts were over in a second but you have suffered so much more. Thank you for being with him at the end. I know you loved him and I'm so sorry for your loss. We'll all miss him terribly."

Sarah stroked Rachel's hair and the older woman looked up at her. Sarah's face was positively glowing despite the tears that ran down her face.

"I saw him in a dream, Mrs. Westcott. I was walking beside Jesus but He let go of my hand and started walking away. I was going to run after Him when I noticed someone holding on to His other hand and I recognized his walk. He turned around and smiled at me. It was Caleb and he was radiant. He asked me if I could deny him that pleasure and that we would all have a joyous reunion soon enough."

Rachel's face lit up then. "Thank you for sharing that with me Sarah. I'll cherish that thought forever."

Moving over with her family once again, she squeezed her husband's hand and looked up into his sweet face.

"It's going to be okay, Stephen. I'll tell you what she said afterwards." She smiled then and Stephen was relieved to see peace fill her countenance. Paul went up to the pulpit to deliver his message of hope.

"Caleb was a Christian and we all knew where he was going but Caleb has been taken home early to be with his heavenly Father. He often spoke of the glorious day when he and Jesus would be together, so although we are feeling the pain of his loss, we cannot forget that he is now basking in the presence of the Lord whom he served with his whole heart, mind and spirit. We don't understand why someone with so much to offer could be taken so young. How could a loving Father have allowed this tragedy to happen? I can't tell you that today. God's ways are beyond our finite comprehension but we must believe that Caleb's untimely death has served God's purpose for something. We can thank God for giving us Caleb, even if it was for such a short time. He was a blessing to us all and will be sorely missed. Let's bow our heads in prayer."

As the service continued, the songs of praise were sung with a rising crescendo. Tom couldn't understand these people. They were supposed to be devastated and upset. He expected them to sob and cling to each other in grief. He would have enjoyed watching that. But something had happened today that was totally beyond his grasp. These strange people were smiling through their tears and singing out to God as if he were right there or something. Tom was utterly baffled. Shaking his head in confusion, he pulled away from the crowd and snuck away to be by himself. He needed to think.

After the service, the whole town moved down the street to meet at the cemetery. They stood beside a newly dug grave and as Caleb was lowered into the ground, families everywhere pulled their youngsters closer and gave thanks that they still had each other.

Sarah was taken back to the clinic where she would convalesce for the next three weeks. The doctors were going to try and get some meat back on her bones and see that her ribs healed completely before sending her home. Kate wished she could take her home now but saw the reasoning behind their decision. Sarah was still too weak to walk and had a lot of stiffness and pain. She needed more care than Kate could give her at home. At least Sarah wasn't too far away and she could visit with her every day. Working there helped.

The Westcott clan would find healing much sooner thanks to those special words which Sarah had spoken. It helped them to focus not so much on their loss, but rather on Caleb's happiness. He was finally home and they couldn't argue that fact. The family was closer than they had ever imagined. Jonah had settled right down and was a pleasure to live with. The loss of his big brother had affected him in a very positive way. He had also seen Jacob change completely with Christ now in his life and he had rededicated his own life to Jesus, much to the delight of everyone. The healing had finally begun.

CHAPTER FORTY-SEVEN
THE HUNT

A Canada-wide manhunt was on for Jim Adams and Tom Erikson. The police reported in their television briefing that they had received a hit in AFIS, from the prints found on Paul's car. Tom was wanted for escaping prison following a murder almost twenty years earlier. They figured the two men must have been working as a team. Jim had killed Caleb Westcott and was also wanted for questioning in the death of Nico d'Arva. It was possible the two had killed the other five people found buried on Jim's property. Jacob had finally notified the police of the change in Jim's appearance just before he took off. The new information was immediately televised and a revised composite sketch accompanied the news bulletins. He was listed as being of medium build with shoulder length cropped blond hair. He had shaved his beard off but it was possible that he was sporting one again. He had a very distinguishing mark, that being a long scar running from the left side of his nose to the corner of his left eye. He dragged his left leg a bit after injuring it in an accident.

The woods around his place were scoured as everyone looked for some clue as to his whereabouts but nothing was found. Jacob had also informed them that

Jim had taken to riding a motorcycle but he didn't know the make of it. He just told them that it looked fairly out-dated like it had been around for a very long time. It's as if he had fallen off the face of the earth.

As soon as Ruby saw the composite on the news she immediately knew where the guy was holed up. She got on the phone and called Cal Davies right away. Cal had seen the reports as well but he hadn't seen Jim around town.

"I know where that guy from the news is staying, Cal! He's the one who killed Caleb and he's living right in our own town," she said excitedly.

"You can't be serious Ruby? Are you sure?" he said, knowing that Ruby was seldom wrong.

"Sure, I'm sure!" she retorted. "He's been staying over at the Silverline Motel for over a week." Cal was just about to hang up when Ruby interjected with something else. "Oh, and I almost forgot. You know how the pictures said that he had dirty blond short hair? Well, the other day he came into the diner with it dyed black. And he had grown a goatee and a mustache. But it didn't do a thing to hide that scar. One other thing Cal! He had coloured contacts in his eyes that changed them from blue to brown."

She seemed embarrassed for a moment which was unlike Ruby.

"Well it's hard not to notice details when we hardly ever get visitors to our small neck of the woods," she stammered. "When I noticed his different hair colour and stuff, he just blew me off saying that he was working in the theatre in Brandon and was doing a new play next month. But I didn't believe him Cal. The guy was lying through his teeth, or my name isn't Ruby!" she said huffily.

Smiling, Cal thanked her profusely and hung up knowing they had finally gotten a break in the case. Hoping this would lead them to the killer Cal called for backup and phoned a couple of other police stations while he was waiting. He also called the motel manager to warn him of the possible danger he was in.

He felt the wind go out of his sails when the man informed him that the guy had checked out that morning but he didn't say where he was going. He didn't have a vehicle parked in the parking lot. When the manager asked if he would need a lift to the bus station, the man had just smiled and told him that his car was in the shop getting the radiator fixed. The manager had only been in the area for the past five years so he didn't know much in the way of local stories. He wouldn't understand the commotion that would be made when Cal determined that the man had not registered under the name of Jim Adams but rather Tom Erikson and he did have a large scar on his face. It was almost as if Tom wanted to bait the police and everyone else for that matter.

Cal had been in Poweetan long enough to remember hearing that name. He started making some phone calls. Because of Ruby's quick thinking, Poweetan was swarming with local police, R.C.M.P. and two homicide detectives from Fulson by midday. Before dark they were scouring the woods all around the town but no sign of Tom could be found. Finally, as darkness descended, they had to grudgingly call off the search until morning. Tomorrow they would do a house to house search and check out the lake area.

A twenty four hour security detail was to be posted around the clinic, the Winchester home and the Westcott home. Tom had already hurt these people enough. Families were warned to stay indoors and to travel only in two's or more until the guy could be found. Now that Cal had a real name to go on, he issued bulletins across the States and Canada in the hopes of finding out anything about a Tom Erikson. Cal went over to Kate's house to personally warn her of the danger, but she wasn't home. Rachel hadn't been able to help because she had been unconscious for most of the kidnapping. She couldn't even recall what he looked like. Jacob was home and was able to put the positive proof on the table. Cal was telling him something that Ruby had said about a limp. That had jarred a memory that was hidden in Jacob's mind. Jim had talked one night about being in a big mudslide on Mount Killaloma and how he had gone headfirst over an embankment and rolled under some thick brush. Much later he had crawled out of the woods with his shattered leg dragging behind him. The doctor had been unable to set it properly because he had waited too long to get it looked at. Everyone had just assumed that the mud had claimed his life because no trace of him was ever found. How wrong they had been. And it had cost them all dearly.

Kate and Paul had just walked into the house when they overheard Cal talking with Jacob. All Kate heard was Mount Killaloma and instantly her ears perked up. Silently she stood and listened to the two with growing concern. What was Cal saying? It just couldn't be true Kate thought as she felt the wind knocked out of her. She and Paul had been out of town for half the day and were just now hearing about Tom.

"Why are you asking about Tom?" she asked Cal. "He died a long time ago in a mudslide, or didn't you know?" she said with bravado she didn't feel.

As if he were talking to a child, Cal gently spoke to Kate although his voice sounded like it was coming from a million miles away. He explained how Ruby had recognized a picture of Jim Adams and told him how he was staying at the Silverline Motel. I spoke with the manager Pete Jones about him but he said he only had one guy registered and he had gone by the name of Tom Erikson, not

Jim Adams. He checked out this morning. I have sent officers to the clinic, and Stephen's house and there are more officers coming here. They'll be watching over all of you until we catch the guy.

He didn't need to say any more. There was no way it could just be a coincidence. Tom had come back to finish what he started over twenty years earlier, only this time he had killed her godchild Caleb, had almost killed Sarah and had just about destroyed Jacob with drugs. When she realized that Jim was really Tom, she just about threw up. She had unwittingly allowed her son to move in with the man of her nightmares and her daughter to visit him. How could that have possibly happened? He was supposed to be dead. Everyone had thought so!

Paul had to catch her from falling and led Kate to the couch in shock. She just kept saying over and over again… "They said he was dead! How can this be?"

Paul left Jacob with Kate and went into the kitchen to speak to Cal.

"Where is the guy now?" he asked when Kate was out of earshot.

Cal looked at him with sympathy. "They haven't found him yet, Paul. The guy checked out of the motel early this morning and he hasn't been seen since. Poweetan is full of cops right now so he won't get far. Don't you worry! We'll find him," he said with much more hope than he felt.

"We're going to do a sweeping house to house search in the morning. If that doesn't turn up something, nothing will." Cal got up and grabbed his hat off the table. "I'm sorry you had to hear more bad news Paul. I'll just let myself out."

"Let us know as soon as you hear anything, Cal. I don't care if it's in the middle of the night. We won't be sleeping much as you can well imagine," he said with obvious fatigue. He watched quietly as Cal walked down the front steps. Would this nightmare never end?

The next morning dawned cold and snowy. Accumulations had been heavy during the night and the only footprints that could be seen in Poweetan were that of the occasional deer and wolf. By eight o'clock, the police had been out in force for about an hour roaming about the woods looking for any sign of Tom Erikson. Albert had taken up a helicopter and done many sweeps over the town and surrounding woods, trying to see anything that didn't belong, but it was as if Tom had completely vanished.

By nine o'clock, the house to house inspection began in earnest. A police dog was let loose after sniffing a piece of Tom's clothing which had been left behind in the house. But again their search was futile. The motel manager was approached again by Cal.

"Are you quite certain you didn't see a vehicle?" he asked for about the fourth time.

"Honest Cal. He wasn't driving anything that I saw. I asked him if he wanted a lift to the bus station but he said his car was in the shop getting the radiator fixed. That's all I know."

Cal was at the end of his rope. Where had the creep gone? There were no tracks, no clues, nothing. Perhaps they should extend their search to include outlying towns and villages. He could have gotten by them. He would suggest that later. When Rachel heard the news from Kate about who the police were looking for, she just about went crazy.

"You mean to tell me that the man who killed my son was the same one who almost killed him when he was inside me twenty years ago?" she screamed into the phone. "Everyone said he was dead! Isn't that what they said, Kate?" she cried out in distress.

Kate knew that she was treading on very thin ice so she chose her words carefully. With great love and gentleness she talked to her friend and tried to get her to calm down.

"You have to understand that we all thought he was dead, but we were all wrong Rachel. I feel just sick inside for what he's done to your family and mine. But we just have to have faith that this time they will catch him once and for all and that will be that. You've seen for yourself how serious they are in catching him. The man is insane and no doubt has been for years. The best thing you and I can do at this time Rachel is to pray. Pray that God will allow Tom to be caught and that this nightmare will finally be over."

Rachel had to agree with Kate. They could pray. When all else failed, God didn't. Hanging up the phone, she dropped to her knees and began to petition her God.

Sarah was blissfully unaware of the massive manhunt going on around her. She had been getting lots of well needed sleep and was resting as comfortably as she could with a good book. Jacob had left earlier after having a visit with her. She had missed talking to her brother for a long time. He had been so unreachable before but now things were so different. He was on fire for the Lord and it truly showed. Sarah was delighted to hear what he was going to do with his newly found faith. He was going to help out at the youth centre and go to bible study and about ten other things. Sarah had to laugh. She wondered where he was going to find the time to do it all but she wasn't going to be the one to throw a damper on his fire. He would find out soon enough that a person couldn't do all the work by themselves. They had to learn to delegate but that would come when he matured in Christ. Sarah was just so happy for him. Too bad Caleb hadn't been alive to witness the transition in Jacob's life. He would have been amazed.

Thinking of her lost love set Sarah to feeling melancholy once again. She wondered if the pain would really ever go away or if it would stay with her for the rest of her life like a dull toothache reminding her of things that could have been. She picked up the book that had dropped to her side and tried desperately to read the blurry lines in front of her face. Giving up, she set it down and closed her eyes. There would be no more reading this morning. Perhaps it was best just to sleep and maybe she would forget the hurt, at least for a short time.

Jacob had to pass three men in navy blue fur-lined coats on his way home from the clinic. Those guys are everywhere, he thought to himself. Surely they would find Jim, or Tom or whoever he was. He felt foolish for being duped by the guy for so long. How could he have been so stupid and blind? He just thanked God that he had seen the light in time to save his sister's life. She seemed to be doing okay physically, but she didn't talk much about what had happened to her down in that cold cellar. He knew that she would have to deal with that before she could be totally healed. And that would come in time, he thought. He figured that it was the same thing that was told to recovering alcoholics. Just take life one day at a time!

Before he knew it, he was trudging up the front steps to his house. He didn't even remember walking up the street, so engrossed in thought was he. He flung open the door and called out to his mom. Kate walked into the front room and looked questioningly at her son.

"How's Sarah doing this morning, Jacob?" she asked. "I'll be going over later on, but the police are doing a house to house search and I had to be here."

"She's doing better today, Mom! She still didn't talk about the cellar but I'm sure it will happen soon," he added hopefully.

"I'm sure you're right son. I just want her to come home as the same girl who left here in late August. I suppose it's just wishful thinking though. She'll never really be the same, will she?" she said with eyes misting over.

"I guess not, Mom," he said sadly. "None of us will be."

"It's getting cool in here today. I think we need to get a fire going in the woodstove. Will you go out to the shed and bring some wood in for me please?"

"Sure Mom. I'll just change into some old clothes first. You'll be basking in warmth before you know it," he said with a boyish grin.

Kate looked at her son with love and noted with pleasure how much he really looked like his dad when he smiled like that. The hair colour might be different but they had very similar mannerisms.

Paul tried without success to write his sermon for Sunday. He couldn't concentrate with policemen going over the whole place and making a lot of noise. He was trying to expound upon last week's message about forgiveness and was looking for that special something that would click for him. That's the way it usually worked when he was letting God's Spirit inspire him. Absently he chewed on the end of his pencil and tried not to get too distracted but it wasn't easy. Maybe he should just call it quits for the day. He would probably work better at home in his own den than here. He decided to give it thirty more minutes and then he would pack things up.

Kate would be pleased to have him home for the rest of the day. Paul did have ulterior motives too. He really didn't want his family to be alone, today of all days. Until they caught that maniac he feared for the safety of all of them. None would be able to sleep right until the police either jailed the freak for life or killed him. And at this point in time, Paul wasn't sure what he would rather see. His head screamed "KILL HIM," while his heart said pray for his black soul because he doesn't know Jesus. There was a war literally raging inside his head and Paul was torn in his feelings.

How could he stand up and preach on the forgiveness of God when he couldn't forgive the man who hurt his loved ones? He felt like the ultimate hypocrite saying one thing while thinking something totally different. He would need much time in prayer before he could preach this message. Surely God would understand his dilemma? Dropping his head into his hands, Paul cried out to his Lord for help. He would not be able to do this alone.

Tom tried to stretch his legs but he was pinned into his hiding place. He was covered from head to foot although it had taken a while to pull the awkward stuff upon his own body. He had to laugh to himself at the blindness of the police. They had opened the door to his hideaway and he had held his breath as the dog came in and started sniffing around. All of a sudden he had started to whine but after a quick search was conducted, the police concluded that Tom must have come in here to hide and then left again. Not one of them attempted to pull away his covering and he mocked their foolishness. What a bunch of idiots they were. Maybe the smell of this place had masked his odour. It was really pungent in here. Whatever the reason, Tom was just glad that they hadn't stumbled across him. Someone was on his side for a change. Luckily, he had come in here late last night and the snow that had been falling so heavily must have covered up his tracks. Talk about divine intervention, he snickered to himself. He would have to get out of here as soon as possible. He was cramped beyond endurance and needed to stretch.

Without realizing it, the cops had just insured his escape by flooding the surrounding area with footprints galore. One more set wouldn't matter one way or the other. He would wait until darkness had fallen and make his way through the woods. Hitchhiking out of the area wouldn't be altogether out of the question if he kept a hat pulled low on his face and his jacket pulled up high on his neck. Actually, it would be expected in this weather. Things were falling into place nicely. He would take off for now, and when things cooled down around here he would come back. His decision made, he tried to settle as comfortably as possible until he was again disturbed from his thoughts.

Jacob took an extra few minutes to shovel a path from the back door to the woodshed. Their yard, like everyone else's had footprints going all over the place. His job completed, Jacob pulled open the door to the shed and hauled his sled up to it. Pulling the wood to the back door was much easier than carrying it, he determined. He loved the smell inside the shed. It was pungent and earthy. He started to grab pieces of wood from the top of the pile. Too bad the police had knocked some of the wood over. The least they could have done was clean up their mess he thought idly. In the muted light it was hard to see in the shed. He had often told his dad that they should get a light or something put out here. As he bent over to pick up a large piece of ironwood, he screamed in fright as something latched on to his hand and wouldn't let go.

It didn't take him long to figure out that it was a hand but that didn't help matters either. Why was a hand coming out from under a wood pile? As his imagination got the best of him, he yelled for his mother. His words were cut off as with super human strength the wood went flying in all different directions and up stood Tom Erikson.

He was larger than life it seemed and it was only a matter of seconds before that dreaded knife was being held to Jacob's throat. He went absolutely still in his captive's arms and prayed that his mother hadn't heard him. He didn't want to see her in danger. And Jacob prayed like he had never prayed before.

CHAPTER FORTY-EIGHT
PAUL'S FAITH IS TESTED

Kate stopped what she was going and looked out the back kitchen window. Had Jacob just called her? She set down her tea towel and went to the back door. She could see his sled sitting just outside the door to the shed with some wood on it. Had he hurt himself she wondered with growing alarm? Pulling open the door, she peered out into the snow that was beginning to blow. "Is everything okay, Jacob?" she called. "You haven't hurt yourself, have you?"

Jacob felt the pressure on his throat and called out to the best of his ability.

"I'm fine, mother. I just banged my finger on a piece of wood," he called back to her.

Kate started to go back into the kitchen when she pulled up short. Jacob had just called her mother. He had never called her that before because she had told him a long time ago that she didn't like it much. Instantly Kate went on the alert. Something wasn't right out there. She wasn't sure what was going on, but felt that her son was in trouble. She quickly ran to the hall closet and pulled out Jacob's hunting rifle. Albert used to take some of the neighbourhood boys on hunting excursions into the woods and Jacob was fairly adept at bringing home rabbits.

As she drove some shells home with shaking fingers, Kate remembered the Christmas that Jacob had asked for a gun. Paul had just about freaked out, but when it was explained to him that it would only be for hunting, he gave in. She could still see Jacob's eyes as he opened up his gift on Christmas morning. He had shown Kate how to use it one summer about three years earlier. She had done poorly when it came to knocking cans off the fence post. She just couldn't get the hang of it. The kick back hurt her shoulder and Jacob would always laugh at her.

Kate felt in her heart that she might need to be accurate today. Something was very wrong but she felt strong and sure of herself. Cocking the gun, she snapped it back into place and tucked it under her arm while racing for the front door. She would go around the side and try and circle back behind the shed. That way she could surprise anyone that may be in there with Jacob. Going as quickly as possible, she came to the back of the house and hopped lightly over the small fence.

The snow was almost six inches deep and made the going a little tougher. Squinting as the snow started to fall more heavily, she made her way over to the side of the shed. Taking aim and holding her breath, Kate stepped into the door opening. Quickly she took in the scene before her and pulled the trigger without a moment's hesitation.

The knife flew out of Tom's hand and he opened his eyes wide in surprise and shock. Where had she come from he wondered through the haze of pain and numbness that was quickly washing over him? He grabbed at the hole just below his right shoulder and felt his warm sticky blood seeping out freely, soaking his hand. He fell to his knees and Kate grabbed Jacob out of the shed and shut the door.

Kate started as Paul stepped up behind her and took the rifle from her stiff fingers. That's when she started to shake uncontrollably. She had just shot a man! Jacob held her close as the sounds of people yelling reached their ears. The police had obviously heard the shot ring out and were on their way over here.

Kate watched in horror as Paul went over to the shed door and pulled it back with such a force that he just about ripped it off its hinges. He looked down at the man cowering in his own blood and felt a rage swell up inside of him. This was the man who had hurt his family and killed his daughter's boyfriend. If anyone deserved to die, it was him. Shaking in anger, Paul reached down and picked up a large chunk of wood. He brought it up over his head and just completed his arch when someone grabbed the wood and held it in place.

He looked around in confusion as he saw Kate and Jacob standing at least two feet away from him. Who had grabbed the wood he wondered? There was nobody else around him. Kate was saying something and he had to strain to focus on her words. As if from very far away, he heard her saying something about God and that He was the only one who had the authority to take a life.

Again the war raged on, as Paul fought the conflicting feelings bouncing around inside of him. He wanted this man to die. He hated him more than anything for all the horrific things he had done. But in his heart, reason finally won out. He had no right to take another human's life. The guy looked like he wasn't going to make it anyway. He was not to be this man's judge and jury. Only God could judge him fairly.

Stepping back on shaky legs, Paul lowered his arm. How easy it would have been he thought in horror. All he had to do was think what Tom had done to Sarah and he was sure that he could have brought his arm down all the way and crushed the man's skull. Then what had stopped him? Paul was certain now that he had been stopped from killing Tom. Was it the Lord, or an angel? He turned and ran back into the house. Quickly he phoned Dr. Verstegan and told him that a man had been shot and needed help. There was no need to call Cal because he could see him running past the side window already, along with many others.

Paul felt like he had just been put to the test and he sighed as he just now realized that he had won. No, that wasn't entirely correct. He couldn't have stopped killing that man in his own power. God had given him the strength to stay his arm. He had been sorely tempted to do the wrong thing but he hadn't succumbed. Just like Jesus in the wilderness he thought with relief and thanked God.

He hadn't killed the man but he didn't think he would ever be able to forgive him either. He had taken too much from them. Paul pulled his jacket a little tighter around his chest and hurried outside to be with Kate and Jacob. Kate was talking with one of the detectives as others were with Tom. Paul came up to them just as Kate was being told that the shooting wouldn't be held against her. Nobody could blame her for trying to save her son's life, considering how many lives this man had already taken.

Just then, an ambulance pulled up in front of the house and within minutes two men trudged through the snow bearing a stretcher. They bent over Tom and ministered to his needs while shaking their heads at the officers around them. They didn't hold out much store for his survival. He probably had a matter of hours to live although they would do their jobs to the best of their ability. Tom was carried away and the Winchester family went back inside to resume their talk with the police. A couple of officers had gone in the ambulance with Tom. There was no way they were letting him out of their sight even if he was dying.

Doctor Verstegan worked on Tom while one of his nurses took down the patient's history. Tom was still lucid and able to talk although he was getting weaker by the minute.

"...and do you have any medical problems that we should know about," she was saying.

"I have O- blood and can only receive blood from another person who is O-," he gasped out in pain as the doctor cut away his clothing from the wound and started to clean it.

"That's going to be a problem as I see it because you've lost a lot of blood and we don't have any O- in my office right now."

"That's the only legacy my biological father left me."

Dr. Verstegen looked over at his nurse and beckoned her over to the other side of the room.

"He's going to die before we get to Fulson if we don't get some more blood into him. This guy needs a transfusion quickly. Please check the files in the computer. We might get lucky and find a match from Poweetan. If not, we're going to have to have him airlifted to the hospital in Fulson. And I don't think he'll last the trip. Go!" he added hurriedly.

It took almost seven minutes before the nurse finally came back into the room. She was very pale and the doctor looked at her strangely.

"What's wrong, Sylvia? You look like you just saw a ghost! Did you find a match or not?" he asked.

"You won't believe it sir. There was one match in all of those files," she said in dismay.

"Well don't keep me in suspense girl. Spit it out!"

She looked at the doctor in dread. "It's Rev. Winchester, Dr. Verstegen! He is a perfect match."

The doctor looked at her in disbelief.

"You've got to be kidding? Wait until he finds out. He'll go crazy. I'm afraid to even ask him, but if I don't, then this fool will die. Don't be surprised when he says no. And I wouldn't blame him one bit."

"There's one more thing you should be aware of," Sylvia began. "I know this blood type is hereditary in a lot of cases so I think this could be more than just a coincidence. When I was filling out his forms, Mr. Erikson told me that his stepdad's name was Erikson but that his real father's name was David Allen Winchester. Don't you think it's strange that this David guy has the same last name as Paul and they all have the same blood type?" she said in a strained voice.

Doc Verstegen shook his head in wonder. Could it be possible? He would have to ask Paul what his father's name was just to satisfy his own curiosity. When the doctor phoned their house, Paul just assumed that Tom had finally died and he couldn't say that bothered him much either. When the reason for the call became clear, Paul was absolutely speechless. Kate watched her husband when he went silent and wondered what was wrong. He yelled something into the phone then and slammed the receiver down on the hook. He stood there trembling and Kate went to him and put her arms around him.

"What is it dear? Is Tom dead?"

Paul sat heavily down onto the couch and just stared right ahead.

"Do you know what that doctor had the nerve to ask me? He says that Tom has a blood type that they currently don't have on hand. It turns out that I'm the only match they can find in the whole town. Can you believe it? He wants me to give that creep my own blood to possibly save his life. What a joke! I'm just waiting for him to die. I don't want to see him live. I want him to pay for killing Caleb and destroying our daughter's life."

His shoulders sagged in defeat as he was faced with another test of faith.

He hadn't killed the guy earlier when he wanted to but could he save him? That was not something that Paul could even begin to cope with right now. He didn't even want to think. He just wanted to escape to his room and never come out. God was asking too much of him. Ten minutes later there was a knock at the door. It was Dr. Verstegen and he looked at Paul apologetically.

"I know this is very hard for you to digest Paul and I'm sorry that I had to spring it on you, but the guy is barely hanging on to life. As a doctor, you know I have to do everything possible to keep people alive."

Paul felt like the wind had been knocked out of him.

"You can't be serious…not after all he's done?" spit out Paul in anger. "This is wrong on so many levels! You can't believe I would even consider what you're asking of me, can you?"

"There's something else that I think you should know about. Sylvia filled out his forms and found something very unusual. The first is that this type of blood is hereditary. Tom said that his mother remarried and that's where he got the name Erikson. His natural father's name was David Allen Winchester. Have you ever heard of him?" he asked hopefully.

The doctor turned around and looked at Kate when she gasped. Paul had told her all about his terrible past before they were married but he hadn't mentioned his father since. It was a sore spot for him. She went quickly to his side but he was as motionless as a statue. All the life seemed to have been drained from his features.

"I think you had better go, Dr. Verstegen," said Kate. "I'll get Paul to call you back shortly. We need to be alone right now," she said.

"He won't hang on for long without that transfusion, Paul. Think about it please? Nodding to the couple, the doctor reluctantly left the house and headed back to the clinic. He had obviously hit a nerve somewhere and it baffled him. He hoped Paul would phone back quickly while the guy still had a fighting chance. He was also glad that Sarah was in the back part of the clinic. She had no idea who was in the front room and he wasn't going to be the one to tell her.

Paul looked at Kate and just shook his head in bewilderment.

"What are the odds, Kate?" he asked quietly. "You don't think that we could actually have the same father, do you? I mean, it's totally unthinkable, isn't it?" he said uncertainly.

Kate looked at her husband and shrugged her shoulders. She didn't understand it any more than he did. It was just like pulling an April fool's joke on somebody and finding that it backfires in your own face. Paul gave a great big sigh and came to a decision.

"I have to go and talk to him, Kate. I just have to know one way or another. I'll never rest with these wild thoughts running through my head. There's no way they could be the same person. After all, my father left me in New York. This guy's father could have been born anywhere in the world."

He talked on in a steady stream as if he were trying to convince himself and then went to the closet to get his jacket.

"You had better get mine out as well, Paul. You're not going to face this alone. Your family will be there for support just in case you need us," she smiled.

Jacob came out of his room and overheard the last part of the conversation.

"I'm coming with you," he said as he pulled his boots on in the foyer.

Together they headed towards the clinic holding hands to gain strength from each other. Their nightmare wasn't over by a long shot.

Paul and Kate entered the clinic while Jacob joined them after seeing his sister. "I overheard the doctor and nurse talking, Dad. Do you think what they're saying is true?"

"I don't have an answer for that, Jacob. But I'll soon find out. They walked to the end of the hall and were greeted by the doctor.

"Have you come to a decision yet, Paul?" he asked

"I need to talk to him alone first. Please just give me a few minutes," he said in a tone that was clipped. Paul excused himself as he walked in front of two officers who were guarding the room.

"Do you want one of us to go in with you?" the one policeman asked.

"That won't be necessary. I don't intend to be long," said Paul.

Paul drew up short when he saw Tom. Lying pale and deathly still, he hardly looked like the menace Paul had made him out to be. Even from this side of the room, he could hear Tom's laboured breathing as he struggled for life. Paul wanted to hate him with all his heart but for some reason, seeing him like this, Paul only felt a great pity and sadness for a life that had been wasted. He walked over to the bed and looked with disdain at the forlorn figure lying there. What a pathetic creature, he thought to himself.

Then he came to a decision which was not easy for him. God was asking him to forgive this man who had caused him so much grief. He just knew it. That was the last thing he wanted to do and then it clicked for him and things all fell into place. Had it been only last week that he had preached on the forgiveness of God? God had forgiven him when his life was a mess and he deserved only punishment. How could he do any less than what God had done for him? His focus had been all wrong. He still hated Tom but with God's help he may have the courage to forgive him. And what better way to show forgiveness than by offering his own life-giving blood to save Tom's life? That was what grace was, after all. It was being offered something wonderful when we don't deserve it. That settled in his mind, Paul quietly left the room and went to talk with the doctor. He had some blood to donate!

Kate couldn't have been more proud of her husband than she was at that very moment. It had taken a lot of guts to do what he was doing and she knew that God was working on his heart. Jacob on the other hand was completely baffled. How could his father forgive that evil man? Kate looked over at her son and smiled with a deep sense of peace. She could read what he was thinking, just by looking at his face.

"You'll understand what he just did when you mature in Christ, Jacob. He didn't come to that decision in his own strength. He had some big help," she said. "One day it will make perfect sense to you. Trust me, Jacob," she added.

About twenty minutes later, Paul walked down the hall. He seemed to be fully at peace considering what had just transpired over the past several hours. He joined his family and waited until the doctor would allow him to go back into the room where Tom was. The family prayed together as one. Nobody had told Sarah what had happened. They didn't want to upset her unnecessarily.

Rachel and Stephen had been told the news but they wouldn't come to the clinic. They couldn't understand why Paul would give that monster his blood. It made no sense and they were dealing with things such as anger and betrayal. Their friendship would be sorely tested over the next couple of weeks but in the end they would see the rightness of his great act of mercy and compassion.

Finally the doctor came out of the room, wiping his hands on a towel. He looked up as the Winchester family waited expectantly.

"Thanks to you Paul, we've done all we can for now. The bullet exited clean through his back but it did a lot of damage inside him," he began.

Kate hung her head in shame. If only it could have been a different way she thought but knew she would do it all over again to protect her child.

"There's no way I can repair any of the damage right now because he won't make it. He's too weak to undergo surgery. Tom's in God's hands now. You can go on in and see him if you want to Paul," he said.

Paul rose and went back into the room. This time he did so with a clean heart. He had done all that God had expected of him and more. He felt like a better man for it. Paul looked down at the man in the bed again. Tom was looking back at him, with bewilderment.

"I understand from your records that your father's name was David Allen Winchester. Is that correct?" Paul asked quickly but with a quiet authority he hadn't possessed even this morning.

"Who wants to know?" said Tom with a hint of his old nature bubbling up beneath the surface.

"I knew a man once who had the same name only he came from New York," Paul pressed on with determination.

That drew Tom's attention in an instant and all of the former haughtiness left him.

"My father originally came from New York," he croaked our weakly.

"Can you describe what he looked like? I'd really like to know," said Paul.

"The creep left my mother when she was giving birth to me but I did steal a picture from one of the photo albums at home when I left. They were together for almost five years before I came along. I keep it in my wallet although it's pretty scrunched up now," he added. Paul decided to press the issue one more time although he could see that the light was fast fading from Tom's eyes.

"May I have a look?" he asked hopefully.

"Be my guest. My wallet's over there with my clothes. I don't think I'll need it anytime soon," he laughed and then started to cough.

Some watery blood trickled out of the corner of his mouth. Without thinking, Paul got a Kleenex and wiped it away. He went over to the wallet while tears squeezed out of the corners of Tom's eyes. Nobody had ever shown him kindness like that before. This man should hate his guts but first he had given his own blood and now this visit. He couldn't understand why he would care about the person who had hurt his family. Tom wondered absently why he was so interested in his father, even if he did know a guy by the same name. That kind of threw him for a loop. He watched Paul with fascination.

Paul withdrew the wallet and skimmed through the few pictures looking for a familiar face. He had just about given up in resignation when he saw him. His father was staring up at him from trembling fingers. He began to weep softly as realization finally sank in. Slowly he walked back to the bed and looked at Tom through blurry eyes. Tom looked back at him in obvious confusion.

"Did you find what you were looking for?" asked Tom.

Paul held the picture out to Tom. "This is your father?" inquired Paul.

When he saw Tom nodding his head mechanically he dropped down into the chair beside him.

"This is a picture of my father as well. I don't know how this is possible but this makes us step-brothers!" he said as he withdrew a picture of the same man from the back of his wallet.

For once in his miserable life, Tom was speechless. First he looked at the photo and saw a younger version of his dad standing beside some woman. He stared at the man before him and as he looked he could see a vague resemblance. But where Tom's face had been permanently disfigured by hardship, anger and hopelessness, Paul's was fairly glowing with something that Tom couldn't begin to fathom.

And then something else struck him like a blow to the stomach and his head reeled. This man had just given him his own blood before he even knew they were related. Even after what he had done to Sarah and Jacob and yes, even to Kate over twenty years earlier. And still he had given of himself? Tom finally was broken and God worked on that broken heart until he looked up at Paul with tears in his own eyes. He knew there wasn't much time left for him but he had to know what it was that Paul had, that he didn't.

"How could you do this, knowing all you know about me?" he asked weakly.

Paul knew what he had to do without a moment's hesitation. Perhaps he was called to the ministry for just this moment in time. He took Tom's hand and told him about the salvation that Jesus offered. All he had to do was admit that he was a sinner in need of God's grace, repent of his sins and invite Jesus into his heart to be the Lord of his life. Tom wept like a baby for the first time in over a quarter of a century as he gave his broken heart to Jesus for mending.

CHAPTER FORTY-NINE
THE HEALING IS COMPLETED

Paul heard the soft noise of the door sliding open and looked up to see the doctor coming into the room. He looked at Paul with questioning eyes and then at Tom. His breathing was getting shallower by the minute but it was his face that caught the doctor's attention. It was positively radiant, as if he had just been touched by God Himself. Paul felt a small squeeze on his hand and glanced quickly down at the man lying there. There was only time for a brief smile on Tom's face and then the light completely disappeared and he peacefully passed away. Paul looked up at the bag of blood dripping into Tom's arm and smiled.

He had just been handed the biggest test of his life and he knew that he had passed it with flying colours. If it had been up to him, he would have let this man die and possibly even taken his life himself. But with God's strength alone, he had learned not to judge others and then he had learned the biggest lesson of all. He had been able to forgive an enemy, first by giving some of his own blood and second by telling him about the life giving blood that only Jesus could offer. Paul spent a final moment with Tom and regretted the years of separation. Perhaps things could have been different if they had each other from the start. Maybe Caleb and all those other people would still be alive.

And then Paul nodded his head slightly as he said goodbye.

"We may have been half-brothers in life, but now we are true brothers in Christ. That is fitting," he said as he quietly left the room, leaving the doctor behind with his mouth hanging open in surprise.

Paul joined his family in the hallway. He looked at his wife and son who had changed so much over the past couple of weeks. They all turned to find out what was making the shuffling noise that could be heard coming down the hall. There was Sarah, who was walking on her own with the help of a cane. They drew into a circle and hugged and prayed and laughed. Their ordeal was finally over and as Paul told them about the last half hour spent with Tom, they were truly amazed. A family who had been torn by grief and upset had just been healed thanks to the saving grace and goodness of God.

And that same grace would eventually bring healing to the Westcott family and to the rest of the community. All it would take was a little time and a lot of prayer. And time was something they would have lots of, as the snow fell heavily from the sky and covered the ground with a new white robe.

ABOUT THE AUTHOR

Debra resides in the very small community of Duntroon, Ontario. She and her husband Steve have four beautiful children who are now adults. Debra was a lay pastor for 11 years at Knox Presbyterian Church in Horning's Mills. She still does pulpit supply when needed, at various churches in the area. Debra works as a call centre rep in Collingwood for Vitality Assurance Vacations. In her free time, she enjoys hiking with her dogs; reading; writing and biking with her husband—he on his motorcycle and she on her scooter.

ISBN 978-1-77067-182-9 (Hardcover)
ISBN 978-1-77067-183-6 (Paperback)
ISBN 978-1-77067-184-3 (eBook)

Debra self-published her first novel, "A Short Fuse Burning" in 2010. It was a Book Of The Year Finalist in "Foreward Reviews," which is an independent media company totally devoted to covering the indie book publishing industry. It was entered as religious adult fiction and was among over 1200 entrants in all fields.

SYNOPSIS

No one knew how bad things were going to get, or if they did, the message didn't get out to millions of people. Matt Ellis and his wife Kerry had just got married when the world turned upside down for them. First it was the earthquakes, and then it was the disappearance of thousands of people, Matt's parents among them. The young couple tried to cope under perilous circumstances, with their young son Stephen and best friends Stuart and Rachel. But trying times tore the couples apart as the world was visited by every imagineable kind of horror. The only thought most people had, was how to survive. And they would do anything to protect themselves and their families. But in the end, would it be enough to save them?